SYVILA WEATHERFORD

BLESSINGS FROM THE FOUR WINDS

ISBN: 978-1-09838-989-5 (print)

PREFACE

IN 1985, I accompanied my father on what would be his last trip to his childhood home in Enid, Oklahoma, to visit relatives who also descended from his Indian or Native American grandmother. His cousins lived, interestingly, in houses side by side in a cul-de-sac. As our motor home pulled into the cul-de-sac, people began streaming out of five houses.

I asked my father, "Which ones are our relatives?"

Looking out the window at them with pride he replied, "All of them."

From a family of eight siblings, five were still living and, along with their descendants, were there to greet us. After introductions chased by tearful kisses and hugs, we were invited into one of the homes where preparations for dinner—no, it was more like a feast—were underway. A large dining room table was covered with platters and bowls of delicious food they had prepared, a variety of seasoned meats and cooked fresh vegetables picked from their backyard gardens. What started as a customary, festive family reunion evolved into a roundtable of sharing memorable stories. As we all sat in a large living room facing a crackling fire in the fireplace, each of my father's relatives took turns sharing stories about the escapades of their grandfather and his Indian wife. My siblings and I were spellbound, and eventually shocked! These were stories about which we never had an inkling. It wasn't long before I realized they were astonishing recounts of a real person's life that should never be forgotten. I quickly found a pen and paper and jotted down notes.

The story I am about to share with you does include some creative licenses taken in naming characters, towns, and places to connect real events, and also altering the names of real persons for the usual reasons. For example, it was never made clear which tribe my great-grandmother belonged to. Some relatives said Choctaw; others, Osage. Both tribes had reservations in the Indian Territory, but I have written this story based on her being Choctaw. However, the core of the story I am about to share with you is based on the notes I took in that living room.

INTRODUCTION

By the year 1885, Union supporters, as well as ex-Confederates, had reconvened their lives in American society, while millions of former slaves and their descendants were far from realizing the American dream. Many handicapped with the inability to read and write, their daily lives saw combat with death by disease and starvation. Negroes with a trade stood better chances at getting by, but at a fraction of the income of their White counterparts. Some were successful at leveraging their knowledge and skills developed during slavery and passing them on to the next generation after slavery, enabling independent enterprises to sprout; but it was more of an exception than the rule.

Leveraging his skills is the goal of our story's main character. The story picks up with him rushing to a job with pay capable of ensuring such leveraging and freeing him from a lifetime of servitude.

CHAPTER 1

START OF THE CATTLE DRIVE

———

"YOU'RE doing great, buddy. We'll be stopping soon," says a solitary rider who pushes his horse to a faster gallop along a tree-lined trail on a warm summer night. Moist air brushes past the rider's face as he and his horse speed down the trail. With the sun dipping into the west horizon, his back finds relief from its hammering rays. But no relief from his stress because he's a Negro traveling alone through Tennessee, Arkansas, and Texas, states that were once a part of the Confederacy. And so, the rider hastens to complete his trip.

The stars in the sky are tiny polka dots on a large black velvet canvas, creating a darkness that cloaks every object on either side of the road beyond recognition. A latent fear fuels his imagining the precarious cloaked objects to be Klansmen or die-hard ex-Confederates lying in wait for a lone Negro man. The rider quickens his pace; he is counting on the shadowy cloaked objects on either side of the road to remain frozen, at least until he passes them by. "Let's get to Indian Territory, then we can ease our pace," says the rider, his pelvis in a perpetual negotiation with his saddle.

The rider has made this trip across these states three times before within fifteen days, each trip consisting of riding thirty miles a day, followed by watering, feeding, and resting man and horse overnight; otherwise, the horse is ruined. However, this time his departure was unavoidably delayed. He left his home two days behind schedule, only leaving himself thirteen days to cover the 440 miles by horseback, barring bad weather, dried-out water holes, or an attack. He can't be late. His future depends on it. Assessing his trip status, he is already nine days in, and yet to reach the Red River in the Indian Territory. Known as the "the plains," that territory has a long, rich history with cultural ties to Native American peoples. Before the territory became the state of Oklahoma, its lands were set aside by the U.S. Government for the relocation of Indians. Many tribes were given large parcels within the territory for their homes, including the Cherokee, Choctaw, Creek, Chickasaw, and Seminoles.

The year is 1885. Much of the unrest between the Native American peoples and the U.S. Government has been settled. However, the recent years were bloody, and the peace is held together only by a document called a treaty, and the fragile peace it provides teeters on the memories of slaughtered loved ones and the "Trail of Tears." And as for legally signed treaties, history will show, honorable men treated them as law, while the greedy eventually broke them for one reason or another.

These tribal lands are part of the land the lone rider will travel through. They are forty of the miles comprising his 440-mile trip. The rider knows danger recognizes no borders or jurisdictions. Staying alert not only equates to arriving safely and on time, but surviving!

The rider approaches the Texas border during the last days of May in the heat of an impatient summer. At the end of each day's ride, the rider makes camp and tends to his horse before bedding down. As if the darkness isn't enough to unnerve him, there is also the quiet. Sounds once heard across the plains during prior trips have disappeared into a solemn quiet. No prairie dog howls, no crickets; not even the rustling of leaves or grass is heard. It is a still night of heat, dampness, and silence—a foreboding night that envelopes the lone rider, Will Lawton, and his horse, Rodeo.

Since they left Tennessee, Rodeo, a chestnut brown horse, seventeen hands in height, adorned with a white star-like marking on his forehead, and white leg markings around his lower legs and hooves that give him the appearance of wearing white socks, has kept that fast pace set by Will. Will, twenty years of age, stands six feet tall on sturdy legs, with broad shoulders, and is of medium weight. His hue depends upon the season of the year—brown rust in winter to a burnt cherry brown during the height of summer. A plain tan-felt farmer's hat hides black kinky hair that he oils with a scented hair tonic for church socials, and that his mother keeps short by attacking it every spring and summer with lamb shearing scissors. Will's face features striking thick black eyebrows atop piercing dark eyes above a narrow-bridged nose ending in a wide set of nostrils. When he laughs, his full, moist lips draw back into a dimpled smile, revealing ivory white teeth.

Will is on his way to join a cattle drive. Based on the distance left to travel, he is running out of time to arrive before the herd is moved out from the Hastings Ranch in Texas near Waco. A late arrival would amount to a personal catastrophe. It may cost him his treasured cattle driving job, a job he acquired by sheer luck, and a job capable of providing him enough money to buy his own farm. With only hours remaining to make it to the Hastings Ranch, Will finds himself crossing the Texas border, blazing through flatland riddled with high grass and weeds. He fears the cattle will be moved out at sunup, and the trail boss may be forced to replace him. *Must make better time*, he says to himself, as he anxiously crosses the Red River.

He is beginning the tenth day of his journey. The trip is thoroughly planned out—down to the stops each day for rest, camp, and water sources. Not knowing the condition of Benton Creek, located near the end of his trip, Will decides to stop at the Red River, dismount, rest a bit, and let Rodeo have a drink. As Rodeo laps water from the river, Will frantically contemplates his options. He reasons his best bet is to catch the herd as near to the ranch as possible. When he gets there, if he can slip in among the other drovers, most will conclude he had been there longer than he actually was. After about two hours at the Red River, feeling somewhat refreshed, he and Rodeo leave the river at a moderate trot.

Will soon reaches a point where the terrain elevations are rugged. They are traversing a course where the land repetitively rises by three to five feet, and then gradually goes down again. This frustrates Will. He dismounts and walks ahead, directing Rodeo through the uneven elevations at a slower pace. Although the path is one flattened by numerous riders over time, the path comprises a mixture of rocks and mounds of dirt causing Will to be careful to let Rodeo secure his footing on each step. He tries to guide Rodeo's steps to areas void of clumps of small rocks that may get lodged in the pad of his foot. Remarkably Rodeo refrains from wandering toward tempting vegetation but maintains steps single-file or parallel to Will's. "You're doing just great, buddy. Single-file. Single-file through here. Good, boy," says Will directing Rodeo.

A few miles farther, the path transitions into a well-traveled trail created by marched-over grass and exposed dirt. He remounts and weaves along the trail until it pours out onto an even lower flatland made up of patches of green and brown grass and red clay. The trail becomes much easier to traverse, and this portion stretches out for miles. Will's spirits lift. He and Rodeo can make good time now. This flatland, however, is no sanctuary, as the grass and bush are low, and during the day, it can give up the location of anything moving quickly to escape its void. At night, the cloak of darkness offers some defense and security against predators and pot-shooters. What it is ideal for is pathways for moving large herds and providing bountiful grazing land. This flatland is fertile with different types of grass and plants, and is so level and sparse of trees, it gives great visibility for keeping watch over a grazing herd.

After a restless night's sleep on blankets and saddle bags, Will relieves himself near bushes away from camp, returns to break camp, packs up, and continues on his way. "My last days are slipping away," Will murmurs to Rodeo. Soft pressure to Rodeo's sides moves them out from camp. As they trot out Will experiences a rush of cleverness to have beaten ol' mister sun's appearance. He is nearing the end of what normally is a fifteen-day trek southwest toward the Hastings Ranch. He knows arriving late is not going to sit well with Tom, the trail boss. He and Tom had discussed the dangers of the travel and how long it would take to make his trip from Tennessee to Texas. Before this trip, Will had successfully made his way to the Hastings Ranch on schedule, that is when the trail boss asked him to get there. How would he explain arriving after the designated time they agreed to?

It is dangerous for a Negro to travel alone such a long distance. News of Negroes being lynched is often circulated among Negro churches and communities. Will knows to be on guard while traveling roads at night and, when possible, to tag along with others who can be trusted. Usually, a wagon train heading west is a good option. They regularly can use extra hands to scout the trail for the easiest passage, sources of freshwater or quarry, and to help stave off wild animals. On his return trips, Will fears being robbed of his cash pay. Whether on a return trip or not, he is particularly watchful of anyone eyeing his fairly new saddle, holster gun, any of his gear, and of course his prized possession, Rodeo.

For a young Negro man in 1885 in the Midwest, there aren't many jobs available that pay well. But of all the good-paying jobs available to any young man, regardless of race, cattle driving is high on the list. While the days are long, full, and require facing the outdoor elements around the clock for weeks at a time, once the trail boss places that pay of twenty-five dollars for each month on the drive in a cattle driver's hands, he forgets about the miles of scorching heat, eating dust, smelling cow dung, and squatting to defecate just shy of a rattlesnake strike.

What keeps Will going is his dream to buy a farm. In later years, he was heard saying, "As I rode through the plains many times on those early trips, I had no idea that all I would come to hold precious and dear in life would be found right here—the farm, the house, and my mate."

Will approaches his next designated rest stop, a water hole called Benton Creek. The creek is almost dried up. It serves as a refuge for travelers weary with thirst out on the plains. Will uses it for a quick stop for him and Rodeo to stretch and quench their thirst on the creek's remaining pool. While Rodeo sucks in small amounts of the creek's water, Will buries his canteen in it. He is late and too near the Hastings Ranch to dawdle for long. Yet, he wants to give Rodeo a once-over because, once they do reach the herd, he can't rule out he and Rodeo being put to work immediately, and unable to rest after their long trip. He does have the option to swap Rodeo for one of the backup horses. But it's not the same. Rodeo reads him like no other animal; he's like an extension of his body. Part of what his father taught him about horses was not to abuse them by running them too hard or too long, even though they are willing to give each time you ask.

Although he has made record time, he is long overdue at the Hastings Ranch and is hoping to see the herd any minute. His body is tired and aches to stop for a short nap. However, it is only a few more miles until he should see the herd. Will shakes off the desire to stop, and he and Rodeo push on.

As they climb a hill, Will notices the sky, miles ahead, transitions from a black starlit canopy to one resembling a dark gray puffy blanket hovering above. This explains the lack of animal sounds out on the plains. The resident wildlife has most likely sensed a storm and gone to ground. Maneuvering Rodeo to a vantage point near a crest in the hills, he has an almost panoramic view of the valley below. Off in the distance, southwest of him, the only sign of life Will can make out is a large herd of animals grazing in a flat, grassy area just twenty miles out from the Hastings Ranch. *It's got to be the herd*, Will thinks as he shoulders his tension.

Nearby, nearly fifty feet from the herd, light dances up from a campfire and shimmers off the dark gray sky. Surrounding the campfire are several cowhands who are taking Mr. Hastings' cattle to market. It has been a long day for them too, and it doesn't help that they are short one man—Will.

The campfire must have been burning for a while because the current flames are low, close to dying out, and no one appears to be stoking it or adding more wood. A few hands sit around the fire making small talk, while others are asleep on their bedrolls. Ten drovers; Oscar, the cook; and Tom, the trail boss, make up this crew. Four of the cowhands are away from camp taking their turns standing guard around the herd. Each guard is perched on a steed from the Hastings Ranch: one to the north of the herd, another to the south, one east of the herd, and one to the west. The herd is a mixture of Texas longhorns, short-horn bulls, and cows. There are no calves yet, since any spotted pregnant cows have been weeded out before the trip. But as certain as the sun will rise, the crew expects calves to drop during the drive. When that happens, mother cows and their newborn calves can have trouble keeping up with the main herd and the pace of the drive is threatened. And then, their fate rests with Tom.

The cowhands are hired to drive Mr. Hastings' cattle to the shipping depot at Dodge City, Kansas, northwest of the Hastings Ranch. Assuming no snake bites, drownings, rustlings, or Indian raids, at the end of nearly two months, each head of cattle will be delivered, corralled, counted, and sold. Will and the other hands will collect their monthly pay and become another drive's pay richer. The pay scale for each drover depends on their job on the drive. Regular drovers earn thirty dollars each month. A good cook can claim up to forty dollars each month, and the trail boss garners one hundred dollars each month per drive. Tom, as the trail boss, is given discretion on the pay for Zeb, his second-in-command or ramrod, and Matt, the lead scout. Will is paid twenty-five dollars each month to be the horse wrangler, a different pay rate than the regular drovers. Under certain circumstances, Tom also has the discretion to pay bonuses, causing some drovers to jockey for a chance to do something extra to earn the bonuses.

"You better ride out and tell those girls to keep a sharp watch tonight," Tom demands of Ben, one of the drovers. Ben is a tenderfoot working his first cattle drive. Tom adds while staring up at the sky, "The air smells of thunderstorms."

Dry thunderstorms are common in this part of Texas: just lightning, no rain. They sprout up suddenly, can last from five minutes to several hours, and surprisingly, may be followed by bursts of Biblical downpours. However, two seconds are all that are needed to create a disastrous setback to a cattle drive. In those two seconds, a bolt of lightning can strike close by, spook the cattle, and a stampede erupts. It would take several days to round them all up again, and unfortunately, you won't get back every last one.

As Ben rides out to pass on Tom's warning to the drovers on guard duty, muffled rumbling thunders in the cloud above him. His horse rears up, and he pulls tightly on the reins to regain control and then gallops to the first guard. But it is too late. Suddenly, a lightning bolt cuts through the dark gray sky to the ground. Resting cows are shaken, and a run ignites. It starts with a rotary motion with frightened cows yelping and mooing. Next, the rotary motion speeds up. Weaker cows get pushed and kneaded by stronger ones. Then they break out into a fast gallop trampling anything in their path. The ground quakes under the weight of the thousands of stomping hooves.

"We got a STAMPEE-EEDE!" Tom yells. "A STAMPEE-EEDE! Get on your feet!" Sleeping cowhands are startled awake. Jumping to their feet, they realize that their greatest fear has come to pass. Scrambling to their gear and horses, all are at a loss as to how they are going to stop twenty-five-hundred tons of beef from making a frenzied escape across the wide valley. The lead steers break out of the pack and lead the charge, heading northeast. Moving like a locomotive engine, the lead steers are the front end of the charged run, streaking through the valley, curving slightly from right to left, with a mass of heavy flesh formed by the remainder of cows following in hot pursuit.

Startled, Ben finds himself in the midst of rushing cows. Fearing being trampled, he quickly struggles to move himself and his horse out of their path. Drake rides up on him fast and shouts, "Get into it, man! This is a stampede!" Then Drake rides away yelling, "Whoo-hoo, whoo-hoo!" Ben surmises this terror is having an altogether different effect on him—some kind of an adrenaline rush.

The crackling sound of the storm's thunder coupled with the roar of thousands of hooves pounding the earth sends chills of fear and excitement through the Hastings' crew's veins. After swiftly mounting their horses, the remainder of the crew takes off to try to slow or stop some part of the wild run. Tom takes off on his horse, Jack, going at the highest speed he can kick out of him, racing to catch up to the lead steers. The lead steers are carefully selected bulls that dominate the others and are impulsively followed by the majority. This phenomenon is due to the dominance hierarchy of cows, making these lead steers too valuable to sell. While Tom races to the front, behind him, the cowhands gallop up to sections of the herd and try to cut into them and cut them off from the main herd. Shooting their guns, twirling white rags, snapping whips, using any tactic they can think of, they try to scare the cows into changing course or skidding to a stop. Sporadically, a cowhand gains the attention of a couple of cows and spooks them out of the pack, but the bulk of them continue a northeast heading.

While climbing onto the crest above the flatland overlooking the valley below, Will hears a thunderous sound, immediately recognizable. From the edge of the crest, he peers down and spots sprinting steers leading a cloud of dust rumbling in his direction. "A stampede. The herd is in a stampede!" Will says out loud. He spurs Rodeo with just his heels to head down the hill where he can get a better view. Thoughts race through his mind, specifically the need to stop them. He hears his father telling him, "*An animal is reluctant to challenge some-*

thing perceived to be bigger and fiercer than itself." Now, reasoning the herd wouldn't try to run uphill toward the crest, but would turn away toward the more level ground, his mind begins to calculate how best to take action to get this chaos under control. Will knows that he's got to force the lead steers to make a hard right turn away from the crest, which would slow the whole herd down.

Snatching a light shirt out of his saddlebags with his left hand, and grabbing his pistol in the other hand, Will aims Rodeo to head farther down the hill, twirls the shirt high in the air, and shoots his pistol. He guides Rodeo by squeezing his calves against Rodeo's sides just behind the girth, accompanied by soft kicks, to deftly move down the hillside from the crest onto the flatland some fifty feet below. Once near the bottom, he kicks Rodeo harder to pick up speed, moving perpendicular to the out-of-control animals coming at him one hundred feet away. The fast-moving herd is coming in his direction at top speed, and he is worried about getting Rodeo too close to the bulls' horns and gored by them.

His predictions, though, are bearing out. As he surmises, when the steers detect the land gradually rising to meet the bottom of the crest, they instinctively seek the more level ground and begin turning right. His outbursts of shirt-twirling and gunshots spook them, reinforcing their decision to turn right. Will tries to appear to be a big, loud, mysterious force, presenting an obstacle the herd would want to avoid. Once they initiate the right turn, Will bears down on them, even more, twirling the shirt, shooting, and yelling, "Hiyah! Hiyah!" spooking them more and more into the right turn. He knows the drill. He knows once you get the attention of the lead steers, you have the whole herd. Riding alongside and getting closer and closer to the lead steers, Will closes in on them, but as safely as possible. By maintaining the chaotic commotion to exact a turn to the right, the lead steers succumb and turn. It's working! They are turning, turning hard. They are even turning back into Tom and the approaching drovers, who hurriedly scamper out of their way, allowing the majestic bulls room to head back. They are heading back toward the original grazing area.

As the hands tactically weave in and out of the herd to break the pace more and more, it becomes apparent that the worst is over. They are turned. Also, thank God the lightning has stopped, allowing the cattle to gradually calm down and come under the control of the cowhands. They are now slowed to a trot, and eventually will slow to a walk. The stampede is over, thanks to Will.

Most of the hands, including Tom, witnessed an unknown rider suddenly appearing, coming down from the crest, riding toward the herd, and bravely spooking them into a turn. This will definitely be the central topic of discussion around the campfire the next time the crew gathers.

Will trails the herd as it enters the grassy area near the origin of the run. A few cowhands slowly drive the cows into one main grouping, attempting to get them reassembled and simmered down. Other hands are riding out looking for strays, but Tom calls them all back in. He feels rounding up the strays is work that can wait until tomorrow. The bulk of the herd is back under control, and it is just too dark to go on a hunt for strays. It is hard enough finding the camp without the fire going. So, it would be nearly impossible to spot brown cows at night under the dark sky.

Exhausted and sitting on Jack, his horse, Tom is hunched over leaning on the saddle horn. He musters strength to yell orders to Ben and Clancy, "Return to camp. We'll get the strays first thing light. Pass the word!" Recognizing Will coming his way Tom, with spent energy, raises his arm and in one huge wave beckons Will to ride to him. Will approaches him gripped with anxiety.

"It's 'bout time you showed up!" Tom shouts, adjusting himself in his saddle as he glares at Will. "I ought to make an example of you showin' up late. But then you go and be a hero tonight."

Will smiles, his anxiety eases.

"Go on into camp, and get some rest. You can help round up strays in the mornin','" Tom bellows.

Will turns and proudly rides into camp. Even Rodeo appears to have a swagger in his stride. Tom and the others head back into camp as well. There are only a few hours until dawn, so everyone is eager to get some quick shut-eye. The crew, physically and emotionally drained, enter the camp welcoming the decision to start rounding up strays at sunup. Will enters camp behind the chuck wagon, dismounts, and guides Rodeo to a makeshift hitching post. This hitching post consists of two long ropes, one end tied to the chuck wagon and then strung between two posts, really two five-feet long lumber boards brought from the ranch and hammered vertically into the ground. An entire set of these posts is kept in the chuck wagon, used to create a makeshift corral for the backup horses. But because of the ominous weather, Tom chooses to tie the horses securely, rather than allow them to roam untethered in the makeshift corral.

Will positions Rodeo with the group of horses already tied there, but places him on the end nearest to the chuck wagon, securely tying his reins to one of the ropes. He removes his saddle and gear off Rodeo's back and then provides Rodeo a bucket of water to help him cool down. The group of horses includes the backup horses brought from the ranch that Will quickly looks over to see which have been selected for this drive. After his quick review, he carries saddle and gear into camp, cornering the chuck wagon, and once on the other side of the wagon, he spots his good friend, Oscar, the cook.

Oscar hovers over the fire illuminating the camp. When the cow-hands make their hasty exit from camp to recapture the herd, he takes it upon himself to find more wood and stoke the campfire to build up its blaze until everyone returns. Anticipating Tom will assign another set of the drovers to guard duty, Oscar puts the coffee pot back over the flame. The campfire provides not only light and is the core of Oscar's kitchen, but its bright light also staves off unwanted predators seeking stealth entry into the camp. While bending over, stoking the fire, drowsy with fatigue, Oscar's focus switches between fortifying the campfire to glancing out into the darkness, trying to interpret the variety of shapes, sounds, and movements. With his focus elsewhere, he does not notice Will dropping his saddle and gear next to the chuck wagon, thirty feet away, and slowly creeping up behind him.

Within about two feet of the nervous cook, Will leans in letting out a bear-sounding growl, "Grhooouw!"

A startled Oscar leaps into the air and turns to face what he thinks is the most ferocious predator in the wilderness, but only finds Will with that big, wide, dimpled grin. "You better be glad I don't have a gun in my hand. Else you would have nothin' to grin about right now," Oscar says letting out a deep breath.

Will chuckles, remembering that Oscar once mentioned his main fear on the drives is the increased chance of coming face to face with a bear, snake, or wolf. All of which are in abundance out here in this untamed territory.

"What took you so long? Tom was all over me. Threatening to fire you. Warning me that you being late looked bad for *you* and *me* since I recommended you to Mr. Hastings," Oscar admonishes.

Will replies, "My work with the Applegates' inventory and veterinarian check-ups ran later than I thought. I couldn't walk off." Will's main job is working at the Applegate Ranch near Covington, Tennessee, primarily helping with the raising and training of horses to sell, and fieldwork harvesting crops. He works that job all year, except for the four months he has permission from his employer, Mrs. Lorraine Applegate, to work cattle driving.

Will and Oscar are the only two Negro men on the cattle drive. Although Oscar is part African and part French-Canadian, to the other White drovers that makes no difference; they take delight in calling them both "darkie," "boy," and "nigger." The hands are less free to name-call on Oscar, though, because of the attention he receives from

Mr. and Mrs. Hastings, but Will is fair game. It is Oscar who suggested to Mr. Hastings they needed to bring onboard someone skillful with horses. After the cows, horses are the next important animal on a cattle drive. Oscar's suggestion made sense to Mr. Hastings, so he hired Will to join the crew as the horse wrangler.

Over time, Will developed into a bona fide cowboy. Completing three and now on his fourth cattle drive, Will is well on his way to being a regular drover. He grew up around horses, cows, and goats. There on the Applegate Ranch, he benefited from working one of the largest and successful horse-breeding ranches in the region. The Applegates began making their money from cotton and horses, and now are well-to-do Whites with family roots stemming back to the origin of the country. Mrs. Applegate's deceased husband is Orin Applegate, and his family helped work on the statehood proposal for Tennessee. The Applegate name carries a lot of weight in that state.

When the Applegate Ranch first began, Orin Applegate had a junior partner, Sir Jeffery Clements. Clements hailed from Manchester, England, and had worked in the stables of the Crown. He brought a level of horse training, care, and breeding unmatched in the United States. Great estates near and far sought out horses from the Applegate Ranch. Sir Jeffery pushed the ranch's sales past its forecasts with the help of his protégé, a young Negro lad he met on his travels: Will's father, James Lawton. James was also exceptionally knowledgeable about horses, and assisted Sir Jeffery in overseeing all of the training on the Applegate Ranch, be it for riding and racing horses, horses for fine carriages, or work horses. When James arrived at the Applegate Ranch, he met a young female slave named Harriet and was smitten right away.

When James died, Will was fifteen. Will and his mother, Harriet, took the body back to Toronto, Canada, for burial near his father's people. While in Toronto, Will saw another way of life for the Negro. He saw Coloreds and Whites living in households in close proximity, shopping at the same general stores, taking lodging at the same hotels, and eating at the same restaurants. If there were any distinctions made between members of the two ethnic groups, it was based upon the ability to pay for services. For the most part, they lived in harmony. Many times, though, Will's mother would caution him about staring, especially when he would happen upon Coloreds locked into serious conversations with Whites and sometimes speaking French. This was a totally new experience for a young Colored boy, who grew up seeing Negroes refused admittance to White businesses, seeing them being told to go around to the back of a store to transact their business, or being asked to come back the next day at the store merchant's whim, regardless of the urgency of their matter. This integrated environment was motivating and reassuring to Will that he was indeed equal to his White counterpart. He became more determined than ever to make something of himself, but not necessarily following in his father's footsteps on the Applegate Ranch as a horse trainer. His mother and other mentoring elders close to the family voiced pride in how well he was growing up to be just like his father, and that he was lucky to be a young man with a trade, surrounded by all of the tools to perfect that trade.

Will, however, had other ideas for his future. His father taught him well about horses, providing him the impetus to sell his services to others. He gained permission to work in town at the livery stable, boarding and tending to their horses. This was only the beginning of his lifelong plans. Every chance he got to go to town he would check to see if any cattle drovers were there. He was eager for a chance to give assistance at the livery stable or hang on the fence where the drovers' horses were corralled during their stay. It delighted him to hear the stories about their experiences and travels when they came to the livery to pick up their horses. Afterward, he would re-tell the stories to his mother, exactly what he saw and heard, repeating the exact tone and gestures. Repeating the whole experience allowed him to relive that experience as if it was happening again to him for the first time. Over time he balanced his book-learning received from his mother and their pastor's wife with armchair cattle-herding skills acquired from the stories he heard. As he got older, he could see how the accumulation of all his skills, book-learning, and experiences were paving the way for him to have his own farm.

When Will reached sixteen, he was already six feet tall with broad shoulders. Because he was so tall at an early age, his mother feared he would be mistaken for a full-grown man who appeared to be callous in his words or actions as opposed to just being young and naive. His eyes seemed to always be squinting, probably due to working long hours in the bright sunlight. Because of his eyes, his mother told him to look away from any White man he addressed, since squinting eyes may be perceived as intimidation or showing disrespect. But Will did neither. To his fortune, he grew up in a town where most knew him and his family, and assumed he meant no ill will to anyone. The town's White business owners would come to his rescue whenever a White stranger in town mistook him for a worker for hire. Will might be in town on Applegate business and a White traveler just arriving would yell at him because he ignored their request for him to carry their bags into a hotel or board their horse. Will usually just walked away without saying a word, which would anger the White traveler even more.

Harriet, Will's mother, is in charge of keeping the inside of the Applegate home clean and organized; an expert at keeping all manners of things cleaned and shined. Even Will, she kept well-groomed. Every night there was a ritual of cleaning teeth, hair, and a quick wash-up. She often told him that you have to take pride in yourself so that others will see that pride, and they, too, will respect you. Harriet would further expound, "First you love and appreciate yourself, then it's very easy for others to love and appreciate you. But if you don't think much a nothin' about yourself, what is the next person to think of you? Understand?" Every day ended the same way in the Lawton house: wash up for bed, and give thanks to God.

While her husband James was alive, Harriet encouraged him to take the lead in Will's upbringing. She reasoned to give a boy a good foundation, it was important for James to imprint certain masculine and gentlemanly behaviors and attitudes on Will, while she filled in with viewpoints based on sensitivity and faith. However, after James died, she changed her approach with Will. She was mother, teacher, and disciplinarian, and felt filling James' shoes required her to be firmer than she wanted for Will's own good.

A tall, slender woman, Harriet had smooth rust-brown skin, small eyes, delicate nose, and lips. As a young woman, she was attractive and shy and did not lack suitors. After James arrived at the ranch, he earned his own cottage before proposing to her. She poses a striking figure and has developed into a person well-liked and respected. After the Applegate family members, Harriet wields the power at the ranch.

She usually wore her coarse black hair in two braids on each side of her head, which were then brought across the top of her head and hair-pinned down on both sides. Sometimes she covered her head with a headcloth tied in the traditional manner of a female Negro field slave. She started by folding the headcloth into a large triangular shape. The largest corner of the headcloth was on her forehead and the base of the triangle wrapped around the back of her head. After wrapping the base or bottom of the headcloth around the back of her head, the other two corners were pulled to the front and tied into a knot on top of the largest corner, securing it as the knot tightened against her forehead. Dangling ends from all three corners were then rolled and tucked under the cloth to give a neat appearance. Now, in her later years, her hair is combed back and pinned into a French roll.

Harriet had worked at the Applegate Ranch since she was a little girl and a slave. While her family was freed by the Applegates at the end of the war, not much changed for them. They remained working as servants on the premises, receiving diminutive pay after adjustments for food and lodging. Carrying on the family's work at the ranch, Harriet became the most knowledgeable about the main house's upkeep and eventually advanced to supervising the weekly tasks: cleaning, doing the laundry, cooking, and hosting. Mrs. Applegate greatly depends on Harriet to keep her household running properly and to always be prepared to receive any number of guests planned for, or otherwise. Now that Harriet is older, she opts to allow younger servants, well-disciplined in their presentations, to serve guests in her stead. However, Mrs. Applegate so appreciates Harriet's management of the household and staff, when Harriet is ailing, Mrs. Applegate sends for her doctor to tend to her until she is back on her feet.

Mrs. Lorraine Applegate is of medium height, slender, and was once a real Tennessee beauty. Her face is comprised of clear smooth skin as if you are viewing a painter's smooth brush strokes on a pale-peach canvas. As you get closer, the peach-colored cheeks give way to sparsely scattered faint freckles, burgeoning crow's feet at the eyes and grin lines around her mouth. When she speaks, her words are slow but intentional, in a steady Southern drawl. Her turquoise-blue eyes are accented by brown eyebrows and flaxen-brown hair. She usually wears her hair pulled up off her shoulders with bangs. On festive occasions, Harriet styles her hair in a bouffant hairdo with the hair raised high on top of her head, sometimes with a large French roll in the back and tresses hanging around the crown of her head. Since Mr. Applegate's death, she seldom wears her hair down.

Though they are employer and servant, she and Harriet often engage in friendly, female banter. "You're only forty-five years old," Harriet tells her while pouring hot water into the full copper bathing tub in Lorraine's bathroom. "There's still a lot of living for you to do and fun to have."

"My fun is keeping this ranch afloat. The living? Well, it will have to find its way in between running the ranch and getting my boys securely on their feet."

To this, Harriet replies, "Those boys are grown men now. Surely you have time for yourself to get some happiness."

"Yeah, right. I'll let some man take me off, and I come back here and find that the boys have let the ranch crumble and permitting high-class whores to run through this house."

They laugh, and Harriet says, "You know good and well your boys are more respectful than that."

"I know. I just get a kick out of saying whores." They laugh again.

Lorraine was twenty-two when she finally met and married Mr. Applegate, ten years her senior. The marriage came with a son, Grant. By twenty-three, she gave birth to her one and only natural child, a son she named Jason. Will grew up alongside Jason, two years his junior. Whatever Mrs. Applegate did for Jason, Harriet would find a way to provide something comparable and less costly for Will. For example, Jason had many memorable birthday parties. Mrs. Applegate would invite all of the children of prominent townsfolk to a decorated back porch and yard, where attending guests would feast on fried chicken, potato salad, green beans, corn-on-the-cob, and watermelon, climaxed with a large decorated cake. Since Harriet directed the kitchen staff to orchestrate these events, it took little effort for her to recreate, on a smaller scale, a birthday party for Will in an area near her cottage on the ranch, positioned upwind from the barns, stables, and corrals. She usually invited her pastor and his family and other Coloreds that lived nearby, most revered Will's father, James.

Despite the differences in their stations in life, Jason and Will became friends of a sort. When they were little, Jason and Will would climb to the top of the barn, watch horses giving birth, or race their horses to a nearby creek. Where Will only attended school three to six months of the year because of the ranch's schedule and the weather, Jason and several other rich White boys worked with a tutor in town that prepared them for boarding school. Jason gave one of his old spellers and arithmetic books to Will and would help him sometimes if he had questions. He would encourage Will to learn to read well, and understand how to figure the numbers properly, by repeatedly saying, "A man has to be able to read the road signs toward his fortune, and a man has to be able to add and subtract to avoid being cheated as well as to determine the amount of his fortune." This is something Jason heard from his tutor. As they got older, their friendship did not allow Will to enter Jason's social circle of other rich White boys. Their relationship became confined to warm greetings on the ranch, Will putting Jason's horse in the barn when asked, and Jason providing Will brief tutoring sessions when Jason wasn't otherwise occupied.

One spring, Mrs. Applegate asked Will's father, James, to select a horse for Jason from among the new foals. A gorgeous black steed was selected that Jason named Dash. James taught Jason to ride and how to care for the horse, which fell to others when Jason became otherwise occupied, which was often the case when Jason got older. Seeing this, that same spring, Harriet insisted that, at the first opportunity, James was to find a horse for Will. James knew good and well responding to that request wouldn't be so easy. The Applegate family made good money selling the horses they bred, and they were of such fine quality that the amount of money James would have to raise would make the purchase an impractical one. Unless Mrs. Applegate was moved to give a horse to Will, James concluded there would not be a horse for Will coming from that ranch.

That following summer, a circus came to town, and James was summoned to their camp after the circus manager made inquiries. James was needed because one of the performing horses, the horse the circus manager rode in the show, was about to give birth. Its protruding stomach made the manager fearful to continue the troupe's travels with her in that condition. Some of the circus performers wanted to move on and just leave her boarded at a stable. Brewing discontent with how the pregnancy was slowing the tour schedule was bordering on mutiny. The circus manager had had the pregnant mare since her birth and was not going to jeopardize her life or that of her foal to keep a travel schedule. James was a godsend. He tended to the mare as he had done hundreds of times to pregnant mares ready to give birth at the Applegate Ranch. The foal was born healthy and a beaut. The mother was allowed to nurse her suckling until it was able to be on its own. The circus manager had, of course, paid James for his services, and recognized his special gift for handling horses by showering him with compliments barely discernable owing to his accent.

One evening, several months later, as Harriet, James, and Will sat down for supper, a knock was heard at the door. James rose from his chair to see who it was. When the heavy wooden front door opened, he saw a thin dark-haired foreign man, who vaguely looked familiar, standing outside the door. But what was absolutely familiar was the animal at the end of the reins held by the man. With only the dim light coming from inside the cottage, James made out the young muscular colt bobbing its head as if to say hello.

The dark-haired man spoke low with an Italian accent. "A gift to you for your kindness." By this time, Will had run to the door with a lit lantern and peered out to see the man and the unique colt, unique because of his coloring and temperament. Applegate stock was usually a single color, mostly all black or all brown and occasionally black bay horses. This animal was all chestnut reddish brown except for a white star-shaped mark on his forehead, and just his lower legs and hooves were white as if he was wearing white socks. In addition, he was comfortable around strangers, not showing any signs of fear or being skittish. James took the lit lantern from Will and raised it high to get a better look at their visitors. Recognizing the man to be the one that stood by as the circus horse gave birth and paid him for his services, James also noticed the coloring on this colt matched perfectly to that of the foal born almost a year ago.

"This is truly a surprise," James replied. "Is this the same colt born that night?"

"Yes," the man answered. "It is, and he's yours now. I only ask that you raise him with love and kindness, the same love and kindness you showed to his mother on the night he was born."

"Dad, wha . . . what breed is he?" Will stammered.

"He appears to be a Hanoverian or European breed of horse, although his mother resembled a Welsh cob," James answered.

Will, bumping into his father, broke through the cottage doorway making his way toward the colt. He, eleven years old, and the horse, one year old, locked eyes on each other. As he came closer to the colt his steps slowed. Using his training, he raised the back of his hand toward the colt's nose, allowing him to learn his scent. Next, he began gently rubbing his face, and, at that moment, he met his best friend for life, the one he would come to know as Rodeo.

Around the age of fifteen, Will started taking excursions into town. There he hung around the livery stable observing and eavesdropping on conversations of travelers, especially cattlemen. Mrs. Applegate didn't object because it was so soon after James died, and everyone wanted Will to get through that. One day, after he turned seventeen years old, he mounted Rodeo and snuck away, riding all the way to Memphis. Fortunately, on this excursion, he met another young Negro, Oscar, who was the cook for the Hastings Ranch and on the cattle driving crew. Oscar had taken the train to Memphis and was in the café in the Negro part of town. On his way to the Hastings Ranch in preparation for a cattle drive, Oscar met Will and struck up a conversation. Will sat captivated listening to Oscar describe previous drives. Oscar and Will took to each other naturally, like long-lost brothers. It made sense to Oscar, given Will's skills and desire to go on a cattle drive, that he put in a good word for him with Mr. Hastings. Thus began Will's dream come true—making money cattle driving.

Oscar did a good job of convincing Mr. Hastings and Tom that they needed someone reliable and good with horses, and selling them on Will being that person. That's why Will's failure to arrive by the start of this current drive was eating away at the "reliable" portion of that sell. Working the cattle drive indeed changed his life for the better. After each drive, Will was able to save most of his pay. With the money he earned at the Applegate Ranch, he estimated needing only one or two more drives before he had enough to buy a small farm and supplies outright.

———•———

Back at the cattle drive near the campfire, Oscar complains to Will, "You'd better check in with Tom. He gave me what-for about having to start this drive short one man. It took all of my pull with Mr. Hastings to keep them from firing you before we left the ranch." Then in a low tone, Oscar says, "I promised them you were on your way and would not let us down."

"Thanks, O. I appreciate you standing up for me. But I just made your work a whole lot easier. Don't cha know I'm a hero tonight? I just saved everyone an extra two days of work." Will brags, as he puts one foot forward, leans on his rear leg, places both hands on his jacket's lapels, and proclaims, "I turned the herd tonight and stopped the stampede!"

"You, stopped the stampede?" Oscar asks.

"Yes, I did."

"Well, I guess I'm going to get an earful of this the whole drive," Oscar complains while smiling.

"I may get a bonus!" Will blurts out, eyes glaring.

"Well, congratulations! But, please, no more missteps from here on out. You need to find a way to get here on time," Oscar says.

"OK, O. Just ignore me being a hero," Will says as he goes to get his saddle and blanket and looks around for a spot to bed down.

"Just work to keep this job; that's all I'm asking," Oscar fusses, yawning and following on Will's heels to get his bedroll to bed down near him.

"Work to keep it?" Will stops and turns around to confront Oscar. "Thanks to this job, I've got over three hundred dollars saved, and after two more drives, I'll have enough to outfit myself for some farmin', and on *my* land! Do you hear me? *My* land!" Will says pointing his finger at his own chest. "Have no doubts about me and this job. You just watch your own self, cookin' for Mr. and Mrs. Hastings for the rest of your life. I, for one, look forward to not hearing 'Wash the horses,' 'Groom the horses,' 'Clean the stable,' 'Fetch this,' 'Come now.'"

Oscar doesn't back down. He remains in Will's face. "I appreciate the work the Hastings gave me. I receive a fair wage and I live comfortably. But I have plans, too!"

"OK, let's hear them," Will says, they remain face to face.

"I've told you before. Someday, not sure when I will open my own restaurant. I've already picked out a name, The Andre. It's going to bring fine dining to some lucky town."

Ben, who often butts into their conversations, comes from tying up his horse behind the chuck wagon, and interjects, "Oscar, they'll let you buy, cook, and serve the food, but I doubt you'll be naming the building." He ends this comment with a laugh that starts as a low chuckle and escalates into a louder belly laugh. Oscar picks up a piece of bark near his foot and throws it at Ben. Ben jumps to miss being hit, but continues his laughter walking away.

"We need to be more careful lest our dreams are heard by the wrong party and get plucked out of our grips before we take a good hold of them," Oscar says leaning in.

Returning to making his pallet, Will replies, "I doubt if Ben will repeat what he heard."

Beginning to make his pallet, Oscar responds, "I can't take that chance of such information getting back to the Hastings. We're not traveling with a bunch of do-gooders here."

"Gotcha," Will says. "O, I just have to say, you've truly been a great friend to me. I can't help but encourage you to go after your dreams."

Glancing around to see if anyone is listening, Will continues, "Let nothing anyone says or does discourage you. You are an exceptional cook, and you deserve your own diner."

"Restaurant, Will, not diner!" Oscar mildly scoffs.

Oscar's full name is Oscar LeGrande Kintoole. He's about five feet eleven inches and has tan-colored skin with black curly hair. His distinguishing features are his black bushy mustache and a brown derby perpetually perched on his head. Tom tried to convince him to wear a wide-brim Stetson so he wouldn't suffer a heat stroke, but Oscar clung to his derby.

He hails from Montreal, Canada, born to an African immigrant and French-Canadian debutante. His parents are an unlikely pair, since his mother met his father while he was working at her father's restaurant, the famous LeGrande Restaurant of Montreal, owned by Phillipe Andre LeGrande. Phillipe LeGrande was not necessarily a man harboring racial prejudices; however, he had high aspirations for his beautiful daughter, Yvette. He had a difficult time understanding how she turned down the invitations and amorous attention from eligible young bachelors in the upper echelons of their society for Oscar's father, Mantee Kintoole, a kitchen porter and a poor African kitchen porter at that. Once the relationship was known, it just fueled gossip among Phillipe's friends and restaurant patrons. After Yvette eloped with Mantee and returned to settle in Montreal, Phillipe could not shake the shame of his beautiful and rich daughter marrying a poor immigrant. He paid Mantee his regular salary and offered something extra to be discreet about the marriage. Mantee refused the something extra, but still was discreet while they worked at the restaurant. Yvette and Mantee understood Phillipe's concerns. It was a matter of survival. No matter what they thought personally, their ability to maintain a comfortable living depended upon the many patrons and lavish celebrations Phillipe hosted for prominent guests from around the world at the LeGrande. Phillipe found the people most appalled about the union were his American customers, and

Phillipe's business was all he had. Therefore, he and eventually Mantee and Yvette protected his business for the benefit of the entire family. As a result, Oscar's parents would only vacation in Europe where they were free to take romantic carriage rides through a park, chase one another through the Mediterranean's surf, or hold hands on an evening stroll after dinner. What mattered was that they were together.

Both of Oscar's parents spoke French and taught Oscar to speak both French and English. During his teenage years, he began working in his grandfather's restaurant. He initially ran errands and cleaned up after closing. He enjoyed opportunities to work with his father, who now assisted Phillipe with buyer and manager duties. Oscar eventually worked his way up to a kitchen cook. Once in the kitchen, he knew the top spot was that of a chief chef, a position Grandpa Phillipe shared with another excellent chef from France. Grandpa Phillipe could not hide his pride in Oscar. He took out time after closing to demonstrate to him his secret techniques, and Oscar became quite good, but evidently not good enough for Phillipe to assign him a top chef position. Consequently, at seventeen, Oscar left his family and home for the States to make his fortune with his skills.

In America, there were plenty of jobs to be had as café cooks or cooks for rich families and estates, but that was not a part of Oscar's ultimate plans. While bumping around, working as a short-order cook in street cafes, he heard one could make real money working cattle drives as a cook. The cattlemen were notorious for raising cane if the food on the drive was lousy or ran out on the trail. These uprisings happened frequently because the trail bosses would recruit just about anyone to do the cooking, and the cooks they hired were usually inexperienced at estimating the amount of food supplies required, not to mention the dishes they prepared would either be too salty, too tasteless, or bordering on spoiled or rancid. Another skill desired was the ability, when the food ran out, to improvise a halfway decent meal with what could be scavenged on the trail: making a meal from deer, rabbit, or fish, if they were lucky. Oscar took the notion to maximize his opportunities by selling his services to the highest bidder. And he did, to Mr. W. John Hastings of Waco, Texas. Upon learning Mr. Hastings had a large spread out in the West and was sending herds of cattle to the Dodge City railhead station, Oscar sought him out. He took the train to Waco, and found his way to the Hastings Ranch. As he climbed the steps leading to the main house's grand front doors, he took a deep breath and then knocked. Once gaining an audience with Mr. and Mrs. Hastings, he introduced himself as having been under the tutelage of great chefs of Montreal, possessing skills in the finest French cuisine, and asked if he could cook that evening's meal. Mrs. Hastings was very impressed after he informed them of his time working at the LeGrande in Montreal, Canada. She knew of this restaurant. She was further enticed when Oscar asked them to dress as though they were going to an elegant restaurant in Paris, France, and to expect to dine by candle-light at a table decorated with fancy tablecloths and napkins.

As a final impressive touch, Oscar wrote down the menu on small cards and placed them at two place settings set up on the Hastings' dining room table. The hand-written menu was thus:

<u>M E N U</u>

Mushroom soup

Lettuce salad with celery and marinated tomatoes

Beef Toreadors in red wine sauce

Sautéed string beans in butter sauce

Mashed potatoes with garlic and butter flavoring

Buttermilk biscuits

Chocolate Puffs

Iced Tea

Upon reading the menu, Mrs. Hastings was ecstatic. Initially, Mr. Hastings was standoffish. However, after the couple consumed the dinner, he summoned Oscar from the kitchen to the dining room and offered to pay handsomely for what he had cooked, adding that Oscar should state his fee to serve as their regular cook and no amount would go without consideration. However, Oscar stood steadfast in front of them making his case. He wanted to be hired on as the cook for the cattle drives so he could see the country and earn pay at a rate higher than a regular cook.

Wrinkle lines forming in her forehead, Mrs. Hastings asked, "Cook for the cattle drive? You are too talented to be cooking on a cattle drive."

Staring intensely at her, Mr. Hastings interrupted her, and then turned to Oscar. "Mrs. Hastings and I will talk it over. In the meantime, you can stay over for the night in the bunkhouse, where the ranch hands sleep." Mr. Hastings could see working the cattle drive was important to Oscar. Indeed, he could use him in either job. What he didn't want was for him to walk off because Mrs. Hastings wanted him at the house full time.

The next morning, Mr. Hastings agreed to Oscar's request, as long as the time between cattle drives would be spent at the ranch tantalizing him, Mrs. Hastings, and occasionally their dinner guests with his fine cuisine. Oscar knew there would be a fight getting time off to go home to Canada to visit, but he couldn't risk losing this opportunity he had skillfully crafted together by bringing up an additional term to negotiate. Therefore, Mr. Hastings' offer was gladly accepted and agreed to as is. As the new head chef of the Hastings Ranch, Oscar was directed to move into a small bedroom near the kitchen, which was an upgrade to the sleeping quarters in the bunkhouse. In the small bedroom, Oscar has a wardrobe closet, bed, chair, lamp, a desk to write on, and a wash table stationed below a small wall mirror. The wash table was only large enough for holding a water pitcher and a washbowl and includes rails on the sides for hanging bathing cloths.

———◆———

Back at the herd, the cattle appear to be settling down after the stampede. Tom and the others return to camp all dusty, sweaty, and worn to the seams. Tom assigns four other drovers to work guard duty for the remainder of the night. Will and Oscar are sitting on their bedrolls near the chuck wagon when Tom approaches.

"Will, first light you can head out due west and round up any strays." Will nods in acceptance.

Zeb, a veteran cowhand standing by the campfire sipping a cup of coffee, says, "Hope we've seen our last lightning bolt for a while."

Tom makes a quick response in a loud and firm tone before grabbing his bedroll out of the chuck wagon, "Well, if we do, we've got to be on the ready to just," Tom makes a circular motion with his finger, "round 'em back up again. We got to make Dodge City on time."

Oscar leans in speaking low to Will, "Tom's under a lot of pressure. He has only ten weeks tops to get this herd into Dodge City and this is the largest herd he's ever driven—twenty-five hundred head. To add to his worries, Mr. Hastings promised the crew some free time in one or two of the towns on the way." Despite Tom pleading to Mr. Hastings that they usually get drunk and arrested for all kinds of disorderliness and mischief and that there was no time to spare, Mr. Hastings tells Tom to give the crew time to blow off steam. He does, however, leave it to Tom to find the right time and place for the drovers to unwind. Mr. Hastings is operating under the notion that it's best to sacrifice a couple of hours to keep a good crew together that returns to work year after year, rather than losing any one of them.

"With you here now, Tom should be feeling some relief. But allowing these cowhands to break loose drinking, gambling, and skirt-chasing on this drive will be a real test of what Tom is made of," Oscar continues.

The next morning, everyone wakes up cranky. Some have had only about two hours of sleep. No one has much to say, except for

Oscar. Donning his derby, he clangs the cook's bell, which is a trian-gular-shaped metal that rings out as you quickly pass a metal spoon from one of its sides to another. He clangs it hard, accompanied by his yelling, announcing breakfast to the countryside. "Breakfast ready! Come and get it!"

The drive is only two days out from the Hastings Ranch, so break-fast is still quite impressive. They respond to Oscar's clanging and yelling with a human stampede. Breakfast features scrambled eggs with garlic seasoning and grilled onions, crispy bacon, grits, biscuits, and coffee. There is a lot of pushing and shoving among the crew in the serving line, jockeying to get ahead of the other to be served. The pushing draws to a halt when Tom or Zeb appear among them. But this time, when Will walks up, the other drovers clear a path for him to enter into the front of the line.

"Part the Red Sea, gentlemen, we are among gods this morning," Pepper says. They all laugh, but make room for Will to proceed to the front of the line. Will, well aware of their fondness for practical jokes, hesitates before accepting their offer, but then moves to the front of the line.

Pepper continues, "A man brave enough to face down stampeding long-horns—"

"Or stupid enough," Clancy interjects, causing low chuckles.

Pepper adds, "Before I was so rudely interrupted, I said to face down stampeding long-horns deserves the first serving of breakfast. Chef Oscar, will you do the honors?" Pepper bows to Will and waves his hand motioning for Oscar to serve Will first.

After they finish eating, different ones either verbally say the breakfast was "deeee-licious," or tip their hats at Oscar to express "good meal." Oscar is proud to acknowledge all of their compliments with short nods. This is goodwill he wants to maintain and can use when dealing with Mr. Hastings in the future. The drovers pack away their bedrolls, strap their saddles on their horses, mount them, and head out to start rounding up the strays. Usually, Oscar kills the fire and makes the chuck wagon ready for travel, but they are staying put until the strays are rounded up.

It takes most of the morning to drive in enough strays. Every steer spotted within eyesight is brought back. Any remaining lost ones may have been captured by thieves, predatory animals, or lost to the elements. After Tom and Zeb do a scan in all directions and consult one another, Tom gives the signal for everyone to prepare to move out. In response, every hand gets to their assigned trail positions.

Lead steers

Tom	C	Zeb
Rodrigo	A	Matt
Clancy	T	Bear
Pepper	T	Drake
Chris	L	Ben
Will	E	Oscar

Tom and Zeb are the most experienced, so they ride up front flanking the lead steers and the front one-fifth of the herd. Behind Tom, moving vertically toward the rear of the herd, are five hands: Rodrigo, the Mexican caballero; Clancy, the gambler; Pepper, the quick draw; followed by Chris, the ladies' man; and Will, wrangler for the backup horses. On the other side behind Zeb, who fought in the Civil War for the Confederates, are the scout Matt, who scouted for the Union Army during the Civil War, and three more hands: Bear, who is as big and strong as a grizzly bear; Drake, another who fought in the war for the South; followed by Ben the tenderfoot; and Oscar the cook, driving the chuck wagon.

Mr. Hastings keeps a good stock of riding and workhorses at the ranch. Several are brought along as backup horses for the drovers in case the horse they are riding becomes exhausted or injured. Will wrangles eight backup horses this drive and usually travels behind the herd and close to the chuck wagon. His key to managing all of them together is to train them to come when called, give them treats, and regular grooming. During the majority of the drive, the horses trot untethered, enabling them to graze frequently. If there is a threat or need to move at a certain pace or along a narrow path, Will can tether them all by stringing ropes from one to the other.

To get the chuck wagon ready for travel, Oscar fastens down his supplies and utensils inside and mounts the wagon's front bench. He is free to ride parallel to the herd, in the front or the rear. Grasping reins connected to two harnessed mules that pull the chuck wagon, he looks Will's way and gestures a nod of "Here we go again." Mounted on Rodeo, Will nods back at Oscar, and then whistles and makes clicking sounds with his tongue to signal to his remuda that it's time for them to join him and to start slowly moving forward. The crew moves the herd out.

CHAPTER 2

FORK IN THE ROAD

———

IT was only fifteen days ago that Will left to join the current cattle drive. He left on a Sunday, a sacred day to his mother. Harriet considers Monday through Saturday as work days at the Applegate Ranch, and Saturday nights to be a time to replenish one's stamina and soul. In that vein, their family adopted the habit of Saturday nights also being bath nights. That works out well because they precede Sunday mornings, a time when members of their tiny household rise early, dress, and scramble to be on time for Sunday church services.

"Why don't you bathe first, then I," Harriet said to Will as she carried clean bathing cloths for washing and drying the body through her bedroom and into the bathroom. Watching the pot of water boiling and bubbling on the pot-bellied stove, Will considered he would be in hot water with Tom if he didn't leave soon. His work at the Applegate Ranch, which delayed his departure for the drive, involved a scheduled inventory and veterinarian check-ups. Based on Oscar's letter informing him when the next herd was scheduled to leave the Hastings Ranch, Will should have left the previous day! He gathered himself for how he needed to explain this to his mother, knowing it will surely trigger an argument since he wanted to leave tomorrow, Sunday; a day etched in her mind as reserved for worship. She was in the bathroom filling the bathtub with cold water they brought in from the well.

Will responded to Harriet, "You know, I've got to get on the road, Momma." He gasped and continued, "Might I?" He breathed in and exhaled. "Can you give my regards to Pastor and Mrs. Walker?" He heard nothing from her. She remained out of his view preparing the bathtub in the bathroom. *Maybe she didn't hear me*, he thought. He moved nearer to the doorway of her room and looked her way flinching, anticipating a backlash, but went on and completed his sentence. "And I miss services and head out early tomorrow morning?"

Harriet, in a fast, demonstrative strut, exited her bedroom, which is next to the bathroom where the bathtub is located. After half-filling the tub with cold water, she was awaiting the water heating up on the stove. Checking the pots to see how hot the water was, she replied rather resolutely to Will, "No, I think it's fittin' that we goooo and give thaaaaanks for our blessings. You're blessed with work here, work moving your cattle, and more importantly, you need to pray to the Lord to watch over you on the road to your moving cattle job. Don't take for granted the blessings you've received. You can pack before church services in the morning, attend services, and then leave."

Will frowned at her and shook his head in disbelief.

She looked back at him in a stance with her hands on her hips and continued, "A couple of hours won't make any difference. You finished up all your work here yesterday. You need to get a bath and a good night's sleep, then you're on your way tomorrow." She resumed monitoring the pots. "I think this water is ready."

Will removed the pots of hot water from the stove and carried them through her bedroom to the bathroom, frowning and sulking. He felt he wasn't being a man of his word to Tom. He had gotten to the drives on time three times now, and for this one, his fourth trip, he will be late. However, after a bit of sulking, his bad mood eventually subsided, after realizing she was right. He thought to himself, *I do have a first commitment to this ranch. I had to finish up the work here at Applegate, bathe, and rest up.*

Early Sunday morning, Will accompanied Harriet heading up the road from the Applegate Ranch to the white church building where they attended church services. It is a small church with eight pews on each side of the main room. A small room in the rear of the building serves as the pastor's office and for storage. Will and Harriet entered behind others hurrying to take their seats. Sliding into a pew next to the last on the right side of the church, their entrance into the main room was of no consequence to anyone, except a couple of young ladies seated in the front on the left side who turned and spied a quick look. The two young ladies were the pastor's daughters who grew up with Will: Rita Mae and Martha Jane Walker.

Church services routinely proceed first with a hymn, followed by notices and announcements. A church member, Mrs. Fenton, at the front of the main room near the pulpit spoke loudly to the congregation so her voice will be heard around the main room. "There will be a bake sale, a church basket lunch at the lake, and we should not forget about our sick and shut-in." She talked for a few more minutes, followed by another hymn, the sermon, the offering, and finally the benediction.

For that Sunday's sermon, Pastor Walker was in rare form. He preached on the story of Job. How Job's faith was tested by having everything he had taken away from him: his money, possessions, property, and family. At the end of Job's test, God restored everything Job lost twice over. Pastor's voice stirred the congregation with emphasis, "The lesson iiiis, your faith should comfort you equally during the harvest as it does during the drought. During the harvest, it's so easy to praise the Lord. But as your condition changes for the worse, meaning you enter a drought, what do you do during that drought? Do you keep praising the Lord's name and waiting on the Lord? Or do you fall down weeping, forsaking your faith? You'll never be ready for another harvest after the drought, if you give up on your faith, lose your faith during the drought! You need to hold tight to your faith. You need to till the soil and ready the seeds for planting. At the first signs of the evening dew, drop those seeds into that tilled soil, and reap the harvest that you have sewn. For salvation comes in the morning. Do you hear me, my brothers and sisters? Joy comes in the morning. During the drought, look not at the sunbaked land, not at the dried river bed, but cast your eyes to the heavens and know that all prayers—I said all prayers—are answered. The land will be soaked once again, the rivers will overflow once again. After all is lost, and you're spent beyond spent—still, I say," and the pastor raised his right arm vertically into the air pointing his index finger toward the heavens. "Still, I say, wait on the Lord to ready the soil. Your joy comes in the morning. Look to the heavens and know that your salvation is on its waaaay!"

Members of the congregation jumped to their feet, shouting the Lord's name, some clapping hands and praising God, looking up toward the ceiling. Many repeated loudly, "Thank you, Jesus! And God is Good! God is Good!" Harriet spread her arms, stretched out on both sides, palms facing up. With tearful eyes looking up smiling, she exuberantly exclaimed, "Thank you, Jesus! Thank you, Jesus!"

After church services finally came to a close, the attendees greeted one another and began dispersing, some toward the pulpit in the front of the main room to greet and thank Pastor Walker for today's message, while others proceeded through the aisles to the doorway exiting the church. Those exiting filed out to awaiting wagons, horses, or to begin their stroll home. Harriet and Will joined the strollers making their way down the road, which is a wide dirt path, heading in the direction toward the Applegate Ranch. Surrounded by other worshippers walking, some talking, some singing in pairs and threes, and making an effort to not kick up the dirt along their path, two young ladies, Pastor Walker's daughters, Rita and Martha, hurried to catch up to walk alongside Harriet and Will.

"Afternoon, Mother Harriet. Afternoon, Will," emerged sequentially from each of the young ladies' lips. Harriet and Will responded in kind almost simultaneously, "Afternoon. Afternoon."

Rita waited for an appropriate pause after the greetings, took a deep breath, and then gushed, "Did you enjoy the services?"

Harriet replied, maintaining her cadence, "It was most uplifting. My soul can feast off that for the rest of the week."

Everyone smiled.

Rita glanced at Will and asked, "Were the services uplifting for you too, Will?"

Hearing his name, Will looked her way, and their eyes met, causing him to blush and reply, "Ah, yes, it was very uplifting."

The parties continued strolling and soaking up the afternoon sun.

Rita is a petite-figured girl, very smart, and Will always enjoys her company. This Sunday her black hair was neatly French-braided with ribbon weaved through it. Her smooth reddish-brown skin framed her face memorable for her enchanting olive-shaped eyes and heart-shaped lips, which she dabs with red lipstick. Martha is a bookend to her older sister Rita, except she takes on more of her father's features with stocky legs, though maintaining a petite figure as well. Both girls are shy, but anyone observing them would notice Rita has her cap set for Will.

Rita barely contained her excitement in preparing to blurt out the next question, a most desired request. "Mother Harriet, you and Will are welcome to join us for dinner tonight. My sister and I are cooking smothered chicken, collard greens, mashed potatoes, and buttermilk biscuits." Martha Jane looked at Rita in a congratulatory fashion for her getting it all out without stammering. Immediately after extending the invitation, Rita raised her eyes and looked with a deliberate aim at Will's face, expecting to capture his positive response any second. Even Harriet glanced his way as if to pull the positive response right out of him. But Will, so preoccupied and worrying about his trip, had allowed his mind to drift elsewhere. While walking, he had angled over to the outer edge of their path, jockeying to see how much more road was ahead. He was anxious to get home. Upon hearing Rita say again, "We're inviting you and your mother to dinner?" he moved back into lockstep with their small group and collected himself.

"Oh, Miss Rita, that is most kind of you and your family. But . . . I, uh, I am leaving this afternoon . . . traveling out-a-town, and have to beg your apologies."

Harriet glared at Will and then responded to the Walker sisters, "Unfortunately, I must also extend my apologies. I have to see to it that he gets on his way properly." Will stepped away again to the outer edge of the path to get a clear view of the road ahead. As they approached the Applegate Ranch boundaries, he shifted his head from side to side peering through those walking in front of him. He was curious to see if Rodeo was in the pasture near the path awaiting his return as he had done times before on Sundays.

The Walker sisters were approaching their turn off from the path. Both parties acknowledged their goodbyes, the Walker sisters giving a soft nervous wave goodbye, Harriet and Will nodding theirs. The Walker sisters turned right, heading toward Pastor Walker's home, while Harriet and Will turned left toward their little cottage located on one side of the stables and corral on the Applegate Ranch.

Harriet opened the door to their cottage preparing to enter. Will made a beeline toward the barn to gather his gear and Rodeo.

Harriet stopped and said in a commanding tone, "May I have a word with you?"

Will made an about-face and followed her inside the cottage. "I know that tone; what did I do now?"

"It's more of what you didn't do. I can't think of a better choice of a young lady to court than Miss Rita. You let that girl muster up enough courage to invite you to supper, and you were no more interested than . . ."

"Momma, I'm leavin' within the hour. I made my apologies like a gentleman. What more could I do?"

"I know. It's just she's such a nice girl and she seems to like you—for now. But I'm gonna stay out of your personal affairs." Harriet turned to walk into her bedroom, but again hesitated and turned around saying, "Wait, I need to say this. If you are ever interested in a young lady, you have got to make an effort to show her you are interested, show her that you are willing to give her some of your time. Spending time together allows you to get to know her and her to get to know you."

Will grinned and replied, "I get it. She needs to know if I go fishin' in the morning, do I get tore-down drunk in the evenin', do I spend all day training my horse, and most of all," he walked over to her and leaned in to kiss her on the cheek, "do I have a meddlin' momma?"

After allowing him to plant his kiss, she pushed him away and, waving him off, said, "Go get ready for your trip."

Throwing his head back and brandishing a big smile, he turned and left through the door of the cottage. Before closing the door, he shouted back to her, "When I get back, we'll go to dinner at the Walkers'."

———•———

On the tenth morning of the cattle drive before sunup, Matt makes a mad dash to an area behind the chuck wagon to relieve himself. Will sees him and finds the appropriate moment to approach. He catches Matt on his way back to the camp area, but still behind the chuck wagon where others cannot hear or see them.

Lowering his voice, almost to a whisper, Will asks, "Can I ride with you to scout Red River?"

"Why would I choose to take you over the rest of these cowgirls?" chides Matt, also responding in a whisper, taking his hat off, and combing through his hair with his fingers.

"Because I'm good company, good conversation, and I'm reliable— well, except for being late to the drive this one time," Will says squinting one eye and holding up one finger.

"Yeah, then there's that. I give you one thing: you're very sure of yourself," responds Matt. "But what about the horses you're supposed to play nursemaid to?"

"That won't be a problem," Will says.

"Well, if you can square that away, so Tom won't be down my throat."

"It'll be taken care of."

"I'm gonna head out tomorrow morning," Matt says. "I'll collect a rifle at the chuck wagon, then head out."

Will is going to call in an IOU. Rodrigo never went to school. When he shared that bit of information with Will, Will explained that he had some spellers that were useful for learning how to read. Will brought one of his spellers to share with Rodrigo, and he was quite grateful. Will plans to approach Rodrigo that evening to get him to cover him herding the backup horses.

At the end of the day, the drovers come in to eat and rest. Some sit on empty food crates; others, on their saddles or the ground. When Oscar announces dinner is ready, they form a line so that Oscar can serve them. He knows how much food has been prepared and doles out enough on each of the drover's tin plates to ensure everyone gets a good serving.

Drake stands first in line, two men ahead of Will. Sporting a half grin, he addresses Will. "Ah—Will, I never paid tribute to your heroism days ago. I guess you'll be informing your sweetheart that you are a stampede hero."

Oscar loads Drake's tin plate with beans, rice, pork chop, and biscuit. Will cuts his eyes at Drake then looks away thinking *I'm not goin' to give this sideways turd the time of day*. Drake smirks at Will moving out of the line to find a place to sit. Will avoids Drake because he knows one he is a Confederacy sympathizer, and two he feels free to call him a nigger at his leisure. Will never responds to him or gives him eye contact; he just stays in line, collects his food and keeps a watch out for Rodrigo.

Drake continues teasing Will, getting louder saying, "Then again maybe you don't have a sweetheart." Holding the smirk on his face, he surveys the crew for someone to bolster his comment.

Chris, also in line, chimes in, "Drake, he's a little young to be handlin' a woman. Now you take me, for example. When a woman sets her eyes on me, she sees a protector, a provider, and," swaying his hips and wrapping his own arms around his body simulating kissing someone, he continues, "a lover."

Zeb finishes Chris's boasting saying, "And she will see someone who'll leave her in the blink of an eye!"

The drovers let out a low chuckle. Soon, they are all seated with their meals in a half circle around the campfire. Pepper joins in the conversation, "Any woman is just plain trouble."

"Don't like women too much, huh, Pepper?" Chris taunts while seated smiling and eating.

Pepper responds, "Don't cause me to wipe that grin off your face."

Tom walks up. "There will be no wiping, arguing and fighting on this drive; else I dock your pay."

Rodrigo has come and gone through the serving line, and is sitting at the far end of the half circle near the chuck wagon. Will gets up, moving to sit near him.

Chris, seeing Will moving around, elects to tease him. "I'm wondering, Will, after all these nights on the trail, have you learned anything about women from my stories of conquest?"

Rodrigo pauses from eating and yells, "Yeah! He learned you are sly like a fox, and slippery like a snake." A few drovers let out a chuckle.

Zeb finishes Rodrigo's statement. "And the gentler sex tangling with a fox or snake never stands a chance. From all we have heard, Chris, you are bad news for any woman."

The drovers nod to one another remarking, "Yeah, that's for sure." And their laughter peppers the air.

Clancy joins in, directing his comments to Chris. "Chris, your stories have a lot of drama. Jilting ladies after you give them a ring and promise to marry them, or romancing a widow with children and leaving 'em. And our favorite, the beautiful lady you went on and on about as the *one* who turned out to have an outlaw, brute of a husband that was trailing the herd to try to catch you alone. Now, I avoid drama by being entertained by the ladies at the saloon. Of course, you can criticize my choice. But, there's no drama."

The crew goes at Chris about how outlandish his escapades are, while Tom discusses supplies and the route with Zeb and Oscar. Will finds this to be a good time to corner Rodrigo and make his request.

"How long will you be gone?" Rodrigo asks, a frown crossing his face.

"Just until night at the most," Will answers.

"Now, I got to get someone to cover my section. And what do I do about Tom?" Rodrigo asks, gaping his mouth open and leaning his head to the side.

Will looks around nervously, then speaks quickly. "Stay in the rear by the chuck wagon. Tom goes around the herd only once and will probably think you're on a break. As long as you have all of them and they're moving fine, there's no reason for him to say anything to you."

"He can tell us apart, Will," Rodrigo says shaking his head.

"It will be OK. They're a good group of horses. I'll owe you after this." Will stands up to leave.

"Yeah, and I'll decide how you pay up. Just, go on," says Rodrigo waving him off with his hand.

It's the eleventh morning on the drive. Zeb rides out to Tom to get any instructions for the day. "Eleven days and only about 140 miles," Tom says to Zeb curling his lips. "This is rotten pace. They can move but so fast when it's hot like this. With our luck, we'll arrive early winter and end up pushing the cattle over ice-slick hills, just lettin' 'em slide down into Dodge City."

"That would be a sight," Zeb says with a grin. "Pounds of beef crashing into storefronts, upheaving posts and troughs," he adds and laughs.

Tom knows a herd of cattle doesn't move vertically, lined up one behind another. Sure, there are lead bulls that the bulk of the cows follow, but for the most part, they trail the lead bulls lined up almost horizontally. They can stretch that line out as far as twenty miles, depending upon the size of the herd. The drovers have to flank each end and follow in back to herd stragglers back into the main group. Without the drovers, one or two a day can wander too far to the left or too far to the right, and then lose sight of the others and be killed or lost for good.

During one of his daily rounds, Tom rides out to Clancy and yells, "Bring 'em in." Clancy nods in acknowledgment and begins waving his hat and wrangles some that were lagging out to the side to hurry along to catch up with the others. The herd kicks up plenty of dust, and leaves enough droppings to keep a horde of insects and flies busy.

Tom rides around the back of the herd to the east toward Ben and yells the same message to him. "Bring 'em in." Ben was expecting Tom to deliver that instruction about now. Since the day started, a little before daybreak, he has been doing all he can to keep his laggers moving back into the herd. That way, if he trades off to take a break, no one would complain about how bad his section had gotten. While Tom checks the herd in Ben's section, Ben decides to use this opportunity to ask him a question. He rides over to get close to Tom. "Would you mind if I go with Matt to scout Red River near the Texas border to pick a spot to cross?"

Tom frowns and replies in an annoyed tone, "Why are you asking me this? You know that's Matt's job, and he makes the call on who he wants to take or not take. But since you brought it up, ask Drake to cover for you, and go find Matt. Tell him to go now and scout where to cross and not to forget we need supplies."

Ben rides south-east, and finds Matt and Oscar fully engaged with a cow in labor. As he gallops up to the two, Matt falls back, stretched out on the ground, squirming to brace himself against the recumbent mother cow to pull the calf out of her womb. Using his feet, he pushes against the cow's backside, his hands firmly holding onto two front hooves of a calf still inside the womb. He's pulling the hooves, and the mother cow is mooing and yelping like crazy. The head of a new-born calf slithers out covered with bloody innards of the birthing mother cow. Ben stops nearby, dismounts, and gapes at the scene. Although this is a common sight at the ranch, he's fairly new to han-dling cows, and a newborn calf unfolding out of its mother always stops him in his tracks. Between the cow's pushing and Matt's pull-ing, only one-third of the calf has emerged.

Straining his arms and legs to dislodge the calf's hips and hind legs, Matt yells, "It'll die if I don't get . . . get it completely out right now!" Bloody liquid oozes out in a pool, soaking the ground where Matt is lying. The mother cow's head is rolling, and she continues making repetitive loud mooing and yelping sounds of distress and pain.

Oscar yells, "Is she hurting?"

Ben blurts out, "How did this happen?"

"How do you damn think?" Matt fires back wrestling to get more of the calf out.

"I mean, I thought we weeded out the ones carrying calves," says Ben.

Oscar chimes in, "Well, you missed one." And with that, the rest of the calf slides out of the womb covered in blood, mucus, and red-dish gunk. The mother cow stops the loud mooing and twists her head around to see what is happening to her new baby behind her. Matt carefully pulls the calf clear of her into a patch of nearby grass. Oscar brings more cut grass and lays it under and around the calf as if to make a nest. Matt shakes the calf's head to ensure it has opened its eyes and is inhaling air.

Ben yanks himself out of the gaping stare and informs Matt of his purpose for riding over there in the first place. "Matt, Tom wants you to go now, and scout ahead on where to cross Red River."

Matt gets up and assesses how much cow liquid has drenched his shirt, pants, and boots. Oscar says, "You can rinse off here by the wagon, or wait till you get to the river unless you want that mother cow mistaking you for one of her offspring. She's already picking up the scent that something of hers is close by."

By this time, the mother cow gets up, walks rather wobbly over to her calf, and begins licking its face and body. This is the first promising sign. Mother cows lick their offspring after birth to remove remnants of the birthing sac the calf has lived in all those months inside the womb. Removing parts of the sac from the nose and mouth ensures the newborn can breathe freely. Also, the licking cleans the newborn's fur and simultaneously contributes to bonding between mother and calf.

Will rides over, and is amused by his discovery. "What kinda pow-wow you got goin' over here? Tom is going to bust a gut when he sees you three are out here birthin' calves—and how did that one get into the herd anyway?"

They had tried to avoid newborn calves because they slow down the drive. The newborn either doesn't walk, walks too slow, or wants to stop and nurse. However, the newborn does need time to nurse so it can receive the necessary proteins and antibodies found in mother's milk. Those nutrients help it stave off infections, illnesses, and helps it survive. Similarly, some mother cows have problems after giving birth. They may lie there a while, recuperating. You can't blame them, but time is not a cattle drive's friend. Therefore, it's better to leave near-term pregnant cows at the ranch where there's plenty of time for them to give birth, to get on their feet after giving birth, for the baby to nurse, and for the mother cow and calf to bond.

Matt walks over to his horse that is tied to the chuck wagon and says, "Well, I'm outta the nursemaid business. Oscar, it's in your hands now. You know Tom's under pressure to get this herd in on time." Looking at the calf he continues, "Bring it along, leave it, or kill it for dinner?"

Ben gasps, "Oh, no I'm not gonna watch this." He quickly remounts his horse and takes off back to the herd.

Matt mounts his horse and inquires again, "What's it gonna be, Oscar? You want me to do it? It may be better all-around if we do it quickly, and save it some misery. Although, I don't know what you can do to get the mother back in the herd. They usually hover around the dead carcass of their baby for a couple of days before they move on. If you can't decide now, ask Tom. I've got to go scout Red River and get your supplies." Matt looks over at Will.

Oscar surveys the mother cow tending to her newborn. The newborn latches onto her nipple. This is another good sign, causing him to direct Will and Matt to go on their way, saying he will take care of the mother and calf.

Matt and Will ride to the northeast end of the herd. Tom could not be seen. From the sun's position, it is about two hours before high noon, and Matt wants to get the hot, sticky cow guck off him. "Will, I'm ready to ride out. Did you . . .?"

"It's all taken care of. I can leave now, too!" Will says, allowing a wide grin to creep across his face.

Oscar allows the calf to finish nursing, and then he grabs it and bundles it in an empty cotton flour sack. Mother cow's mooing erupts and she charges at Oscar, but she is still too weak to aim at him with any precision. Oscar successfully scoops up the calf and loads it into the back of the chuck wagon. Mother cow staggers over to the wagon and watches his every action intensely. After Oscar situates the calf in the rear of the wagon where the mother has a clear view and can see no obvious harm is coming to it, she quiets down and sniffs the wagon. Oscar mounts the wagon bench in front, grasps the reins, and motions to the mules to pull off slowly, going at a pace slow enough for the mother cow to keep up. He has no idea of when or whether she will get back into the march with the others, but he does not want to let the herd get too far ahead of him. Out on the plains, there is safety in numbers. He stays with the herd and at times speeds up so by sunset he can find a place to stop, set the calf out of the wagon, allow the mother and calf to continue bonding, and wait for the drive to stop for the day. Luckily, Tom stops the drive near the place Oscar is waiting, and he tells Oscar to make camp there. To keep the newborn out of sight, Oscar moves the hitching post for the backup horses twenty feet from the chuck wagon. He creates a mini-corral using wooden stakes and ropes to restrict the mother and calf to an area on the side of the chuck wagon opposite to the campfire. A direct view of them from the campfire area is blocked by the wagon. If any of the drovers notice her, Oscar hopes they will think she's one of the twenty-five hundred that just meandered over near the wagon. By moving the hitching post for all of their horses, Oscar further hopes each drover will ride into camp, tie their horse, proceed to the scrumptious dinner he has prepared, and eventually drop off to sleep without even seeing the mother and calf.

Returning to other events of that morning, Matt mentors Will on scouting on their way to the Red River. "Scoutin' is a big responsibility. You gotta keep your bearing, know the route, and find a clear path for our large number of travelers. You hear what I'm sayin', boy?"

"Do you say that to annoy me, or are you just being funny?" Will asks. Ordinarily, Will would have verbally pounced on Matt about calling him *boy*, but so far Matt always gives him pointers about how to do things on the trail, and he doesn't want bad blood between them.

Chuckling, Matt replies, "Oh, I'm just funnin' with you. It's a long ride, three hours. I'm not gonna talk sweet to you the entire trip. I tell you what. Why don't you call me a name?"

"I tell you what, why don't you tell me more about scoutin', and leave out the insults?" Will replies.

Leaning on his saddle horn, Matt continues with his narrative, "You can't be out here just ridin' like you're taking a little trip or somethin'. You gotta see if there's enough area for clear passage, enough grass for grazing, a good place for a camp at night. Now that's the easy stuff. The hard stuff is lookin' to see who else is out here. Watch for tracks of animals, especially predator types. Snake skins, carcasses, or skeletons reflect a predator that might feed on our herd. Are there tracks of renegades, drifters, and the like? Look for camps others cleared out of. Examine the camp to figure how long ago they cleared out, and the number in their party."

"How long you been scoutin'?" Will queries, adopting the same relaxed posture in his saddle.

"I learned during the war with the South, and only by accident. As a mere tadpole serving in the Tennessee Regiment in the Union Army, I was drafted to help scout when the regular scout got wounded. The regular scout was my uncle whose heels were never more than twenty feet from mine. I followed him around like a puppy. There are some things a man teaches you by speaking, by punishing, and by example. I was lucky; the only man always around me was my uncle, a man of few words and a man by his very nature loathed violence. So, I learned by example."

Matt and Will ride for two more hours before reaching the Red River.

In some places, the river is as wide as fifty feet, and in other spots, it narrows to twenty feet. The water is clear near the shallow parts, but everywhere else murky and it is difficult to determine the depth. The riverbank in spots gradually slopes down to the water's edge while in other places there is an abrupt drop up to four feet. Matt rides alongside the river going in a northerly direction, observing the current, speculating on the depth, and checking the river banks for how easy their travelers could climb in and out of the water. He eventually finds a spot about twenty-five-feet wide with no drop on either side. There are some trees and shrubs nearby offering him partial seclusion, so he dismounts, ties his horse, and begins peeling off his shirt, boots, and pants.

Matt glances over at Will. "I'm gonna wash up here. I'll check the depth at this crossing. You do a hundred feet circle of the area ahead. See if you can find a better spot for crossing, and report back."

Will crosses the river and continues north along the right side of the river about ten paces away from the water's edge to avoid muddy riverbanks. He scans the riverbanks on both sides and out into the grass about fifteen feet or so. Along the banks, the grass is thicker than out on the open plains because of the moisture. The grassy banks are great hiding places for insects, swamp rats, and the feared water moccasins. From tidbits of conversations with Matt, Will knows what to scout for around the river. The best crossing for the herd is one with low water depth, weak current, and banks with a gradual grade on both sides. He also looks for signs of hunting parties or others occupying or passing through the area. Unsure of what will show up, his focus is on being able to give Matt a good report. Therefore, Will tries to be as observant as possible.

The sun blazes. Will's shirt is drenched with sweat, so he removes it. His body glistens from the new sweat fostering on his skin. So near the swirling water, he is tempted to leap in for a quick cooling. He and Rodeo do pass a shady spot ideal for them to dive in and refresh themselves. After about one hundred feet, he pulls the reins to the right motioning Rodeo to start turning around to go back, anxious to return to that inviting shady spot. But then he hears water splashing just ahead. He and Rodeo aren't alone. The splashing sounds are coming from an area just ahead of where the river bends to the right. Will dismounts Rodeo so he can walk nearer to the water. He moves along the river's edge; the riverbank along this section rises two or three feet. The brush and trees thicken as he continues walking, Rodeo trailing behind him. He hears water falling, rushing rapidly across rocks, and occasional splashes, like someone's diving in. Up ahead the river drops down three feet and crashes, creating a short waterfall. Easing up slowly, he drops Rodeo's reins and motions to Rodeo his hand signal to stop. Continuing to ease his way closer, stealth-like, he gets close enough to peer through high reeds and thin overhanging tree limbs to see someone else bathing in the river. It was a *she*, a *beautiful she*. In the water her long black hair snakes behind her as she swims around a large boulder, about three feet round; its top breaks through the clear water surface with about another eight feet of the boulder extending beneath the water. With the three-foot waterfall as a backdrop, she and the river etch a memorable scene in Will's mind. As he spies on her, she leaps out of the water and perches herself on top of the boulder revealing a drenched full, voluptuous body under an even more drenched thin cotton undergarment. He is mesmerized, because the drenched undergarment she wears does not disguise her body at all.

Will has never seen a woman unclad before. Without breathing, he gazes intensely. The only woman whose body parts he has ever caught a glimpse of belong to his mother, and only because in their small four-room cottage sometimes you can't avoid getting caught dressing, or getting in or out of the bath tub. Of course, he never stared like this at his mother, and without breathing too. Will and his mother are always cognizant of the other's need for privacy by using blankets for partitions, and respectfully announcing, "I'm dressing," or "I'm bathing." But this is an entirely different situation—it is not his mother, and he can't look away. He's even discovering nerves and blood vessels coming alive that he had never felt before.

Always getting impatient when standing in one spot just a bit too long, Rodeo makes a low whinnying sound and steps forward nudging Will to move along. As Rodeo nudges him forward, Will, agitated, loudly whispers back at him, "Stop. Wait." The girl on the boulder hears a rustling sound in front of her and dives into the water. She circles the boulder, then peers from behind it to see who it is. Feeling he has no reason to hide, Will walks from behind the trees and reveals himself. He walks forward, bare-chested, and puts his hands in his pockets hoping to make his six feet frame appear less alarming to her. She remains behind the boulder appearing frightened and assessing her options for escape. Continuing to approach, he clears his throat and speaks loud enough to be heard over the falling water sounds, but speaks slowly with care. "Good afternoon. This," he says trying to keep his voice from quivering, "this seems to be the spot for a taking a dip." He waits and smiles.

She says nothing.

He can sense she wants to make a run for it. "Please, don't be afraid. I mean you no harm." He licks his lips and tries to calm his nerves. "My name is Will. What's your name?"

She looks around from one side of the river to the other to see if there are others present. Finding some comfort that others have not yet appeared, she floats to the opposite side of the river, but then realizes her clothing is on the other side, twenty feet in front of him.

He takes a deep breath, swallows, and attempts to get out another inquiry without stammering. "Do you live around here?" Wishing he could put his shirt back on that he has tucked away in his saddlebag, he continues, "I took off my shirt because it is so hot." He is running out of things to say to draw her into a conversation. "Are you from the . . . the Indian village near the trading post?"

She still makes no reply to him.

Feeling she can grab her clothes and escape back into the water if need be, she slowly swims over to his side, twenty feet in front of him, keeping her eyes glued to his every movement. He stays in place, again to keep from alarming her. When she reaches the riverbank on his side, she is reluctant to climb out. Feeling the transparency of her wet undergarment exposing her naked body, she shouts, "Turn around!"

"OK, I will . . . No need to be afraid," he assures her. He turns slowly and searches his mind for something else to say. "As I said, uh . . . my name is Will. I'm from Tennessee. Have you heard of Tennessee? I live there on a big ranch. We raise and train horses, and I do a bit of fieldwork during the crop season. There's . . . there's no reason for you to be afraid of me. My mother raised me to be a gentleman. I'm really a nice person once you get to know me." He is gaining confidence. "I hope you stay and talk."

While he is talking, she draws herself out of the water and grabs her dress. She slips it on over the wet undergarment and then slides on her moccasins. The dress extends to just above the ankles and is made of brown cotton material with a white ornate trim made in half-diamond shapes, and the moccasins are made of tan deerskin.

He listens to hear if she is still there, and says, "I'm turning around, now."

Slowly backing away, continuing to glance around for others, she says, "Why are you here?"

Will smiles because she hasn't run off. Turning, he replies, "I'm scoutin' for a place to cross the river. We're bringing twenty-five-hundred head of cattle through here."

She looks him up and down, and then scans over his shoulders to the left and then to the right, and sees Rodeo. She slowly turns her body around but keeps her head facing back and her eyes intensely focused on him.

Walking away, she says, "Don't follow me."

Will sees a water moccasin come shimmying out of the bushes along the grassy path she is walking, directly in front of her.

He points and yells, "Snake!"

She stops, turns her head, and spots the snake ahead in her path. She backs up quickly as Will runs forward, grabbing her arm and pulling her back toward him and Rodeo. She stumbles and falls against his wall of a chest and looks up into his face. Her countenance fades from alarm to gratitude. His eyes move from the snake, which swiftly makes its way into the water, to her captivating eyes and inviting lips. Her eyes, to him, resemble black pearls floating in white cream. He can see she is no longer afraid of him, but can't decipher what she is now. But he is enthralled by her. Scents of a mixture of lavender oil and incense emanate from her hair, from her burnt tan skin, skin he's now finding to be soft to his touch. Completely without thinking and with no hesitation, he leans down and kisses her on the lips. Maybe she is still gathering her footing or has never been kissed before because she is looking into his eyes watching him make contact, and does not pull away. He gently holds his mouth to hers, mingling their breaths and carefully wrapping his arms around her waist. She seems to be accepting it all. The passion igniting him seemingly passes to her. But just as unplanned as they enter into this amorous embrace, they exit. She makes the first move, using her two hands to abruptly push him back away from her. As she pushes, he immediately releases his arms from around her waist and stumbles backward toward Rodeo. As if awakening from a deep sleep, he struggles to get out an apology that is swelling in his throat. But before he can get it out, she turns and flees up the path along the river. He watches until losing sight of her before he mounts Rodeo to better see which way she is running. He rides in her direction, keeping an eye on her. She is now moving along a trail and going away from the river heading north toward structures off in the distance. Will realizes the structures are part of the Indian village next to the fort. Up ahead of him, the river becomes very shallow, about four or five feet deep. There, he chooses to cross the river and head back to where he left Matt.

Matt is tightening his saddle on his horse. "Did you see anything?"

Yeah, I did, Will thinks, remembering his amorous encounter downriver, and then he responds out loud to Matt, "Yeah, there's a shallow spot four to five feet deep just up from where the river drops. We can go through there much easier."

"OK, show me, and then we can go to our next stop, the trading post for supplies, and then we head back."

Will follows Matt to the trading post two miles north of the Red River. Built as part of the Fort Townsend complex, the trading post sells goods, food, and supplies; some of the goods are produced from the nearby Choctaw Indian village. Fort Townsend guards the area near the border between Texas and the Indian Territory. As they ride up, Will scans the Indian village not too far away. He wonders if that could be her home. Matt ties the reins of his horse to the hitching post in front of the trading post. Will stays mounted. Matt observes him staring in the direction of the village.

"I'd stay clear of that village if I were you. They don't like strangers wandering in," Matt advises, giving Will a lingering look. Then Matt turns and walks into the trading post.

Will hears what he said, but after washing up at the river and putting on a fresh shirt, he ventures toward the village anyway, riding Rodeo slowly so as not to alarm anyone. The village is comprised of a large number of varied structures. Most are round structures made with logs vertically staked into the ground and thatched roofs covered with palmetto leaves and grass. These structures are called *chukkas*, and there are summer chukkas and winter chukkas. The summer chukkas are built with lighter pine wood and the same grass-covered roofs. Most chukkas have a hole in the middle of the roof to allow smoke to escape from the fire pit built in the center of the floor. Inside the chukkas, there are seats made of river cane that can also be used for beds, which are built three feet off the ground all around the walls. There are also pavilion-like structures built with no walls, four or more supporting posts, holding up grass-covered roofs. These pavilions are located near the center of the village complex adjacent to a large fire pit and appear to be used for assemblies and group activities. Further down are more modern buildings made of brick. A large garden is located at the end of the complex nearer to the trading post. In an area down from the trading post is a clearing where young Indian boys are playing a stickball game, running and falling on each other and laughing. Will dismounts, tips his hat at two elders sitting nearby, walks over to the children, and says, "Hello." The children move back staring at the stranger.

Will continues, "I have a smart horse. Would you like to see the smart horse do tricks? Let me show you."

Will turns to Rodeo and says, "Hat." And using his mouth, Rodeo grabs Will's hat, shakes it, and places it back on Will's head, not securely but good enough to make the children marvel.

With his back to Rodeo, Will says, "I'm tired. Let's sit down." Will sits on the ground, and following special cues, Rodeo too sits by folding his front legs under him, lowering his back section and folding his hind legs until he is completely down, and then raising the front of his body by extending his front legs.

By this time other adult villagers, men and women, gather to see the horse show. Among them is *her*, the one he is hoping to find.

Will then asks Rodeo to stand and do several actions sequentially on verbal command. "Walk straight . . . Stop . . . Turn right . . . Walk . . . Stop . . . Turn left . . . Walk . . . Stop."

The crowd looks on in amazement and chats with one another.

While everyone is mesmerized by Rodeo, Will maneuvers Rodeo with starts, stops, and turns over to near where she is standing.

The show comes to an end and Will bows. "Thank you, everyone," he says. "Isn't he a fine horse?" He walks over to Rodeo and rewards him with pieces of carrots he keeps in his saddlebag. Many of the villagers see that the horse show is over and walk away. Others stay asking one another, "Where did this Negro man come from?"

She stands near a dwelling second in from the outside across from the garden.

Patting Rodeo and looking her way, he says, "Hello again."

"What are you doing here?" she asks in a low tone.

"Just passing through." There are others still watching. A few determine he is not a threat and walk toward the interior of the village. He rubs Rodeo's neck and continues addressing her, "I'm so glad to see you again."

"I can't be seen talking to you," she responds looking around and seeing two spectators lingering, trying to determine whether or not she knows the Negro man. She walks over to a dwelling and bends down to get a bowl of water from a container stationed against the dwelling. Speaking a little louder, she says, "Here's water for you and your horse." She knows she is being watched so she deliberately pretends to be admiring the horse, and not the man.

Will accepts the bowl of water with a "Thank you." He takes a drink, then says to Rodeo, "Here you go, buddy," holding the bowl so Rodeo can get a drink before returning the bowl to her.

"Now you have to go. Others will talk and ask me how I know you."

Will, speaking really low, says, "About earlier, I'm so, so sorry. I don't know what came over me. I'm normally a true gentleman. Can you forgive me?"

She responds in a low tone, "I'll forgive you if you go, *now!*"

Will can see she is firm about him leaving, so he mounts Rodeo and rides back to the trading post. As he approaches, Matt stands holding two burlap bags of items he has purchased. He had been sitting on the porch of the trading post, wondering where Will had gone until he saw the show he and Rodeo was putting on, and the exchange with the pretty Indian girl.

"I wouldn't go barking up that tree," he says, throwing his head to point in the direction of the village. "Some young brave most likely has his eyes on her, so you, Master Will, do not stand a chance. She's what you might describe as beyond your reach for courting, and to try to do so would start a regional incident. Why do you think that fort is over there? We've finally got peace in this land. Don't give cause for folks on both sides to grab their weapons and be up in arms. Understand?" Matt advises again. Looking at Will, hoping his words stuck, he throws one of the bags to Will and continues, "Here, carry one of these bags."

The two make it back to the herd by chow time. Will and Matt are at the tail end of the serving line. After all the drovers have their plates filled, Will asks Oscar if he can talk to him.

"Sure, let me cover these pots and I'll meet you by the wagon," Oscar answers.

Will finds a spot to sit near the chuck wagon, and Oscar finally walks over and hangs up his apron before sitting down on an empty crate.

"What happened to mom and baby?" Will asks.

"They're still back there on the other side of the wagon bonding. I let Rodrigo in on it because I needed help moving the hitching post. He estimates giving them another two days, and they should be able to march in the rear of the herd," Oscar replies. "What new adventures do you have from scoutin'?"

"Well . . . I met . . . uh . . . a girl."

Oscar looks puzzled. "When? Where?"

"At Red River," Will answers.

"At Red River? What was a girl doing at Red River?"

"She was, uh . . . bathing."

"Bathing?"

"It was unbelievable, O. I just walked up, and saw her, and uh . . . I . . . I couldn't move. I could only stare," Will explains.

"I'm sure you did," Oscar says grinning.

"No, it wasn't like that. She was just so beautiful; I couldn't look away. And then, well . . . I kissed her."

"You kissed her? This adventure is getting better by the minute. It's much better than Chris's tall tales. Who was she?"

"An Indian girl from the village nearby," Will answers.

"Indian!"

"Not so loud," Will urges.

"Indian? I've got a bad feeling about this. We don't need an angry Indian father or brother after you, because guess what? It can block the herd from getting through, and that would anger Tom and Mr. Hastings! And that's not good for us. Remember all our plans?"

"No one's getting angry," Will replies.

"OK, you saw a pretty girl. That's always nice." Oscar puts his left hand on Will's right shoulder and speaks to him with direct eye contact. "Put her out of your mind. Let's get to Dodge City, and get paid. We can find some girls in Dodge City, or we go to another town and find some girls." Oscar pats Will on the back and stands up. "Right now, I've got to go check on the new woman in my life and her newborn."

CHAPTER 3

CROSSING THE RED RIVER

———

AFTER sweating out twelve days driving the herd north, the Hastings crew approaches the Red River. The Red River is recognized as the northern border of Texas, and the land north of the river is known as the Indian Territory. The drovers tighten and smooth the herd's flanks, preparing them to enter the portion of the river designated by Matt for the crossing. When they reach the area to cross, Tom yells, "Squeeze 'em in, and send 'em over." As the drovers guide them nearer to the river water, the cattle become uneasy. The crew holds a perimeter around them by riding close along their flanks and bearing down on them with their horses. These tactics are used to block the cows from breaking away from the herd, finding their own place to cross resulting in fatal injuries or drownings. Hearing Tom's verbal signal to cross, the drovers increase their hat-waving and yelling to get the cows in their section to step up moving into the river. They incite the cows in the rear to push forward, forcing the cows in the front to move ahead faster. After the lead steers pick up the pace, the remainder of the herd crowds up behind them, involuntarily treading on their heels. They stumble into the river splashing water and mooing.

As the water rises over their hooves and then to their shoulders, the mooing and yelping grow louder, reverberating from one group of cows in the water to another group just entering the water, and together their collective mooing bombards the air. It's all one can hear for miles. Each cow's eyes glare open wider with surprise when their bovine bodies submerge, and buoyancy overtakes them allowing them to swim. One after another, groups of cattle enter the water forming fronts that spread up to as much as thirty feet, causing the drovers to streak across the river attempting to bunch them back together. Where the water is shallow, they walk; where it is much deeper, they swim. The loud noise from their unsynchronized collective mooing keeps everyone on edge. The crew continuously fights the spreading and is also on the lookout for anything threatening their crossing in or near the water, such as sinking mud, loose rocks, and particularly water moccasins. The drovers battle to keep the cows bunched together crossing where it is most shallow. But they are spreading out into sections of the river beyond where Matt designated. In these sections the depths and river beds are unknown. Even more deadly are the varying slopes and heights of the river banks, where the cattle have difficulty vaulting out of the water and are bound to break legs, fall below the water line, get trampled, and drown.

Tom sits on his horse, Jack, about one hundred feet away from the river on the exit side of the crossing. He watches as the twenty-five-hundred head of cattle make their way through the river, their heads bobbing up and down in the water, maintaining a loud mooing chorus. Groups of steers reach the other side, dragging themselves up onto the riverbank, some slipping after the first try, but eventually exiting the river soaked and winded. Once a group of steers is out of the water and onto dry land, their mooing gradually subsides, while those groups remaining in the water maintain their mooing at their highest volume.

Since the crossing is occurring in the morning, Zeb has instructions from Tom to move the herd inland, a far enough distance out from the river to an area capable of accommodating the entire herd. The area should be suitable for all of them to settle in, dry off under the warm sun, and graze the lush grasses near the river. Because the market pays best for plump, healthy looking cows, rather than starved, dehydrated looking ones, occasionally, cattle drives intentionally stop, to let the cattle feed and fatten up.

This crossing so far has been a good one. Not a head has been lost. If their luck holds, the next river crossings along the trail will go well, too. After the bulk of the cattle crosses, Will follows closely behind to cross next with the eight backup horses. Will is never sure how the horses will react to being submerged in water up to their shoulders, especially those crossing for the first time. Of course, Rodeo is a pro at swimming. Will times his crossing to allow the horses to mingle with or at least see the straggler cows entering the river and swimming across. By mingling the backup horses with the straggler cows and Rodeo, Will hopes the horses stay calm and are less likely to get spooked by the splashing water and walking on the river bed's unfamiliar, uneven terrain. He unties them from the rope and allows them to go freely into the water. Using his lariat, he motivates them by waving it at them and shouting, "Hiyah!" The backup horses splash in, struggle through, and finally bolt out on the other side.

Oscar holds back, wanting to be the very last to cross. He chooses to be last because he has the calf on board, and is being trailed by the mother cow. He also wants to cross without drawing Tom's attention. But taking the chuck wagon across is fraught with its own peculiar dangers. Because of those dangers, Zeb instructs Drake and Rodrigo to ride back and assist in steadying the wagon through its crossing. Oscar guides the wagon mules to the river. The mules step into the water's edge and begin bucking and attempting to back up, but Oscar flaps the reins and yells at them, spurring them on. They jerk and hee-haw, and eventually begin moving forward. The water rises to the mules' shoulders, causing them to make their contributions of loud intense sounds, "Hee-haw, hee-haw," but they keep moving, pulling the chuck wagon through the water. As the water rises above the wagon's wheels, the wagon bed sways and twists from the force of the river current. The uneven river bed causes the chuck wagon to rock back and forth wildly. This jerking motion invokes the calf on-board to cry out. There is a pure domino effect, since it isn't long before the calf's cries spark the mother cow to answer with her loud mooing as she swims through the river in hot pursuit. Drake and Rodrigo leap into the water and work their way over to the wagon to stabilize it. They apply pressure on both sides attempting to stop the swaying and rocking and help keep the wagon moving straight ahead. Upon reaching the riverbank on the other side, the mules are taxed pulling the wagon free of the river bed, through the muddy banks, and onto dry land. Once free of the mud and rolling on solid earth, Oscar keeps the wagon moving to about fifty feet away from the river's edge. It is impossible now to avoid Tom's view since he is keeping watch, perched on Jack stationed between the river and the main herd. Oscar stops, exits the wagon's bench, and unloads his exasperated passenger, the calf. The calf leaps and darts over to its mother, who is just exiting the river. The calf is so happy to be free from the wagon, it bucks and skips all around the mother. Tom sees the calf for the first time. Realizing this, the cowhands still near the river sense an uneasy tension in the air. Sensing the tension are Will, Drake, Rodrigo, and Oscar. Drake, the ex-Confederate, wasn't aware of the calf and elects not to ask the Negroes, Mexican, or Tom about it at this point. Will decides to play it off and proceeds to perform his duties as normal. He whistles and rounds up the backup horses with carrot treats. By putting them back into a group formation, he is now able to ride over to Tom with them and ask, "Rest or move out?"

Tom says, "Rest."

Will yells to Rodrigo to grab the sticks and rope out of the chuck wagon for the makeshift corral.

Rodrigo yells back, "Say, por favor." After retrieving the makeshift corral parts from the chuck wagon, Rodrigo carries them to Will.

Drake looks up at Tom, and then back at Oscar. "I'm gonna get out of these wet pants." Tipping his hat at Tom, Drake rides back to the herd. As Rodrigo helps Will set up the corral, he enviously watches

Drake leave. He doesn't want to lose pay for appearing to play any part in harboring a calf.

Sitting on Jack, Tom watches the animated calf frolic to-and-fro in front of its mother. He turns to examine the herd, which is settling in and grazing. Noticing that some of the crew either got soaking wet or are choosing to go shirtless and rinse off their sweat, he decides it would be an efficient use of time to break for the remainder of the day, dry out, and rest a bit. He could make the most of this downtime by going to the trading post, purchasing any additional needed supplies, and checking in at Fort Townsend for any activities of interest in the region. As trail boss, he knows it's essential to learn if there has been an incident, or if there is someone on the loose in the area endangering others, or could be a threat to his men or the herd. The fort receives complaints regularly from settlers traveling through, from inhabitants of the reservations, and the fort's own periodic scouting reports. But first, for several reasons, Tom has business with Oscar. He rides Jack to the chuck wagon. Oscar is busy checking to see if the Dutch oven and other boxes of supplies near the back of the wagon have shifted, presenting a danger to the calf since he may be riding a couple more days.

"Oscar, when was the calf born?" Tom demands.

"A day ago," Oscar replies, continuing to work in the back of the wagon.

"It's nursing OK?"

"Yes," Oscar answers.

"Well, once it's weaned, both go back into the herd."

Oscar says nothing.

Tom throws his head back and stretches. He again addresses Oscar, "Meet me at the trading post in about two hours. We can make sure we are well stocked for the remainder of the drive." Tom turns Jack toward the herd and heads in the direction of Zeb.

Will and Rodrigo set up the makeshift corral, stringing rope around sticks bored into the ground, and then drive the backup horses inside the corral. These horses are trained to respect any kind of enclosure.

Smiling in jest, Rodrigo says, "It looks safe for you to go check on your friend and his baby. I leave you now." He, too, rides back to the herd.

Eager to learn what Tom said, Will makes sure the horses are settled in before riding to Oscar in haste. "Did Tom say anything about the calf?" Will asks.

"Nothing important; he just asked about it. It's just another cow to him," Oscar says. "He did ask me to meet him at the trading post." Oscar finishes working inside the wagon before he exits it, walks to its front, and climbs onto the wagon bench. Oscar continues, "I need to head over there."

Will finds Oscar's last comments of particular interest. "I'll follow you over to the trading post. Let me get a cover for the horses," Will says.

Will finds Rodrigo and asks him to keep an eye on the horses once more. Rodrigo snatches his hat off and slaps his thigh. "Again, mi amigo?" Cocking his head to the side he continues, "Are you really the horse wrangler, or am *I* the horse wrangler?"

Will, riding Rodeo, and Oscar, on the chuck wagon, make their way to the trading post. To their amazement, the calf and mother cow follow the chuck wagon. They stop and assess the situation.

Surprised at this development, Will says, "Mother and calf keep trailing this wagon. Now, this *is* a problem. They think this chuck wagon is their lead steer. Where it goes, they go!" Will begins to chuckle. "Tom—ha ha—won't understand this," Will says with more chuckling.

"What part of this is funny?" Oscar blurts, pushing his derby up off his forehead. Then he too breaks down laughing. "We're hanging on to these jobs by a thread, and along comes this little innocent calf that's gonna snip that thread, and we're done." Oscar puts the calf in the wagon and proceeds to the trading post.

Once the chuck wagon arrives at the trading post, Oscar sets two buckets near the wagon, one containing feed from which the cow immediately begins to eat, and the other contains water. His objective is to use the buckets to keep the mother cow and calf occupied, deterring them from wandering away from the wagon. With them tethered by the buckets, Oscar enters the wagon taking an inventory of foodstuffs, seasonings, and other supplies. After having their fill of feed and water, the calf and mother cow lie down next to the wagon.

Will had dismounted Rodeo and has been looking toward the village, scouring it for a particular inhabitant. Not spotting her, he devises a plan to flush her out. Using marching instructions, he sends Rodeo over into the village into a clearing in front of all the dwellings and maneuvers him down near the dwelling where she gave him water. He verbally cues Rodeo to march lifting his front legs high one at a time. Then he signals him to turn right sharply, and make two left turns, resulting in him facing the dwellings. Children playing at the far side of the clearing area naturally stop what they are doing and gather near, watching with amazement the "smart horse" obeying verbal commands. After the impromptu show ends, Will walks over to the children and asks if anyone can find his friend with long black hair. One child leaves running. Soon she appears, coming out from the center of the village carrying a basket of plants.

She approaches Will stepping briskly and angrily. Satisfied that she came at all, he pays no attention to her anger. She steps right up to him and makes a hard stop directly in front of him breathing heavily. With a tone of annoyance, she asks, "Why are you back here?"

He smiles and takes off his hat. His squinting eyes dance quickly from her face to waist, then finally settling on her face. Disguising his nervousness, he says, "Good afternoon. What do you have there in your basket?" Peering into her basket, he adds, "They are not the prettiest flowers I've ever seen."

Still annoyed, she looks down at the basket, returns her eyes to him, and responds, "They are not flowers. They are for medicine and cooking." She pauses, and beckons him with her hand to follow her. She walks him and Rodeo to the edge of the village nearest to the trading post. "You must go. You must not make trouble for me or you."

"What kinda trouble? Are you spoken for?" Will asks.

"What do you mean?" she asks.

"Is someone courting you?"

Her eyebrows furrow even more.

"Ahhh, let me explain." Will holds his two hands out in front of him, palms facing, and says, "Man and woman." Then while moving his hands from left to right he says, "Courting, courting, courting." Then he brings both hands together, palms touching, fingers curling around the opposite hand, and says, "Husband and wife."

She puts her basket down and says, "No!" Putting her two hands out in front of her, palms facing one another, she says, "Man and woman." She moves her hands in one sweep from left to right, and then similarly brings both hands together, palms touching, fingers curling around the opposite hand, and says, "Husband and wife. No courting, courting, courting."

Will raises his thick eyebrows, gulps, and says, "Hiyah! Ha ha. Well, that cuts out the chase." He gets tickled by her version and covers his mouth with his hand to muffle his chuckling.

"Is that why you came back?" she asks. "For courting, courting, courting?"

"Well, I did want to see you again, and . . ." Before he can finish his statement, an elderly woman comes out of a dwelling, second in from the outside across from the garden, and calls her in their language, a language that Will doesn't understand.

Giving him one last piercing look, she firmly says, "Go!" She turns immediately and leaves striding toward the elderly woman. He watches her walk away. Her hair is pulled back into one long braid and after she suddenly turns for a last quick look at him, he watches the braid swing like a pendulum above her hips before she and the elderly woman disappear into the dwelling. He commits to memory which dwelling.

Feeling dejected, Will mounts Rodeo and quickly gallops back to the trading post. Having taken in that whole little scene, and finding it very entertaining, Oscar, with arms crossed, is leaning against the wagon smiling. "Is that the girl?"

Will, embarrassed, answers, "Yes."

"Woooo, you're right; she is pretty. No wonder you couldn't take your eyes off her. I'm looking at her from over here with her clothes on, and . . . well . . . uhhh . . ." Oscar unfolds his arms and stands up straight compelled to advise his friend wisely. "But listen here, Will. You can't court this girl. I think you would be breaking a territorial law or something."

"No courting, courting, courting," repeats Will in a high-pitched voice, mocking her, and oblivious to what Oscar is saying. He is so frustrated from this last encounter with her, he's in a little emotional turmoil, repeating her words. He feels he's not getting anywhere with her. At least not getting where he wants to go.

Oscar slaps him on the arm, frowning and insists, "Are you hearing me?"

Will looks into Oscar's face and says, "O, there's nothing to worry about. She and I are ... are just friends, that's all."

"Friends?" Oscar says.

"I'm gonna head back to the herd before Tom comes," Will says and then leaves.

After a while, Tom arrives at the trading post, and sees the calf and mother cow. "Oscar, why are they here?" Tom demands.

Feeling he can hide it no longer, Oscar throws up his arms and blurts out, "They've bonded to me. To get them to keep up with the march, I put the calf in the wagon so the mother cow would follow. Now, they think we, including the wagon, are all one pack."

Tom takes off his hat, wipes the sweat off his brow, and says, "As I said, they go into the herd after the calf is weaned. Now, what supplies do we need?"

It is the start of dinner time on the drive, and drovers are coming back into camp. Word quickly gets around the camp that Oscar is making pets out of a mother cow and calf. The calf and mother cow are no longer sequestered with ropes by the chuck wagon, but still, they seem to want to graze and lie down near the wagon. Oscar is making every effort to wean them from him. That night, the mother cow and calf are grazing on the side of the wagon opposite the campfire. The drovers are passing through the serving line, getting their grub, and finding a seat not far from the fire. Clancy sees the calf and mother cow. He goes around the wagon, scoops up the calf, and runs toward the other drovers, who are seated and eating dinner. Mother cow follows, chasing Clancy and mooing loudly.

"Look, look, here's Oscar's family," shouts Clancy, causing members of the crew to laugh.

Oscar stops stirring the beans in a pot hanging over the fire. Pointing a serving spoon, Oscar shakes it at Clancy and demands, "Take them back to where they were. Take them back!"

Clancy continues scampering around the camp to avoid the mother cow; both calf and mother are yelping and mooing. His antics draw mild laughter from the others who are trying not to anger Oscar. Oscar throws the spoon at Clancy; it bounces off him and hits the dirt. Enraged, Oscar yanks off his apron, throws it to the ground, and leaves his serving post. He walks away from his simmering pots, taking long strides and yells, "Serve yourself!" He goes to the rear of the chuck wagon. The crew continues to chuckle at the cow chasing Clancy until someone whispers loudly, "Tom's coming. Tom!" Clancy rushes to return the calf where he found it, behind the wagon, the mother cow following. Chris runs to pick up the spoon, rinse it off, and picks up Oscar's apron. Tom ties his horse and walks into a scene of Chris calmly placing the apron on the back of the wagon near Oscar and carefully putting the spoon near the pot over the fire. The drovers quickly hush their laughter and substitute it with either looking down at their plates and eating their food, or pretending to be in serious conversation with each other. Tom walks over to the simmering pots, looks around at everyone in the camp, and senses something isn't quite right. For starters, Oscar isn't there serving the food like he normally does to prevent a drover from taking a heaping portion. Instead, Oscar has his back turned to everyone, giving off a vibe of anger.

Tom addresses the crew, "Listen up! We've got a few more days before this sojourn is over and we can get paid. I know you're tired. Some of you have sore backsides already, but we've got to complete this drive on time. I don't know if something just went on here. But I'm gonna repeat myself. It would be unfortunate and cruel to short your pay over arguing, fighting, name-calling, teasing. Have I exhausted the list? Let's say anything disruptin' this drive. Is that clear?"

"Yes, boss. Yes, boss," each of them repeats attentively.

For the next thirty days, Oscar keeps the calf out of the wagon so the two have a chance to rejoin the herd. However, the calf is still drawn to the wagon, so the calf and mother cow make their march alongside the chuck wagon. One night near the end of the drive, the crew sits around the fire having filled their bellies with Oscar's cured pork, beans, creamed corn, and biscuits. Chris takes the floor as usual describing how he will use his pay to wine and dine some lovely lady in Dodge

City. His performance features him wrapping his left arm around his body, stretching his right arm high in the air like a flamenco dancer, and saying, "I love dancing with you, mademoiselle."

Next, Chris responds for the mademoiselle saying, "Ooooo-la-la, qui, qui, monsieur."

Then Chris says to mademoiselle, "May I have a little kiss to celebrate our night together?"

Pepper interjects as the answering mademoiselle, "No, no, monsieur. You smell of many cows' poo-poo, and that is faint compared to your horrible breath." Bursts of laughter come from the crew.

Chris drops his arms a moment and says, "Mademoiselle would not be that rude to me." Returning to his dancing pose, he continues, "I shall buy you drink and a scrumptious dinner, and then before the night is done, I will make mad, passionate love to you."

Again, Pepper jumps into Chris's presentation and responds for the imaginary mademoiselle, "Oh, monsieur, I shall drink your drink, I shall devour your scrumptious dinner, and then I will unfasten my corset."

Enticed, the crew says, "Oooooh."

Pepper continues, "And plant a long, juicy kiss." Chris's grin gets bigger and bigger. He leans in puckering his lips as if to kiss this imaginary mademoiselle. But Pepper finishes with, "On your friend Pepper!" Chris drops his arms again and frowns. The crew roars with laughter at Chris. Listening in, Tom and Zeb smile at their antics, too.

As the drive crosses the Dodge City boundary, Tom sends instructions around the crew in preparation for entering the city. Oscar falls behind the herd to let all the cattle be driven in first. The crew is instructed to drive the cattle right down the middle of the main street and stream them into the stockyards where they are counted upon entry. There, they will wait to be loaded onto train cattle cars destined for Chicago and other Eastern cities. Mother cow and her calf, immediately behind the chuck wagon, are the last of the herd to arrive.

Oscar stations the wagon near the entrance to the stockyards. He exits the wagon bench and physically directs the calf through the main gate of a stockyard. Oscar waits inside the stockyard for a few minutes. The calf skips around him. Mother cow is apprehensive. She won't go in. When Oscar comes out, Clancy comes over trying to scare her in, but she still refuses to go in. To get her to go in, Oscar re-enters the stockyard and walks in much farther than before. Seeing Oscar, the calf runs to him, bumps him, and shoves its head under his hand. Not expecting this show of affection, Oscar looks down at the calf as if to say, "I've grown fond of you, too." Mother cow finally strolls into the stockyard. Oscar darts out, and the gate is shut. The calf watches him mount the wagon bench and pull away. The calf runs to the closed gate. Oscar doesn't look back.

After the lead steers are brought out of the pens, the station manager at the Dodge City railhead meets with Tom and Zeb in his office. The count is good. They estimate less than five were lost to the stampede and river crossings.

"I'll telegraph exact numbers to Mr. Hastings this evening," Tom says shaking the station manager's hand. He exits the office, and tells the crew to get the backup horses boarded, except for the three slated for auction. He orders everyone to meet him in front of the Great Western Hotel in three hours.

Oscar pulls up at the livery stable and asks for the mules to be boarded and the wagon wheels to be checked. Already there, tending to Rodeo, Will walks over to Oscar. "Can't wait to get my hands on those greenbacks," he says rubbing his hands together.

"I dunno if I even want pay this time," Oscar groans.

"It's the calf, isn't it?"

"Yeah. It was hard leading it to slaughter," Oscar says laying his head back and exhaling a huge breath.

"O, after all is said and done, they are Mr. Hastings' property. And he sent that property here to Dodge City to market. He's paying us to bring it here."

"I dunno, Will. It's just that the calf is not even a year old. It should at least get a couple of years to live; that's what's bothering me." Oscar hammers his fist down on his knee.

"What we need is a good hot bath, a good meal, and some whiskey." Will slaps him on the back.

The crew meets Tom in front of the Great Western Hotel. After Tom is sure everyone is accounted for, he moves them all through the large hotel lobby to a private corner in the hotel's massive parlor. Each of the crew receives their pay for their work on the cattle drive. After paying the crew, Tom says, "We're scheduled to leave for Hastings Ranch after four days. So, you've got this time to let your hair down and take some time for yourselves. But avoid foolish, unruliness and getting yourselves jailed. Meet at the livery stable after four days and we'll head out from there." As different ones receive their pay, there is grinning, kissing the money, and talk about how it will be spent. Among the bonuses paid that day, Will receives a bonus of thirty dollars for stopping the stampede, and Rodrigo and Drake earn a bonus of ten dollars each for helping get the chuck wagon across the Red River.

While some take over the saloon and dance hall, others have private parties in their hotel rooms. Will and Oscar head to the Negro section of town where they are free to get hot baths, something to eat, and rent a clean, comfortable room with two beds. Their room isn't fancy like the one Tom has. In their room, Cotton cloths cover the windows, not damask or taffeta drapes. Metal-framed beds with cotton sheets and wool blankets are pushed against the back wall, not a wood-framed bed with fancy bedding and bedspread surrounded by decorative throw rugs.

Will and Oscar's days in Dodge City are uneventful compared to their comrades'. Oscar writes and mails letters to his family in Canada. Will does the same to Mother Harriet. On one occasion, Clancy and Chris invite them to meet up in the saloon. They are even invited to so-called private parties in their hotel rooms. However, drunken gatherings usually end badly for Negroes who mix in with loud, drunk Whites. Will and Oscar have worked too hard to put themselves in a position to make something of themselves, and not to get charged for disorderliness and jailed. Knowing they would get the brunt of the punishment; they politely decline and wish Clancy and Chris a great time. Oscar does make an acquaintance with one of two young Negro ladies patronizing a local café. Will agrees to engage the other young lady in conversation, but he won't go any further, which messes up Oscar's plans to romance the lady he has chosen. However, Oscar wins out when Will spends one night with Rodeo while Oscar entertains his young lady in their rented room.

Every night Will checks on Rodeo to make sure he is fed, has water, and is comfortable. During their fourth and last night in town, while checking on Rodeo, Will hears a faint, low cow mooing sound coming from the rear of the stable. Following the sounds, he walks to the rear of the stable and peers into a stall. There, with straw piled in to make extra soft padding, is a calf and cow. He brings a bucket of water, they drink, and the cow quiets down. Staring at the calf by dim lantern light, Will isn't sure it's Oscar's calf. He runs to their lodging and tells Oscar, "A calf and cow are in the livery stable. It looks like your calf." Given his current heartache about leading the calf to slaughter, Oscar frowns at Will.

"No, it really looks like him," Will insists.

Oscar enters the stable, and follows Will to the stall. When he gets near, the calf leaps in the air kicking and bucking over to the edge of the stall appearing to recognize Oscar. Oscar opens the stall and hugs him. Will watches the intense warm reunion.

"How? Ha, ha . . . How did he get here? How did they both get here?" Oscar asks.

Hearing the voices in the rear of the stable, a worker comes to investigate. He looks to be sixtyish, White, and irritable from being awakened from a nap.

"What you boys doing back here?" the worker asks.

"Where did this calf and cow come from?" Will asks.

"Why are you concerned about another man's property? These aren't your animals. Wait, I know you. Leave, or I won't let you in anymore," says the worker to Will with a scowl.

With that, Will beckons Oscar to come away since he needs access to the stable regularly to check on Rodeo. They exit the stable and continue their speculations.

"Why would they be hidden there? Maybe they've been sold to someone—some butcher!" Oscar worriedly speculates as they both stand outside the stable.

"OK, let's not jump to any conclusions. I'm for just going to Tom and asking him straight up what's going on," advises Will.

They walk into the lobby of the Great Western Hotel. As they look around, not another Negro is in sight. The male clerk at the front desk sees them entering and immediately composes his face as if to say, "Your kind is not welcome here." Oscar pushes Will behind him and takes the lead. Taking his derby off and holding it in his hand, Oscar begins with, "We'd like the room number, suh, of a Mr. Tom Morgan of Hastings Ranch. We are his servants, and we needs," Oscar engages a poor-pitiful Negro voice, "aaah . . . I say, suh, we needs ta ask Mr. Morgan if he wonts his shoes shined, bath drawn, horse stabled . . . ah, ah. I have a list here somewhere if you wants to look it over." Oscar appears to be looking through his coat pockets for something. "In fact, it may be better if you, suh, could ask Mr. Morgan, what he needs tonight."

Will chimes in holding his hat in his hand, "Yes, suh, that would help a great deal, if *you* ask him because if he's been drinkin', he might not act too kindly to someone disturbin' him."

Oscar picks up the presentation, "Oh yes, you must approach him with caution; he's known to take a swing at-cha."

"He's in room 215," the desk clerk answers, looking at them over his spectacles. "Do not disturb the other guests."

Both go upstairs, leaving the front desk maintaining serious expressions. But once they are out of earshot of the desk clerk, they burst into laughter, having to resort to using their arms over their mouths to muffle the chuckling sound, else they may disturb the other guests. Oscar knocks on the door, while Will moves off to the side leaning against the wall by the door numbered 215. Tom yells from inside, "Who is it?"

"Oscar."

Tom cracks the door open, and then opens it farther and invites him in. "Come in."

Still holding his brown derby in one hand, Oscar walks in but stays near the door after Tom closes it. Tom *is* drinking. But he actually appears more relaxed and friendly than he is on the trail. He asks Oscar if he wants a drink.

"No, thank you," Oscar replies.

Tom fought for the South in the Civil War. He served as captain of a regiment under Colonel Hastings. That's where they met. After Tom returned home to Petersburg, Virginia, there wasn't much left except for pain and sorrow. His house was destroyed, and his wife and son lay in a city hospital on death's doorstep. He tried to find work, but none could be had. Old friends tried to console him after his family was buried, but he retreated to the bottle, blaming himself for leaving them to fend for themselves. He got caught up in the revelry of the South's cause and never examined its spiritual and political implications for the country he loved. As a consequence, he developed a hate for his fellow man. He would frequent the local drinking taverns and invoke arguments that turned into melees. He was very bitter. The last time he started a brawl, he was jailed for disturbing the peace. The sheriff warned he would fine him his horse, saddle, and weapons since he had nothing else of value. While jailed, he contacted Mr. Hastings and asked for a job and a place to pull his life together. Hastings did better than Tom asked. Hastings boarded a train from Waco, Texas, to Petersburg, collected Tom, and brought him to his ranch in Texas. After sharing his plans to drive cattle to Dodge City, Hastings asked Tom to be his trail boss. Tom, now, never drinks on the trail and minimally at the ranch. But occasionally, the stress of ramrodding a dozen or so grown men for most of the year at the ranch, and about three months on the six-hundred-mile cattle drive, gets drowned in whiskey during layover days in Dodge City.

"Did you find lodging?" Tom asks.

"Yes, no problem there," replies Oscar. Thinking he better get on with the reason he's come to Tom's room, he says, "The calf."

"You and that damn calf," Tom responds.

Oscar summons up enough nerve to continue, "I saw the calf in the stable. What's going to happen to it?"

"Have a seat."

Oscar settles into the nearest chair.

Tom sits eight feet from Oscar. He takes a swallow from a glass of whiskey he had poured from a bottle already half-empty sitting on an adjacent table. "You know . . . Have you read the passage in the Bible about God telling a family to take in a one-year-old, unblemished male lamb, and keep it for four days? At the end of the four days, the lamb is to be slaughtered, roasted, and eaten completely by the family. 'Leave no signs of it,' God said. Well, as I see it—that calf is turning out to be your sacrificial lamb. You have bonded with that calf and now you can't come to grips with its purpose for being here. All of that cattle we drove over six hundred miles are going to market!" Tom raises his voice. "Their meat will become steaks and stews; their hides will become belts and boots." He collects himself and lowers his volume. "It's a hard world, Oscar. And if you plan to live in this part of the country, you need to harden up.

"Having said all that, I saw the little touching scene in the stockyard, how that calf ran to you, so playful, and rubbed against you so trusting while the other cows were being led away. I must have been overcome by the tender scene, because I had him and his momma pulled out of the stockyard and taken to the stable." He pours another portion of whiskey into his glass resting on the adjacent table. "This is gonna make an interesting conversation with Mr. Hastings in a few days. Pick them up tomorrow when we head out. Use my name."

Oscar rises from his seat, heads toward the door, and stops to ask, "Why did you tell me the story about the lamb?"

"I heard the story when I was a boy, and it stuck with me. I often wondered how did the children of the family feel, keepin' that one-year-old lamb for four days, knowing that at the end of the four days, they were going to kill it and eat it. On the farm, my grandpa always said it's easier to think of critters as food if you don't get too close to them and start naming them. I suspect you got too close."

The next morning begins the day the crew will depart Dodge City for the Hastings Ranch. Will rises before sunup, while Oscar sleeps. He keeps the noise down as much as he can while dressing and packing his belongings. He is almost out the door of their room when he hears Oscar say, "Is it time to get up?"

"No. Go back to sleep. I'll meet you at Fort Townsend," Will says.

"The Indian girl?"

"See you at the fort," Will says loaded down with his gear, closing the door gently behind him.

Will put bridles on the five remaining backup horses and, using ropes, strings them together again. Controlling all five reins he heads out of Dodge City on Rodeo with the backup horses at full gallop.

After being cooped up in the stable, Rodeo and the horses enjoy romping out on the open road. After hours of riding at a faster than usual pace, Will stops, makes camp, feeds, and waters his traveling companions. This will happen about eight times over the three-hundred-and-fifty miles from Dodge City to the Red River. To hinder horse thieves, he selects campsites where a view of them is obscured from the road. He misses the help his crew would have provided with securing the horses, but he had to leave out when he did. He needs the extra time alone.

When they finally make it to the Red River, he stops to let the horses drink and splash around in the river. He too rinses off and changes his shirt. After securing them off any traveled trails, he plants himself in the grass on a small hill above the Indian village where there is a view of the dwelling she disappeared into the last time he saw her. He has brought only Rodeo with him because the other horses are adapted to waiting patiently; Rodeo is not. A child is playing nearby in the clearing, and he picks his moment to get the child's attention by waving him over to the edge of the clearing by the hill. He comes down the hill, squats down, and asks the child if he can go get his friend with the long black hair that sleeps in that dwelling, and he points to the dwelling in question. It isn't long before she comes around to the side of the village he is spying on. She looks up toward the high grass below the trees where she is told he is waiting for her. She sees Will and Rodeo. Will is squatting down to be camouflaged by the high grass. Carrying a basket of herbs, she casually walks to him, going up the hill, and looking around to see if anyone is watching her.

"You are not smart like your horse," she says, slowing her approach to him.

Will takes his hat off, smiles, and says, "Hello," desperately hoping they have a good session today. His heart is pounding. He contemplates how no one had prepared him for having such strong urges toward a woman, or is it just this particular woman? He has been around girls before, and he had no problem following his teachings to always behave like a gentleman. But for some reason, an element of male bravado creeps into his reasoning when it comes to her.

They see two men of the village returning from the trading post. She squats and beckons Will to get down low. They both sit down. Will instructs Rodeo to get down as well.

Watching Rodeo squat and eventually lay down, she marvels at his control over Rodeo.

"I'm here. What do you want?" she asks.

His eyes and facial composure soften, and he remembers and repeats what his mother said. "Just . . . wanting to give you some of my time." She jerks her head to one side, frowns, and looks at him confused. She leans on her hands attempting to get up. He grabs her arm and asks her to wait. Her eyes fix a piercing stare down at his hand on her arm, and he immediately removes it. This is not the reaction he was anticipating. "Wait! I'm . . . I'm very interested in the plants you collect. Tell me about the plants in your basket."

"This is what you come for?" she asks, returning to a seated position.

Desperate to look sincere with this new approach, Will answers, "Yes."

After taking a deep breath, she looks at him. "First, they are not just plants; they are herbs." She looks into the basket and begins picking up each herb, one at a time, identifying it. "This is called squirrel's tail, and is good for healing cuts or open wounds on the body." As she says that, she uses her finger to poke Will in his side. "Like when you are cut with a knife." He flinches and smiles to the extent his dimples appear as she's poking him. She smiles a little, too.

"Next, tea tree is used for . . . ummm . . . helps make the body throw off water. This one is mint. It is good for itchy skin. Wild ginger is for stomach pains."

As she talks, he watches her lips, fantasizing about kissing her again and going further.

"And I know you see this one on the trail, blackberry. You probably eat it or give some to your horse. It's good for in the mouth when you are hurting around your teeth." She takes her finger and rubs her gums. But unsure if he knows what she means, she brings her finger up to his face and attempts to rub his gums. Healing sessions require her as a healer to examine, touch, and probe her patients. Still fantasizing, he comes back to himself and sees her hand coming toward his face. He gently grasps her wrist, turns it toward his mouth, and gently kisses the inside of her wrist. He remembers Chris saying women really like that and he'd be surprised at how they respond.

No such luck for him. This completely irritates her. She snatches her wrist back and hisses, "Siti!" That's snake in Choctaw.

While she is scrambling to get to her feet, he pleads, "Oh! I'm so sorry. I don't know what gets into me."

"This is no good," she says.

With that said, he jumps up, grabs her basket, and takes off running. Seeing him race away with her basket, she gives chase, and chases him into the trees, yelling in a low tone so as not to alert anyone in the village. "Give it back. Give it back." Rodeo rises to his feet and follows them, but stops about twenty-five feet away from them when he finds something tasty to graze on.

Deep within the trees, Will stops running and turns to face her. "I'll give it back if you give me one thing," he says.

"What thing do you want?" she asks.

"I want a hug," he says innocently, making a sad face.

"No," she says firmly.

"A tiny, fast hug," he says in a bargaining manner, maintaining his sad face.

"No."

"Let me tell you why I want the hug. This is the last time I will see you for a while. It will be twelve moons until I see you again. That's when we will bring another herd through here. So, can we part as friends, with a goodbye hug?"

"No," she remains firm.

"Then Rodeo and I are going to ride off with this basket." Looking over the basket, he adds, "It will make a nice present for me to take home to my dear mother."

She glares at him. Then thinking someone may soon come looking for her, she surrenders. "Agreed. It will be good to say goodbye to you, but you are to put your hands behind you. No touching!"

"What kinda hug is that?" Will asks with eyebrows raised and a partial smile.

"Noooo, touching." She smiles because she thinks she has outsmarted him. "I will do the touching."

Looking at her bewildered with a hint of a smile, Will blurts out, "Fine!"

She walks toward him, reaching for the basket. He moves his hands behind his body, bringing the basket along too. She comes in very close to him, within an inch. He can smell the lavender oil and incense emanating from her hair and skin. The smell is more intense than before. It intoxicates him. Her face is directly in front of him. He looks down at her with a hunter's grin when prey is easing into the trap. If she looks straight ahead and up a little, she will be staring into the bottom of his throat. However, she keeps her eyes on the basket, and keeps reaching around him for it. Will raises his left arm higher and higher taking the basket up with it. Being six feet tall, he causes her to go up on her tippy toes, bracing herself against him with her left hand, stretching her right arm in the air, and still, she cannot reach the basket. Then she turns her head to look up directly into his face and says softly, "Give it to me." He lowers the basket. She pans her face to the right and watches the basket being lowered with his left hand. He takes his right hand, and he reaches around and places it gently on her waist. Something has taken over and is in motion. He can feel himself breaking his promise to her and leans down angling to connect with her mouth for another kiss. His lips instead connect with her left cheek, and he softly kisses it. His lips keep traveling to the right side of her face to intercept her mouth. Feeling him kissing her cheek, she quickly turns to the left, opens her mouth to say something, and before she can, their open mouths collide. His eyes close, and he lunges his tongue partially into her mouth. Their noses, their lips find a way of fitting together like sensual puzzle pieces. His right hand pulls her in tight to his body. Her eyes close, and she feels lit up inside like a torch ablaze. While her right hand is floating in the air looking for the basket, her left hand is squeezing his muscular arm near the shoulder as if holding on to a thrilling ride. This time the kiss is more passionate and lasts for a while. Neither gives signs of stopping. Then, both abruptly, almost simultaneously, break free and step back to catch their respective breaths. Her chest is pounding, and her face is flushed. He puts his hands on his hips, tilts his head back, flexes his legs and shakes his head to gain clarity. He has ridden wild stallions and never got this off-centered. This is new.

Then he remembers how this whole thing started, and he still has the basket in his hand. He steps toward her. "Here's your basket," he says while handing it to her. Looking at him, she accepts it not saying a word. She turns slowly and walks uneasily back toward her dwelling. Still keeping out of view, he follows her to the place where she can comfortably descend the hill. He follows her because this *is* the last time he will see her for a while. After getting down the hill, she turns to look at him once more. Standing stiff as a statue, his hands at his side, he is powerless to move until she is out of his sight. She disappears into the dwelling, second in from the outside across from the garden.

Not far from inside the trees where this romantic escapade ensued, Will has stashed the backup horses. Checking to make sure all five are there, he mounts Rodeo, gathers the five's reins, and slowly rides over to the main gate of Fort Townsend. Forty feet from the fort's gate, he sets up to wait for his crew. He plans to keep a lookout for Oscar in the chuck wagon, which will indicate Tom is approaching and that will give him time to look like he too is riding up after giving the horses a thorough watering at the Red River. This is his cover story for riding ahead of the crew from Dodge City.

Rodeo never likes standing in one spot very long, so just about the moment when Will begins to drift off, to nap while lying under a tree, Rodeo gives Will a nudge, asking him to get up. It is great timing, because he opens his eyes and sees the chuck wagon emerging off in the distance. Will gets up and pats Rodeo saying, "Good boy." He mounts Rodeo and grabs the reins of all five horses. Steering them toward the fort, Will lines them up facing the road which leads to the fort's entrance. There they stand at attention, waiting for the others.

Seeing Will up ahead, Clancy challenges Ben. "Race you to Will." They sprint off racing to meet Will.

"We wondered where you ran off to with our horses," Clancy says.

"How long you been waitin', Will?" Ben asks.

"Not long," Will replies, looking expressionless. By this time the complete drover armada rides up, parading behind the lead steers. Oscar nods hello with a slight grin. Pepper, Chris, and Rodrigo are on one side of the chuck wagon. On the other side, Tom is followed by the calf and mother cow, which are flanked on the right by the wagon, and flanked on the left and back sides by Drake and Bear, respectively.

Pepper asks, "How you like our little herd?"

"Don't know why you chose to travel alone, forgoing our help with makin' camp and wrestling with those horses," Tom says. "But now that we are all together, let's all go in. Remember, we leave out in the morning."

At the fort, the crew corrals the lead steers and Oscar stables the mules, the calf, and the mother cow. Will does the same for Rodeo and the backup horses. As a general rule, the soldiers stationed at the fort give the cowhands a wide berth. They give them a particular look of curiosity and surprise at their traveling with only the calf and cow, but say nothing. Viewing the crew as wild, undisciplined cowboys, the soldiers limit their interactions and conversations with them, while the cowhands on the other hand, engage them discreetly, seeking whiskey and other spirits. After dinner in the mess hall, Will and Oscar make excuses to leave the group and retreat to the unattached chuck wagon to sit and get caught up.

"Did you see her?" Oscar eagerly asks.

"Yes. It wasn't good between us at first. But, by the end, we kissed again."

Oscar gasps. "You've gone further with this girl than most married couples. Two kisses. Is she now your intended fiancé, betrothed?" asks Oscar with a low chuckle.

"Betrothed? O, I don't even know her name," Will confesses.

"Well, that doesn't seem to be hindering anything," Oscar replies. Will starts to reply, but Oscar is enjoying teasing Will too much and continues, "The next time we talk, you'll have a papoose and didn't take the time to marry." Oscar chuckles. Will picks up some rope in the wagon and throws it at Oscar. "But tell me, Will, how far are you taking this courtship? You don't know anything about her. She may not be free to choose her mate. Her people may have promised her to someone. And more importantly, her people may not approve of you. I'm just telling you this to save you some heartache."

"Oscar, I'm not after her people or their approval," Will says with a smirk.

"You are not being serious," Oscar replies. "You're not thinking this through."

"Look, O, the drive is over. We're headed home. As far as I'm concerned, she and I are just two friends who said goodbye."

Unexpectedly, Tom walks up. "I'm glad I have the two of you here. There's been a complaint submitted to the captain of this fort. The complaint is about a Negro man with a horse with white feet entering the Indian village uninvited, pursuing one of their girls. It's hard for me to say I don't know this person since one of my drovers *is* a Negro who *rides* a horse fitting that description. You should know the chief's name is Chief Samuels, and he has a son named Nashoba. Nashoba has eyes for this girl. They are the source of the complaint. Now, I don't know how either of you mixes into this, whether or not the calf is involved, but, for the record, I'm ordering you two to avoid the Indian village from now going forward."

After the crew rested overnight in vacant barracks at the fort, they stagger to their feet the next morning to dress and get chow in the fort's mess hall. They stagger because the night before whiskey had been scavenged and passed among most of them, and now only hot black coffee before they travel will save them from Tom's tirade.

Will travels with the crew to his usual turn-off point on the trail. He hands the backup horses over to Rodrigo, Clancy, and Chris. While they continue on their way to the Hastings Ranch, he detours toward his home in Tennessee.

———•———

"You're gonna turn into a prune," shouts Mother Harriet.

Will sits sunken down into the bathtub soaking his naked, travel-worn body in warm soapy water. Drifting in and out of a daze, looking out the small bathroom window at the full moon, he thinks of her, and wonders if she thinks of him. He has been in the tub for over one-and-a-half hours.

"Do you need more time?" Harriet asks. "I have plenty to keep me busy, but I don't want you to fall asleep in there."

"No, I'm . . . I'm done," he says as he stands up, wraps a large drying cloth around his body, and steps out of the tub. He dries himself and heads to his quarters in the cottage. Harriet has the fireplace blazing, so the cottage is nice and toasty. "I'll put some pants on, and empty the tub," Will says.

"No need. Put your sleeper on and go to bed. You need your rest. I want you plenty rested for tomorrow's church services."

"Oh, no, Sunday—do I have to? I'm really tired, Momma," Will says groaning.

"You should never be too tired to give thanks for safely returning home with all your limbs, a clear mind, and receiving your good pay and—"

"OK, OK, church in the morning," Will says.

The next day, church services proceed the same as usual. Pastor Walker speaks this Sunday on the story of Joseph.

"Now, Joseph had many brothers, but his father, Jacob, favored Joseph and Benjamin over all of his sons because they were born to him by his true love, Rachel. You remember the story. Jacob had to work for seven years, and the land owner tricked him into marrying Rachel's sister, and then finally after working seven more years, he was able to marry Rachel, the one he really wanted. So, Jacob had several wives, and in turn, had children with each of the wives. But the sons he loved the most were Joseph and Benjamin, those born to him from Rachel. The Bible story teaches us that Joseph was out in the field one day with his stepbrothers, and their jealousy got the better of them. The brothers taunted and bullied Joseph and ultimately sold him to a caravan on its way to Egypt. The brothers went home and told their father Joseph was killed, and as evidence presented Joseph's bloody coat to their father. Their father wept and wept, and clung even tighter to Benjamin since he was the only surviving child born to him from Rachel.

Joseph arrived in Egypt and was put into prison. Sometimes our lives fall into a crevasse, and we are not sure if we will make it out or not. God says don't choose despair; wait on the Lord.

In Egypt, while in the prison, Joseph interprets another prisoner's dream. He interprets the dream to say the prisoner will be released from prison, and indeed he was released. After the prisoner's release, the prisoner returned to a high post in Pharaoh's court, and this former prisoner, in turn, rewarded Joseph with a high post in his household as a servant. After a time, Joseph is summoned to interpret one of Pharaoh's dreams. His interpretation causes Egypt to survive years of great famine. His saving Egypt prompts Pharaoh to make Joseph the most powerful man in the land, only second to Pharaoh. Did I say don't despair, but wait on the Lord?

In time, Joseph's brothers deeply regretted the pain they inflicted on their father through their jealous deed. During the famine, the brothers were forced to go to Egypt to buy food, and eventually learned what happened to their brother. Oh, see how the Lord worked in the life of Joseph. He was raised high among men, but he would never have achieved that greatness without having been pushed into the crevasse, pushed into prison by his very own brothers.

Oh, my dear ones, when others rebuke you, even your family, or circumstances push you over the edge, do not despair. The Lord has a plan for you. You cannot see it until the Lord manifests it in your life. But you must pray for his guidance and grace."

The church again is electrified by the sermon. All stand praising the Lord, and then join in singing the last hymn, followed by the benediction, and the attendees are dismissed.

Harriet is so spirit-filled, she goes down front to thank the pastor for his sermon. Will moves to let people by and finds a space at the door where he can stand and wait on his mother. As Rita Mae hurries out of the church, she passes him and says without stopping, "I'll have supper on the table by 5 p.m., but you are welcome to come earlier."

Will raises his thick eyebrows, surprised, and yells, "Thank you," at her, but not knowing why.

Harriet finally comes to him and motions they can proceed out. After strolling partway, Will asks, "Did you accept an invitation for dinner at the Walkers' tonight?"

"You said when you returned," Harriet says looking at him surprised.

"I know . . . um . . . um . . . I need to talk to you about something."

"Oh, what is it?" Harriet asks, raising one eyebrow.

Before he can speak, a trickle of rain starts. "We better get a move on it," Harriet says. They run for the trees along the path leading to the ranch. They wait a bit. The rain is light, but doesn't let up. They sprint for the cottage much farther. By the time they settle in and get the fire going and get dry, Will loses his courage to discuss with his mother the girl living in the Indian village. He doesn't know where to start. Besides not even knowing her name, her being Indian, him kissing her twice, and he could never tell her about the kissing; this doesn't amount to a relationship his mother would understand or condone. He decides not to tell Harriet.

———•———

The elder woman that shares a dwelling with her is named Liola. She, who has kissed Will twice, is afraid to share these developments with Liola. Besides him being a Negro, how would she explain spending time with him? And the kissing—no she could never tell her that part either. Such actions are not in line with her culture and are considered conduct that is dishonorable and shameful. She decides not to tell Liola about him. But every time her mind reminisces those romantic interludes with Will, those thoughts heat the blood running through her veins. Relief only comes from exhausting herself with long walks. "The next time for gathering," she suggests to Liola, "let's search for herbs in a meadow farther above the grassy area." This area is reached by passing through the spot east of the village where he kissed her for the second time. She walks briskly as they pass through the area. Once they pass that area, she settles down, and they start their gathering. They stay out there for hours walking around, squatting to cut plants, and placing the plants into the baskets they carry.

As they gather herbs, the chief's son, Nashoba, which means wolf in Choctaw, returns with a hunting party from the north carrying deer and rabbit meat. They transport the meat in a travois, a small cart pulled by one of the horses. Passing through the same meadow, Nashoba spots her and Liola. He instructs the others traveling with him to leave one of their horses, forcing two of the villagers to double up on a horse. Nashoba takes the reins of the extra horse and rides over to her and Liola, pulling the extra horse.

"Is the gathering good today?" Nashoba asks.

She responds, "Yes, we gathered good samples today. Why did you stop here?"

"You need to ride back. You must be tired after all the gathering."

"No need. We can walk back," she responds.

"But I am already here. I will give you a ride home."

She and Liola exchange glances. Liola smiles at her before going to mount the extra horse. They set their baskets on the ground. Nashoba dismounts and he and the girl lift Liola onto the extra horse. From there, Liola swings her leg over and sits upright. Nashoba expects the girl to be lifted onto his horse so he can sit behind her and hold her tight against his body. However, she asks him to lift her onto the extra horse. She climbs on and sits behind Liola. Nashoba gives them their baskets, and they slowly move toward the village.

Nashoba is six feet tall with coal-black shoulder-length hair, a chiseled chin, long, narrow nose, wide mouth, inset eyes, and a muscular body. He maintains the fitness of his copper-colored body by his daily activities of running, climbing, lifting, and routinely playing stickball. He attributes the muscles in his arms to be from tightening the tension on his bow and competing shooting arrows at targets. While he and his friends are occasionally chastised for their excursions off the reservation, they never have to be asked to help a villager to build or repair their chukka, work in the garden, or assist his father, the chief, with his many responsibilities. He is admired around the village by the men, women, and children, and everyone knows he has eyes for she that lives with Liola.

Nashoba is disappointed with the riding arrangements, but is still glad to escort them to their dwelling. Upon their arrival, Nashoba hops off his horse and assists her in dismounting, using this opportunity to touch her body and be close to her. Then Nashoba assists Liola. Liola takes her basket and disappears into their dwelling. She has her basket, thanks Nashoba, and starts to follow Liola inside.

"Wait!" exclaims Nashoba, causing her to stop near her dwelling's entrance. He stands with a wide stance leaning back into his legs, his chin raised high. "Your time is near to choose a mate, or do you want someone to claim you? It is better for you to choose."

"And have you challenge whoever I choose?" she asks.

"I am next in line to be chief. What woman would not be proud to stand by my side?" he says, his hands patting his chest.

She takes a step toward him, her chin extended and pointing a finger at her chest. "I train to be a healer. That is what Spirit has chosen for me. There is no space for a mate and children in a healer's life."

"Has Liola filled your head with such foolish ideas?"

"Is it foolish for me to want more than building a chukka, making, washing, and mending clothes, gardening, cooking food? Oh yeah, and having babies too?"

Abruptly mounting his horse, Nashoba says, "We will speak on this again."

———•———

Will sits there at the Walkers' dining room table, surrounded by his mother, Pastor Walker, Mrs. Walker, Rita, and Martha. It is a familiar room. Many times, Mrs. Walker has invited him and other young people in for tutoring, Bible study, and Rita and Martha's birthday parties. Now, he is there feeling as though he is in someone else's skin.

"Dinner is delicious! Whom should we thank?" remarks Harriet, slyly glancing at Will.

"Rita prepared the chicken, cabbage, mashed potatoes, and apple pie, while Martha made the cornbread," announces Mrs. Walker. Will was quiet during dinner, drifting in and out of daydreams. Fortunately, Mrs. Walker and Harriet hadn't been together for a while to talk so, each found loads to get caught up on during dinner: from new fabrics at the general store to recent betrothals and births. Will finishes eating, fiddles with his napkin, and begins moving his fork around on the plate. Harriet kicks him under the table.

"Thank you, Rita and Martha. This was a really enjoyable dinner," Will blurts out.

As Rita and Martha clear the table, Rita asks, "Would anyone like your pie now?"

"Yes," Harriet says.

"Yes, for me too," Will says. "But I'm gonna walk around a minute to let the food work its way down."

Pastor Walker starts to get up to walk with Will, but Mrs. Walker kicks him under the table. "I guess I'm taking my pie right here," Pastor Walker says, looking at Mrs. Walker confused.

"We can take our pie out on the porch, Will," Rita suggests.

"OK," Will nods.

Rita and Martha serve Pastor Walker, Mrs. Walker, and Harriet, and Martha places a slice in front of her seat at the dining room table. Rita carries two forks and two saucers each with pie out to the porch, where Will waits at one of two wooden chairs on either side of a small wooden table. Her heart is beating fast because she really likes him and wants their relationship to move past meeting at church services, community dances, and family outings to the lake.

"Here you go, Mr. Will," Rita says. He begins rising from his seat when she draws near. She motions for him to remain seated.

"Oh, so I'm Mr. Will to you now." Will smiles stiffly and accepts the pie.

"Only because you are such a hardworking man, traveling across territories, seeing the big cities," Rita says.

"Wait, I think you are making cattle driving out to be some kinda highbrow job. It's really a dirty, stinky, long, hard job where I never get enough sleep, can't bathe, and go sometimes days without clean water."

She stares at him with amazement. "I had no idea it was that bad."

"Yes, the only redeeming feature is the pay. I can work that hard at Applegate Ranch doing a similar job, and would get about one-fourth the cattle drive pay."

"What do you plan to do with all that pay you've received?" Rita asks.

"I have the same dream I've always had, to work my own farm," Will says.

She smiles and says, "I know you will get your farm, Will. You are a hard worker. You don't give up easily, and you're a good person." She wants to talk about seeing him more, but does not know how to steer the conversation that way. "Have you thought about sharing your life on that farm with someone?"

Will knows there are expectations between her parents and his mother. He is fond of Rita, and before these last few months, he would have started courting her. He had known her since childhood. But things have changed for him, on a grand scale. His heart is drifting through a gate controlled by another, who is the gatekeeper. He respects Rita and wants to be honest with her.

"Farm life, in the beginning, will be hard, and a gamble until I get my first crop. At first, there will be no house. I will have to clear the land and battle the weather until I can get inside. I think there are very few women that would be anxious to live that kind of life. I envision having to tough it out alone, at first."

Rita withdraws from wanting to press him on the subject of courting. He has given her a lot to think about. Her home life, in comparison to most Negro girls, is exceptionally comfortable and safe. She has her garden, her duties at the church, a social calendar of tea parties, dances, and she enjoys canning and quilting. She also has, in the back of her mind, to someday go to nursing school. From what he is saying, following him would remove her totally from a way of life she has become accustomed to; and will limit her choices. Although Will has a striking physique, handsome face, and a cuddly mild nature, he will have to do better at wooing her to get her to leave her life here for a farmhouse that's not even built yet!

CHAPTER 4

THE TAKING

———

THE moon has cycled to full moon eleven times since he last saw her. Work at the Applegate Ranch has helped fill the void of time. What did gnaw at him was the absence of his father because he has no adult male in his life acting as a consort, someone to whom he can divulge his current feelings, advise on how to resolve them, or particularly how to control them. Not even his closest friend Oscar is available, at least until he returns to the Hastings Ranch. This is his state, for the time being. But every day he eagerly tackles the work before him, and before long, his work at the Applegate Ranch stands complete, remarkably earlier than expected. He bids his goodbyes to the other workers there, and packs water and food for his trip to Texas. Harriet senses an edginess about him, but can't get him to share his thoughts before he and Rodeo depart. As with every one of his departures, she starts the night before, sending up a stream of prayers to protect his way.

While munching on boiled eggs Harriet has packed in his saddlebags, Will approaches the entrance to the ferry that carries travelers across the mighty Mississippi River. Will's trip to Texas always begins with him and Rodeo crossing the Mississippi via a ferry at Memphis. The ferry is located on banks of farmland owned by a farmer named Moody. Moody built the landings on both sides of the river, and he and his sons operate the ferry to generate supplemental income. At the ferry's entrance, there is a wooden sign posted, hand-written in black paint, listing the fares to cross.

Fares

Man on Horse	5 cents
Man in Wagon	10 cents
Livestock	1 cent for 2

Moody's ferry is a barge-like structure, a platform that floats on four small canoes or pontoons, which can carry only one wagon and team, six horses, or eight people without a high risk of someone or something accidentally toppling overboard.

As Will moves nearer to the entrance of the ferry, he spots a lone middle-aged White male with two satchels within arm's reach. He presumes him to be another traveler waiting to cross. Sitting on one side of the ferry's platform, gentlemanly dressed, pants rolled up, bare feet dipped in the river, the lone White traveler tugs on a stick fitted with a fishing line. He is actively engaged, pulling something out of the water caught on the casted line. Not seeing any of the usual ferry operators about, Will decides to stop near the outer edge of the landing to dismount. The White traveler briefly looks Will's way and slightly dips his head, which according to most at the time is a good enough greeting from a White man to a Negro. Will nods back.

As he continues reeling in the fishing line, he rolls the line around the stick. His efforts climax into bringing a squirming fish to the surface. Grabbing his catch with his bare hands, he yanks it out of the water and onto the ferry platform. From an inside shoulder holster, he removes a pistol. Holding the fish down firmly he bashes it in the head with the pistol handle and remarks, "There! I got supper. Now if only the damn ferryman will show up."

Will and Rodeo maintain their distance, not sure which side of the law this character is on. Examining his tailored attire and well-made satchels, Will guesses he's either with the government, a tradesman, or may even be a gambler. Once the White traveler packs away his catch, he gives Will and Rodeo a thorough once-over. "Where you headed, lad?" he asks Will.

Reluctant to offer up his travel plans to strangers, Will replies, "Marmead, sir. Just north of here."

Looking quite perplexed, the White traveler replies, "Never heard of it."

Will thinks, *That's reasonable since I just now made it up.* "It's a Negro settlement, sir, not far from here."

"Oh, well, safe travels," scoffs the White traveler. Removing his hat and wiping sweat off his brow, he continues, "My name is Gilley. I'm on my way to Little Rock." Gilley repositions his hat on his head, and begins putting on his socks and boots. Then Gilley asks, "And your name, young man?"

"My name is Will," Will says nervously, still limiting how much personal information he will share. "How long you been waitin' to cross?"

"Long enough for me to relieve myself in the river twice, and catch this here dinner. Not of course in the same spot, mind ya," the White traveler says, chuckling as he reaches into his pocket for his timepiece. "I sure would like to know what hours they keep runnin' this ferry."

Will looks toward the Moody home. "I see some men coming now, headed down from the main house," he says.

Four men walk up, none of them Farmer Moody. One of them, a spokesman, asks, "You folks waitin' to be ferried across?"

Gilley eagerly responds starting calmly, then ending loudly, "Yes, I have been here hopin' for just that very thing for the last *three* hours!"

One of the men rolls his eyes at the remark. The spokesman for the four continues, "Moody was waitin' for more than one to arrive.

It's not worth it for him to send all four of us down here to ferry only one traveler across."

"You *mean* he's been lookin' at me out here bakin' in this sun?" Gilley blasts.

"Now hold on, sir. We are tryin' to run a business. And a business doesn't run on charity and thoughtfulness. But, if you ever find yourself stranded out here again, you're more than welcome to come up to the main house; there you can refresh yourself while you wait for the ferry. Most folks around here know how Moody likes to do things."

Three others and a child wanting to cross come down a lane to the ferry landing, pay their fare to the spokesman for the four, and pack onto the ferry. After Gilley pays and boards the ferry, the spokesman beckons Will to come forward. He accepts Will's fare, but directs him to board and remain in the rear to isolate Rodeo's droppings away from the other folks on board.

The shore slowly drifts away behind them as the ferry gets underway floating out into the river. The four men steering the ferry use long paddle posts against the imposing waterway, alternating between digging into the river bottom and paddling the water to steer the ferry. The river's current naturally, with no paddling at all, carries the ferry downriver. So, the four push against the current to get lateral movement toward the other side, aiming for the matching landing across the river. Will stands, legs spread in a wide stance, bracing himself for any unexpected tips or dips. Unexpected ferry jerks cause Rodeo to anxiously step around and whinny. Will calms him by rubbing his neck and whispering, "Easy, boy."

The ferry's platform floats freely on the water, moving slowly but steadily across the river with gentle horizontal twists and rolls, giving its passengers a sensation of hovering above rather than floating on the water. By the time the ferry reaches the middle of the river, the swells and undulations lull Will into a disconnected space. Unresolved questions he's had overtake him. Such as how will he acquire his farmland? To buy the land outright will deplete most of his savings, leaving his survival that first year dependent on the success of his crops. The first year may be in jeopardy since the land must be cleared and made ready for planting, and he cannot forecast how long that will take. And if it's a large parcel cut out of wild uncultivated land, he may not see a crop until years two or three. Another way to get land would be by sharecropping, but that means he would have to work someone else's land and share in the crop revenue with the landlord. That could take years.

Will lets out a deep breath as if exhausted by these mere thoughts. His mind, after momentarily wondering, returns to the present — the ferry crossing; scrutinizing how much farther they have to travel across the river, and how Rodeo is accepting his confinement. Drifting back into his reverie, he considers how easy his goal would be attained if he were a smart White boy like Grant or Jason. Smart White boys always somehow get land, while Negro boys have to work endlessly, toiling for years on someone else's land. Unfortunately, the struggles don't end there. It is too soon after slavery for a Negro farmer to expect fair trade for his crops. Where a basket of corn sells for five cents on the market, a Negro will be offered two or three cents for the same basket.

The ferry finally reaches the other side. The platform's wood creaks, and generates scraping sounds as it rams into the wooden landing. Two operators nimbly jump off the platform to secure it tightly against the shore. After the platform is secured, passengers in front make their way off the ferry onto the landing, and take one of the roads leading inland. Gilley picks up his satchels, walks off, and stops near the far edge of the landing. Will begins leading Rodeo off, but one of the four operators yells out, complaining, "Negra, you left something," as he points to four three-inch balls of Rodeo's dung clumped on the ferry platform.

Gilley, who is still on the landing, looking at a paper he drew from his inside coat pocket, turns upon hearing what was yelled. He vigorously interjects, "Surely the fare covers *that!*"

Connecting eyes with Gilley, Will waves his hand to stop him and says, "It's OK." He doesn't want any trouble with this crew. After all, he has to use this ferry to cross the Mississippi to get to and from Tennessee. In the past, every time he crossed Mr. Moody was present and never voiced any complaints about Rodeo's dung. Hell, they move wagon teams across. So, this is something personal arising with *this* operator. The complainer of the four exhibits a smirky grin and says, "Here, boss," as he hands Will a shovel. Will begins scooping up the droppings and dumping them into the river. While he's shoveling, the complainer intensely eyes Rodeo and his saddlebags, tightening his lips with jealous contempt. He moves closer to Rodeo to get a better look, making Will feel uneasy. To unsettle the complainer, Will whistles and cues Rodeo to skin his lips back to display and grit his teeth, an act he typically performs for the vet. Seeing Rodeo's teeth like that, the complainer backs up. Next, Will directs Rodeo to take lateral steps to line up for a clear exit off the platform. He then signals Rodeo to march forward moving him off the platform and onto the landing. The operators see Will with his back turned to Rodeo, whistling and saying single words. They miss his glances at Rodeo making sure he is following his instructions and is moving off the platform safely. They wonder how the horse is being controlled or whether he is acting on his own. After Will is done shoveling, he keeps a cap on his seething anger as he returns the shovel to the complainer. But the complainer and the other three operators, as well as Gilley, are shaken, spooked by a horse glaring his teeth and then marching forward raising his legs high, marching riderless off the platform. These actions are akin to the animal being possessed or the presence of menacing spirits.

Flabbergasted as to how to ask about what just happened, Gilley frowning approaches Will. "Did you teach him to do that?"

After rewarding Rodeo with carrots, Will nods. Then turning his sights from Gilley and staring at the complainer he speaks loudly, "Animals are just plain unpredictable. It pays to never turn your back on them." Will looks back at Gilley who still bears a pronounced frown. Tipping his hat at him, Will says, "Thank you, sir, for offering your support. Safe travels to you too." He mounts Rodeo, and clicks his tongue signaling to Rodeo to head out.

Rodeo's hooves pound the dirt roads of Arkansas at a comfortable trot. Will holds his stride at a moderate, steady pace so that each day's ride wouldn't tire them both out too quickly. The road is quite familiar since they have traveled this way many times before when heading to the Hastings Ranch to join the drive. This will be trip number five. They average thirty miles a day. Between the hundreds of miles ahead of them are sites he's scouted for planned stops to rest or make camp for the night. He knows how long he and Rodeo can go a stretch at a time before they need to get water or take a break from moving. Moving too slowly overextends the trip, and racing Rodeo at maximum speed invites injury and prolonged fatigue for both of them. While riding, Will remembers advice from his father: *Treat a horse as an extension of yourself. If you like having use of their four legs, use them with moderation, lest you abuse them and are left with using just your two legs.*

Will is no longer a rookie at traveling alone for long distances. He prizes his learned capabilities formed from several sources: teachings from his father about horses, especially how to attain their complete trust and control, the knowledge gained from the other drovers like Tom and Matt, and from understanding his physical ability to complete the almost two-week odyssey to the cattle drive. He enjoys being on the cattle drives, listening to the other drovers as they swap stories, some comical, and techniques about wrangling cattle and horses, cross-country trips, visiting big cities, and the notorious tales of romancing women.

Will plans his stops for water at natural springs, rivers, and creeks. Hunting trips with his father have prepared him for trapping rabbits, hunting deer, catching fish, and scavenging for food on the road. He remembers another of his father's sayings, *Clean 'em, skin 'em, and preserve 'em to eat later*. His scouting skills come in handy when searching for food. Thanks to Matt, he is expanding his scouting skills to include the invaluable ability to track prey, spot predators, and, most importantly, ways to disguise his tracks.

For this fifth trip to the Hastings Ranch to join the cattle drive, he left the Applegate Ranch extra early, giving himself almost a month to arrive. He hopes arriving early will smooth over any of Tom and Mr. Hastings' doubts that arose from his late arrival for the last cattle drive last year. With all this time at his disposal, he also thinks about using the extra time to scout out additional possible campsites or to just arrive early and spend time gallivanting around with Oscar.

After five days of riding, rest stops, and camping, Will finally reaches Pleasantville, a stop on his trip where he can have a long rest in a real bed and delicious meals. Pleasantville is a small, plain town with a population of six hundred people, providing basic services and businesses. The main town or the White section of Pleasantville includes a store, saloon, barbershop, restaurant, hotel, bank, livery stable, transportation depot, school, and church. It mostly serves as a way station to bigger towns. Travelers passing through provide news from across the territory and is a side benefit for the citizens of such small towns.

On Will's first time stopping in Pleasantville, he rode into town going smack down the middle of the main street. It never crossed his mind he was doing anything wrong because he so often rode into his local town, Covington, outside of Memphis, entering via the main street. There, the Whites are ... marginally friendly; but not even that in Pleasantville. If he rides into Pleasantville again, after being told to proceed to the Negro section, he will be jailed for disturbing the peace, or worse. So, Will doesn't bother chancing fate by riding down the main street. Instead, he rides past the main entrance to the town, and picks up a side road taking him behind stores and shops with storefronts facing main street to the end of town where the Negro people live.

There are no rooms to rent to Negroes at the hotels and boarding houses on the main street of Pleasantville. And no need to ask. The town vigorously enforces its rules of no Negroes in any of the White business establishments. And there are "Whites ONLY" signs posted as reminders. Negroes occasionally defy the rules out of desperation or an emergency and attempt to trade at the White businesses. They are either sent around to the back, asked to come back another time, or arrested. Newly arriving Negro travelers like Will know to seek out other Negroes in town to inquire about food, lodging, or other services needed.

Pleasantville, like most burgeoning towns, has Negroes working as servants, maids, field workers, and general laborers. These work-ing people have to live somewhere nearby, thus the Negro section of town. Also living in the Negro section are educated Negroes, who work as schoolteachers, doctors, politicians, businessmen, ministers, and legal advisors. Among this group are persons who serve as the Negro community's rule makers and elders.

Will and Rodeo, therefore, abide by the town's mandate and pro-ceed down the side street behind restaurants and shops facing the main street of Pleasantville. That side street takes them down to the back of the last store. From there the side street continues for two hundred feet and branches off into several small lanes, which mark the transition to the Negro section. The several lanes lead to the Negro church, school, other small buildings, and a tent city occu-pied by Negro families and migrants. Will takes the lane leading to the tent city.

As he approaches the tent city, the day is winding down; the west-ern horizon slowly swallows the sun. He notices a couple of elderly Negro men who are relaxing on crates under two large shade trees. He rides to them, dismounts Rodeo, and asks, "Why is it so busy this evening? Is Mrs. Pritchett's boarding house full up, and I got to find space in the tent city?"

Looking at Will's fine saddle and new boots, one of the men replies, "Mrs. Pritchett should have room for you." He points to Mrs. Pritchett's boarding house among a cluster of buildings at the end of one of the other lanes, and explains that the area is buzzing with migrants looking for work and travelers seeking to sign up for the wagon train. "Yeah, the tent city is near full up. Don't waste your time lookin' for a spot," the man continues. "If you have enough money, your best bet would be to rent a bed at the boarding house. There you can water your horse, get a bath, a clean bed, and a good night's sleep."

Will heads in the direction in which the man points. Rodeo trails behind him, his reins loosely held by Will. As Will and Rodeo draw nearer and nearer to the boarding house and cafe, the aromas of pot roast, sweet potatoes, and collard greens dance potent in the air. Will boards Rodeo, and then enters the boarding house and café through the rear entrance. It's after sundown when he arrives and checks in with Mrs. Pritchett. He is assigned a room at the end of the second floor just large enough for a bed, coat closet, dresser, small table, chair, and chamber pot. The bathrooms are at the bottom of the back stairs, and the outhouses are outside next to the makeshift stable where Rodeo is boarded and resting for the night. By the time Will has dinner, it is late, and even later by the time he gets a bath. The bathrooms are just that, rooms each having only a large oval tin tub for bathing. Mrs. Pritchett keeps boiling water on hand, and gives buckets of it to Will to add to buckets of cold water for his bath. Will eases his body into the hot bathwater, allowing him to escape into a cloud of steam. A sigh of relief oozes out of his mouth and every pore of his body. He has no idea he is that tired. After his bath, he retreats to his room and falls into a deep sleep, dreaming of lavender flower blossoms floating down a river to a waterfall.

The next morning, the sound of a clanging bell that could awake the dead shakes Will awake. While yawning and stretching, he hears other tenants opening and slamming doors, and shuffling down the stairs. He quickly dresses and joins the procession to the café for breakfast. Standing at the bottom of the stairs holding a huge bell, Mrs. Pritchett greets the boarders with, "Good mornin'! Get you something to eat, and don't be late." When she sees Will, she apologizes for having disturbed him so early, and explains that some of the men have jobs in the White section of town and out on farms. She wakes them early so they can get something to eat and get to work on time.

Will enters the café located on the first floor of the boarding house and takes a seat at a table near the window. At this establishment, Mrs. Pritchett is what you would call the chief cook and bottle washer. She is a stout woman with thick rounded breasts and hips. Her hair is salt-and-pepper gray and styled in thick braids. Everything about her is thick and stout: her arms, legs, and the loving attention she pays to each of her customers. Her skin is dark brown, and her face slightly patted with face powder, with round-shaped eyes that reek of wisdom. She is a handsome woman. Her nose is narrow atop small but full lips that she keeps covered with ruby red lipstick. Although she is a widow, she never accepts the advances of drifters and strange travelers. She is a smart woman, smart with her money, perhaps ahead of her time. She boasts, "I'm content to run my boarding house, my café, and keep my trust in the only one I can always rely on, the Good Lord."

She takes Will's order, yells it to the cook, glances around the dining hall to make sure others are getting their orders in, and then bends down and begins chattering away at Will about the goings-on in town.

With one hand on her hip and the other pouring coffee, she goes on and on about the crowd gathering for the wagon train and how long their journey will take. Will watches her dart between the main entrance of the boarding house, the café's entrance, greeting guests, pouring coffee at other tables, and back to her one-sided conversation with him. He has been taught to respect his elders, so he gives her the same respect he would give his mother. Although he can't imag-

ine his mother leaving the Applegate Ranch, and making a living running a boarding house, she could certainly do it. But she has become
so accustomed to the gentile life she has created there at the Applegate Ranch, she would be put off by a bunch of drifters and strangers
sleeping under the same roof as her. As Will gets to know Mrs. Pritchett, he learns she has lots of help. She has three sons: one works as a
cook in the café, one runs their stable where Rodeo is boarded, and
the other assists her as a cashier for the boarding house and café.
While deep into her one-way gabfest with Will, she occasionally looks
up at one of her sons or other workers, and using only her eyes points
to where they should go, and then returns her focus to Will. Will
answers her with polite comments as she imparts her compilation of
important news, or plain gossip about prominent individuals in the
town, or about just common folk passing through. He nods, raises
eyebrows, and expresses one or two "Hmmm, hmmmm." She seems
bent on making conversation with him. Perhaps he looks too confident. He is often mistaken for a man of more years than he has. For
some reason, he is the person in the café today to whom she chooses
to divulge her juicy tidbits of information.

The cafe is filling up. Men are pouring in from the small rooms
upstairs and down. Others are coming in from the tent city. In the
back behind the cafe, those with very meager means are lining up for
handouts. She has an agreement with the general store in the White
section of town to allow purchases the night before for restocking
her pantry, readying her establishment for the next day's onslaught
of customers. With this agreement, she can cover all her constituents'
needs, and she doesn't have to go to the White stores or farmers'
stands during the café's busiest hours to restock her shelves. Yes, there
is more than the usual number of people in town, and she is feeling
the brunt of it. Her sons ease some of her pace, allowing her an opportunity to swing back around to Will's table to tell him about the wagon
train leaving from the transportation depot on main street. Will keeps

his eyes on his food and coffee while nodding to her comments until she says they are on their way to Texas. He looks up at her.

"Aren't you on your way to Texas?" she asks searching his face for a response.

"Yes," Will says.

"Your odds of getting there safe are better if you join that wagon train. That wagon train will travel over the plains, you know. And the plains, let me tell you about the plains. They are full of snakes, renegade Indians, and days without water. Do you hear me? No water! Believe me, I've heard stories from others." She points at persons around the café dining room. "Different ones have tol' me stories of losing a rig because their wheel broke, they couldn't find any water, and somebody died. Oh, my goodness, it gives me the sweats to even think about it."

Will toys with the idea. He has ridden with a group before, but you have to be careful whom you join up with. Traveling by wagon train wouldn't cause a problem timewise. As of now he has twenty-five days before he is due at the Hastings Ranch. At most, the wagon train will have him arriving in Texas within fifteen days. Besides, he has a weakness for sitting around campfires swapping stories like he has done so many times on the cattle drives.

Mrs. Pritchett continues pleading that traveling on the wagon train would make his trip to Texas safer, and any party he joins would appreciate his help as an extra man. "Unless you aren't going straight to Texas." She pauses, intensely looking him in each eye.

Will finally agrees. "I'll join up with them." He isn't sure he agreed to shut her up, or to keep her from probing further into his business. He hurriedly finishes his breakfast and joins the exodus out of the café.

It does not take him long to gather his things and saddle Rodeo. He rides down to the transportation depot where folks are assembled in the back of it, off the main street. He ties Rodeo to a nearby post and merges into the crowd, searching for the right group to join for the trip. There is an orderly commotion. Numbers and names are being called out, and money is being collected. He surveys the crowd gathered there with unintimidating eyes, limiting his search among the Negro travelers.

The crowd gathered at the transportation depot is becoming restless and eager to move out. They are mostly Whites from the North, foreigners from Europe, and Negroes. All are dressed for a long trip, wearing hats, bonnets, capes, carrying satchels, trunks, and every type of bag or knapsack. There are brand-new handsome wagons in front, more used ones in the middle, to very worn, tattered ones in the rear. Gabe Tremble, a gray-bearded White man who is the wagon train master or leader, sits at a small table up front, signs up each party, takes names, and accepts travel fees. It is $1.29 for each individual and $0.49 if you are part of a party. Gabe is a fair man and has made this trip many times. He takes Whites, Coloreds, Indians, Mexicans. As long as the travelers abide by rules of decency and respect, they are welcome to stay on his wagon train. But if they choose to be underhanded, rowdy, or a drunkard, Gabe does not hesitate to oust them from the fold, even if it is in the middle of the desert.

Will spots a family that looks like they could use his help. He approaches the head of the Harper family. Mr. Harper is a stout man in his early forties. Will explains to him that he is going only as far as the Red River, but would appreciate joining his party and serving as their extra set of hands. In return he would share in the watering of the horses in the evening, checking the wagon, setting up and dismantling camp. The Harpers consist of a father, mother, their daughter Marigold, and young son Harris. Mr. Harper is actually Reverend Harper, a minister who is taking his family to a new region to start a ministry. Reverend Harper asks Will where he is from and if the Lord Jesus Christ is his savior. Will replies Tennessee and, with no cynicism in his voice, exclaims that Jesus is the only savior he knows of. With that, Reverend Harper glances around at the faces of his family and announces, "Family, this here is Will Lawton. We would be delighted if you, Will Lawton, joined us on our journey."

Gabe gives the order, and the wagons begin to move out, one behind another, Negroes traveling in the rear of the wagon train. Gabe has scouts and armed patrollers who will cruise down the line on guard duty and checking on why a wagon isn't keeping up the pace, or to see if they are having wheel problems. Once the wagon train is underway, horses and wagons kick up dust and debris, requiring travelers, walking and riding, to wear bandanas over their noses and mouths. And this is only matched by the hellish heat. As Rodeo trots alongside the Harpers' wagon, Will monitors him to ensure he doesn't get overheated or dehydrated. Sweat rolls down Will's brow. He wipes his forehead only to feel another drop roll down to replace the one wiped. His tan wide-brim hat becomes so soaked around the crown of his head it sticks to him.

For the first two days of travel, Reverend Harper's daughter, Marigold, hardly says a word to Will. She considers him to still be a stranger, and she feels it isn't proper for her to initiate conversations with a strange man. Marigold is brown-skinned with shoulder-length hair that she wears in one long braid, or she pins the braid up and ties a yellow cotton cloth around her head. She has dark brown eyes, eyes that are bright and warm and glisten when she laughs. Her nose is short and round, and she has a small mouth with curved thin lips that pucker when she pronounces her words. Anyone can tell she is educated because she pronounces each of her words distinctively. This is expected since her father and mother put a lot of time in on these children. The Harper parents have tutored them, and tout how smart and well-mannered both of their children are. In days when Negro families range from barely surviving to having a comfortable living, considering ..., the Harpers are to be commended for their efforts to encourage their children who are blessed with an education to serve the broader community and be role models.

It isn't until three days into the trip that Will is surprised to see Marigold waving him over to the wagon to get some fresh-cut watermelon. Will rides over, reaches out, and accepts her offer of a slice. He then asks if it is OK to get a slice without the rind for Rodeo. She nods yes, hands him the slice with no rind, and smiles.

For several nights, Will joins the Harpers for dinner cooked by Marigold and her mother. The food is always delicious. Entering the second week of dining with the Harpers, Will begins to feel uneasy. He senses that he is being selected as a possible suiter for Marigold. *Are the Harpers teaming up on me?* he wonders. He is given hefty servings of food, encouraged to get seconds, and urged to applaud the culinary expertise of Marigold. Often space is left next to him for Marigold to sit after she serves everyone. Finally, after days of this, Will decides to diplomatically put an end to the possible matchmaking attempts. He decides to do it when the wagon train reaches the Indian Territory. Will thinks what he is about to do is appropriate because they are nearing the Red River, which he associates with his current true romantic involvement, and he needs to resolve his feelings about that before he can move on to someone else. When they pass through the Red River Valley, he is overcome by the reality that just over the horizon is the Indian village where *she* lives, and where he is barred from visiting. For now, he must focus his mind on heading toward the Hastings Ranch and putting his feelings for her aside for a while. However, he needs to talk to Marigold so that he can help her avoid any embarrassment.

The Harper party has finished dinner. Will picks up a lantern and invites Marigold to go for a short stroll. "Let's walk to the other side of the wagon," Will suggests. The camp is created by allowing the wagon train to divide into two groups. The first group of wagons stops, and the other half keeps moving up until its first wagon becomes even with the first wagon of the first group, making two parallel lines of wagons with space between the two lines. In the space between the lines, campfires are set up for cooking, warmth, and light. As Will and Marigold turn to leave, Mrs. Harper calls out, "Stay within sight of the camp, please." One of the norms at the time is that it is unladylike for a young, unmarried woman to be alone with a man.

Marigold's eyes glisten more than usual that night as they head to an area twenty feet from their wagon. Feeling the relationship may be entering a courtship, she walks with confidence, gliding her body around stones and shrubbery in their path. She is elated to be alone with him and welcomes the speculations that they are courting. Walking with her chin tipped up, she thinks, *I'm educated and a reverend's daughter. My prospects are unlimited. Any man would be proud to claim me.*

They finally come to an area with a few standing and downed trees where he thinks they can talk privately. Will pulls down a tree limb, hangs the small kerosene lantern on it, and keeps a hawk-eye lookout for any indigenous wildlife. He clears his throat and begins to speak nervously. "I need to clear something up. I want to say, I hope I have not led you to think that I wanted anything more than to be a friend, and a help to you and your family. I'm really just passing through right now." Marigold is stunned to hear this of all the remarks that he could have made to her in this romantic setting. Will, too, is stunned he got it out on the first try. Normally, he would keep his feelings bottled up inside and just muddle through everything. But he can tell his mind and body are going through some kind of metamorphosis. He is driven to be with a certain young woman, and has no stomach for misleading Marigold or anyone else for that matter.

Marigold is actually enraged inside, but she refuses to show it. "I see. You speak like a man that knows exactly what he wants."

"I think I do, but I may be wrong. I mean, things may be different by this time next year," Will says.

She doesn't let this disappointment completely discourage her. She will keep her options open with him, keep cooking him good food, smiling, and will definitely get his post information so they can stay in touch.

Thinking what he set out to do is done, Will grabs the lantern and ushers Marigold to head back to camp. She is looking away from him when he says, "You are very pretty, smart, and clever. You will do just fine, Miss Marigold."

Glancing at him momentarily she responds, "Thank you, Will. You are most kind with your compliments. You said you wanted to be friends; I hope then that you will give me the satisfaction of receiving your post information so that we can stay in touch as friends." Saying these words leave a bitter taste in her mouth.

They walk back to the camp taking slow, deep breaths. Will hopes that the air has been cleared. He feels his mother would be proud of him for correcting this situation. Marigold too accepts that, although Cupid did not make his appearance with them this night, a strong friendship bond is possible and can still lead to romance. There is a way about Will that she really admires. She has watched him; how strong and deliberate, he would set up their camps, handle their team of horses, and go hunting for their game. She has watched his eyebrows jump with expressions, and dimples in his cheeks appear and disappear with each chuckle. Yet he is so soft-spoken when speaking to Harris her brother, or about his family and friend, Oscar.

By the end of the second week of traveling, making camp, and breaking camp, Will comes to his departure point. It is near the city of Dallas, Texas. He says his goodbyes to the Harpers, and rides off into the wide openness. As he rides toward the Hastings Ranch, his mind is torn between giving up his pursuit of the Indian girl completely and searching for a way to win her over once and for all. Just thinking of her skin, her smell, even her stubbornness, all of it gives him a rush throughout his body. He can't imagine what making love to her will be like. He droops his head and says what he's thinking out loud to Rodeo, "I must be in love. It's been a year and I can't think about anything or anyone else." Rodeo whinnies. "OK, except for you, buddy. I'll never *not think* of you. As Mrs. Walker would say, 'That sounds like poor grammar, Will Lawton.'"

Will arrives at the Hastings Ranch, and according to his plans, this may very well be his last cattle drive, although he is wavering on that idea. He checks in with Tom.

"Good, you made it," Tom says.

Arriving early, Will gets to work right away selecting the backup horses and continuing the training of others. Later that day, Tom rides over to the corral where Will is working. "What did you decide about FireTip? Is he ready to travel, or do you want to hold off?"

FireTip is a wild horse that came to the ranch hungry and malnourished. Matt lassoed him and locked him in a corral by himself because he kicks and bites anyone or anything that comes near him. Will has made some headway with him using techniques taught to him by his father. In fact, Will is the only one FireTip would let ride him. He stays unsaddled year-round until Will arrives at the Hastings Ranch. Mr. Hastings wants to sell him, but the horse is labeled by the other ranch hands as loco. Tom suggests a long trip may work some of the vinegar out of him, as a last resort to making him a sellable horse. Will imagines another use for him.

"Yes, let's take him on the drive. We'll see how he behaves," Will says to Tom.

The bunkhouse is where the ranch hands sleep and spend their free time when they're not working. Mr. Hastings has installed bunk beds, personal storage closets, and two outhouses nearby. Oscar sleeps in the servants' quarters in the main house. When Will finds him, he is busy in the kitchen preparing one of the last dinners for the Hastings before the pending drive.

"When did you get in?" Oscar asks as he bounces from one pot to another, checking and stirring contents.

"This morning. Saw Tom and started working," Will says while proceeding to enter the kitchen.

Oscar sees him step inside and immediately holds up his right hand as he continues to stir with his left hand. "No, no you can't come in. You'll have to talk to me from the doorway." Will stops and stays on the porch. Oscar continues, "Mrs. Hastings just had the maid clean this entire kitchen this morning."

"I do need to run something by you," Will says biting his lip.

"I'm listening," Oscar says while stirring gravy in one pot, and then mashes potatoes in another.

———•———

Mr. Hastings rides out to the south pasture to survey the herd in preparation for the approaching drive. He finds Tom out there. "Have they all been branded?"

"Yes, colonel."

"Don't call me that. At least not when we are alone. Lest I call you captain," says Mr. Hastings.

"Understand," Tom says. They both smile in agreement. "We should be ready to leave in two days. I told the crew they can have a long night in Waco tonight. Drink and be merry, but no arrests. After tonight, they will have all day tomorrow to rest up, and then the day after be raring to go in the early morning."

———•———

After hearing what Will had to share, Oscar removes his brewing pots from the flames, stops tending to them, and sits down at the small kitchen table staring at Will. "You need to get this girl out of your head. We were told to stay away from the village. You can't chase her anymore."

Trying to make his point, Will extends both hands, becomes animated while talking. Cognizant of where they are, he pleads in a low tone seeking Oscar's understanding, "I have a plan. I just have to buy myself some time."

Oscar shakes his head in disagreement. "No, you shouldn't . . ."

Suddenly, Mrs. Hastings enters the kitchen. Oscar jumps up. She asks, "Is the food ready? It must be. You are taking a rest." Seeing Will in the doorway, she says, "Oh . . . ah . . . hi . . . ummmm . . . young man." She throws her right arm up in Will's direction, flexes her wrist as though that will bring his name to her mind.

"It's Will, ma'am," Will says after taking off his hat out of respect.

"Of course. Will," Mrs. Hastings says giving him a slight nod as a greeting.

Oscar answers her question. "Almost ready, ma'am. I need to finish browning the meat, mashing the potatoes, and then dinner can be served."

"Good! John is having some railroad men and politicians to dinner, and they may even stay over. Unfortunately, they will dine in heaven tonight, and be thrown to the wolves tomorrow, if you're not here."

"Oh, it can't be that bad. I've shown you and the maid some pointers," Oscar says.

"Yes, you have. But I know Mr. Hastings didn't marry me for my cooking. But our love has grown because he pays you for your cooking. If only I can get you outta that cattle driving. Any chances?"

"No, not yet. I'll know when it's time," Oscar says.

While they are talking, Will leaves for the bunkhouse to find an empty bed for the night. Oscar looks at the empty kitchen doorway where Will stood, hoping he will consider the advice he gave him about the Indian girl.

The cattle drive leaves the Hastings Ranch, and the travel up to the Red River is uneventful, except FireTip is along for this drive. He keeps the camps lively. Will has to constantly go to the makeshift corral and separate him and another horse from fighting. He finally ties him off to the side and puts Rodeo with him for company. For some reason, they get along.

"Can you find a way to behave yourself?" Will asks FireTip, speaking in a soft low tone, almost nose to nose with him, and rubbing his neck. Rodeo shakes his head, indicating FireTip can't behave. "Ha ha haaaa," erupts from Will. "Well, then you will have to teach him," Will says to Rodeo chuckling hard holding his stomach, and then commencing to rub them both.

Following the herd, the backup horses kick up their portion of dust and prance about. Occasionally, Will races them ahead of the herd, allowing them a chance to stretch their legs and run the vinegar out of FireTip. Because FireTip outruns the other horses, Will often lets him run untethered, but calls him back if he gets too far away.

Along the trail, Will gathers dried weeds, vines, and branches and packs them into one of some old flour bags Oscar keeps in the front of the chuck wagon. Oscar comes across the bags while looking for something in the wagon, and concludes Will is collecting kindling for future fires.

Will asks Matt if he can ride up to the Red River to scout the crossing again. While Matt can take whomever he wants on these scouting excursions, he doesn't let Will know he prefers taking him because he makes an extra effort to help him spot things of interest. He finds Will has a curiosity about him. Matt says, "OK." Now, Will goes to Rodrigo begging him to watch the backup horses. After some going back and forth, Rodrigo finally agrees, and it involves ten dollars. Rodrigo also insists, "OK, but take FireTip. I have no patience for him."

Riding Rodeo and towing FireTip, Will rides over to Matt. Matt frowns looking at FireTip and asks with skepticism, "Is he going to give us trouble?"

"No, he's good with me and Rodeo," Will says.

"Alright then, let's move out."

Matt and Will arrive near the place of the last crossing; it appears acceptable, but Matt wants to have other choices. He suggests Will go west and he will go east, looking for other good options for the cross-ing, and meet back when the sun is straight up, or high noon. They have to pick a crossing point every trip because waterways change. Changes to the river happen because of the weather, flooding, the riv-er's current wearing down the banks, and human actions. This time Matt asks Will to try to avoid what he calls "the wildlife" and laughs. Will rides around, observes some Indian women washing clothing near the shallow part of the river, but sees no signs of her. He stops and dismounts to let Rodeo and FireTip prance around. Both have big egos. Rodeo only prances to keep FireTip in check. FireTip sometimes runs up on Rodeo and stops just short of ramming him as a bluff. Will whistles. They both go to him, and he gives them carrots. There is a lot on his mind. He is glad Matt has allowed him to join him, so he can get away from the others and think clearly.

It is time for him and Matt to meet where they parted hours ago. After a short discussion comparing sites identified, Matt selects a spot for crossing, and then they head to the trading post. Matt wants a cigar, and Oscar wants any fresh vegetables and fruits if available. They reach the trading post, dismount, and tie their horses. Will tells Matt he'll wait outside. His heartbeat speeds up as he scours the village for a sign of her. He doesn't dare move in that direction, nor does he have the guts to send Rodeo over. He is heeding Tom's orders. Frustrated at having his hands tied, he bites his lip and continues to scan the area. As fate would have it, she exits her dwelling, comes within his view, and eventually looks directly at him.

He thinks, *It's as if she shot an arrow at me and it hits me right between my eyes. Get it together, Will. Make your move now.*

Staring back at her, he raises his arm and points to the river, his desire pulsating through his raised arm. If she doesn't respond or responds in the negative, he will be crushed. Finally, after what feels to him like an eternity, she nods, giving him a sensation of euphoria. Hoping his legs don't buckle, he leaps up the steps and enters the trading post. Inside he tells Matt, "I'll meet you back at the herd. I want to run some vinegar out of FireTip."

Will arrives at the river and ties Rodeo and FireTip to small tree limbs that are capable of breaking in the event they need to get away from a snake or something. He walks along the side of the river to the spot where they first met. Not seeing her, he wonders if she just nodded to get him to move on. He thinks, *After all, it has been a year since she's seen me.* He paces back and forth, thinking, *Oscar may be right. This relationship is impossible.*

"I can get in a lot of trouble if she and I are caught together. I have to consider what may happen to her, her reputation, as well as what may happen to me," Will whispers to the river and the reeds.

She finally walks up, sweaty and beautiful. Her presence silences his concerns. His feelings for her come roaring back. It takes all of his strength to calm down his muscles.

"You are back. What do you want now? To finish dishonoring me?" she says.

"Dishonoring? Ahhh . . . I hope we can somehow be friends," Will says.

"Friends! A friend doesn't grab the other friend, and force themselves on them as you did to me," she says.

"I didn't force myself—wait, and I didn't come here to argue. The reason I came to see you is to tell you I want to buy you some boots, as a farewell present. They are genuine leather and will make it safe for you to do your gathering in the tall grass, where there may be snakes. But I need your foot size."

She sees Rodeo and FireTip.

"Whose horse is that?" she asks.

"Never mind the other horse. Can I measure your foot?" Will asks.

"After you tell me whose horse that is?" she insists with her head cocked to the side.

He stands there biting his lip, feeling both anger and passion at the same time. He tactfully answers her, "He belongs to the Hastings Ranch. OK?"

"These leather boots—you will buy them for me?" she asks.

"Yes."

"And why are you buying me these boots?"

"Well, to make up for . . . if I've offended you in any way."

"Hmmm. OK," she says.

"Right. I have a strip of cloth. Let me lay it next to each of your feet to see how long and how wide." She stands still, and he stoops down low by her legs and feet and takes measurements. He can smell the oils and incense emanating from her. After finishing taking the measurements, he stands up and says, "Thank you."

"When do you bring me the boots?" she asks.

"OK, now, that's where we have a problem. I'm not allowed to enter the village anymore, thanks to your suitor, Mr. Nashoba. You will have to watch for the chuck wagon coming back this way after one full moon. Did you get that? The chuck wagon will come by headed to the fort. But I will be here at the river waiting for you after one full moon. I'll be here with the boots. Agreed?"

"Agreed," she says.

She saunters toward FireTip, and he warns her, "I wouldn't get too close; he's a little wild."

"Wild, like me?" She gets closer, close enough to rub his neck, and then his face. FireTip whinnies low like her touch is soothing to him. Will watches in astonishment. Next, she unties the reins, grabs a hand-full of his mane, throws herself up onto his bare back, and takes off. Will runs and hops on Rodeo and chases after her. FireTip is tan in color, and she is a caramel color, wearing a tan cotton dress. They are moving so fast tearing across the valley, their coloring blurs together as if they are one entity. She skillfully handles him. Anyone viewing them would assume they were born together. Fortunately, she heads away from the direction of the herd, and away from the direction of the Indian village. Some male villagers passing by hear him yell at her, "Come back with my horse!" They find the scene funny and laugh. She rides to a green oasis where there is a dozen trees still standing, shading green grass and a water hole, like a scene that had been painted there. It does not match the rest of the surroundings of fading green grass across red-clay dirt. At the oasis, she hops off FireTip and says, "I like this horse." FireTip lets her cup her hands around his mouth, and he licks them looking for a treat. Will dismounts and gives her a few pieces of carrot to feed him.

"He likes you, too," Will says. And then there she goes again staring at him, making his muscles quiver.

"Tell me something," she says. "When you return with the boots, that will be the last time I see you?"

"Yes," he says. He was hoping she was feeling a little passion also and would favor him with another kiss.

"I suppose after I get the boots, you will want another hug."

"No, no, not unless you want to," he says smiling from inside out.

She comes closer to him as if daring him to reach out and grab her. "Maybe you want to hug and kiss right now for the boots. We are away from the village, and you seem to be sweating a lot. The women elders of my village tell me to watch for these signs when a man is in season. He will sweat and pant and stare at your body, like you are looking at me now. They also say a woman's body can make a man weak with passion, and he is easy to control."

"I'm sweating because it's just plain hot. Are you toying with me? I do have feelings, you know," Will says trying not to stare at her body.

She comes even closer, speaking low, "You put your mouth on me and did something I could not tell anyone about. It was too, too . . . It's not for unmarried people." Raising her tone, "Do you do that with other girls, other Negro girls?" she asks.

Will responds quickly. "No. I myself do not do that with other Negro girls." Will knows that to be partially true.

"We can go back now. I will wait for you to come back with my boots. And we'll meet at the river, where you first dishonored me! Ha ha," she says loud, laughing. She grabs FireTip by the mane again, leaps upon him, and takes off going back to the river. Will follows her back. At the river, she skids FireTip to a stop, hops off, kisses FireTip, and runs to her village. FireTip begins to trot after her, and Will whistles the signal to stop. He halts, turns around, and comes to him. Will takes his reins, and the three race back to the herd.

Matt has already returned alone from scouting. Tom sees him come into camp and asks, "Didn't two of you ride out to scout?"

"Will is wrestling with FireTip. He'll be along soon," says Matt.

"He didn't by any chance go over to that Indian village, did he?" Tom asks.

"No."

Oscar sees Will ride up, corral the horses, and grab a plate for dinner. Everyone else has been served and is eating. Drovers are coming up for seconds, but Will is allowed to get his first serving before seconds are served. But Oscar is beside himself. He is eager to get an update from Will. To have privacy, Oscar asks Will to follow him over to the wagon. Oscar sits with bated curiosity. Before Will can sit and get comfortable, Oscar demands, "Did you see her?"

"Yes," Will says.

"You mean you went into the village anyway?" Oscar asks, leaning toward Will.

"No, she met me at the river where I saw her bathing. We talked and then we went for a ride. She rode FireTip."

"Surely you jest. She rode that loco horse?"

"Yeah, she even likes him, and he likes her. And, he's not loco. Don't call my horse loco."

"Your horse?" Oscar replies.

"Yes, I'm gonna work out something with Tom. No one at the ranch can handle him, so I might as well take him."

"My word, you've got a story to tell. We are sitting on the best story out here. I know the crew would love to hear this one. But unfortunately, it's so bizarre you can't share it with a soul, let alone our gossiping crew."

The crew makes it to Dodge City, driving the cattle into the stockyards. After receiving the count, Tom telegraphs Mr. Hastings the revenue and payouts. Will boards Rodeo, FireTip, and the other backup horses. He arranges to meet with Tom in the hotel parlor later that evening.

Earlier that evening after the crew is paid, Tom retreats to the hotel dining room where he polishes off a steak, roasted potato, and wine for dinner. Carrying his glass of wine from the dining room, he finds a seat away from others in the parlor where he can finish the glass and eventually talk privately with Will. Will enters the Great Western Hotel, removes his hat and maneuvers past stares from the front desk attendants and other hotel workers. He enters the grand parlor and approaches Tom. Will nods. Tom invites him to have a seat. Will gets comfortable and waits until Tom finishes taking a sip of his wine.

"Well . . . ?" Tom says with eyes focused on Will.

"I wanted to know what's going to happen to FireTip?" Will asks, his eyes scrutinizing Tom.

Tom takes a sip from his glass of wine, and then he looks up at Will. "What do you want to happen?"

"I want him. He's no good to Mr. Hastings. He can't keep him or sell him. He's too wild, but he obeys me."

Tom returns to staring at his glass of wine, swirling it around in the glass. Will decides to give him a moment to contemplate his offer. Tom's decision has grave consequences for Will. Holding his hat in his hand, Will looks around the enormous parlor at the various room adornments: large pictures on the wall of former owners and landscapes, large flower pots, lengthy thick drapes. Other patrons enter the parlor, glide onto cushioned seats, and whisper their conversations. Tom continues thinking and sipping his wine. He does dread the return trip to the ranch wrestling with FireTip all the way. And he notes Will is right, the prospects for a sale of the animal are poor.

"Ah, hell. Take him! I'll clear it with Hastings when we get back. Thanks, Will, for providing another interesting conversation I have to look forward to with Mr. Hastings."

Will's plan is coming together. The crew wraps up their stay, and they and the chuck wagon leave Dodge City heading south to Fort Townsend. Their plans include lodging at Fort Townsend before continuing on their way to the Hastings Ranch. As they approach the Red River, Will hands off the backup horses. Oscar lags behind the crew to say goodbye to Will. Thereafter, he races the chuck wagon to catch up with his crew as they approach the gates of the fort.

Will rides to the Red River, to the place where they first met. He waits at the river for her. About an hour or so passes, and the time is approaching dusk. He is getting anxious.

She finally comes right before sunset, wrapped in a light tan deerskin cape, wearing a red blouse, a tan wrap-around skirt, tan leggings, and moccasins. Her hair appears freshly braided with ribbon intertwined, and she's emitting the usual intoxicating scents of lavender oil and incense.

"I'm glad you finally came. But we need to hurry. I need your help," Will says speaking with urgency.

"What do you need my help with?" she asks with a frown on her face.

"It's Rodeo. Please come now," Will says before he calls FireTip, who races to him.

"How can I help him? Where is he?" she asks looking around.

Will hops onto FireTip's bare back. "Well, if you just look at him and see what you can do. You're a healer, aren't you?" He lifts her and she swings her leg over. "We need to hurry. I don't want him out there on the plains alone too long," he says. Once she's seated in front of him, he holds her tight and secure, and takes off, directing FireTip to moderately gallop along the road toward the oasis.

After they arrive, he says, "He should be near here." Will calls Rodeo's name. Out from behind the trees where he had hidden him, Rodeo emerges and gallops up next to them on the road. Rodeo gallops dragging a string of tree branches, vines, dried weeds, and twigs strewn together on a rope. The objective is to drag the ground to erase the tracks made by FireTip and Rodeo. Will gives them the signal to continue moderately galloping, single file, Rodeo to trail behind FireTip.

She realizes what is going on. "You *lied* to me! Take me back! Take me back!" She starts squirming, trying to get down.

"Be still; you don't want to fall off at this pace." He holds her tight, gripping the reins with his arms pressing into her breasts.

———◆———

At the village, Liola has been waiting for her in their dwelling. She has cooked dinner and has been waiting for her to return home. It is getting late, and there are no signs of her. Liola walks around the village, looks out in the fields where they usually gather herbs, checks the garden, and looks around the trading post. She asks one of the children to find Nashoba. He enters her dwelling, walking jovially with ease, glad to have been summoned to this dwelling. "What do you need, Liola?"

She speaks in their language, saying in essence, "I am worried. She has not come home or sent me word. It is not like her to say nothing by this time of the day."

"Oh, don't worry. I'm sure she is late coming from the river where she may be washing clothes or her hair. I will find her for you," Nashoba says reassuring her, and then departs.

Liola thinks, *This one is not fond of washing clothes. I do all the washing clothes. She does cooking and healing, but no washing clothes.*

Nashoba rides his horse down to the river, scans the neighboring fields, asks families in the village, and no one has seen her. He goes to the trading post and goes inside to ask their workers if they have seen her. As Nashoba exits the trading post, two male villagers, Talako and Koi, close friends of Nashoba, ride up. Talako says in Choctaw, "We hear you are looking for your woman. We did see her weeks ago riding on the Negro man's horse. She was smiling and happy, so we kept going."

Nashoba's jovial mood dampens.

"To tell you the truth, she seems to always be talking to him," Koi says smiling at Talako. "I'm afraid if I had to guess where she is, if she is not here in the village, I would guess she went to visit him." Koi and Talako exchange smiles and nod at each other.

"And after I find her, remind me to cut your throats for saying such things," Nashoba says.

"We are just trying to be honest with you," Talako says. He continues looking around shrugging his shoulders, "Where is she going to go around here, and not come home?"

"She might be hurt or taken by the White men in the fort," Nashoba says gritting his teeth.

"Oh yes, she's been here for years, and yet today the men of the fort take her?" Talako says questioning Nashoba's logic.

Nashoba grows angrier and tells them to get some torches and ride with him back to the river. When they reach the river, Nashoba says, "Look for tracks!"

Northeast of the river, Koi yells, "Here! There are deep tracks, maybe two on a horse heading east." They gallop east following the tracks found at the river. When they reach the oasis, the tracks disappear, almost like they have been wiped away.

"Do you see which way they went?" Nashoba asks.

"No, nothing this way," Koi says.

"Or this way," Talako says.

"We have to keep going. Maybe they kept going straight that way," Nashoba says pointing east and gazing at the eastern horizon.

"You don't know that. And we can't go off tracking a ghost," Koi says.

"Ah," sighs Nashoba gritting his teeth more and balling his fists. Realizing Talako and Koi will not follow him riding east, he races back to the village.

Nashoba barges in on his father, the chief, who is having dinner.

"Father, may I talk with you?" asks Nashoba.

"Is it urgent, or can I finish my meal?" says Chief Samuels.

"It's urgent, Father."

"Very well. Aaahhh . . . what do you need?"

"I need you to speak to the captain at the fort and tell him we have a girl missing." Nashoba paces back and forth as he explains. "We are not sure, but we think one of the Negro cattlemen took her against her will."

"What makes you think one of the Negro cattlemen has her, and what makes you think he took her against her will?"

"She has been seen with one of those Negroes several times, talking, riding one of his horses, smiling with him, and yes he took her because she is to choose me when her time comes. And I would choose her to stand with me."

"Sit down, son. First, I will contact the captain at the fort because I am responsible for all of our people in this village, and I need to try to find out what happened to her. Second, I want to discourage you from leaving the village to look for her. We don't want to bring unnecessary trouble upon us until we know what we are dealing with. Third, you may very well be chief one day. Being chief requires you to listen to your people, just as I have listened to you. And when you listen, you have to listen with an open mind because when a person comes to you, they usually desire something, and that desire can sway the way they make their request. For example, do you want our young girl to be found to secure her safety, or to secure her away from the Negro man so that the way will be made clear for you to have her? And have you considered—and I am going to make some assumptions here—assuming there is no blood, no body, no signs of a fight, or screaming heard, that she could have gone willingly? As chief, you cannot look at the problem from one direction. Four directions in this world give us guidance to move through it, and for making decisions. As chief, you must look at the problem in multiple ways to find a solution, like looking from four directions. Study what each offers, their consequences, implications, to be thorough. See what each direction teaches you before you come to a decision."

The chief does set an appointment to meet with the captain at Fort Townsend and report that one of their Indian girls is missing. He gives the captain her name and description and explains that, days before she went missing, she was seen riding a tan horse alongside a Negro man. Both the horse and the Negro are possibly associated with one of the groups driving cattle through the Indian Territory. The captain dispatches a telegraph message to the Hastings Ranch.

———•———

Will and his captive ride in silence for over three hours. Refusing to be outdone, she sheds not a single tear, but settles in to watch the approach of the eastern horizon—coming towards her, revealing itself, layer by layer. Green fields emerge from behind golden hills, then those fields disappear into clusters of trees. Her captor keeps a steady pace, holding the reins with one hand, and gripping her stomach with the other.

Their first stop is at the Glover River. There, he dismounts and looks up at her with an apologetic expression. She remains seated on FireTip. Then she grabs the reins, kicks FireTip in the sides, yells, "Hiyah! Hiyah!" and takes off. Will casually turns, and then whistles, giving FireTip the signal to return. FireTip slows and turns carefully as though he doesn't want to throw her. Kicking her feet, she screams, "No! Go, go!" FireTip whinnies and jerks confused, but obediently trots back to Will.

"Come down," Will says with his hand on her thigh. He raises his arms out to catch her. She hops down. He continues, "I don't want to do this, but I'm going to have to tie you up so you won't run off and hurt yourself, or run off and someone else gets you and hurts you. I have to take responsibility, and watch over you to keep you safe."

"Keep me safe?" she yells as she hits him. Then they wrestle, him trying to tie her wrists, her trying to pull her wrists away from him. "I'm not one of your horses to be lassoed and trained," she lashes out.

He finally gets control of her wrists, ties her hands, and puts a rope around her waist. At that moment his father's words come rushing back to him, that a gentleman takes responsibility for the circumstances he creates. He feels bad about tying her up, but those feeling are dwarfed by the fear of being caught by her Indian suitor. He imagines Nashoba, the chief, and the soldiers from the fort are hunting for her by now, and he thinks, *We need to get out of Indian Territory.*

CHAPTER 5

FINDING A WAY

———

NOW riding separately, Will and his captive, her hands tied, a rope around her waist tethered to him, arrive from the Glover River to their next stop on the journey to Will's home. Two months ago, Will had found this place while scouting on his last trip en route to the Hastings Ranch. It appears to be an abandoned shed. The outside walls are weather-beaten, surrounded at its base by unrelenting wild grass. Upon entering the shed, the smells of old wood, dirt, and dried fodder compete for prevalence. The shed has a slanted roof and four sidewalls. The front wall includes the apparatus for two large hinged doors that have fallen off, and now are outside and lean against the structure. Weather-beaten and dilapidated as it is, Will and his captive have been riding for hours, and he finds it quite suitable to shelter them for a night's sleep. Desperate to put the Indian Territory behind them, he can justify pushing himself, but not her. He doesn't know if dragging the broken tree limbs and twigs behind them has successfully camouflaged their tracks. However, he does know everyone in his party, including the horses, is exhausted. They will have a rest here.

After helping her down off FireTip, he carries her to an old barrel in a corner of the shed and props her up on it. He ties the rope on her waist to a two-by-four board, forming part of the bottom of the loft above them, and ties her ankles together as well. It is nearing dusk. She sits there, eyes heavy with fatigue, but opens them momentarily to look out the large opening where the two doors should be, and spots a hooting owl in the distance. She thinks, *Only a hooting owl is witness to my captivity in this run-down shed.* She can cry out, but only pines, oaks, and turning Bermuda grass will hear her.

Will nervously unloads gear and supplies from the horses, and puts out fresh feed and water for Rodeo and FireTip.

"Do you want some water?" he asks her.

She gives no reply. Her nostrils detect the smell of garlic, followed by the faint scent of lavender and incense emanating from the deerskin cape that remains wrapped around her since he stole her. The lavender and incense scents bring to mind familiar smells of the comfort and safety of her village—of home. She leans back against the wall and takes a nap.

A short while later, she awakens and looks around. She doesn't see him at first. Her eyes are drawn to the light emanating from above, and then she hears him working above her in the loft. He sees she is awake. "Get used to the garlic smell," he says, as he sprinkles chopped garlic around the loft where they are to sleep for the night. He brags, "It's an old trick I learned from the guys on the drive. Spread this around your camp and the snakes, spiders, and critters will avoid you like the bubonic plague."

Rodeo and FireTip are tied up across from her in another corner of the shed. On the way out to the Hastings Ranch months ago, Will had stashed in this shed some provisions to last them one week. The provisions include a lantern, coffee, candles, corn, a bag of beans, and feed for two horses. He wasn't sure Tom would actually give him FireTip, but because everyone on the Hastings Ranch is so leery of him and tired of separating him from other animals, he at least expected to be able to bring him home for a temporary stay, to give them some relief.

He had estimated, riding at a moderate pace, and without any mishaps, it would take nine or ten days to get from the Indian Territory to Tennessee. And mishaps could be anything from die-hard ex-Confederates taking a potshot at them, to other Whites or Negroes accosting them, thinking they have more than they had. It is unusual for just plain folks to be out on the open plains. Most folks travel in groups like wagon trains. But just in case they don't, he plans to keep an eye out for strangers and stop as needed to hide or rest. He even has enough money for them to get rooms at a boarding house for a comfortable stay whenever they have to stop in towns. And between the towns, they would have to lodge in vacant, abandoned sheds or barns he has scouted out. His fear is that word would have been sent out from Fort Townsend that an Indian girl is missing, so he prefers avoiding towns where such news would be circulating. He has also brought his small drover's tent that is shared with Oscar on cattle drives. Back at the Hastings Ranch, Oscar notices the tent is missing from his storage closet, but he knows Will feels free to use it after the drives for when he is traipsing back and forth across the country, so he doesn't give the missing tent another thought.

Depending on the tied ropes to restrict her movement, Will continues making the shed ready for their stay that night. He darts in and out of the shed, dragging out bundles of dried hay and sweeping out leaves and other debris. He takes dried brush, fashions it into a makeshift broom, and sweeps the weeds and small pieces of splintered wood away from the area in the loft where they will sleep. He also clears the area around the bottom of the ladder on the ground leading up to the loft. Much debris is swept out of the opening for the double doors. He guesses this worn building is probably a storage area for harvested corn or hay. There is no main house in sight, so it could be at the far end of one large farm. Whoever built this shed hasn't put a lot of thought into it. They also don't bother keeping it up. So that gives Will confidence that no one will be coming around to check on its contents, or whether it's occupied.

Will has a blanket tightly rolled and tied to his saddle, and additional ones he stashed in the shed. Using those blankets plus her deerskin cape should suffice in keeping her warm and creating soft bedding. After he finishes sweeping out as much debris and dried hay as possible, Will leans the large doors against the structure, covering most of the opening to keep the warmth and invited entities in, and the coldness and uninvited wildlife out.

As he finishes positioning the doors, she jerks forward, stands up, squinting her eyes, and holding her knees and thighs together, letting him know she has to pee. Expecting this moment, he quickly unfastens the one rope around her ankles and wrists, but keeps the rope around her waist and another rope around her neck linked to one ankle. This last tie allows her to stand to almost her full height, but she must arch over to one side as she staggers to walk. With the rope around her waist, he leads her outside to another area surrounded by garlic. Pointing for her to do her business there in the center of the garlic, he holds the rope, but turns his back to her and walks ten feet away, giving her some semblance of privacy. He hears the weight of the skirt, which falls below her knees, rise against her skin. Liquid sprays down to the ground, seemingly like an eternity. He anguishes over treating her like this, but now it is a matter of kidnapping, and no law would be understanding of him: no Negro law, no White law, and in no way any Indian law. In fact, Indian law probably calls for his immediate death on the spot. When he walked her out of the shed, he did not relish seeing her this way. She, who is lovely, spirited, but detests him, is now subdued. He will still keep his guard up because he sees taking her has not won her over, and she could very well be lying in wait to strike back. His mind rambles in distress about what he has done, empathizing that the rope bound about her neck is a fair premonition of a noose tightening around his. In the short time that he had reasoned how sensible it was to take her against her will just so she could of all things "get to know him," he now perceives his actions to be those of a madman. The women elders in her village called it "a man in season." Is this a condition his mere masculinity created, since he feels powerless against it?

She stumbles away from the "elimination area," and he takes her back to the shed.

"I know you can't be enjoying what I have done to you. Let me explain. I thought this would be a way to . . . well . . . For heaven's sake, I can't even explain it. Ahhh . . . to get some time to get to know one another, if you can believe me."

She returns to stand near the barrel; her eyes stare at the wall to the left of him, giving him no sense of connectivity with her at all, almost as though she is alone in the shed.

"OK, let me get this all out now since I've started. He bites his lip and looks up before releasing the next thought from deep inside. "You, are the first girl that when I first saw you—it was like a fire was lit inside of me. I've been fighting a desire to touch and ...I just wanted us to be able to spend some time together away from the village, away from the cattle drive—just you and me. Otherwise, you would never have considered me as a possible suitor."

Her eyes now glare in that piercing way, not at him but still at the wall, in defiance, completely ignoring him and despising the predicament he has put her in.

"Well, you don't have to say anything. I understand perfectly how you feel. Please know I will not harm you, and actually, I would glaaaadly take you back if I didn't think I would be killed! So, we'll just have to make the most of . . . my foolish mistake until things cool off and I feel safe enough to take you back and right this situation." Looking at her, he lets out a sigh of relief that he has explained himself. Next he says, "I've cleared an area for us to sleep in the loft. You can go up."

As if on cue, she abruptly turns and marches to the ladder to climb up to the loft, almost running him over and rejecting his extended hand offering assistance. She climbs up to the loft, situates the deerskin cape and blankets around her, and lies on the soft pallet he has made. He comes up and reties her ankles and wrists. Feeling the heat of her anger, he changes his plans and beds down on the ground below at the foot of the ladder.

The next morning, she awakes to a piece of bread, a warm cup of beans, a cup of water next to her, and her wrists untied. Will had gotten up before daybreak and prepared their breakfasts. It is still dark while he saddles FireTip and Rodeo, gathers up any usable garlic that was sprinkled around, and mentally maps out this day's ride. She raises her head and looks down at him on the ground level with the horses. They lock eyes, and she abruptly turns her head to look down at her ankles. Getting the message, he runs up the ladder and unfastens her ankles. Before motioning for her to go down the ladder, he rolls up the blankets and grabs the food that she has left untouched. He gives her untouched food to FireTip and Rodeo, and repacks the eating utensils. Her wrists are rebound before he lifts her onto FireTip, who is now adorned with a blanket saddle that was also stashed there weeks ago on his trip out. She takes hold of FireTip's reins, but remains stationary until she gets a tug via the rope around her waist tethered to Will. Will mounts Rodeo, takes one last look around the shed that sheltered them their first night under one roof, and they are off. Holding tight to the rope around her waist, he leads the way out of the shed and down a road of uncertainty.

Several times a day, they see a rider in the distance, and dart behind trees or circle away keeping a distance between them and the rider. Occasionally, a rider far off would stop dead in their tracks to try to understand what they are seeing. The earlier they get out on the road, the less likely they are to see anyone. Since settlers routinely quit work at sundown, and most riders avoid night riding unless it is an emergency, close to dusk becomes a good time for them to travel as well. When they stop, she uses the time to examine the vegetation, and dig up certain plants that she cleans, chews and swallows for nourishment. If they pass fruit trees or berries, he stops and lets her eat her fill. As a general observation, he finds her diet to be quite varied compared to his road diet. She isn't getting meat, because he can't leave her to hunt. So, while he prepares beans and scavenges corn, she continuously ingests fruits, greens, and berries. He admires how her people practice preventative medicine by using treatments found in God's garden, the natural landscape. At the trading post, goods are offered that are produced by her village, such as a plant for improving eyesight, cleaning teeth, moving bowels, and fighting infections. Another observation he makes is how she sometimes sits and chants words quietly to herself in a spiritual nature, similar to reciting a prayer.

When they reach thirty miles outside Pleasantville, the rains come. Will sees a rider head in the direction of an abandoned hut he had scouted out earlier for their third stop, so he has to change his plans for where they will stop for the night. He finds a seven-foot space between two boulders on high ground far off the trail, and strings the tent covering between the two boulders, securing the covering on top with heavy rocks. This will at least get them out of the rain. He wears himself out creating the shelter, carrying her from the horse to the shelter so she won't get her feet wet, and making a small campfire under the shelter. The best he can do for Rodeo and FireTip is to station them under a tree with a thick canopy of branches. From all the work setting up camp, he gets soaked and can't dry off. His body heat is depleted; he's sneezing, feeling run down, feverish and miserable.

Once they settle under the tent covering, the rains slow, but annoyingly continue with a light sprinkle. Shivering beneath a blanket, he turns to her. "I bet you know just the herb to clear this cold out of my system." She doesn't appear to be forthcoming with suggestions. "Well, I'll have to eat something and build up my strength to keep going. We're not that far from a friendly town, Pleasantville. We can get fresh provisions there, get a hot bath, and sleep in a real bed," he says.

Light rains continue sporadically. She decides to make him corn soup and gives him water, after seeing him choked up with mucus, sneezing and blowing his nose. The rain finally stops completely. She motions to go out. He feebly rises and follows her to an area not far from the "elimination area" where she snaps a plant from out of the ground, roots and all. Then she snaps another before they return to the shelter. Determined not to speak to him, she works her mouth motioning for him to chew. She heats water in a cup, tosses in the plants, transfers it to another cooler cup for him to drink from. He drinks the broth and chews a little of the stock. As he eats what she has prepared for him, her eyes soften with compassion. He thinks, *The healer in her cannot be held back by ropes.* Along the trail, he had allowed her to harvest food from fruit trees and vegetable fields they passed. She had intended to not eat anything he offered her, but to ravage the figs and wild berries found growing along the road. Now, their roles are reversed. It is time for him to eat what she offers him. She intently watches him sip and swallow the herbal broth. Her eyes are like a paintbrush, making a slow stroke down his body from his mouth, neck, chest, to his stomach. Using her hand, she checks his forehead for fever.

"Thank you for doctoring on me. You are returning my bad and awful actions toward you with kindness. Thank you. I can feel some relief even now. You are really a good healer," Will says gratefully. "Wha . . . what did . . ." He slurs his words and keels over into a deep sleep.

Once he is down, she scurries out of the shelter, pulling and tugging at the ropes that binds her neck and wrists. She pulls the rope off her wrists with her teeth, and then removes the one around her neck, scratching her skin and leaving superficial scraping marks on her neck. Leaving behind only the ropes on the ground as evidence of her once presence, she takes off. Mounting FireTip bareback, she heels him to giddyup, making tracks.

After riding about an hour at full gallop, she happens upon a camp of Negro people, two men and a woman, sitting under a raggedy canopy next to a wagon with a small fire going. It is night now, and she needs a place to camp. Although this gang looks dirty, underfed, and clammy, not at all clean and healthy like Will, she doesn't fear them. If she had seen them before her time with Will, she probably would have kept going. However, she fears getting found by White men, more than getting found by Negroes. She slowly approaches them and asks if they know of a nearby Indian village. One man is stout, the other man quite skinny, and the woman is also skinny with dirty and matted hair under a hat. The men wear black linen suits over long johns. The lady's dark brown dress is so dirty, it may have started out orange in color. All three have dusty hats like they have been out traveling and camping in the elements for months.

"No, we don't know where one is, but we can find out tomorrow when we get into Pleasantville," answers the skinny man anxiously looking to the left and right of her.

"Oh, you're going to Pleasantville?" she says as she dismounts FireTip. "I hear it is a friendly town."

"It 'tis, it 'tis. Very friendly. Sit a spell and partake of our fire and shelter. We glad it stopped rainin'," says the skinny man as he reaches inside his coat and pulls out a gun. "I think you are going to make us three wealthy folks."

Her eyes bulge out of their sockets, and she extends her hands in front of her, palms out. "What's the matter?" she asks.

The skinny woman steps forward and asks, "What you up to, Jake? This little Indian lady means us no harm. Why you don' gone and pull a gun on 'er?"

One hand maintaining the gun on his captive, Jake gets animated using the other hand and gestures to the other man. "Earl, you 'member how we been trying to think of some way to raise enough money to go to the new territory? Well, this little lady right ch-ere is goin' to help us do that very thing." Licking his lips, he continues, "She's mighty pretty, and will fetch a nice price in Pleasantville."

The woman waving her hands at Jack lashes out, "Are you stupid? They abolished slavery, fool! Who do you expect to sell her to now?"

"There are work slaves, and then there are other kindsa slaves, and there will always be a need for the other kindsa slaves. She's young! Well, hell if we find an old geezer he may give us the whole estate for her." Jake turns to her, "Or young lady, the geezer may give his estate to you. Have you thoughta that?" He walks around her sizing her up. "I really don't care. I jus' want to see what the little lady will bring us in greenbacks," Jake says, still aiming his gun at her.

Jake tells Earl, "Get a rope and tie her in the wagon," while moving past her to get a better look at FireTip. "We need to tie up this horse as well. He looks like he'll fetch a good price, too." Jake gets too close to him, and FireTip rears up and charges at him, snapping his teeth, attempting to kick him and bite him. Jake runs back scrambling to get away from him, now aiming his gun at FireTip and shouts, "This horse is loco! I may have to shoot him."

This prompts her to yell, "No, let me tie him to the wagon. He'll calm down if I do it." They let her.

Still disturbed from being chased by FireTip, Jake says, "Yes, this horse is gonna be sold or ate, since we have absolutely no need for him at-tall."

Earl puts her inside the rear of the wagon and ties her up. Tied to the back of the wagon FireTip is calm as long as he can see her. That night, the two men sleep outside on the ground around the fire, and the woman sits up in the wagon staring at her. She, their new captive, thinks, *Another night, another rope.*

Will awakes with a headache, blurred vision, and looks around frantically. He notices that FireTip is gone, but Rodeo stands safe and content. He is surprised Rodeo didn't stir him first, and wonders if she put something in his drink too. Still groggy, he packs and loads up as fast as he can. He knows his riding is going to be awkward since he has to carry her blanket saddle and all their supplies until he finds

FireTip. He mounts Rodeo and looks for tracks. Their tracks are easy to spot because the rain had stopped falling when she rode out. After determining the general direction of FireTip's tracks, he rides that way. He gallops along the road looking down at the conspicuous tracks that indicate FireTip is at full gallop. Since she is frightened of snakes and most predators, he assumes that she will stay on the road. After an hour, the tracks lead him to an abandoned camp twenty feet off the road where the fire cinders are still warm. He notices foot prints of three others and wagon tracks deep in the mud with FireTip's tracks less deep than before following close behind. Pleasantville is only twenty miles away in the direction the wagon travels. Thinking they are taking her and FireTip there, he looks carefully along the road for more tracks, but heads straight for Pleasantville. He begins to think about what could happen to her. What if a stranger sees her and avails himself upon her? He worries that, if something bad happens to her at all, it is because he took her from her protective village to a land gone mad with racial hatred and desperation, a country recuperating from a war based on race. Or perhaps she will find a family on the road, like the Harpers, working their way through the countryside, and will extend warm hospitality to a lost young girl. His mind races from one extreme to the next.

Entering Pleasantville, he takes the detour to the Negro side of town as he has done so many times. The tracks appear to lead to tent city. That could be good or bad news, depending upon who picked her up. He's still wobbly and needs to think through how he's going to search through that big encampment. So, he heads first for Mrs. Pritchett's. She is delighted to see him again and asks about his dear mother. After she checks him in, he says he needs to get over to tent city right away. Then he weakly carries his gear upstairs and dumps it in the room. When he returns downstairs to exit the boarding house, Mrs. Pritchett examines his demeanor and decides to intervene. She blocks his path, squinting her eyes, looking into his. "I can see the fatigue and remnants of a serious illness in your face. You look like you need to eat, get some water, and rest."

"No, no, I really need to keep moving," Will says. Too spent and too much of a gentleman to push her out of his way, he considers his options for getting out of the building.

Holding her hand up, Mrs. Pritchett says, "I tell you what. At least eat something, and then you can go over there."

He acquiesces and turns toward the café, holding his arm over his growling stomach. She prepares a plate of baked chicken, yams, cabbage, and stewed carrots, a dish he usually orders. While he is eating, she chatters about some ex-Confederates that came and shot up tent city, running many of the good folks out, and leaving some destitute, ornery folks who held their ground, but now require a stiff hand to ensure they live cooperatively.

"They say many fights have broken out over there among plantation workers and migrating Negroes seeking a new life, but, thank God, they've calmed down tent city. We've got some folks patrolling through there now. Some migrating in won't work, say they don't want to work for anyone else, yet they want to eat. They won't abide by anybody's rules, and they're angry. So, the menfolk of this town had to go in there, clean it out, and will continue to do that. They'll send those troublemakers on their way, and allow the sensible, decent ones to stay on," Mrs. Pritchett speaks while jerking her eyes around the dining room, looking for empty coffee cups or neglected patrons.

Will chomps on his dinner like it is going to run away.

She leaves performing one of her rounds of the dining room, but returns with a water pitcher, pouring him a cup of water. Her acute curiosity doesn't miss Will's damp hat laid on the café table and unkept, dusty clothes. She's never seen him dirty and untidy before. "You look like you have been on the road a while. See anything interesting in your travels? I must rely on travelers like yourself to keep me posted on information outside of Pleasantville."

"Well," he swallows a mouthful of food so he can talk, "I saw an Indian girl galloping by fast. I'm kinda wondering if anyone else around here reported seeing her?" He returns to stuffing his mouth and chomping.

"Maybe that's the Indian girl some of those troublemakers have in the back of a wagon in tent city. They say she stole some food from them, and—"

Will jumps up. His chair falls over slamming the floor. His foot grazes the table leg almost knocking the table over, leaving his food swirling in his plate as he tears out the front of the café.

Mrs. Pritchett gasps, "What's the matter?"

Bumping into a man entering the café, Will leaps off the café's porch, but stops and turns back to retrieve his gun from his saddle-bags up in his room. Mrs. Pritchett and other patrons watch his alarm-ing behavior through the window. Her attention span is short-lived when the man Will bumped at the door asks for a menu.

With a gun in hand, he returns to his mad dash of a run, rushing over to tent city, and begins scouting for the certain troublemakers Mrs. Pritchett had so amply described. While searching for a wagon, he makes inquiries about an Indian girl. When he is told a group in the back may have one for sale, hair on his body bristles. He finds the parties in the very back of tent city with the wagon cover closed tight at the ends and FireTip prominently standing content, tied near the rear of the wagon, which means she has to be close by. Otherwise, merely being tied up or corralled is sufficient criterion for him to bite anyone near or go on a wild rampage tearing up the place. With his gun resting in his holster on the side of his hip, loaded and ready, he walks indeterminately, casing the area near the wagon, behaving as if he merely wandered back that far by accident.

Jake is the first to spot Will and elbows Earl. Jake comes from the front of the wagon. "Howdy, young gent. You lookin' for somebody?" Jake asks.

"No, just tryin' to find a friendly game of poker. I got money to spend and nowhere to spend it. Do you gents play?" Will's adrenaline rises as his eyes bounce back and forth between Jake and Earl.

"Well, even if we dids, the folk runnin' this place would frown on it. They don't like gamble-ling. We want to stay for a while, so we want to abide by they's rules. But I tell you what we can do for you. How much you got?"

"Nearly one hundred dollars." Will folds his arms cocking his head to one side. "It's my whole year's wages from cattle driving."

"One hundred dollars! I ain't never seen that much in one spot, mister," Earl shouts. "Lemme see it! Lemme see it!"

Leaning in speaking low, Will replies, "No, it's best not to flash that kind of money, lest you gonna buy something really special, I believe."

Moving over to the wagon, Jake pulls back the canvas and beckons Will to walk over. "Well, what about this?" pointing at his estranged traveling companion. "Is this worth some of that one hundred dollars? She's wrapped in a nice deer-skin cape, and ready to go. She does cookin', cleanin', rub your tired feet down, and anything else you got need rubbin'," Jake says making a half-grin and snickering.

"What kinda shape is she in?" Will steps where he can get a clear view of her.

"Good shape," Jake says.

"I mean, you haven't beat her, or harmed her, have you?" Will asks tightening his lips.

"Naw, no, nothing like that. Though I wanted to put a bullet in that horse of hers. She's in good condition." Jake beckons Will to come closer to the wagon. "You can check for yourself. Get 'er out here, Earl. Let the man see our prized merchandise up close." Jake moves away still making the half-grin, allowing Will to get a clear view of her. Jake continues, "Now you have to understand, she's not what you call a 'willing worker,' so you may have to take some authore-ta-tive measures to help her understand who's the boss, and how you want things done."

Earl unties the rope around her ankles, and allows her to step down from the wagon. She looks up and sees Will, with less defiant eyes now. Hands tied, she drops her head and stands limp. Will realizes that she has probably not eaten since she left him because she wasn't able to eat from the fields like she did while she traveled with him. Will walks over to her, grabs a chunk of her hair, and pulls her head back as though he's examining her. He whispers, "When I tell you, get behind me."

"She looks familiar." Pulling his gun, Will turns around and shouts, "In fact, this is the Indian girl I married four days ago in Indian Territory. She ran off with my horse." He looks at her and says, "Untie FireTip."

Jake, Earl, and the woman go for their guns, but are stopped when Will threatens to shoot. Will looks at the one held captive and orders, "Tell them, that you are my wife." She limply unties FireTip, rubs his neck, and then leans against him. Holding them at bay, Will yells again, "Tell them!"

She raises her head and says faintly, "Yes, I am his wife."

"You see that! Now she and I and the horse are going to walk out of here, and if you don't bother us anymore, I won't get you put out of tent city for wife and horse thieving. But if any of you show your faces around me again, I'll report you to the people patrolling around here and get you thrown out for good, or worse!" Will says.

"We didn't know who the horse belonged to. You can't accuse us of horse thievin'," shouts Jake, frowning. It seems they are more afraid of being labeled horse thieves than being accused of kidnapping and attempting to sell her.

She and Will back up slowly into the area behind the tents. Will whistles for FireTip to follow. As FireTip comes around from behind the wagon, he rushes to the front of the wagon to charge at and scare Jake and Earl one last time. Will keeps the gun aimed at them so they won't shoot FireTip either. When they are out of view, Will cuts her bonds and hops on FireTip before lifting her to sit in front of him. They quickly ride over to the stable where Rodeo is boarded. No one follows them; at least they don't see anyone.

Will helps her to the back of Mrs. Pritchett's boarding house, and up the stairs to his room on the second floor. Once inside he tells her to make herself at home while he goes and gets something for her to eat, he leaves locking the door behind him. Mrs. Pritchett is surprised to see him back. However, before she can get a word out, he tells her that he needs another plate of baked chicken, yams, cabbage, stewed carrots, and a biscuit, and a bath ready in about an hour. She says, "Oh!" And looks puzzled, but after her eyes follow him upstairs, she orders preparation of the plate.

Back in his room, she is so exhausted and spent from that terrifying experience she passes out on the soft bed. It is only after he brings food into the room that she stirs. The aroma of the seasoned chicken revives her and summons a ravenous appetite. She scarfs down the food, smacking and licking her fingers. When she finishes, she takes a deep breath and says, "Thank you for coming after me."

Before she can remember that he is the cause of her getting into that situation, he says softly, "I have hot water waiting downstairs in a big tub for you to take a bath. Come now."

They both leave the room and march down to the first floor where Mrs. Pritchett has sanitized a tub and poured in hot water. On seeing the two of them coming down the stairs, Mrs. Pritchett forms a big grin and waits in the doorway of the bathroom. Her eyes skip past Will and start bulging with curiosity at his new companion.

"Hellooooo. Will, I thought you were traveling alone. Who is your friend?"

Will is disappointed Mrs. Pritchett is still in there working, and before he can generate an answer for her, his companion says, "My name is Niabi."

He is stunned to hear her name for the first time and equally stunned that she has freely resumed talking.

"Nice to meet you . . . Nee-yah-bee?" Mrs. Pritchett brandishes an even bigger smile, waiting to hear more.

Niabi replies, "Yes, you said it correctly."

"Well, Will is a fine gentleman, so any friend of his is a friend of mine." She clears the doorway to the bathroom and asks, "Whose bath is this?"

"It's hers, ah... my friend's bath." Will extends his hand ushering Niabi to enter the bathroom.

After Niabi goes in, Mrs. Pritchett steps between them and says, "You did say *friend*. So, Will why don't you go back to your room, and I will get this little lady started, and," Mrs. Pritchett sees how dirty the clothing is Niabi is wearing, "I will get her something clean to change in to. My niece left something here I think can fit her."

With that, Will gets out of their way, but only to the foot of the stairs near the outside of the bathroom. He takes no chances that either those troublemakers or some other boarder might decide to take his captive. After a few minutes, Mrs. Pritchett exits the bathroom and gently closes the door behind her, carrying Niabi's old clothes and the deer-skin cape. When she sees Will, her big grin returns. "Well, Mr. Will, is this the Indian girl you saw galloping by? You are some kind of tracker. Are you going to tell me what's going on, how you met her, or are you going to leave me to wonder in agony?"

"There's nothing to tell. I'll settle up with you for the room, meals, and bath when I leave in the morning." Will avoids eye contact with her and remains seated on the stairs expressionless.

Hearing only that, Mrs. Pritchett looks at him annoyed, and says, "She can keep the dress I'll give her. I'll wash up these things." She holds up the deer-skin cape in the air examining it and adds, "This one will have to be spot-cleaned." She gives Will another annoyed look at his refusal to let her in on the whats and whys, and then she makes a sharp turn throwing her head in the air, heading back toward the café. Will realizes that he has insulted an ally by withholding the only treat she loves—information. And if it wasn't for her snooping for information, he would not have learned where Niabi was being held. But he can't bear to tell her the truth, and she doesn't deserve to hear lies, so saying nothing is his best alternative.

Niabi finally appears in the bathroom doorway, wearing the dress given to her by Mrs. Pritchett, and smelling of scented soap, clean skin, and hair. Her old outfit was a cotton blouse with long sleeves, and a wrap-around skirt that extends to below the knee, and leggings covering the leg from the bottom of the knee to ankles. The dress given to her from Mrs. Pritchett is light blue linen, high neckline, three-quarter length sleeves, narrow ankle-length skirt accented with matching light blue stockings. Her hair is still damp so she wraps a cloth around it and follows him back to the room. She walks in, and sits on the bed, staring at a brush given to her by Mrs. Pritchett. She avoids eye contact with him.

"I want you to lock the door till I return from taking my bath. I have a key so if you're sleeping, I can get back in," Will says.

She makes no reply.

Downstairs, he finds an empty bathroom and fills the tub with warm water. As he soaks in the tub, his feelings are caught in a whirling pool. By her words, actions, and demeanor, he feels she obviously wants to be away from him, but will stay put after her harrowing ordeal.

After his bath, he leaves the bathroom and does a final evening check on Rodeo and FireTip. FireTip must be glad to be back with his pack, because he is acting well-behaved. The peace found in the sta-ble is a reprieve to the rejections and denial of any level of forgiveness prevailing back at his rented room. He will just have to live with it for a while, at least until he can return her to her people.

When he returns to the room, she is finishing braiding her hair. Fatigue overcomes him, and he doesn't see a reason to sit there trying to stay awake, keeping watch over her as he did when he first took her. The day has been long and full for him too. He unrolls his bed-roll and stretches out on the floor next to her bed, tipping his hat over his eyes, as he does in camp on the cattle drives, but also at least until she extinguishes the lamp in the room. While braiding her hair, she had already scanned the room examining the furniture, a table with a water pitcher, a large bowl and wash cloths, and the modest cotton curtains covering the window. Now she sneaks periodic glances at her captor lying on the floor. She can smell the pine soap scent on his skin and he's used a little of his hair tonic. She thinks, *He must have shaved because the little peach fur that was on his face is gone. And he must have oiled his lips too,... they look soft.*

Done with her hair, she douses the lamp, pulls the blanket over her, stretches out on the bed, and falls asleep. He doesn't know who fell asleep first, but he remembers drifting off, wondering if he can ever put a rope on her again, and wondering what she will say tomor-row, now that she is talking.

CHAPTER 6

BONDING

———

WILL hates lying. He was raised to honor his mother and father, and the way he does that is to represent them in the world outside his home. Their teachings included being honest, standing by his word, being respectful, and acting with dignity. This behavior does not reflect what he did to Niabi. He hates tricking her to accomplish the kidnapping, and he hates lying to her about the first girl he has passionately kissed. The fact is, she isn't the first. The first time is like most first times, branded on our brains. We never forget them. He recalls the first time.

I was fifteen years old, and it was a day before a big event taking place at the Applegate Ranch. Being an age where I could be useful to my family, I was helping my father dress and groom some horses for the event. The Applegate Ranch has been the most prosperous horse ranch in the region, and sometimes had grand events that drew prominent townspeople, politicians, and many dignitaries from neighboring towns. The Applegates were always having something, like auctions, races, and parties to boost their horse sales. The exact event skips my mind, but what doesn't skip my mind is a visiting guest for that event, Miss Catherine Applegate. She is Mr. Orin Applegate's niece, his brother's daughter, and Grant and Jason's cousin. She had come to attend the big event, for which we servants were helping them prepare. Catherine had blazing red hair, brilliant green eyes that sat inside peachy, freckled skin. She was 5'7" of frisky and defiant energy. One day Catherine, Jason, and Catherine's companion named Ellie, who was a meeker and more mild-mannered girl, were all playing a stick and hoop game in the backyard next to the main house. During play, they were yell-

ing and cavorting throwing the hoops until one got away and rolled down the lane. This caused their play area to expand beyond near the main house. They continued throwing the hoop longer distances and before you knew it, they were down near the stable where Father and I were working. When Catherine saw me, she stopped in her tracks and motioned for Jason to come to her. "Who is that handsome boy there?" she asked Jason.

"That's Will. He and his family work for us on the farm. They are our paid servants," Jason said.

"Servants, hmmmmmm, does that mean we can get him to do anything for us?"

"You're a hoot, Catherine. Have you forgotten we abolished slavery? You can't get him to do anything, any more than you can get me to do anything," Jason said.

"We'll just see about that," Catherine said. The three returned to playing and tore out running back toward the main house.

Later that evening, I was in the barn saddling Rodeo to take an evening ride. I don't like for Rodeo to stay confined for too long, and he even hates being cooped up too long. I like to let him romp and stretch his legs to keep his limbs flexible and his stamina up. When I exited the barn, I saw another lantern approaching from the direction of the main house. It was Miss Catherine. She asked me to saddle a horse for her to take a ride, too. "The moonlight is just screaming for me to ride around under it," she said. I had no idea what she was talking about. I asked her if she knew how to ride, and she said, "I'm an Applegate, boy! If you know what's good for you, you'll saddle that horse now, and be quick about it."

I bit my lip to stifle responding to her for fear it would cause more remarks I wouldn't appreciate. In case she was lying about her riding ability, I saddled the mildest horse in the barn. If she were to get injured, I would be the one blamed. After she mounted the horse I saddled for her, she turned and said, "Well, come on. I'm not going to ride around in the dark by myself." Then she took off. I quickly mounted Rodeo, and rushed out of the barn, racing down the lane that leads to the far end of the property to catch up with her. We galloped to the far *south pasture. The moon was full. Maybe that was why she was so edgy. She stopped her horse in the back of the field behind the pasture fence, dismounted, and walked over to the white fence bordering the pasture. Leaning back against the fence, looking up staring into the sky at the moon, she spread her arms wide resting them on the top of the fence. It was an eerie scene, her leaning against the fence like that, head back, facing up and lit up by moonlight.*

She then turned her gaze at me and said, "Come here, Will." I had no idea what she was up to. But I was at her mercy since I couldn't leave her out there alone.

I dismounted Rodeo and said, "What do you want?"

"Come and see, or are you scared of girls?"

I admit I became intrigued as to what kind of game we were going to play, so I walked over to her.

She stepped forward, put both of her hands on my face, and planted on me a full-on kiss. After my initial shock, I attempted to remove her hands from my face, but abruptly stopped when she sensuously slid her tongue all the way into my mouth. I became beguiled. Every muscle in my body stiffened up. Holding me at bay with just her mouth, she used her hands to place mine on her hips and pushed her body into me, kissing even harder. I felt like a stick of dynamite went off in my brain. I liked every bit of what Miss Catherine was doing. Every limb gradually came alive, and I began embracing her tightly against my body. I learned quickly this game Miss Catherine wanted to play. Then she eased up on the kissing, and her lips swept across my face to my left ear where she began to nibble, and asked me so softly that I could barely hear her, "Do you want us to take off all our clothes and make love?"

I wanted to, really bad, really, really, really bad, but I collected myself, took two good breaths, released her from my embrace, stepped away from her, and said, "Miss Catherine, I, uh . . . I, uh . . . I have too . . . too much respect for Mr. and Mrs. Applegate and my own parents to bring dishonor on them. You and I doing . . . that would not be right."

She walked toward me, took my hands, opened my arms, and attempted to re-insert herself back against my body, a body that was now quivering with excitement and anticipation. Next, she said, "Silly boy, no one needs to know. It will be our little secret."

I broke away from her again and said, "Miss Catherine, you need to go back to the main house, now!" I hopped on Rodeo and pleaded to her to come back to the main house. She stuck out her lip, hopped on her horse, and tore out going to the main house passing the barn. I got a little nervous when she passed the barn because I needed to put the horses up for the night, and I didn't particularly want to draw questions about why we were together at night. But I continued riding behind her to make sure she safely got back to the main house's back porch. More lanterns were moving about. Jason and Ellie were looking for her. Jason saw her ride up and saw me following behind her. "Where did you two go?" he asked with a devilish smile.

"Oh, I had your boy escort me on an evening ride after dinner. It was quite pleasant." Then she looked at me as she went up the porch steps, and said, "You can take the horse back to the barn. I have no further need of it." Jason continued smiling shaking his head and went into the house. She opened the door and, before entering, turned all the way around to face me and said, "Thank you for tonight, Will. But don't you dare think I'm through with you."

I told my father everything about that night, everything! He rolled on the floor laughing. "Ha ha. That Miss Catherine is a wildcat, but she got a hold to a housecat in a lion's body."

"It's not funny, Dad!"

"You're right, son. She's a misguided young woman, who's probably passing into her woman stage, and is a little hot-blooded. Some women drink ice tea and fan themselves, and others, like Miss Catherine, just act out on their emotions. You have a grown man's body, son, and will attract girls, women, and even feel things yourself. You just have to remember that the difference between a man and a gentleman is that a gentleman weighs the consequences for his actions, consequences for himself and the woman before he acts. And if he does act, he takes responsibility for those consequences. I am proud of how you handled yourself, because if she had gotten with, say old Clarence, who helps out in the garden, she woulda learned firsthand the whole story of Adam and Eve, Sam-

son and Delilah, and Sodom and Gomorrah all in one night." Then we both had
a good laugh.

—————•—————

The next morning in Pleasantville, Will wakes up late. Late for him because he usually rises before sunup. The curtains are still closed, yet the sun, barely tipping the horizon, drives rays of light into their room signaling a new day is upon them. His eyes make a tour around the room and settle on a figure that's sitting still, legs folded with its back erect on the bed. He rubs the sleep out of his eyes so he can see clearer. This figure indeed is his traveling companion. Her body resembles a stone statue: no facial expression, eyes closed, only her lips are slightly moving as if quietly chanting a private prayer. Gazing at her, Will thinks, *This young, vibrant woman I took from her home has matured before my very eyes into a person of conviction and prayer. Taking her, made me so less than the gentleman my mother and father raised me to be. I am what Mrs. Applegate called her relative who took two horses and never paid her for them: a scoundrel. What was I thinking of, but myself?*

Will moves back the blanket covering him where he lay on his floor bed pallet, and rises to his feet. Reluctant to interrupt her, he speaks softly to Niabi. "Are you wanting something to eat?" There is no response. He waits, and then he says, "The cafe here has a mighty good breakfast. And I'd like to thank Mrs. Pritchett for her help before we leave. She is a good friend to have, and one of the finest ladies you could meet in these parts." Still, no response from her. Not even a glance his way. He continues preparing himself to leave the room, tucking his shirt in his pants, and rolling up his bedding and blanket. She had slept in the dress Mrs. Pritchett gave her while her blouse, wrap-around skirt, and deer-skin cape are being cleaned. Preparation for her to leave the room is just standing and walking out. All she carried from her village are the clothes on her back. Now she also has a brush from Mrs. Pritchett.

Using a little louder tone, Will says, "Well, I'm hungry, and I'm
not about to let you out of my sight again. So, let's go downstairs and
get some food." Still, no sign of life stirs from her. She remains in the
seated position on the bed with her eyes closed. He steps to the door
and cracks it open. Footsteps in the hallway grow louder, several footsteps as though people are checking into rooms while others are rushing on their way downstairs. The foot traffic of so many others nearby
startles her. She unfolds her legs, stands up, folds her blanket, and
joins him standing by the door, as though to finally accept his repeated
invitations to breakfast as the best of two odious alternatives. Still, she
gives him no eye contact and utters no words.

They exit their room, proceed down the hallway, and downstairs
to the cafe. Many are coming and going, talking, eating. In the middle, Mrs. Pritchett seats patrons, mostly male farmhands and laborers. Now and then, she makes a comment that ignites an uproar of
laughter. He wonders if there are notices out reporting a missing
Indian girl, and if he is exposing his situation unnecessarily by coming into a public dining hall. But Mrs. Pritchett's cooking has him
spoiled, and after dealing with his self-ridicule for kidnapping her,
and Niabi's persistent refusal to communicate with him, he reasons
he can use some kind words, a smile, and a delicious meal, all hall-
marks of Mrs. Pritchett's hospitality.

"Oh, good morning, good morning, young people. Come on in
and sit right here," Mrs. Pritchett says as she shows Will and Niabi to
a table in a corner that is ideal for privacy. It is almost intuitive of her
to consider seating them there as though she senses Will's need to be
as inconspicuous as possible. Will follows Mrs. Pritchett to the table
with Niabi trailing close behind him. Once they get to the table, he
remains standing there waiting for Niabi to reach her chair. Once she
reaches the table, he pulls her chair out from the table and motions
for Niabi to sit down. She sits down, and he scoots her chair under
the table. His mother had told him about doing such things if he ever
attended a really nice dinner with a young lady and they were all

dressed up. Harriet probably had seen such practices at a formal Applegate affair. Niabi reacts to his gallant action by glancing back toward him with a look of instant, momentary surprise. After they are seated, Will thinks, *I ought to show her exactly who the man is that kidnapped her. Yes, the kidnapping is foolish and reprehensible, but now it's a done deed, and I have a chance to reset the scales on my judgment. I will prove to her that, yes, a daring, adolescent kidnapped you, but a very gentle, kind, loving, mature and hardworking man is taking care of you now. And if I can't convince her that I would be a good suitor for her, then back to the village she'll go. I'll safely deliver her back to her home, once I'm capable of doing it without getting lynched.*

Will hands Niabi the handwritten menu.

B R E A K F A S T   M E N U

3 EGGS AND PORK SAUSAGE AND BREAD	15¢
FLAP JACKS AND SYRUP	10¢
GRITS OR RICE	5¢
COFFEE	5¢
MILK	5¢

Mrs. Pritchett can't stop herself from spying a look at their every gesture. She goes about serving and taking orders from other customers, but every free moment she gets, she glances over at Will and Niabi as if to catch some confirmation that there is something amiss, or some intrigue between the two of them. Mrs. Pritchett's facial expression gives her away. Her forehead is wrinkled and her mouth is held in a half gape with ears flaring. If there is a story there between Will and Niabi, she will surely sniff it out before they leave her premises.

Niabi looks around the café, which is lively with people and sounds. This is another new experience for her. Among customers talking, customers filing through dragging chairs out from under the table, and scraping the floor scooting up to the table, she also hears customers placing their orders for eggs, flapjacks, coffee, and milk. Will, quite adept at being in these surroundings, glances around the dining room for other reasons, hoping he doesn't see a lawman or other sort that would have received word about a missing person. When his eyes finally retreat to his own table, nodding at the menu, he asks Niabi, "See anything you like?"

On one of her rounds serving coffee to the patrons on Will and Niabi's side of the café, Mrs. Pritchett swings by. "Are you ready to order?" Niabi doesn't look up from the menu, and Will is afraid that that mere action alone will indicate she is unhappy. Such an indication will alert Mrs. Pritchett that their union is not based on mutual consent. Mrs. Pritchett fixes her eyes on Niabi for a response. Suddenly, he's overcome with a terrifying question: can Niabi read?

So, again to stalemate any further inquiries from Mrs. Pritchett, Will lunges forward with their breakfast orders. "We'll have two orders of flapjacks and two orders of grits."

"Anything to drink?" Mrs. Pritchett asks.

"The lady and I will just have coffee," Will says.

"No. Milk for me," Niabi pushes out.

Will corrects the order. "Ah, coffee for me, milk for the lady." He looks up and smiles at Mrs. Pritchett. Then Niabi looks up into Mrs. Pritchett's face. Not until now had it become evident to Will that he should not have brought her to a public place where there is a high possibility the word is circulating about a missing Indian girl and someone will see her pitiful face and put things together. And such news, if it is out there, will not escape Mrs. Pritchett.

"Do you want something else, young lady?" Mrs. Pritchett asks.

"Some water, yes some water, ma'am," Niabi says.

"Yes, I will get your orders to you right away," Mrs. Pritchett says as she collects the menu.

Will is glad she is talking. He holds the moment sacred by not uttering a single word after she speaks. He also wonders if she read milk on the menu, or maybe she heard someone else order it. He sits quietly for several minutes, until the food arrives, and he only breaks his silence to tell her to use the knife and fork to cut her flapjacks. "It's best to cut them into little pieces, like so." He actually doesn't know what to expect from her at this point. He wouldn't be surprised if she maintains her combatant disobedience by not taking any directions from him. But her childlike curiosity surpasses other inclinations, and she picks up the knife and fork and begins chopping the flapjacks into squares similar to how he did his. Then they both smother the flapjack squares, already covered in melting butter, with syrup, and dive in. She takes a bite, and quickly takes another and another. Will has to tell her to slow down. He surmises the sweetness of the bread, syrup, and enhanced by the melting butter has just taken her away to sugar heaven.

Several times, he has to interrupt his own eating to whisper, "Slow down." She has allowed herself to get so famished that the meal becomes a race to satisfy her hunger.

Again, Will speaks firmly in his loudest whisper. "You're going to make yourself sick. Slow down!" The bottom half of her face is covered with syrup, so he tells her to use her napkin to wipe her face, all the time fighting back a grin. He looks around to make sure she isn't drawing any extra attention. Even Mrs. Pritchett bumps into a wall while staring at how the gorgeous young woman is scarfing down her breakfast like a little pig. With a mouth full of flapjacks, she washes it down with milk, and then gulps down some water. She tops off the whole exhibition by belching loudly. Embarrassed, she grabs her chest. Male workers seated at the table next to them clap, and offer a couple of belches themselves in camaraderie. Will smiles and thinks, *I need to get my little darling home to Momma quick, for some lady-like training for that!*

Unable to keep away any longer, Mrs. Pritchett swaggers over as if part of the cat is out of the bag. "Well, young lady, you were mighty hungry. When was the last time you ate?"

Will speaks up instead. "Mrs. Pritchett, the breakfast was delicious as usual. Would you be so kind and tell us how much we owe you?"

Again, this is not the response Mrs. Pritchett desires. "I will get your bill and check on your belongings right away," she says and slings her body around in sequence: first her head, shoulders, and then hips.

Will pays their bills for livery stable, café and boarding house services, and gathers all their belongings, including Niabi's cotton blouse, the wrap-around skirt, leggings, and deer-skin cape, which Mrs. Pritchett cleaned. They head out to get their horses. In the stall with FireTip, Niabi decides to change back into her original clothes. She finds them more comfortable for mounting and dismounting a horse.

On saddled and refreshed horses, they exit Pleasantville and head northeast toward his home. Will knows it will be safe to travel in the daytime a few miles out from town, but once they hit the open range and nightfall comes, he will have to watch out for clansmen and thieves. He has heard that the James gang is still active in these parts. They aren't known to gun down travelers in their path, but then again, they do not want a witness to their whereabouts.

They ride from early morning until dusk only stopping to eliminate body waste, have a drink of water, and eat something to tide them over until the main meal at dinner. The main meal consists of meat, if he can shoot something. She is quite adept at defeathering fowls and skinning rabbits. Otherwise, the meal is combinations of coffee, beans, corn, any remaining bread, and fresh milk, if they chance upon a grazing cow. Riding along the trail, they may spot a fine dairy cow grazing in a nearby pasture. The desire for fresh milk overcomes her. She stops FireTip and stares at the cow. By now Will knows she loves milk. So, he asks her to stay with the horses. Being this far from her village, she is leery of running away from him now. By this time, she realizes that there are worse things in the world than a kidnapper who is otherwise a gentleman. Keeping his head low, watching for snakes or overseers, he creeps through the grass aiming for the dairy cow. He regards both snakes and overseers to carry about the same venom. Once near the cow, he approaches her gently and speaks the soft tones that will make her feel like there is nothing to fear. He blows on his fingers to warm them, and places a pan right below her udder. Gently, he squeezes her udders, and then gradually a little harder and harder, and the milk finally squirts out. One of her back legs lifts slightly as though to kick him, but he rubs the underside of her belly soothingly, and her back leg drops back down. The fresh warm milk continues to flow from her. Once the pan is three-quarters full, he takes it and retreats back to an awaiting Niabi. Niabi is given the first right to taste the stolen white drink. As she gulps it down, her eyes glisten. Unfortunately, he cannot get a reading on her, why her eyes are a glaze, because she is not speaking to him again. Then it becomes his turn for a drink of the milk. He surmises that her eyes glisten because the milk is fresh and sweet. If it had been served with some biscuits or cake, they would have been in paradise. The pan is passed back and forth between them. While they are drinking, Will keeps a vigilant watch down the road both ways, ready to move Rodeo and FireTip off the road at the first sign of someone approaching. Once the pan of milk is empty, they each belch as if performing a ritual. She belches first.

"That was a loud one," he says. "Here I go, bauuuugggg. Can you beat that?"

Without hesitating, she lets out, "Bauuuuurrrrgggg."

"Wow! I'll beat you the next time. Let's get going," he says.

Based on his home training, Will knows belching is an ill-mannered habit in public, but it is the only activity she allows them to do together. Nevertheless, he thinks, *I really need to have a talk with her about that, preferably before we arrive at my mother's cottage.*

By nightfall, they travel another twenty miles deep into Arkansas. His only complaint about Arkansas is that there are so many poor White folks traveling the roads, and they are still sore about losing the Civil War. Niabi and Will make camp at night, but keep their campfires small. They are afraid of attracting unsavory drifters because that's all that would be moving in the night. The fires are so small, they barely get enough heat from them to keep warm.

After another day of travel, they stop to make camp. "Can you gather some small branches and twigs? Look no farther than fifteen feet from camp," Will says. "I will get out the food." She heads to the outskirts of their small camp and stops cold. Then she begins to slowly back up, walking backward toward Will.

"What is it, Nia—yah? Oh, no, don't shoot!" Will yells. His eyes can make out that it is a Negro man covered with bear fur from head to toe, pointing a rifle at Niabi's head. Intermixed with the coat fur on the hood around his face, his woolly beard obscures his appearance. Without close examination, he could have been mistaken for a bear.

With hands raised, Will continues pleading, "Don't shoot! Please." The strange man still points his rifle at Niabi. "May I offer you some of our coffee?" Will asks pointing one hand at the small coffee pot. With that offer, the man moves his focus away from the gunsight on Niabi, and looks down at their coffee pot and a package of coffee waiting to be brewed.

Moving his eyes back to the gunsight, the stranger asks Niabi, "What tribe are you from, dearie?" Niabi with hands extended just trembles.

"She is Choctaw," Will blurts out.

"Choctaw! Why are you so far northeast?" the strange man asks. Niabi continues to walk backward until she bumps into Will.

"We are on our way to my home in Tennessee. But there is enough coffee, beans, and bread for the three of us," Will says.

The stranger lowers his rifle, and says, "I'll take some of your coffee, beans, and some bread too."

He sets down the belongings he carries on his back, and lowers himself into their humble dirt camp, sitting right in their midst on the dirt, assuming they will not try a revenge attack on him for scaring them out of their wits. He is not afraid of them because he can see that they are just youngsters with no business being out there in the wilderness.

"What makes you think that you can make it to Tennessee on your own?" the stranger asks.

"I have traveled from Tennessee to Texas and back five times now. If we know where the water holes are and avoid the trail bandits, I think we'll be OK."

Niabi finishes gathering kindling and lights a fire and brews the coffee.

"May I ask who you are?" Will asks.

"You first," the stranger says, bouncing his sleep-deprived, blotchy red eyes, from Niabi to Will and back.

"I'm Will, and this is Niabi." That's all he cares to share.

"I'm Dakota Sam. I've been searchin' for goin' on a week now, tryin' to locate some no-good renegades who jumped me, whacked my head really good, and took off with my food and horse. She looks like one of 'em. You see, they had a woman with them. That's why I let my guard down. They sent her in asking for help, and then a gang of them pounced upon me and took everything."

"I assure you that she has nothing to do with them. She's been with me for over a week now, riding side by side from Indian territory," Will says.

As Will pours the coffee, he thinks what a tale he's going to have for his crew on the next cattle drive. Then he remembers that he completed his last cattle drive when he decided to take her. Now, he won't be able to show his face again in the Indian Territory.

Will had heard of someone matching Dakota Sam's description from one of Zeb's stories about a former Negro Union soldier that went loco and continues to roam the backlands, looking for die-hard ex-Confederates and helping runaway slaves.

"Are you the Dakota Sam that fought in the Civil War?" Will asks, handing him a cup of coffee, a bowl of beans, and a piece of bread. Niabi pours herself a cup and curls up under a blanket close to Will, their shoulders touching. Amid his curiosity about Dakota Sam, Will fails to notice that Niabi is finding a sense of security and protection when she is near him.

"Yes, I am. I suspect you've also heard I gone loco, and been terrorizin' the countryside. Well, ya heard right! When I returned home my family's shack was bone empty. My wife and son were nowhere to be found, and all the slaves that weren't sold off were slaughtered to keep 'em from being free. I searched plantation after plantation for 'em. Sometimes gettin' caught by former overseers, chased and whipped, as they said for ol' time's sake. I never found my woman or my child. So ya see, there is nowhere else for me to go, but loco."

"If you give me the name of your wife and child, and the name of the plantation, I may be able to get you some help looking for them," Will says.

"What you gonna do, boy? You just another darkie like me, out here fearing for your life. Not knowin' if any minute some sheeted clansmen or fake-grinnin' good Samaritan is going to string you up for the fun of it, or because God said you be damned cause of your skin color. Don't give me hope. It carries too much pain with it. Proverbs 13:12 says, 'Hope deferred maketh the heart sick.'"

Niabi, whom they thought had fallen to sleep, leans forward and blurts out, " And the verse ends with, 'But when the desire cometh it is a tree of life.'" Will and Dakota Sam's mouths drop open. Will starts to say, "I thought you couldn't read . . ." but she keeps going, "If your woman and child are out there praying to the Great Spirit to reunite all of you, those prayers are wasted because you have turned a deaf ear to the Great Spirit."

Just then Will remembers that the Christian missionaries had a presence in her village and that may have influenced her Bible knowledge. He also remembers that one of her duties in her village is to tend to the sick, especially the mothers during child birth, or on occasion she undoubtedly has had to comfort loved ones of persons passing on to the afterlife, or parents who lost a baby. If she was there with people during struggle or loss, she would have to develop a positive outlook to address tragedy, pain, and heartbreak.

Dakota Sam rears back, stares her down, and then looks at Will. "Where did you get this Indian woman? She has posed a riddle to ol' Dakota Sam that even he must consider in his loco-ness. Ha! Ha! Let's drink to your Great Spirit, little lady." Dakota Sam holds his coffee cup up in the air. "May he know that my words are those of a soldier, a warrior, but my thoughts are from the heart of a mere humble husband and father."

No more words are said. They all stare into the crackling fire canopied by full-leafed branches, drooping from the tall trees surrounding them under a dark sky. Slowly the fire dies down, and with it Dakota Sam nods off into a deep sleep, falling over on his belongings. He never awakes to let out his bedroll and get comfortable. His snoring challenges Will and Niabi to fall off to sleep for a while. Both turn their backs to each other, her deer-skin cape and the blankets keeping them warm. They fall asleep leaning against each other. Dakota's presence somehow quells their fears of animals creeping up, or wayward people thinking twice about attacking them. The three of them sleep until an hour before sunrise.

They all awake and get up before daybreak and quickly break camp. Thinking it would be better to eat while riding since they are out in the country far from any town or civilized people, Will breaks off pieces of bread to quiet their stomachs. But his immediate question is regarding Dakota.

"Do you want to travel east with us?" Will asks.

"Sure, especially if your offer to help find my family is still on the table."

"Good, but we need to find you a horse," Will says.

"I'm still an able-bodied man. I can walk," Dakota says while beating his chest.

"I'm not doubting that, sir. But we . . . we just need to get home soon. Why don't you stay here while Niabi and I see if we can track one down?"

Will and Niabi leave Dakota at the camp. They take Rodeo and FireTip to the nearest water hole in a canyon area. If horses are roaming the hills, they will frequent that watering hole. They wait and by midday, several steeds prance in, thirsty for water. Will grabs his lariat and tells Niabi he will pick out one for her to drive toward him. His eyes focus on a black one that looks nourished and slow. He nods at Niabi and they corner the black one, and after a romp, Will lassoes him. Then the real work starts; Will has to break him in. It takes almost one-half an hour for Will to get near him. When he manages to ride Rodeo close enough to the steed, Will leaps onto his bare back. The new horse kicks and bucks, throwing Will to one side where he almost slides off, but he manages to stay on. At times, the horse tries to reach around and bite, but Will dodges him. Niabi looks on, coming to understand the extent of Will's skills with horses. She flinches each time the horse bucks and throws Will into the air. Will estimates he was "bronco busting" for about two hours.

Will yells to Niabi, "If he doesn't break, I will!" Niabi continues watching, hoping he doesn't break a bone. Soon the black horse tires from his exertions and begins walking normally. Will hops off him, brings him over to Rodeo, and gets carrots out of his saddlebag. He feeds all three horses carrots, so neither one gets upset. Right now, He can't tolerate Rodeo or FireTip acting up on him after breaking in the new horse. They rendezvous with Dakota Sam, and now they are truly ready to move on. Will warns Dakota Sam to watch the horse. "They usually need a couple of days before they get used to being broken in," he says.

Will feels more confident about staying on the road now that Dakota Sam is riding along with them. After Will convinces him that Grant Applegate can help find his loved ones, he agrees to travel with them all the way to Tennessee. They ride, proud and confident, in their saddles. Will rides with his sidearm in his holster, Dakota with his rifle propped on his arm, ready for anything that might touch off. If one White man rides by, he would not give them even a glance. If two, they would stare them down. Three would sometimes stare, and yell out a slur or obscenity. But four White men would give Will and his companions cause to move off the road, something Will and Niabi are accustomed to doing. However, Dakota resists any form of retreat as a first option. His first inclination isn't to retreat. He wants to stand and fight, especially if the odds are good. But Will convinces him that it only puts Niabi in harm's way. And Will has no intention of subjecting her to any further avoidable danger.

The days are filled with navigating the road, scanning on both sides, and spying ahead and behind for trouble. By the end of the day, they are worn out and still unable to let their guard down during and after making camp. Will thinks, *You just never know what is around the next bend.* And the fear isn't always against Whites. As taught by Niabi's experience, there are Negroes too, who are dead set on devilment. Sometimes White folks pass and nod their heads in an awkward greeting at the rare threesome. As they ride to the next stop, Will shares that his anxiety is bolstered from remembering the stories he heard from other cowhands about how easy it is for some folks to string up a man and leave him for dead.

One night at camp, after the three had spent several days together on the road, Dakota commences talking about a string of skirmishes during the war, the Civil war. The Negro soldiers, who had been straddled with mundane duties and errands, were finally allowed to really participate in the battle. But they were still not mixed in among the other troops, the White soldiers. They were assigned to capture a bridge and not let anyone cross.

"We felt good about finally getting a worthwhile assignment," Dakota says. "We held it for two weeks, four weeks, then six weeks. The men started to wonder if relief was ever coming, or what was the overall strategy. Crabtree, a man I enlisted with in Ohio, took a sniper's bullet in the throat. We learned to stay down until we drew the sniper's fire enabling us to circle 'round to ambush him. Then a young fellow, who stayed at my side like a stray pup, was stabbed in hand-to-hand combat with some rebels, who tried to storm the bridge. Thinking our squad was smaller than theirs, and weaker, the rebels charged at us, their twelve to our five. We fought them to the bitter end, losing just one. The bridge became a ball and chain around our necks. We could not stray from it, yet we grew to hate the sight of it. There were dried blood stains in spots on and near the bridge, where life and death struggles occurred. After three months, I sent a scout to Captain Arnold, my commanding officer. The scout took another week to return to tell us that Arnold had been killed, and the forces were concentrating at Appomattox. He said that we were relieved at that post and he had orders for us to go straight to Appomattox for what might be the final battle. Every abled soldier was needed. You can imagine that, by this time, I had hoped the other regiments of Negro soldiers were having a better time of fighting this war than we had. Our enthusiasm to free ourselves from the Ol' South was waning. Now all I wanted was independence from this man's army. But the disappointments I felt serving in the army was a mere splinter in my toe compared to the gash that was cut into my heart when I returned home. My woman and child were gone without a trace. I searched and searched and searched and searched."

Seeing Dakota plummet into a strained mental state, Will interrupts him. "Well, we are grateful you made it through. And we are going to get you some help finding your family." Niabi listens to Dakota tell his stories and watches him unravel when he speaks of searching for his family and not finding them. She looks on as if watching a powder keg readying to explode.

Will tries to further defuse the mood. "I better see to the horses," he says and strolls over to Rodeo, FireTip, and the new addition to the crew; they have named him "Blackie." Will takes out Rodeo's brush and begins to brush him. Rodeo hadn't had a good brushing since all this kidnapping began. Dakota scans Niabi with a roving eye, causing her to tense while she finishes drinking her soup.

Dakota gets up, walks to Will, and speaks low asking, "How did you come about this squaw? And such a pretty one too?"

To let him know she is spoken for, Will says what most honorable men respect, "I'm aiming to marry up with her. I am taking her to my home in Tennessee, to meet my mother." Even though Will doesn't feel threatened by Dakota, he can't take the chance of Dakota sharing what he's seen. So, he wants to establish the story—if a story is going to circulate—that a man is traveling with his bride-to-be instead of a Negro man traveling with an Indian girl. The Indian girl is secondary in the story of a bride-to-be, he hopes. Will walks over to where she sits, squats down and asks her, "Are you OK? Do you need anything?"

She shakes her head. He is grateful for that little bit of gesture from her. He is thrilled since, though not audible, this mere gesture from her acknowledges his existence as a human being.

Another night around the campfire comes, and Dakota and Will get into it about the Bible. Dakota seems to feel that the Bible was hindering the progress of the Negro people and Will disagrees. "It is from the need to know the works of Jesus Christ and the scriptures that many Negroes have come to learn to read," Will says.

"But what have they learned from their reading?" rebuts Dakota Sam. "How to turn the other cheek? That their reward will only be received when they get to heaven? And that they should be proud of their suffering? There is something wrong with all that. I believe we have to stand up and fight for what we want, right now, today. And be willing to die for everything important that we are deserving of in this world."

Will shakes his head. "I am not encouraging turning the other cheek, but I know the first book I ever read was the Bible because that's all we had at the time."

Dakota snaps back. "Don't you question a book that tells you to wait on yours, while you see White folks getting theirs now! Whose God are you worshippin' anyway?"

Then suddenly Niabi jumps in the conversation. "There is but one God. The maker of all living creatures. He dwells in the mountains, rivers, and in our souls. I too wondered why bad things happened to my people. But then I look at the world he created, and I see that there is a perfect order. And this order comes about not by chance or wishing for it, but it comes by tests, trials, and victory. The affliction put on my people has made us cling tighter to our customs and beliefs. We are withstanding the trial. We await the victory."

"Well, Will, you've got a little preacher on your hand," Dakota smirks. "And pray tell what victory are you expecting, my dear?"

"Victories are happening now. With each breath of air you take, the berries on the vine, fruit on the trees around us, the rabbit you will shoot for tomorrow's supper; all are victories given to us, sometimes with little or no effort of our own. We might say that God is not hearing us, not watching us, or not at home, but changes to him happen like a blink of an eye, and happen to us over lifetimes. We are a part of a larger journey that man has been traveling since man began, and will continue until he reaches the destination. In life, we all have a part to play in this larger journey. Our goal should be to make our steps on the right path so that we continue the steps of our great ancestors on this path. They help us along, and can see us through until our time to leave the path."

"My word, you are surprising me every day," Will says gazing at her in awe. "How did you know?"

"That's enough spook and spirits talk for me. I'm bedding down for the night," Dakota says before standing and grabbing his bedroll.

Will continues to stare at her in amazement, wondering how that came out of the same mouth that had been with him frozen silent for over two hundred miles. She slowly unrolls her bedroll and begins bedding down herself. Again, he thinks of Oscar and what tales he has to share with him. He feels excited about the future, and what a fine partner he may have found. Thoughts race through Will's head as he beds down two feet from Niabi. Another evening comes to a close.

They finally reach the ferry crossing. Readying themselves to cross, Will tells Niabi, "This is the mighty Mississippi River, and over there on the other side is Tennessee, my home. Do you know how I can tell my land from any other land? By the rich green grass and the trees as tall as mountains," he says. Her head twists from side to side taking in the view of the vastness of the river.

Will has been pushing the group along so he could time their arrival to be the next night. After they cross via the ferry, he says, "This time tomorrow night we will be sleeping in real beds."

They reach the outskirts of Covington, Tennessee, and it's not that far to the Applegate Ranch. It is here that Dakota says his goodbyes and turns off the road to go find the Negro section of Covington. To help him get settled there, Will throws out some names Dakota Sam can ask for. He decides to separate from Dakota Sam because he knows

Ms. Applegate will frown on a strange man being on her property without prior notice. But he takes his chances showing up with Niabi.

By the time Will, Niabi, Rodeo, and FireTip make it onto the grounds of the Applegate Ranch, it is dark. They both are exhausted; she is even leaning, about to fall off FireTip. Will stops and asks her to lean forward on FireTip and hug his neck, while he takes FireTip's reins and guides them all in slowly. They weave through trees and along narrow paths and lanes heading to the servants' quarters.

CHAPTER 7

THE NEW ASSISTANT

―――――

THE tension Will carried from the Indian Territory subsided dramatically after they reached the ferry crossing. A feeling of peaceful euphoria overcomes him as their horses moderately step along the way getting closer to the Applegate Ranch. Dakota had parted from the traveling party at the turnoff to go into the local town, Covington, Tennessee, after which Will and Niabi continued traveling the road toward the Applegate Ranch.

Niabi murmurs from a drowsy stupor, "How much longer before we camp?"

"We're home; just a quarter of a mile to our beds," Will replies equally fatigued. He can see the cottage. "Just about there," he says almost joyfully. After passing the road leading to the church, they are soon on the lane that passes in front of his cottage. It's late, not a soul is stirring, and all of the cottages on that side of the ranch are dark and quiet. The evening dew drifts across the pastures, dampening the trunks and leaves of trees; the leaves free fall to the damp grass below.

Once outside his cottage, Will sees a lantern in the kitchen window, surely left there by his mother. He helps Niabi off FireTip. She is so sleepy she stands and tips to one side like she's dizzy, so he scoops her up into his arms and carries her to the large wooden front door of his and Harriet's cottage. Using his knee, he presses down hard on the crank door handle and pushes the door open. Awakened by the noise of the large cottage door swinging open, Harriet dons a cotton robe and barefoot runs out of her bedroom saying, "Will, Will, is that you?"

"Yes, Momma," says Will as he walks through into the cottage's front room.

The front room is a combination of kitchen, dining room, and sitting room. On the wall opposite to the one including the kitchen window is a fireplace expelling heat from its abating charred logs. The lantern in the kitchen window gives off only enough light to reveal silhouettes of human bodies entering their cottage. Harriet can't make out whether he is the body being carried or the carrier, so she asks, "Are you OK?"

"I'm fine, Momma," Will answers.

Harriet makes her way to a cabinet where more lanterns are stored, and reaches in for two of them. "Let's get some more light in here. I can't tell who's who," Harriet says.

Maneuvering across the kitchen and sitting room, Will moves slowly, feeling his way with his feet, carrying Niabi to his bedroom. After pushing his bedroom door open, he carefully lays her on his bed and speaks softly to her. "We've made it to my home. You can sleep here. I'm going to put the horses up." With eyes closed, Niabi turns on her side and gets comfortable on the soft bed. Her nostrils pick up a hint of his hair oil coming from somewhere near, and she also feels warmth drifting into the bedroom from somewhere. It feels good. Inclined to open her eyes to explore her new surroundings, her body refuses and claims its rights to rest. She drifts off to sleep.

The light inside the front room increases when Harriet lights the two additional lanterns. Now, able to see Will coming from his bedroom, Harriet speaks low so as not to disturb the unknown guest. "Who is that?"

Reserving his remaining energy to go take care of the horses, he takes a deep breath before saying, "A friend. I'll explain more after I put up the horses."

"I'm assuming I'm safe in here, with the 'friend.' This friend won't jump up and slit my throat while you're gone?" Harriet asks.

"No. Ha ha. No," he replies releasing a weak chuckle as he stumbles for the door, but then suddenly he stops, turns around, and drags himself back to Harriet. "Hello Momma, good to see you," he pushes out. "You have nothing to fear." He kisses Harriet on one of her cheeks and turns to continue toward the door saying, "She'll sleep through the night. I'll be right back."

"A *she?*" Harriet says, looking toward his bedroom.

On his return to the cottage from the barn, Will has a sick feeling mounting in his gut because he doesn't want to tell his mother the truth about Niabi and how she came to be his traveling companion. But to his surprise, Harriet has extinguished all lanterns but the one she carries and has made him a pallet in the far corner of the sitting room. This is routinely done when they have more guests than beds to stay overnight. She approaches him, raises the lantern to get a good look at him before returning to her bedroom, and says, "I made you a pallet, there. Get some rest, son, and we can talk in the morning."

His sick feeling immediately vanishes, and as he lies down a new thought bubbles up and out on his lips in a whisper. "Thank you, Jesus."

Harriet rises early and starts breakfast. She prepares eggs, bacon, sausage, coffee, and biscuits with butter and jam. The aroma emanating from the kitchen flows into Will's bedroom and into Niabi's nostrils. Her eyes slide open, and she gets out of the bed. She scans the strange room; her attention is drawn to a small mirror mounted above a vanity table. On the vanity table is a pitcher full of warm water that sits in a large bowl next to neatly folded clean cloths. In front of the mirror, she tries to tidy her hair, and then using a cloth and warm water, she wipes her face and freshens up. She wonders who put the warm water there. She has used a bowl of water in her chukka to wash up, but she bears the burden of drawing her own water and warming it. After washing up, the bowl is usually emptied by throwing the water outside. Niabi tugs on her blouse and skirt, trying to straighten them up on her, and carries the used water into the kitchen on her way to meet Will's mother.

Harriet turns around and tries to not look so surprised. It was dark when she set the pitcher of hot water in Will's room. Now that they have the help of daylight, she gets a good look at Will's "friend." She had no idea that the "she" isn't a Negro girl. Suspecting her expression of complete surprise is probably causing discomfort for the pretty visitor, she stops the staring and proceeds with welcoming her and determining how to deal with her unexpected presence.

"Good mornin'," Harriet whispers, pointing to a sleeping Will in the corner.

"Good mornin'," Niabi replies, also in a whisper after seeing him in the corner.

"You are not what I expected. You are very pretty, though. I can see why Will would want you as a friend. Come. Oh, let me have that bowl. Extending her hand aiming at a chair at her small kitchen table, Harriet says speaking low, "Please have a seat. I guess you all had a heck of a journey. I've never seen him sleep in that long." Looking at Will, Harriet continues, "He's usually up by dawn. But I'm glad you're up."

Niabi's eyes roam the walls, cabinets, stoves, and a large fireplace. Pots are simmering above low flames in several places. Her eyes finally land on a sleeping Will. She had hoped he would be awake to intercede by introducing her and explaining her presence. But the mother, who regains her full attention, is quite talkative, relieving her of a need to explain anything at all.

Harriet continues, "Please forgive me. But we need to have a conversation that I'll admit I should be having with him, but I'm due up at the main house soon. First, you are welcome in my home as a guest of my son. There needs to be no further discussion or concern about that. Second, the fact is, we live in this cottage rent-free because of my husband's legacy working for years and years to build up this ranch, and I grew up working in the main house. Will is supposed to work here steady, too, but he's been allowed to leave gallivanting across the country doing his cattle driving. While we are allowed visitors, to keep tongues from wagging and guessing, I'll just take you up to the main house and introduce you to Mrs. Applegate as my new assistant. I'm getting older, and it's reasonable for me to have an assistant now. Now, between you and me, you can assist me if you like, or you can roam around the ranch doing nothing. It's totally up to you. But I think you may not like being idle because Will and everybody else on this ranch has to work. So, what do you think?"

Niabi thinks, *Now I know where Will gets his controlling nature from.* "I don't want you to get in trouble, so I will go with you to be introduced to Mrs. Applegot," Niabi says.

"Applegate," Harriet corrects her. "I'm not going to get in trouble. I just know the Applegates frown on us workers letting family or friends move in unannounced, unplanned, and they think they are freeloading or something. But I have family that visits sometimes, and when they do, I let them know, and beyond that, I don't care. But you and Will have caught me off guard here, and there's bound to be questions. This seems to be the best way to get ahead of idle gossip. OK?"

"Yes, OK," Niabi says.

"Well, I've prepared breakfast for all of us. Put whatever you want on your plate, and just eat up," Harriet says as she places on the table the various dishes of food, matching the aromas Niabi smells. "We'll let him know our plans later," Harriet says still speaking low, so as not to wake Will.

Niabi makes her plate from the dishes of food on the table. Hoping to impress Harriet, she eats the breakfast slowly, remembering Will's admonitions about using the fork and knife to cut the food into small pieces. Harriet pours her a cup of coffee, and Niabi watches and copies Harriet adding cream and sugar. Her usual drink at home is hot tea. They both sit there blowing on their respective cups of coffee to cool it down, and gingerly sipping it like two who regularly dine together. When Harriet asks if she would like some milk, Niabi's eyes light up, and she eagerly answers, "Oh, yes, thank you. I would." Harriet pours a glass of milk for her. Niabi drinks almost all of it in one swallow, and then lets out a monstrous belch. "Bauuuugggggrrrgg." Harriet had returned to sipping her coffee, but upon hearing the loud belch, she almost drops her cup. Gripping the table with her fingernails, she looks at Niabi, takes deep breaths, and says calmly and softly, "My child, never ever do that again in front of other people. That is a personal bodily reaction that you should try to hide from others. Hide by either covering your mouth with your hand or using a hanky. It's best to let out the air with no sound, but if you can't, then muffle the sound in some way. And please, never ever do that around Mrs. Applegate. She will fire us both and set us out on the road like trash." Niabi is startled by Harriet's reaction because Will has seen her do this many times and laughed; in fact, he and she made a little game out of it, competing to see who could belch the loudest. That's why hers is so loud. She perfected belching during their competitions and started beating him at it. She thought it was part of *his* culture. Now, she has something else to be mad at him about.

Harriet takes another breath and says, "You know, sweetie, I don't know your name."

Niabi replies, "My name is Niabi."

"That's beautiful. OK, Niabi. Now that you are done eating, let me take a look at you. If I may, let me brush over your beautiful hair a bit, and we are off to the main house."

Harriet brushes Niabi's hair in her bedroom with the brush supplied to her by Mrs. Pritchett, and then tugs on her blouse and skirt to make it look less slept-in. Harriet finds that she likes having a young girl around to tend to. Niabi looks over at Will, hoping he will wake up and end her second kidnapping to the main house. But Harriet is already at the door to exit the cottage, beckoning Niabi. "Come on, come on, we don't want to be late. This is another working day on the ranch."

Exiting the cottage, Niabi for the first time views the grandeur of the ranch: the endless greens, carved by virgin white fencing enclosing clusters of tall majestic horses filing into the corrals. She twirls around gawking at the beauty and serenity of the new place in which she is held captive. Harriet notices her slowing to sightsee. "Keep up," she says. Getting back in step with Harriet, Niabi barely catches her breath before assessing that there is a three-story structure looming at the end of their path, which is the main house Harriet referred to. It looks like they are to go up steps leading to a wide porch skirting the entire back of the structure. Once on the porch, Niabi turns again looking to the left at the endless greens and the edge of a garden, and then to the middle where Harriet's and other cottages sit on the side of a lane in the forefront of the main barn and two stables. Later she will learn that family, staff, and guests' horses are held in the main barn, and animals for sale are housed in the stables. And to the right she sees more servants' cottages, barns, bunkhouse and a track all on an additional expanse of green that stretches a great distance. The breadth of the property is breath-taking.

On the porch, Harriet leans toward Niabi, tugging on her blouse and skirt and patting down the frayed ends of her hair. "You don't have to say anything unless asked. Let me introduce you and explain why you are here." Based on it being early morning, Harriet surmises she will find Mrs. Applegate in her bedroom or taking breakfast in the dining room. Upon entering the house, they find Mrs. Applegate in the hallway, heading toward the back door, coming toward them.

"I don't know if Jason is coming around to the back door or the front door," Mrs. Applegate says to someone stepping away from her, maybe Grant.

With Niabi in tow, Harriet stops just inside the house near the door waiting for Mrs. Applegate. "Pardon me, ma'am, I would like to

introduce Niabi to you. She came home with Will last night, and she
will be working as my new assistant."

"Oh! Well, welcome, Niabi," Mrs. Applegate says, surprised she is
Indian. "I'm afraid you have caught me on my way to town, and unfortunately I don't have time to get acquainted. I look forward to a time
in the future when we can talk." Proceeding toward the back door,
she continues, "I'm waiting for the carriage to be brought around.
Jason is taking me to town." Mrs. Applegate looks out the back door,
and soon sees Jason pulling up in the carriage. Followed by Harriet
and Niabi, she walks out onto the back porch. Still speaking to Harriet, Mrs. Applegate says, "Harriet, you can get—is it Niabi?"

"Yes, ma'am," Harriet answers.

"Yes, get Niabi settled, and let me know if she needs anything."
Jason exits the two-person carriage, and energetically skips up the
steps to the back porch. "Are you ready to—who is this?" says a surprised Jason, sliding one side of his lips up higher than the other. He
moves past his mother to eyeball the visitor.

Harriet says, "This is my new assistant, Mr. Jason. Her name is
Niabi. She'll be helping me in the main house with . . . ah, ah . . . the
upstairs chores and serving. Niabi, this is Jason, Mrs. Applegate's
youngest son." Niabi's eyes twinkle while forming a slight grin at this
very friendly, young and handsome White man. His charm propelled
by an easy smile and fun-loving nature is only equal to his good looks,
comprising dusty auburn hair, dark turquoise eyes, and an agile fit
body.

Jason removes his hat as he walks over to Niabi. "Welcome, Miss
Niabee," he says in a low deep voice. This arousing voice is complemented by him lifting Niabi's right hand and kissing it on the top like
a French man. "I can't tell you what an immense pleasure it is to make
your acquaintance."

"Down, boy. This pretty lady is Will's friend," Mrs. Applegate says.

"Will's friend?" he says and gently lets her hand go. "Well, no wonder he is tearing out of here every summer on his trips south. I would tear out of here, too, if a pretty one like you was at the end of the trail."

Niabi blushes.

Staring into her eyes, Jason continues, "Lovely to make your acquaintance, Miss Niabi." He puts on his hat and tips it at Niabi and Harriet saying, "Harriet. Niabi. I look forward to seeing you around the house, Miss Niabi." Moving back toward the steps, Jason nears his mother and extends his arm to her to escort her to the carriage. Niabi delightfully smiles at him as he leaves the porch. She grew up fearing White men because of the stories of how they mistreated her people, but this White man is attractive, charming, calls her pretty, and kisses her hand like she is a queen. She reserves her opinion of this White man.

———•———

Captain Horton of Fort Townsend seats himself around the large dining table capable of seating twelve persons in the dining room of the main house on the Hastings Ranch. He is accompanied by two of his lieutenants on a detail to scout the area and local towns in response to the recent shots fired near the village, and the report of a missing Indian girl. Mr. and Mrs. Hastings are glad to have him visit.

"I was surprised to learn that you were making a journey all the way down here. Isn't this outside your territory?" Mr. Hastings asks.

"Yes, it is. But we have an alarming situation we are trying to resolve quickly and peacefully," the captain says admiring the display of china and vases decorating the shelves in the Hastings' dining room.

"Alarming?" asks Mr. Hastings.

"It seems an Indian girl from the village near the fort has disappeared. And no one has a clue as to how or with whom. The only lead we have is that one of your Negro cowhands was seen talking to her, letting her ride one of your horses, I believe, a tan stallion."

Mr. Hastings rises and says, "Excuse me a moment." He goes into the kitchen, asks one of the servants to fetch Tom, and asks Oscar to come into the dining room. Oscar removes his sauce-stained apron, and after entering the dining room, Mr. Hastings asks him to take a seat. "Captain Horton, this is one of my Negro workers, Oscar Kintoole." Oscar nods at the captain. Mr. Hastings continues, "He is the head chef in my home, and he also works as the cook on my cattle drives." Now directing his questions to Oscar, Mr. Hastings asks, "Oscar, I'm going to ask you what may be a strange question. By any chance, are you harboring an Indian girl somewhere?"

"Oh, John, that's preposterous," says Mrs. Hastings. "Oscar sleeps in a small room off from the kitchen. Where is he going to harbor an Indian girl?"

Oscar camouflages his nervousness over this line of questioning by maintaining his composure and displaying a calm smile. "No. I am not harboring an Indian girl, anywhere," Oscar answers.

"Of course, you're not," says Mrs. Hastings. "And we are ashamed to have asked you that," she says, looking cross at Mr. Hastings.

"Thank you for coming in here, Oscar. You may go back to what you were doing," Mr. Hastings says.

Tom enters the main house through the back door and passes through the kitchen heading to the dining room. His path becomes obstructed by Oscar's exit through the doorway between the kitchen and dining room. Each acknowledges the other with glances and nods while performing a mutually induced dosey doe to get past one another. Oscar hurries through the kitchen and out through the back door to get some air.

Tom enters the dining room and comes toward the table. "Good evening, ma'am, John, captain." All give a courtesy nod back to Tom.

Mr. Hastings says, "Now, captain, we have only one other Negro worker and his name is Will Lawton. I will let Tom tell us the state he was in the last time seen on the drive." Mr. Hastings now settles his eyes on Tom. "Tom, the captain is here asking questions about our Negro boys and whether they know anything about an Indian girl who has gone missing. It is reported that she was seen with one of our drovers, a Negro, who let her take a ride on one of our —did you say a tan horse, Horton?"

The captain looks at a paper he holds in front of him verifying the descriptions from his notes. "Yes, a tan horse."

Mr. Hastings continues, "Now, Tom, they've seen Oscar just now. What do you know of Will Lawton?"

"Ah . . . Well, Will finished this last drive with the crew. He was paid in Dodge City and traveled back with us. He split off from the crew as he normally does around Red River. Is that what Oscar said?" Tom says.

"No, we didn't ask Oscar about Will. Now, did Will have a reason to go visit an Indian girl at the village?" continues Mr. Hastings.

"Sir, the chief had already filed a complaint at the fort about the men coming too close to the village, so I gave them all, including Oscar and Will, strict orders not to set foot in the village. As far as I know, they honored my orders," Tom says.

"Well, you see, captain, you need to look elsewhere. My men have been back and forth through that territory for years. There would be no reason for them to take an Indian girl. And take her where? They would be seen with her," Mr. Hastings says.

Horton responds, "It's just that the chief's son is very interested in this girl, maybe to be his future wife. So, we're getting a lot of heat on this one."

"Well, there's your answer right there, captain," says Mrs. Hastings. "This girl might not want to marry the chief's son, and just made her a way out of there."

"Is that all, John?" Tom asks, anxious to leave.

"Yes, Tom. You can go back to what you were doing. Thanks for coming up here," Mr. Hastings says.

Tom exits back through the kitchen and looks around for Oscar. He finds him standing outside near the kitchen back door. Tom approaches Oscar in a huff. "I didn't mention FireTip, a tan horse! The captain said she was seen riding a tan horse belonging to the ranch." Tom gets up close in Oscar's face. "Now, I'll ask you—think about what you are going to say before you answer—did Will take the Indian girl?"

"I can only tell you what I saw. I saw Will ride off going east, riding on Rodeo with FireTip next to him. I did not see an Indian girl with him," Oscar says.

"For some reason, I think you are holding something back. But I won't pressure you. Just tell me if the girl is in any danger of harm?" Tom leans forward, his eyes penetrating Oscar's.

"I have to repeat, sir, that I didn't see the Indian girl when Will left for Tennessee. But rest assured, whenever he mentions her . . ."

"Ah, shit, he 'mentions her'?" Tom takes off his hat and slaps his thigh with it, and then steps around, agitated. The tension rises between the two.

Oscar interjects, "As I started to say, whenever he mentions her, he in no way talks about harming her. That's all I wanted to say."

Tom gets in Oscar's face again so he can talk low but firm and not be overheard. "Listen, Oscar, Will has FireTip. FireTip is the only tan horse we have or had in our stock. The captain is looking for a tan horse. Now, I can't even bring up the horse to Mr. Hastings because that links us to the girl. I would suggest if Will has the girl, tell him to get her back to that village, pronto! That's all I have to say on the matter." Tom storms off.

———•———

Nashoba, Koi, and Talako had trailed the captain and lieutenants to the Hastings Ranch. Nashoba guessed the captain would go to the ranch to make inquiries, so he and his companions followed them. They were able to trail them at a distance by following their tracks. Subsequently, the captain was completely unaware of their presence as he led them to the Hastings Ranch. Once the soldiers went through the Hastings Ranch archway, the three tribesmen perched themselves on a hill where they had a view of the entrance to the ranch and movement from the main house to the barn. During their time keeping watch, they only saw the one Negro wearing an apron come out of the main house and go back in, never working with the other ranch hands. They also saw no signs of the other Negro or his horse with white feet.

After spending two days at the ranch, the captain and lieutenants leave the Hastings Ranch to go to the local town, Waco, Texas. Nashoba suspects Niabi is being held at the ranch, but can't figure out which building she could be held in. He devises a strategy to get Niabi back. Suspecting the Negro cattlemen that work for the ranch know where Niabi is, he and his team prepare to sneak on to the ranch and find Niabi or take one or both of the Negro men captive. They are surprised when one of the Negroes mounts a horse and rides out the ranch's main entrance. It's Oscar on his way to Waco to post a letter to Will. Nashoba, Talako, and Koi trail him, but at a great distance to see where he is going. When they see signs for the town of Waco, they back away. They dare not go near a town and be seen. Their only option is to wait near the road on the outskirts of Waco, hoping Oscar will return on the same road heading back to the ranch.

The letter Oscar posts reads as follows:

Dear Will,

I hope this letter finds you and your mother in good health. The captain of Fort Townsend came to Hastings Ranch making inquiries about a missing Indian girl. They questioned Mr. Hastings, Tom, and myself. They learned nothing from us, but I have a great concern for you. If you do have her you should find a way to get word to her people that she is OK. Even, if she's with you and you met with some mishap on the road, they should learn of that too. I'm worried until I hear from you.

Take care of yourself.

Oscar

After Oscar posts the letter at the Waco post office, he heads to the grocers.

Hunkering down among shrubberies and trees, the tribesmen have positioned themselves with a view of the road both ways. Since morning they have been waiting and watching in one spot until the sun passes noontime. Talako and Koi, fifteen feet between them, keep from Nashoba their exchanged glances of discontent. After so much time hiding and waiting and not wanting to give away their presence to anyone, Talako softly speaks to Nashoba, who is ten feet away, "How long must we wait? He may be staying there or traveling on to another place."

"If he's not back by nightfall, we can go back and watch the ranch again," Nashoba replies. "I know he or the other one has her."

After shopping at the grocers for flour, nuts, and jam, Oscar heads back to the ranch. Koi, positioned along the road closest to town, spots him first and squawks like a crow to alert the others. Koi rides his horse to where they agreed to situate themselves for an ambush. As Oscar enters a bend in the road where there is a blind turn to the right, Nashoba, Koi, and Talako leap out on horseback ambushing him. Talako and Koi flank Oscar's rear while Nashoba rides to the front of him, close enough to grab the reins of Oscar's horse, and he does. This confrontation takes place about eight miles from the ranch.

"Give back my reins!" Oscar yells as he looks from one Indian to the other; his horse whinnies and shuffles about.

"Where is your friend, the other Negro man?" Nashoba demands, squinting his eyes at Oscar. "Did you contact him, the one who rides the horse with white feet, or is he back at the ranch with Niabi?"

Sweat pours down Oscar's face. Getting ambushed by Indians has been a worrisome premonition of his. "I have no business with you. I would appreciate you removing yourself from my . . . my path," he stutters.

"No, we are not going to remove ourselves. Where is Niabi?" Nashoba raises his voice. A vein throbs in his temple as he leans into Oscar's face.

"I don't know any Niabi," Oscar says shifting his weight in his saddle.

"We saw your friend with Niabi when she rode the tan horse and he rode the brown horse with white feet. We saw him!" Talako leans forward. A smirk flickers across his face from watching Oscar twist around jerkily to see him.

"I don't know anything about a Niabi, and I didn't see anyone riding a tan horse," Oscar says, breathing heavily through his mouth. He looks forward in the direction of the ranch hoping someone will come along.

"Well, your Negro friend knows something. I'm sure of it! And we are going to hold *you* until she's returned to us," Nashoba says, stabbing his index finger toward Oscar.

"Is he at the ranch?" Talako asks fidgeting in his saddle, too, watching for White riders coming from either direction.

"No. Now let me go," Oscar yells, his face turning ashen.

"No, I want you to write a letter on this paper we have brought, and tell your friend to bring Niabi back to the village. Let him know we will trade her life for yours," Nashoba says waving a sheet of paper above his head.

Koi turns and looks at Nashoba, "How will you send it?"

Nashoba snaps at him, "Don't worry about that! We just need him to write the letter, and put the post number on the outside for his Negro friend."

Speaking in Choctaw, Nashoba tells Talako and Koi, "Hurry. Tie his hands, Koi. Talako, here, take the reins of his horse. We return home." Nashoba is painfully aware that he and his companions should not be found off the reservation. Imprisonment and some form of punishment will come from those that capture him, but he fears the indeterminable amount of wrath that will come from his father, the chief. He had been warned.

Nashoba, Talako, and Koi travel seven days, taking Oscar to the Indian Village where Oscar drafts a letter dictated to him by Nashoba. Nashoba posts the letter at the trading post, which provides postal services for the village and the fort.

———•———

Harriet takes Niabi to the kitchen where the other two house servants are working. "Now these are the other house servants. Later you can meet Clarence, who tends to the garden, and Fred and his staff, who take care of the horses, other livestock, and grounds. In the meantime, this is Ethel and Sheila. Ethel mostly helps me with the meals and is a live-in servant. Sheila and I take care of the personal needs of the family, and cleaning this house from top to bottom. The family consists of Mrs. Applegate and her two sons, Grant and Jason. You met Jason: Grant is his older brother." Harriet pauses and sweeps her eyes over the kitchen. "There's not much to do once we've thoroughly cleaned everything. Most days, it's just a little dustin', remo-vin' trash from the day before, and responding to requests for water to freshen up or bathe. We remove the linen every three days or as needed, and have a wash day at least once a week. If there is a big event scheduled or guests stay over, that can be grizzly. But we can always get help brought in when that happens." Niabi looks over the two ladies, noticing they are very clean, with neatly braided hair, and they wear light gray dresses trimmed in white and covered with white aprons similar to the traditional dresses worn by women of her tribe.

Niabi thinks, *The Great Spirit is sure bringing many experiences my way.* Harriet gives her a short tour of the main house starting with rooms on the first floor, and ending near the front door entryway. To show her the upstairs area, they climb the four-feet wide staircase. Niabi scans the portraits and sconces lining the staircase walls. At the top of the staircase stretches a hallway adorned with more sconces in between small alcoves, which shelter closed doors to other rooms. "This is the office, one of the guest rooms, Jason's room, and Grant's room," Harriet says as she moves down to the end of the hallway to the master bedroom, Mrs. Applegate's bedroom. When Niabi enters the master bedroom, she gasps at the high ceiling, wall-papered walls, and huge four-posted bed with a canopy made of carved pine painted pale lime. The pale-lime wooden bed matches the dressing table in front of a large oval mirror and ornate coat closet. Pale-lime damask drapes cover the windows and match the bed canopy and bedspread; all are bound together by pale-lime printed wallpaper. To Niabi, it is like something out of a dream. Off to one side of the bedroom are glass doors leading to the bathroom where the center piece is a large copper bathtub. Around the bathroom are dainty tables and shelves holding glass and porcelain bottles and bowls filled with scented soaps, oils, bath brushes, and sponges.

After Niabi adjusts to the magnificence of it all, she works upstairs with Harriet changing the linen on Mrs. Applegate's very large bed. She presses down on the mattress and lays her head on one of the pillows. Harriet explains what they are made of. They collect the soiled linen, and Harriet directs her to take it downstairs two floors to the laundry room. Once Niabi reaches the laundry room she gapes at multiple huge washtubs, a cabinet with bars of laundry soap, starch, and bottles of liquid bluing, that she learns is for whitening. On hooks are pails of different sizes, different sizes of washboards with metal scrubbing surfaces, and dollies, a short wooden pole with usually three or four legs, made for stirring or agitating clothes in a washtub. Looking out of the window of the laundry room, she sees three clotheslines where clothes are hung and dried in the hot sun.

It isn't long before Sheila bolts into the laundry room behind her, anxious to get time alone with her. "Did you really snag that hunk of a man, Will?" Sheila asks.

"What do you mean by snag?" Niabi says, furrowing her eyebrows.

"I mean has he kissed you, hugged you, and said you are his girl?" Sheila asks merrily twisting from side to side.

"Well, he did kiss me," Niabi says. Sheila howls and jumps up and down, and then catches herself and says, "I'm sorry for making so much noise. I don't want folks to come running in here, thinking I saw a rat or something, but go on."

"And well, he hugged me, too," Niabi adds. Again, Sheila is ecstatic, covering her mouth with her hand to not let out another howl, and then says, "I love it. I love it."

Niabi does not know what to make of her reactions.

Sheila queries her further, "He must have a fire burning inside him for you to bring you home. Do you know how many girls been laying traps for that stallion, and you got him on a cattle drive? Did you really meet him on a cattle drive? Were you driving cattle, too? If so, I'm in the wrong profession."

Further answers from Niabi are stopped because Harriet walks in looking for her. As Harriet enters the laundry room, Sheila bolts out.

"I wouldn't take up too much time with her. She's a hard worker, but she's irresponsible in her personal life. So, I wouldn't want you to adopt any of her ideas," Harriet says to Niabi.

Ethel comes to the laundry room smiling and informs Niabi, "You have a visitor out back." Niabi follows her upstairs to the kitchen and sees Will outside sitting on a bench near the clothesline. She exits the kitchen to talk to him. He stands up when he sees her approaching.

"So, you finally woke up," Niabi says.

"Yeah, sorry about that. I meant to talk to Momma about you, and how we would introduce you to everyone, but I see she's taken care of that. Ethel says you are her new assistant. Are you OK with that?"

"I don't see how it can be helped now. You have brought me here to be someone's servant. But I have to live somewhere and need food to eat, and you don't have a place of your own. You stole me to bring me to your momma's house!"

"I deserve that . . . but . . ." Bobbing his hand and lowering his tone, he says, "Hey, please keep that stole business quiet. I don't want my mother knowing anything about that, OK?"

Sheila brings out freshly washed linen to hang on the clothesline to dry.

"Hi, Will," says Sheila in a real sexy tone, looking back and forth between him and Niabi like something is going on.

"Hi, Sheila." Seeing how she is looking at him, he twists back to face Niabi. "Is there something I am missing?"

"No, I am the *one missing*!" Niabi yells. Then she looks away from him and gritting her teeth continues, "I will see you tonight, or am I like Ethel the servant who sleeps here in this house, and the day of work never ends?"

"Ha ha ha! Yes, the workday has an end, and you will be paid I'm sure of it. Ethel is the only one who lives in the main house to serve them dinner and to clean up afterward. She's a live-in servant by choice. Mom comes home, and Sheila, well, I don't know what Sheila's circumstances are. Now understand, you can come back to the cottage during the day whenever you want to." Will begins to walk away to go and start his workday. "We can talk about this more, later," he adds. He tips his hat at her, and heads for the barn.

Two weeks go by, and Niabi settles into a routine of accompanying Harriet to the main house every morning, except Sundays. She even receives a small compensation, and is outfitted with her own gray and white maid's uniform with a matching apron. Her moccasins are becoming so unsightly, Mrs. Applegate orders her pairs of white socks and white leather work shoes that Niabi keeps spotless along with her uniform. After the work shoes arrive, Niabi remembers and wonders if Will's promise to buy her boots was a lie, too. But then when Harriet is cleaning her own house, she comes across a box that came in the post addressed to Harriet Lawton; inside are a pair of tan leather boots and a note that reads, "For my friend at the Indian village." Harriet presents the box and note to Niabi. "I think these are for you."

While sitting at the kitchen table, Niabi tries on the boots. They are a perfect fit and are very comfortable. Looking on, Harriet asks, "How did he know your size?"

"He measured me by the river," Niabi says standing, walking around to see how they feel.

"Well, I guess he has another skill on top of cattle driving—shoe salesman," Harriet says, and they laugh.

Another Sunday is upon them. Niabi and Will missed church the first Sunday after they arrived in Tennessee because Niabi claimed she had nothing clean to wear, and Will purposely kept his things in his saddlebag. Well, Harriet isn't taking any chances; she dumps the contents of Will's saddlebags, grabs a bundle of Niabi's soiled clothing, and everything washable gets washed, mended, pressed, and made ready to wear.

"Tomorrow is Sunday, so that means we take our baths this evening," Harriet announces on Saturday afternoon.

"How are we going to do this?" Will asks. Up to now, he and Niabi were taking turns washing up in his bedroom.

Harriet quickly responds, "Easy. I have it all worked out. Will, you will bathe first, so that Niabi and I can have the bathroom to ourselves. That way we can share the scented soaps, body oils, and perfumes received as presents from Mrs. Applegate."

Will finishes his bath, and then relinquishes the bathroom to Harriet and Niabi. After hours of chatting, Harriet and Niabi agree Niabi needs a dress for church services. Harriet has dresses given to her by Mrs. Applegate that are hanging in her closet. She selects one and lets Niabi try it on. Harriet takes it in at the waist and bodice to fit Niabi's petite figure.

On Sunday morning, Harriet takes a long strip of pale green ribbon, also gifted from Mrs. Applegate, and weaves it into a large braid of Niabi's hair. The large braid is then wrapped around Niabi's head, forming a crown of braid and ribbon around her head. The green dress Harriet had taken in at the waist and bodice and the green ribbon are almost a match in color. The dress fits Niabi perfectly. Harriet's dress is made of blue cotton with lace trim around the neck, sleeves, and the bottom of the dress three inches above the hem. Both ladies glide out of the bedroom into the front room primping and modeling their outfits in front of Will, who waits for them so they can walk together to church.

"Wow, you ladies look lovely. That's ah—a beautiful outfit, Niabi," Will says pointing to her dress and hair.

Niabi smiles. "Thank you. Your mother did all this." She twirls around showing off her dress and new boots. "Thank you for the boots, Will. They fit perfectly," Niabi says.

"I'm glad. I'm glad you found something to smile at me about," Will says. Harriet looks puzzled at his comment.

The three stroll to church, Niabi taking in the sun, watching it peep out of the clouds before noontime. Her eyes try to observe it all, starting at the tops of the towering trees that border the dirt road they walk along, to travelers passing by on horseback, in wagons and carriages, also dressed for church. In the distance, she hears people congregating around a large porch leading into a white building with a sign next to it. Niabi reads the sign, which says, "Colored Methodist Episcopal Church, Pastor Edwin Walker."

Inside they find seats in a middle section on the right side of the church. Harriet wants to be near the front, so Niabi can see how services are conducted. After the three are seated with Niabi in the middle, the service proceeds as usual. When the speaker calls for any first-time visitors to stand, Harriet motions for Niabi to stand, but Will, frowning, moves his hand from side to side indicating a bad idea. Niabi is caught in the middle, looking back and forth between Will and Harriet. Harriet reassures Niabi that she should stand, so Niabi stands. Will looks away and shakes his head. Niabi and Dakota Sam are the only ones standing. The speaker in front asks for their names. Niabi's throat tightens. She hears someone clear their throat and turns around to see Dakota with half his beard shaved off, standing two rows behind her row. Dakota says, "Ladies first."

She says softly, "Niabi."

The congregation says, "Welcome, Niabi."

The same happens for Dakota Sam.

Pastor Walker chooses to preach this Sunday about Daniel in the lions' den. "I want you to turn your Bibles to the book of Daniel, Chapter 6," the pastor says. "King Darius threw Daniel into the lions' den because he violated a law restricting his worshipping God. But while in the lions' den, an angel came forth, and shut the lions' mouths, and Daniel was protected until morning. Oh, how unexpected events happen as we travel down life's road. We can have such a pleasant trip, and then come face to face with the Devil, evil-doers, and danger. But because of our love for the Lord, we are safely delivered from the Devil, evil-doers, and danger. We don't have to move a muscle, but we are saved from the Devil, evil-doers, and danger. Just like Daniel, an angel steps in to protect us . . . from? Can't hear you."

And the congregation repeats along with the pastor, "The Devil, evil-doers, and danger." And Pastor adds, "just like Daniel." Pastor Walker continues, "All Daniel did—look at verse 10—all he was accused of was bowing down upon his knees and praying three times a day. King Darius threw Daniel into the den of the lions for that. And in verse 16, it is explained that King Darius actually favored Daniel but was forced to do this to him. King Darius said, 'The God thou servest continually, he will deliver thee.'

Oh, my beloved, if you would just make Jesus your Lord and savior and serve him and his Father God, not just on Sundays, not when you are in distress or trouble, or when on the road when your horse goes lame or your wagon wheel breaks down, but continually call on God to be in your life. Oh, there are times when no human is around to help, and the only help can come from the Maker of Men, the Source of our Manna, the Alpha and the Omega, the Great Spirit on High. Can I get an amen?"

"Amen, amen," says the congregation, including Niabi.

Hearing Niabi say amen so forthrightly, Will is stunned. She had been listening attentively and found the pastor's words ringing true in her life. Was she not in peril when those three no-good vagabonds grabbed her and held her captive intending to sell her, or worse? She saw the Great Spirit come to her rescue—albeit a combination of the vagabonds' inability to make a deal right away, and Will finding her. She can see the Great Spirit at work in her life. Tears stream from her eyes. Will takes out and offers his handkerchief. Although smudged with the residue of his dried sweat, she takes it anyway and wipes her tears away. Harriet looks their way. Seeing Niabi wiping her tears, she puts her arm around her shoulders and begins to slightly rock back and forth, to bring her comfort.

The pastor stirs them all into chants of "Thank you, Jesus" and "Thank you, God." Giving them time to pay homage to God, the pastor gradually brings the service back in line with the scheduled program, and calls for the offering and singing of the last hymn.

After the service, Harriet takes Niabi up to the front of the church to meet the pastor, and Will heads for the door. Sheila watches the trio with special interest, and finds now to be a good time to make her way over to Rita. As Rita greets different church members lined up to greet her, Sheila gets in the line and finally moves to the head of Rita's small greeting line.

"Hello Rita, you're looking so lovely as usual," Sheila says smirking like she has a secret.

"Hello to you, Sheila. Thank you for the compliment," Rita says smiling from ear to ear.

"I wonder if you have met our new visitor, Niabi?" Sheila says, turning to gaze at Niabi with Harriet, greeting the pastor. Rita, still perky, follows her lead and looks at them as well.

"Who is she? I saw her stand as a visitor," Rita says, focusing her eyes to get a clear view of the new visitor.

"I thought you would never ask. She is Will's friend," Sheila answers widening her eyes.

"Will's friend?" Rita says, her mouth half open.

Sheila spells and says his name. "W-i-l-l, Will," Sheila emphasizes. "She is staying at the cottage with Harriet and W-i-l-l."

Rita immediately grows agitated by Sheila's news and scans the sanctuary, filled with departing attendees, for Will. She finds him perched at the entrance waiting on his mother and the friend.

Sheila softly touches Rita's arm and says, "I thought you should know." Sheila moves away working her mouth as though she is savoring a juicy bite of candy.

Stunned, Rita continues greeting church members who had been waiting in the small greeting line while she talked to Sheila. Now and then, she glances over at Will. At one point, their eyes meet and he smiles and nods hello. She forces out a smile at him that is painful, but necessary for appearances.

Harriet and Niabi take their leave from the pastor and head toward the entrance where Will is waiting. He lets his mother pass him first, and then he makes eye contact with Niabi, and the two become flushed and exchange mutual warm smiles. He momentarily forgets he is at church and quickly reaches around to tug her ear lobe farthest from him. She jerks her head around to see who did that, and he gushes a chuckle. "It was me," he says. She continues walking in front of him and uses her index finger to beckon him, like a proper debutante, to bend down and hear her comment. He bends over, matching her small strides and inhaling her intoxicating scents. She whispers in his ear, "You just had to touch me, didn't you?" Their eyes fawn over one another, concluding with more smiles. Witnessing the exchange between Niabi and Will, Rita's heart sinks. She feels ill and abruptly excuses herself to the remainder of the persons waiting to greet her. Fighting back the tears, she quickly scoots to her father's pastoral office in the back of the building. She does not know how long she has been there. Her father eventually comes into the office to change out of his pastoral robe and sees her wiping tears and blowing her nose.

"Oh, sweetie, what is the matter?" Pastor Walker asks. She has a very open and honest relationship with her father, more so than with her mother, so she speaks frankly.

"It seems Will has found another—that Indian girl with Mother Harriet," Rita says and blows her nose into a hanky.

"You don't know that. Harriet said he met her on a cattle drive, and she's just here visiting for a while. Did he tell you that she is more than a friend to him?" Pastor Walker asks.

"No, not in words. I saw the way he looks at her. He never looked that way at me. He looked like a dog in heat."

"Oh, goodness!" Pastor looks up toward the heavens and says, "Forgive us, God." Then he continues, "All I know, he's a good young man. Give him a chance to share with you what's going on before you give up on him. I know you are interested in him. Now, if indeed he wants the Indian girl, you wish him the best and her too, because listen here, my Rita Mae is no consolation prize. My Rita Mae is the Blue-Ribbon winner of the whole contest. Any man lucky enough to win her heart—which means he would have to love her just as much or more than she loves him—and that man will be blessed beyond his dreams. You are smart, talented, skillful, and you'd make a great companion and homemaker for any man."

"Oh, Dad, how can I be sad around you? You can lift the spirits of someone buried. And I love you for it."

Will, Niabi, and Harriet walk along the road leading from the church to the Applegate Ranch. Church attendees are seen ahead moving to the side of the path to let a carriage pass through. As the carriage gets closer to Will, he recognizes the driver of the carriage to be Grant Applegate. Grant sees Will, pulls the carriage to the side of the path, calls out his name, and waves him over to him. "Will, I have two letters for you. They came in the post Friday and I plum forgot to give them to you." Grant hands Will the letters. Will looks at the return addresses and is wondering why one is from Oscar Kintoole, Trading Post Fort Townsend, and the other from Oscar Kintoole, Hastings Ranch.

"Thank you, Grant," Will says. Grant turns the carriage into the path again, and heads on his way. Will quickly opens the letter from Oscar, Fort Townsend. His eyebrows knit as he reacts to the news that Nashoba is holding Oscar captive and will exchange him only for Niabi. And the letter ends, "Do not tell the men of the fort or other White men. Come alone." It is signed "Oscar Kintoole." He opens the second letter, from Oscar, Hastings Ranch. It informs him that the captain from Fort Townsend paid a visit to the Hastings Ranch looking for information about Niabi. But the first letter is quite vexing with contents that Will did not foresee.

Having moved out of the path of others leaving the church, Harriet and Niabi wait on the side of the path for Will. Will walks toward Harriet and Niabi holding the letters, so Niabi cannot see either return addresses, fearing she may recognize the address of the trading post. Unfortunately, they did see him receive the letters and are curious. Harriet asks, "Who sent the letters?"

Spreading open his arms, Will gently touches each lady on their back. "I'll explain later. For now, you ladies go on home. I've got to find Dakota Sam."

Will turns around and walks against the church crowd until he passes the church and then he is among the crowd headed into town. He catches sight of Dakota's blue uniform up ahead. Will runs until he is close enough to yell, "Dakota." The nurturing church members come to his aid and pass the call up to Dakota, a first group yelling, "Dakota," then a second group closer to Dakota calling out "Dakota." Finally, Dakota stops, turns around and sees Will waving like a madman back down the path.

When Will reaches him out of breath, he pushes out, "I need your help." They move under a canopy of trees that block the sunlight, shading the road and allowing cool breezes to swirl through. "I received a letter from my closest friend. He's being held captive by the chief's son in the Indian Village near Fort Townsend."

"Woooo, wooo, chief's son." Dakota Sam shakes his head.

"I need your help to free him," Will pleads.

"Now, son, just the two of us? You want the two of us to go against a chief's son and all the manpower at his command?" Before Will can answer, Dakota adds, "Well, hell, I'm tired of waiting on your Master Grant. I'm about ripe for a little adventure. Now you don't want to get that fort involved? They can bring that chief's son to heel."

"I don't want to give him any reason to hurt Oscar. This is all my fault." Will drops his head and tells Dakota that he took Niabi from the village against her will.

"You coulda fooled me. That little squaw-lady looked like she was just on a friendly cross-country trip, pitching in with makin' camp, cookin'. I never thought one time that she had been kidnapped. So, it sounds like your friend bein' taken is more than for ransom—it's a form of revenge for damage to a man's honor, and by a chief's son too. Hot smoke! Why is the chief's son involved?"

"He is eyeing Niabi for his future wife," Will says.

"For a boy in Tennessee, you sure do know how to make a reputation for yourself in the Indian Territory. Are you planning to keep her? For good?"

"I can take her back with us and settle it all," Will says.

"I think it's a bad idea to take her on this trip. First, the weather will be bad. We'll have to coordinate getting in and getting out fast, I mean moving like foot soldiers on a hit and run mission. And if there is any shooting, you don't want her in the crossfire," Dakota Sam says.

"Let's avoid shooting if we can," Will says, putting up one hand.

"Well, I don't know how you negotiate with someone whose pride is damaged and mad enough to take a hostage," Dakota snaps back.

"By the time we get there, I will think of something," Will sighs. "I'll go pack and get Rodeo. Let's meet where we split off on the way into town, in say, two hours."

About a little over an hour later, Will arrives back at the cottage and enters the kitchen. "Who sent the letters?" asks Harriet. She and Niabi sit at the kitchen table with their eyes glued to his face.

"The letters are from my friend Oscar. He's in a bit of trouble, and needs my help." Will proceeds to get a change of clothing, rations for his saddlebag, and fills up his canteen with water.

"Should I . . ." Niabi asks, widening her eyes and gesturing with her head at Will "go with you?"

"No, it'll be safer for you to miss this trip and stay here where it's safe with my mother. Dakota Sam rides with me."

"Is that the ex-Union soldier you told me about?" Harriet asks, getting pots out to start dinner.

"Yes, Momma," Will says and continues gathering his gear.

After finishing packing, Harriet insists he eats something before traveling. She makes something for them all to eat. Niabi eats staring at him and breathing heavy. Will finishes eating, kisses his mother on the cheek, and gestures goodbye to Niabi. He grabs his saddlebags and heads to the barn to get Rodeo. Niabi follows him out, right on his heels.

When they are away from the cottage Niabi blurts out, "You *said* you would take me home the first chance you got."

Walking steadily, he responds, "I don't know how this trip is going to go. We're gonna be moving fast, and the weather may be against us." He stops, turns, and faces her. "I am responsible for you until I get you back to your village. I can't take the risk of something happening to you. Let me do this, and come spring we can safely return to your village." He turns and continues walking toward the barn. "And when I return you, I may have to drop you somewhere near the village so I have an easy escape."

Niabi, still on his heels says through clenched teeth, "You refuse to take me?"

"It's not safe, Niabi," Will insists.

Niabi stops, skins her lips back, fuming, and storms back to the cottage. He makes sure she is out of sight, and then puts his saddle on Rodeo and a saddle on FireTip. They all gallop out to meet Dakota Sam at the designated place.

Dakota waits where Will asked him, dressed in his grizzly bear coat, sitting on Blackie. The sun tips behind the towering trees, escaping the slight chill starting to hover. These are signs of the winter season preparing to greet them. Dakota sees Will riding up. "Oh, you bringin' her horse for the captive?"

"Yes, he will need a horse and this one is fast and obedient to me. It will also keep a certain young lady from following us," Will says.

Dakota grins. "Smart move."

As he predicted, Niabi waits until Harriet goes into her room to change out of her church clothes. Niabi quickly fills a canteen with water, gets some fresh bread, leaves a note in Will's bedroom on the night table, and slips out of the cottage quietly. She races to the barn, goes to FireTip's stall, and finds it empty. She lights a lantern and frantically goes from stall to stall, and looks out at the pastures for FireTip. Fred Johnson, the foreman, exits the office in the barn to go home and sees her frantically moving around. He goes to her to investigate.

"Hi, Miss Niabi. What do you need?"

"Do you know where my horse is, FireTip?"

"I saw him galloping outta here alongside Rodeo with Mr. Will. Mr. Will gave me no message for anyone about where he is going or when he is returning. He may be back soon."

"Siti!" she angrily cries out.

"I didn't catch that, Miss Niabi?" Fred says, looking her way squinting.

"Nothing, Mr. Fred. I'm going to bed." She takes a deep breath. "Good night, Mr. Fred."

As Niabi exits the barn, Jason rides up.

"Hi, what are you doing out here this fine evening? Is everything OK? Can I get something for you?" Jason asks with wine on his breath from visiting friends at a nearby ranch.

"Yes, my horse," Niabi says.

"Ahhhh . . . yes . . . Your horse is . . . FireStorm?"

"FireTip," Niabi says.

"Oh, sorry." Jason lights another lantern and rides through the barn looking around. "Well, it seems Mr. FireTip is missing. Do you want to borrow my horse?"

Seeing more lights on in the barn, Fred comes back again. "Oh, Mr. Jason. Do you need me to put up Dash?"

"No, no, Fred. I can do it this time. You go on back to your family. I'm gonna put up Dash, and then see Miss Niabi back to her cottage."

Jason puts Dash in his stall and clumsily gives him water and feed. She starts to help him, but her sense of charity has left with Will and FireTip. Overcome with anger, she leans against the closed gate of FireTip's stall, sulking. Jason walks over to her and looks into her eyes. "You know if there is anything you want that is in my powers to give to you, it's yours," he says and points his finger, touching her at the top of her chest. He stands in front of her, plants both hands against the gate on either side of her head, smiling and giving unbroken eye contact. Admiring his auburn-blonde mix hair and dark turquoise eyes, which are only surpassed by his gentle, jovial, and generous nature, she is put off by the smell of wine on his breath and clumsy posture. Although up to this time he has always acted like a gentleman toward her, his wine-influenced ogling of her makes her feel a little uncomfortable. Then she remembers her rage against Will for leaving her.

"Mr. Jason, I am thinking that you are trying to court me."

"Court? Well," nodding, he says, "yes, this could be considered courting." Trying to keep his balance, he spreads his legs into a wider stance, still leaning with both hands against the gate in front of her, and smiling.

Niabi thinks he has that look the women elders spoke of: sweaty hands, flared nostrils, look of fever, eyes staring at her lips and breasts. She hates Will for blocking her chance to catch up with him and Dakota by taking FireTip. So, she decides to entice Jason.

"Mr. Jason, do you want to kiss me?" She wants to drown her anger in Jason's kisses.

"Kiss? Oh, yeah. May I?"

"Yes." Niabi lifts her chin.

His wobbly head comes toward her face, and his lips press down on hers. She waits for the tingles, bells, a rush, anything similar to what she feels when Will kisses her.

Jason finishes, grins, and says, "That was nice."

Niabi looks at him perplexed. "Again, but harder," she says firmly.

"Oh, I didn't realize this is a test." He stands up straight and grabs her by the shoulders, steps into her, kisses her lips harder, and slightly opens his mouth to allow his tongue to gently graze the inside of her lips.

When they are done, he says, "Oh my, I'm getting worked up here. How about you?"

"Yes, I am too. But let's not do this anymore. This is not proper." Niabi turns her face away from his.

"Of course." Jason steps back, perplexed as to what just happened. "I'll walk you to the cottage, I guess," says Jason. "Is that OK?"

"Yes, that is OK," Niabi says feeling a little guilty for using him that way.

The next morning Niabi helps Harriet prepare breakfast. "You've been quiet all morning. Are you sad Will's gone?" Harriet asks.

"I don't know what I feel about him. One day, I like him, then he makes me mad and I want to cut him." Niabi swings her hand in a cutting motion.

"Oh, dear. He can have that effect on people. He's very helpful, thoughtful, and then he goes after what he wants and can be downright inconsiderate. But most love him because, under all that young male posturing, he has a good heart."

"Momma Harriet," says Niabi.

"Yes, honey," Harriet says.

"How did you know Mr. Lawton was the . . . the one for you?" Niabi asks.

"Well, you just know. You meet different young men. Some come courting; others are too shy. You invite them to dinner; you try to get to know them. But there is always the one who will touch your heart in a way that the others can't. His company brings you laughter, makes you feel safe, and most important he should believe in God. The Bible in 2nd Corinthians 6:14 says, 'A couple should not be unequally yoked.' That means you should have ideas in common—similar ideas in faith, goals in life, things you like to do together, and the most important thing is you love and respect each other. I should say that real love drags in all the others. If there is true love between you, you learn to compromise and you can build common goals, faith, all of it because you want to make it work."

"Momma Harriet, I am going to surprise you with the next question."

"Oh, then, let me get my coffee." Harriet pulls up a chair and sits next to Niabi. "OK, I'm ready."

"What if you kiss a man and you feel your skin heating up and bells ringing inside, then you kiss another man . . .?"

"Another man?" Harriet's eyes widen. "Go on."

"Yes, another man, and you feel nothing. Just smell the wine on his breath, and feel his rough skin against your face."

"Well," Harriet pauses, and then restarts, "first, you shouldn't be going around kissing different men; I must tell you that. Second, there is a process for courting. But I think we may have passed that point since there is 'another man' in the picture. You really should court one man at a time, and hopefully, you select the one that you feel has the best chance at winning your heart. And there are no guarantees. You may spend a lot of time with the one you selected, and then he, for whatever reasons, determines he is no longer interested." Harriet pauses again, and then continues. "Now, if I heard you correctly, it seems that the first man made a connection with you. I mean, your inner being or spirit is excited by him. Does he have the same reaction when he's with you?"

"I think so. He has told me once that he can't keep his hands off me," Niabi says.

"Now, has he? Have you two . . .?" Harriet asks gingerly making a face. It takes Niabi a moment before she understands what she is asking.

"Oh, no . . . No, no, we have only kissed two times and hugged one time, unless the first kiss included a hug." Niabi's face reddens.

"Is the first or second man, my son?" Harriet asks.

"Yes," Niabi says softly.

"Well, I think I should bow out at this point because I promised myself I would steer clear of his personal business. That's just a promise I made to myself to protect my nerves."

CHAPTER 8

LIFE FOR A LIFE

———

ONE hundred miles of road winding through meadows and forests is behind Will and Dakota Sam as they maintain their southwest heading. Although this is the same journey Will has made many times before, the urgency to resolve the crisis at their destination makes the journey this time seem much longer. As they travel from one state to the next, Will expects the ground to change from rich black soil to the decorative red clay characteristic of the Indian Territory. However, this trip brings him through the land during a cusp of seasonal change. He will witness the land contort itself from green and bountiful to brown and scant, and then to white and harsh. He expects the land will level out into valleys dispersed among rolling hills flowing into plateaus of weather-beaten plains. But this is Will's first time traveling within the region as it changes from autumn to winter. The vistas of green grass he has become accustomed to will now be hidden by mounds of leaves before transitioning to grass blanketed by new-fallen snow.

Will and Dakota may inevitably be forced to extend their trip by stopping at towns along the journey to gain shelter from torrential rains or deep layers of snow. Snow especially, because horses may weaken from frostbite on long hauls like this. It is truly a land of the untamed and determined. Long rides such as this can put you in thought for hours. Since Dakota is more of a lecturer than a conversationalist, for a portion of the trip, when Dakota keeps his thoughts to himself, Will returns to conducting his usual internal debate. *Where can I acquire land? It most likely will be in the West. Am I cut out to be a farmer in the West? I travel through this land, either to meet a cattle drive or be on one, but never stopping to stay a while and engage with the elements, testing my survival skills. Can food be grown here? What kind of food? The ones we seek, who are holding my friend Oscar, are in league with this land. They were born under these harsh skies, endure the worst seasons, and survive off of whatever the land chooses to yield. They are a proud people made of stamina and grit. They walked the Trail of Tears for God's sake, and survived. Do I have such stamina to carve a living out of raw land?*

The Bible speaks of reaping what you sow. Indeed, my romantic escapade may have cost me the life of my one good friend; no, he's more like a brother. Growing up on the Applegate Ranch as an only child left me unbalanced, as far as casually mingling with others. I either found a reason to say something, or said nothing at all. I either engaged in a game I thought I could win, or I did not play at all. I left no room for exploring possibilities or taking risks. My role model is my father, and he was an excellent horseman. He talked horses, trained horses, bred horses, raced horses, and found time for nothing else with exception of mother and me. I want to be like him, always in control, never off-balance, or feeling inadequate, to be one who takes charge of his future. And so, these thoughts underly my reasoning for taking Niabi. I knew she would have to choose a man soon, and I wanted to be in the running. I saw her and I wanted her. It's as simple as that. What were my choices? How could I overcome the odds that I would never be in the running for her hand? I rationalized all my alternatives. Contrary to what Oscar said, I did think it through—I knew I only stood a chance if she could spend time with me. I brought her to my home, where she could see me for who I was and what I could offer her as a mate. I thought if she really knew me, I would win out. But before I left Indian Territory, right after I had taken her, I came to realize that what I did was all wrong and selfish. I had been heartless to her. Tied her with a rope like a lassoed steer. Took her from the only home she had ever known. Threw her into harm's way, and finally thrust her into a culture with a purpose foreign to her, a culture set up to demean her and her culture. And if that wasn't enough, she's been asked to earn her keep in this foreign environment, asked to take ridicule if she does not catch on. And to stoke the fire hotter, my friend has somehow become a pawn in this drama I've created. I shared with Oscar my hopes and dreams of owning a farm, building a house, and finding a mate. He is learning in a rare tragic form how I go about finding a mate.

Dakota came along without criticizing me for why we are traipsing across the country to rescue Oscar. I will be beholden to him for coming along and not questioning my decisions.

Emerging from his rambling thoughts, Will speaks to Dakota, "In a little while it will be dark. Rodeo's breathing is tightening. We had better find a place to make camp."

"There's no water hole nearby. We'll just have tah make as best a camp as we can with our current supply," Dakota says.

"I've got my drover's tent and blankets," Will says.

Another sunset, and they are about four days away from their final destination. Will feeds the horses, gives them water, and begins brushing Rodeo. FireTip looks on, and Will tells him he is next.

"You take better care of that horse than I have seen people care for their little 'uns. What are you going to do if you ever get stranded out here with nothin', and are faced with starvin' to death or eatin' your prized pet? Ha ha ha!" Dakota laughs while lying in the tent with his face in view through the tent's opening.

Will glances at him and keeps brushing Rodeo. "Rodeo is family. I was there when my dad birthed him, and then he was given to me as a colt, just weaned. So, I'm the only family he has, too."

"Aw stop, I'm gonna tear up," Dakota says, rubbing his eyes.

"No, I could never treat Rodeo like anything but my prized stallion. He is very smart, fast, and reliable, better than the best stallions around." Will continues to stroke Rodeo.

The next couple of days they see snow flurries. If it is just the wind kicking up over the flat plains, our two riders must dart within a canyon or lay the horses down, sheltering in place behind them to ride it out. Dakota tells stories of the Civil War, and how his regiment managed through the snow, freezing ice, and thunderstorms. When Dakota starts talking about slave auctions he saw or heard about, Will knows he is beginning to feel more comfortable with him. He grits his teeth when he speaks of a sale that separated husband and wife, or mother and child. And he ends the story with, "That is ungodly, ungodly I tell you."

One night he talks for hours about different plantations and how they were before the war, about how near the end of the war slaves were sold off, or traded as a survival means necessary to keep the master's family from going under. Even though many White plantation owners had to relocate their families when they lost their land and homes, the slaves had to remain and were the last bit of bartering medium left among the master's possessions. All the grand plantations in the South, and even some in the North, measured their wealth by how many slaves they owned. Dakota preaches and scorns and works himself into a stupor of fatigue before he keels over into sleep.

They experience days of light snow and heavy rain. They can deal with that. Not seen yet is heavy snow, which would pin them down in a town for days. They begin to realize they are lucky that the winter isn't harsher. Knowing they may be able to get into the Indian Territory and back out without too much trouble from the weather gives them confidence.

The morning comes when Will recognizes they are not far from the Indian village. He decides it's best to steer away from the front of the village where most travelers pass to enter Fort Townsend. He finds a trail leading to the woods behind the village. He quietly explains to Dakota that this is the Choctaw village where he thinks Oscar is being held. He points out that adjacent to the village is a trading post that sells goods and products made and harvested by the villagers, and, five miles farther west is the main entrance to Fort Townsend.

"Our scouting should start here," Dakota suggests glancing around and looking up at the trees.

At day's end when the villagers move inside, Will and Dakota Sam creep in closer to the village, and climb high into one of the trees nestled behind rows and rows of chukkas, tipis, and other dwellings and structures. From that height, they have a bird's-eye view of the village and the back of the trading post where there is a large garden. It takes a while for Will to get comfortable resting on limbs in the huge flaky tree. As they fit themselves among the branches, he just knows someone will hear or see all of the debris falling to the ground from the tree. Rodeo, FireTip, and Blackie are tied about thirty feet behind them. Their hopes are high that they will determine Oscar's whereabouts and get him out of there before being discovered.

Dakota scours over the dwellings and inhabitants with his U.S. Army telescope, a souvenir from his tour of duty in the Civil War. Nothing seems unusual. He points out what he suspects is the chief's dwelling, which is extra-large with a pavilion area near it possibly used for gatherings and assemblies. Dakota sees workers leaving the garden area and women calling their children inside. And then something unusual does happen. Playing with a dog, an Indian boy child throws a stick too close to a chukka on the outskirts of the community, forcing the dog and boy to run almost into the chukka. Two male villagers, who look as though they are in idle conversation, immediately lunge forward to shoo the dog and boy away from the area. It isn't the chief's dwelling, nor does it carry any insignia or markings of significance. So, they wonder, can this dwelling be the one where Oscar is being held?

"We'll have to go down for a closer look," Dakota whispers.

"That's my job, Dakota. I've created this mess. I have to take all the risks," Will says while climbing down. Then he stops climbing and looks up at Dakota. "And absolutely no blood is to be spilled during this rescue."

"Then you must be a miracle worker because there's no guarantee we're not gonna get shot at!" Dakota quietly barks, following Will down the tree.

"You can help me by having the horses on standby ready to race out of here once I get back with Oscar." Will continues climbing down the tree.

"I can have the horses ready. Just make tracks out of there. The numbers are not in our favor," Dakota says firmly in a low tone.

As nightfall blankets the village, the human movement grows slower and slower, until the last tribal man tucks himself into a furry pallet by a fire outside of a chukka. There are no guards on duty because these are peaceful times. The fort is nearby, and no Whites would dare venture into the village to cause trouble.

With cut-up strips from flour sacks surrounding both feet to muffle his steps, Will crouches down and creeps into the slumbering village. He maneuvers his way to the designated chukka on the outskirts of the village. He walks crouched down, and then on hands and knees, crawling to the back of the dwelling. Placing his head against a crack in the structure's wall, from the outside he hears nothing. He constantly looks to the left and right for any signs of movement. But all is well. He has no choice now but to take a chance and enter the dwelling to see if this is where Oscar is being held. As quietly as he can, he crawls around to the entrance that's covered by a heavy weaved blanket. Lifting the covering just high enough to peer inside, he sees a small fire in the center of the dwelling. The fire keeps the temperature inside habitable, but has burnt down low and requires more wood. He strains his eyes to see by the flickering fire light, and makes out strange formations in the shadowy darkness. After his eyes adjust, he determines a man is lying on a platform three feet off the ground attached to the inside wall of the chukka. With close examination, he also sees a bushy dark mustache. How many Indians wear mustaches? And one especially groomed according to the "de French way" as Oscar usually brags? It is indeed Oscar. Now to awaken him and get him out without alerting anyone. Will slowly crawls under the entrance covering on hands and knees, scampers over to Oscar, and taps him on the forehead. Anticipating Oscar blurting out something,

Will uses his hand to cover Oscar's mouth. Oscar jolts awake in sheer shock from someone putting their hand on his face, but to his delight, it is his dear friend.

"What kept ya?" Oscar's words are muffled by Will's hand.

Will removes his hand. "Keep quiet while I untie you," Will says.

Zealous over finally being rescued Oscar says low, "I thought I was going to have to write to Frederick Douglass himself to get me outta this fix."

"Shhh, keep quiet; we're trying to get out without being discovered." Will uses a small knife kept on his holster belt and quickly cuts the ropes that tie Oscar to the platform in the chukka. Once freed, Will cautions him to crawl as he does, and follow close behind him out of the chukka. Once outside, from the back of the chukka, they have to cross an open grassy area. Will surveys around carefully to see if anyone is about. The body Will can see is the sleeper in the furry pallet by the fire. If the sleeper's eyes open, he will have a clear view of their escape. Well, they can't chance staying in one spot too long, so Will motions for them both to move out across the open grassy area, keeping their heads down. They run for the tree line on the edge of the village with their heads down. Before they can clear the open grassy area and reach the surrounding trees, a gust of wind blows stirring the sleeper. His eyes wince and crack open for a second, and he notices two large life forms moving away from the last row of chukkas. It startles him because his first notion is that they are animals, perhaps bears or other predators. He rises to his feet and walks forward to get a closer look. Mindful to continue looking around to ensure their escape is undetected, Will spots the risen sleeper looking their way, and tells Oscar, "We got to run for it!" The sleeper still can't tell if he is seeing animals or children playing. But his reasoning soon draws a mental line from the place where he spots the moving figures to the prisoner's chukka. He runs over to the chukka that held Oscar, and throws back the covering of the entrance. Surveying the inside, he sees cut ropes and an uninhabited chukka. He runs to Nashoba's chukka and shouts in his language, "Your hostage is gone!"

Once in the trees, Will and Oscar run upright at full sprint to where Dakota waits mounted on Blackie and holding Rodeo and FireTip's reins. Nashoba wastes no time in grabbing his rifle, running in the direction the sleeper told him to run, and giving out a yelp like a code call.

Will takes Rodeo and FireTip's reins from Dakota and directs Oscar to mount FireTip, causing Oscar to frown, blanched with fear. "You don't mean mount *him*? I'd feel safer with my captors."

"We don't have time for the chatter, gents," Dakota says watching growing movement in the village. After Will mounts Rodeo, he takes FireTip's reins and holds him steady so Oscar can mount him. "Get on, O. I've got him." Oscar leaps onto FireTip.

Dakota whips his horse around and leads the way out of the thick-tree area, followed by Oscar, and then Will. They kick their heels into the sides of their horses, and the animals move out as fast as they can. Dakota has to race Blackie faster to stay ahead of FireTip. Will turns to see if any villagers are in pursuit. When Dakota, in the lead, gets beyond fifty feet of the village grounds, two male villagers appear out of nowhere pointing bow and arrows straight at Dakota and Oscar. In response to Nashoba's yelping code calls, archers lying in wait were signaled to stop a possible rescue and escape.

Dakota yells, "Ambush ahead. Ambush!" Then he charges the one pointing the arrow at him. The archer releases the arrow aimed at Dakota, and it glances off his thick bearskin coat. The other archer fires, and his arrow pierces Oscar's arm. Dakota continues his charge toward his archer, sending the archer who shot at him to the ground. Dakota bashes his head with the butt of his rifle. Remembering Will's admonition to avoid blood being spilled, Dakota whips around his rifle and fires a shot over the head of the second archer, and that archer runs away. Coming out of the trees behind them, Nashoba hears Dakota's rifle shot and, still sprinting, aims and fires his rifle at them. His shot hits Rodeo in the hip, and he cries out in pain. Will slows him, looks around Rodeo's body, and sees blood streaming down Rodeo's leg. Will stops, jumps off raising his hands high in the air, and yells, "Don't shoot. Don't shoot anymore. We are hit. We give up!"

Dakota also stops, sees Will standing next to Rodeo, but tells Oscar, "Keep going! Ride!" Then aiming his rifle at Nashoba, Dakota yells, "Will, come on, I can pick him off from here."

"No! Nobody shoots. You go on, Dakota, and help Oscar," Will yells. Dakota turns and gallops off to catch up to Oscar.

Holding his rifle on Will, Nashoba walks up slowly approaching Will. He tells Will to throw his holster gun over to him. Will complies. As Will turns to look at Rodeo's injury, Nashoba keeps the rifle pointed at Will. Examining the wound, Will says, "Don't shoot me. I am reaching for my knife on my belt to dig out the bullet. Don't shoot. I need to get the bullet out." Will pulls out the same short knife from his holster belt that he used to cut Oscar's ropes. The bullet looks like it's not too deep. He tells Rodeo, "Hold still, buddy. Hold." He presses around the bullet hole. Rodeo emits high-pitched whinnies, but manages to hold still. Rodeo screeches when Will uses the tip of the knife to enter the wound and roll the bullet out into his hand. At that moment, Will looks up and smiles. Rubbing Rodeo, Will says, "Well done, buddy. Well done."

Nashoba now stands right behind Will, holding the rifle on him. "You are the Negro man I was searching for. You are the one that took Niabi."

Talako rides over to them, bringing Nashoba's horse. Speaking in Choctaw, Talako tells him the chief was awakened by all the commotion and gunshots, and wants him to meet the chief in front of the chief's dwelling right away. Nashoba looks at Talako with dread. Before Will and Nashoba can leave the area, Dakota rides back slowly with his hands in the air. Nashoba quickly switches and begins pointing his rifle at Dakota, and tells Talako to get Dakota's rifle.

Dakota says to Will, "Oscar needs patching up. He took one in the arm. If you are going to stay around here, we might as well use their healer to patch him up." Next, Dakota addresses Nashoba, "I assume you are the chief's son. Can one of your gentler men bring Oscar back in? He's unarmed, just bleeding." Nashoba calls one of the archers and asks him to fetch Oscar and bring him back to the village.

Nashoba, Will, Dakota, and Talako make their way back to the village, and enter the pavilion area, a large structure with a roof but no sides, that is located in front of the chief's large dwelling. A subset of lanterns is lit to illuminate the area. The chief steps out of his dwelling wrapped in furs and marvels at the uninvited guests on their land at night. An archer brings a bleeding Oscar riding FireTip to where they are assembled. To stop the bleeding, Dakota crudely fashioned a tourniquet on Oscar's arm using a rope.

Chief Samuels says, "I don't see Niabi, so your plan to exchange her for the Negro man did not work." Nashoba looks surprised that he knows about Oscar being held at the village. The chief continues, "Yes, I knew he was here. I would not be a good chief if I don't have ways to learn what is happening in my own village."

Pointing at Will, Nashoba says, "Father, this is the man seen with Niabi. You must give the order to have him whipped to get to the truth."

Looking at the three Negro men, Chief Samuels asks, "Do either of you know the whereabouts of our Niabi?"

Will says, "Yes, sir. Niabi is at my home in Tennessee."

Unable to contain himself, Nashoba shouts, "I told you! I told you!"

"Silence!" the chief says, and continues directing his questions now to Will only. "Did you harm her?"

"No, sir. I . . . I have the highest respect for her. She is at my home with my mother. She eats at our table, sleeps under our roof in her own bed, in her own separate room. I promised her that I would bring her back to the village before the next twelve moons. I gave her my word."

"Liar! Liar!" Nashoba yells.

"My son!" Chief Samuels says loudly. Then he calms himself to address his son, "Your blood is running hot because you know the truth now about where Niabi is and who took her. Now I say to you, my son, listen to my words with your mind, and not your heart. This chaos created by this Negro man and you requires the mind of a chief to work it out. But this is not my test. Today, this is your test. Work this out, but when you do, you must consider all wants. Consider your wants, their wants, and most important Niabi's wants. I know you will find the right path for bringing Niabi home safely. And now I will return to my sleep."

After watching his father leave and go back inside his chukka, Nashoba walks over and positions himself nose to nose with Will. "I should cut your throat where you stand, and honor our Great Spirit and ancestors with your blood flowing down and soaking this sacred place where we assemble," he says. "But my father desires me to be wise like him. What can you say to cool my blood?"

"I promised Niabi I would bring her home next spring," Will says. "I gave her my word. Now, I give you my word."

"Your word means nothing to me! I captured your friend to flush you out like the spineless, hiding prey you are. We sent you a message and asked you to bring her. Why didn't you bring her now?"

"We were traveling fast. We didn't know what the weather would do. And I would never ever put her in danger. She is safe at my home, with my mother."

"I don't know how you expect me to let you go and trust that you will bring her back," Nashoba says.

Dakota speaks up. "If I may add something to the discussion, I'm sure you don't want the fort captain to know that you have possession of that rifle." Dakota twists his head, looking sideways to get a good look at the rifle Nashoba still brandishes in his hand. "That's not an old rifle. It looks like a Springfield Model 1873. There's not many ways you can get your hands on that. Let's say someone found it on a dead soldier after a skirmish or battle somewhere?"

Nashoba's hot blood appears to start cooling down.

Dakota turns to Will. "I think you are now in a position to barter to get us outta here. Tell him everything you need. Just lay it all out there. I mean tell him exactly what you need."

"I need for you to let the three of us go home. I need your healer to wrap Oscar's wound from your man shooting him with an arrow. I need your healer to help me dress my horse's wound. And once we leave, I give you my word, I will bring Niabi back before twelve moons," Will says with authority.

"Your word, your word. What power do I have over you to make you keep your word to me? You may go back home and I never see you, any of you, again." Nashoba glares at Will.

"I can give you power over me. There is only one other creature walking this earth that I have loved most of my life other than my mother." Will walks over to Rodeo whose blood is still trickling down his leg. "That only other creature is this horse." Tears begin to well up in his eyes. "I will leave him, whom I've never been separated from since I was a boy. I was there when he came out of his mother's womb, and started training him from when he was two years old. He is my one prized possession. Even your children here in the village are my witnesses that he is very smart, obeys my commands, and knows my feelings. I leave him here as proof that I will return in twelve moons." Rodeo holds his head down so Will can hug him around his neck. "Do you accept my word now?"

Nashoba walks away and grumbles, "You equate our Niabi to your horse." Nashoba then raises his tone and says, "Alright, Negro man. I will keep your horse until you return with Niabi. And if twelve moons pass, and you do not return Niabi to this village, I will take your horse, cut out his heart, feast on his smart spirit, and use his hide to make a fine garment for myself."

Liola, Niabi's mentor, wraps Oscar's wound well enough to hold for travel. She blots and treats Rodeo's wound and ties a dressing on him. Will gives them instructions on what to feed Rodeo and to make water available at least three times a day. Liola also fills a bag made of animal skin with personal items she thinks Niabi would need during her visit away from the village. Will and Oscar both straddle FireTip, Dakota Sam is on Blackie, and all three ride out of the village destined for the Hastings Ranch.

It takes a while before FireTip settles down after leaving Rodeo. It is as though he is struggling to keep moving away from the village without him. As they cross the Red River, Will remarks, "I should have ridden another horse for this trip. I should have . . ."

"Will, he's better off healing there, and you'll get him back," Oscar says trying to soothe Will.

After days of traveling in the cold weather, they grow weary, mostly because they are completely out of water. They utilize every second of daylight to travel and only stop to rest the horses. The light snow melts allowing them to periodically stop and harvest what fresh water they can, but they have to keep moving. Will, acting as their lead scout, finds remaining clumps of snow cover the trails making the territory unfamiliar terrain to him. Eventually, Will recognizes landmarks indicating the town of Larrington is close. He remembers once Tom let the crew stop there to let off steam, and he somehow was charged with bringing drunk Chris and Clancy back to the herd by leaning them against their horses' necks and slowly guiding them back to camp.

They avoid a full-out gallop into Larrington to reach drinking water, and instead pace themselves to the edge of town. Finding their way to the Negro section, these battered travelers board the horses so they are watered and fed, and then replenish themselves with food and water before renting one room. After dinner, the three share a bottle of whisky. The two novice drinkers, Oscar and Will, justify their drinking as being for medicinal purposes. Dakota states his reasons are for escaping life's pain. All three stumble to their rented room, and agree Oscar should take the bed. Blankets are scrounged to make pallets for Dakota and Will on the floor. They don't know how long they were sleeping. They were awakened by a maid who comes to change the linen, and is surprised to see the room is still occupied. She is greeted and promised a generous tip to have coffee, eggs, bacon, and biscuits brought to their room.

After they eat and feel well rested, the three depart to continue their trek for the Hastings Ranch. Based on Will's knowledge of the distance, he expects them to arrive in the morning. The days are cool with no more falling snow, and the nights are breezy, which makes it hard to keep the campfire going. During this part of the whole trip, no hour passes without hearing Dakota question why Will could not have ridden Blackie and he walk the whole way. Dakota says that walking doesn't bother him because his Union army regiment walked from Vicksburg, Mississippi, to Lynchburg, Virginia. He says he walked so far that shoes only got in the way of studying the road with his bare feet and toes, studying it for moisture from the last rain, for soft soil which could signal fruit trees were nearby, or feel the pounding from a herd of buffalo headed his way. "Feet are for more than just walkin'," Dakota pitches over the campfire. "Feet are an extension of eyes, ears, nose, and taste."

During the whole trip, Dakota wrangles out several stories, drifts off to sleep, and falls over on his saddle and saddlebags. Oscar and Will sit there wrapped in blankets with knees folded up into their chests, wringing their hands in the night air. On the last night around the campfire after Dakota falls asleep, Oscar says quietly, "I've been meaning to ask you, where did you meet this ol' geezer?"

"Niabi and I happened upon him during my trip home."

"Niabi. So that's her name. Will, I feel bad about you being forced to rescue me, and about Rodeo," Oscar says.

"What's done is done. I had to do something to get all of us out of there," Will says.

Looking up into the night's sky, Oscar continues, "I can't help feeling that it was my fault that this happened. I forced you to give up something so important to you."

"It wasn't your fault, O. It's actually my fault. Niabi did come home with me; I just left out the part about taking her by force."

"What! You told me that day in the kitchen at Hastings Ranch before we left on the drive that you wanted to *invite* her to your home for a visit, but you said nothing about doing something like that to her!" Oscar stares at Will, mouth ajar.

"I know it was a stupid thing to do. But I did it. Just took her. I did nothing else to her. Rest assured, her virtue has not been compromised, Oscar."

Oscar just stares at him and shakes his head. "Well, is she worth all this mess you've put us through?"

"O, I don't know how this is going to end. I had a burning passion for her in the beginning. She hated me, although she let me kiss her. So, I have learned to temper my feelings and have tried to forget how I feel about her, especially since I know she is unhappy, and I have to get her home as soon as I can. She occasionally smiles at me, and that stirs my feelings and gets my hopes up. But I've come to realize, it's really not good, unless the woman feels about you, the way you feel about her."

"What does your mother say about it all?"

"Oh, no, she knows nothing. If she knew, I would be tarred and feathered right now!"

The next day as they move farther south, the terrain covered with patches of ice changes from the prairie lowland grass to grassland especially good for cattle grazing, and they know they are nearing the Hastings Ranch. They stop to get their bearings. Peering through his telescope, Dakota yells, "I see something that looks like a marker."

Will reaches for the telescope, mounts it on his eye, and exclaims, "We're here!" The Hastings archway on the border of the ranch juts out of the ground. And not a moment too soon, because Oscar's wound has reopened from being jarred from the ride, and he complains of pain and fever.

They enter the ranch and aren't three hundred feet past the archway when they are spotted. A maid working on the second floor of the main house sees riders in the distance approaching. She alerts Mrs. Hasting who comes out on her second-floor terrace. She calls to Mr. Hastings who has just exited the house with someone heading to the barn and gets his attention. Mrs. Hastings calls out, "John, riders are coming."

Mr. Hastings stares toward the archway wondering who it could be, and then turns to look up at Mrs. Hastings as if they are sharing the same wish. He motions to Ben. "Ride out and see who it is."

Ben mounts a nearby steed and gallops out to intercept the travelers. As soon as he sees Will and Oscar, he rides back in a frenzy to the yard and yells, "It's Oscar and Will!"

The travelers ride around to the rear of the main house. Will helps Oscar off FireTip, and they all enter the main house through the back door. Will asks Dakota to wait inside the kitchen by the door. "Wait here. I'll get him settled then round up some food and water for us."

Will helps Oscar to his room, trailed by Mrs. Hastings. She throws her hand over her mouth when she sees the bloody wound on his arm. Unable to hold her tongue any longer she says, "We were out of our minds worried about what happened to you. Matt found some tracks outside Waco and said the Indians had you. I told Mr. Hastings to contact the fort, but Captain Horton was still on the road. Mr. Hastings, Matt, and Tom talked and decided to wait until this heightened climate settled. First, the Indian girl went missing, then you went missing. But I knew you would be OK. I knew it, because, who hurts a great chef like you?"

Mrs. Hastings remains at the door of Oscar's room and supervises getting him settled in his quarters. The maid brings water and Will helps him remove his coat and begins removing his soiled bandages. Mrs. Hastings had the maid put fresh linen on his bed weeks before. She asks Oscar if he needs something to eat, perhaps a cup of hot soup.

"I'm OK; you don't have to," Oscar says working with Will to change the dressing on his wound.

Mrs. Hastings sees the extent of his wound and her face distorts into a frown. "Nonsense," she exclaims. "You lie down. I'm sending someone to fetch Doc Stevenson."

"I don't need a doctor. I just need to change the dressing on my wound," Oscar says.

"Doc Stevenson will help with that. You don't want to get an infection, Oscar," Mrs. Hastings insists, remaining in the room's doorway taking deep breaths and fidgeting all the while.

Others are coming to the room. Mrs. Hastings looks back, smiles, and steps aside for Mr. Hastings, who enters through the doorway of Oscar's room accompanied by an elderly European-looking gentleman with more salt in his salt-and-pepper gray hair than black hair, a bushy mustache exactly like Oscar's, and finely dressed.

"Grandpa!" says a surprised Oscar.

CHAPTER 9

REDEMPTION AND REVELATIONS

———

WHILE Niabi is drying the dishes and placing them into the cabinet, Harriet thanks her for cleaning up the kitchen after dinner. As Harriet enters her bedroom to retire for the evening, she reaches into her pocket and remembers she received a letter when the post arrived today. "Niabi, I received a letter from Will," Harriet says. "He says they rescued his friend Oscar, and he and Dakota Sam are on their way back home."

"That is good news," Niabi says, trying to decide whether she is still mad at Will for leaving on his trip west without her and taking FireTip so she couldn't follow him. While he is away, she channels her anger into her work at the main house, keeping herself busy changing the linen on beds upstairs, organizing the linen closets, helping Sheila with the washing, putting the wash on the clothesline, and folding clothes. She has had two interesting experiences, though: one with Clarence the gardener, and another with Grant Applegate.

Harriet had told Niabi about a gardener who tends to the fruit and vegetable gardens on the ranch. "He's a little grouchy," she had said. "You should stay clear of the gardens lest you have his permission to care for, or harvest food growing out there." One morning, while helping Sheila hang the wash on the clothesline, Niabi saw a large dark-skinned Negro man with a puffy face working in the garden on his knees. He was tilling the soil and planting seeds all wrong. He'd be lucky to get any kind of decent crop. Niabi asked Sheila to introduce her to him because Harriet said she shouldn't talk to a strange man that she has not been properly introduced to.

Sheila said, "Come on, then. Seems like you don't have enough aggravation in your life, so you want to put Clarence in it."

As Sheila got near Clarence, he turned around and said, "No need comin' out ch-ere. I put all the veggies I could harvest in a box next to the kitchen door."

"No, Mr. Clarence, that's not what I wanted. This here is Niabi. She's Harriet's new assistant," Sheila said.

Clarence looked at Niabi and formed a sly grin. "Somebody told me an Indian girl was working here, and then I saw your pretty self going in and outta the main house one day. Aren't you far from your home, child?"

Anxious to get back to work, Sheila said, "Well, I gots stuff to tend to. Niabi, this is Clarence. Good day to the two a you." Sheila went back to a basket of damp wash needing to be hung up on the clothesline.

"What can I do for you, Niabi, or are you wanting some of my veggies for yourself?" Clarence asked.

Niabi touched a leaf of his greens. "Your vegetables may not be fit to eat. You are killing the soil by tilling it like that. And what kind of seeds are you planting?"

"Now, hold on there, little lady. You just showed up here, and old Clarence has been working this garden for years. We always have a good crop. And I haven't had any complaints," Clarence said and pulled up a weed growing near his collards.

Back at the clothesline, Sheila heard Clarence and yelled out, "The greens are always a little bitter, Clarence."

"Bitter, hear that?" Niabi said. "She said the greens are bitter. That's because the soil is bitter. You have to taste the soil and balance it out between bitter and weak."

"What are you talking about?" Clarence stopped and eyed her.

"To make the soil less bitter, workers in the garden at my village mix into the soil burnt bone ash. If the soil was too weak, they would add strong elements like ground-up fish parts or droppings from horses or cows. The soil is the womb, and you place the seed in the womb to grow, just like a child grows in a woman's womb," Niabi said.

"I use to add horse poop to the soil. But Mrs. Applegate said the garden smelled, attracted droves of flies, and was too close to the main house since the smell was blown straight through her windows, giving her the vapors," Clarence said. He then paused, looking down at his crops and considering what Niabi said. "You had success with these methods, and the vegetables tasted good?"

"Yes, tilling the soil, the way you are doing it kills the soil. All the natural ingredients for growing are underneath the soil on top, and tilling pulls the good stuff up to the top to be blown away by the wind or diluted in strength when you water. And, we plant corn, squash, and bean seeds all together. The beans add something to the soil. The corn provides a ladder for plants to grip onto as they rise out of the soil, and the squash is a cover to protect new growth and keeps away bugs. There are also methods to draw bees to help the plants spread around an area, ways to save the soil on top from being blown away, and ways to protect seedlings from the sun. There are even ways to surround the garden with plants that give off a more pleasing smell to cover the smell of animal poop. The Great Spirit has given us everything we need. Everything has to work together to grow delicious, healthy food."

Clarence fell back on his butt in the dirt. "Child, you are just full of information. I'm willing to listen and try some of your ideas, and see if they make a difference."

Niabi agreed to work with Clarence. When she returned to the main house, her spirits were lifted high. She finished her work in the main house, which wasn't extensive. At the end of the day, she spoke to Clarence again, and they discussed her helping him in the garden and even adding an herbal section to the garden, where she could continue studying the herbs Liola taught her about. There were uncleared fields near the ranch where she spotted a few different herbs, and she was told it was okay for Harriet to order other herbs through a catalogue at the general store. Niabi was finding life at the Applegate Ranch very rewarding, despite how she got there, and not to mention the small remuneration she is receiving monthly for her services out of ranch revenue. She has saved her money thinking, if Will doesn't take her back, she would buy herself a train ticket.

The experience with Grant started one morning out at the clothes-line on the side of the main house. Niabi had explained to Sheila that her tribe considers a female displaying any part of her leg to be indecent.

Sheila argued back, "That's got to be hard, trying to get work done wearing the long dresses."

"Well, some younger women wear shorter dresses but with leg-gings made of cloth or deerskin that cover the legs from ankle to knee. Like the ones I wore when I arrived here," Niabi explained.

"So, if I'm running and my dress kicks up like so, I'm a fallen woman?" Sheila asked, and they laughed. Niabi kicked her dress up, and it flew above the knees. She and Sheila made "oooo" sounds and fell on a bench near the clothesline with more laughing. While they were tussling their dresses up above the knees, Grant was watching them from his bedroom window. While fastening his shirt's buttons then buttoning his pants, he is enjoying the display below, and expe-riencing an uncontrollable male attraction to one set of the knees. That afternoon, as he worked in the office, Sheila passed his doorway and he called to her, and asked her to fetch Niabi. Curious as to what he wanted, Sheila accompanied Niabi back upstairs and peeled off as Niabi entered the office. Niabi stopped about four feet from the big desk where Grant was seated working. He asked her to take a seat in front of the desk. Where she sat there was a clear view to her left of Sheila standing in the hallway, but a wall separated Sheila from Grant so he was unaware Sheila remained within listening distance.

"Why did you send for me, Mr. Grant?" Niabi asked, dressed in the same pale green dress with green ribbon weaved in her hair like she wore to church with Harriet and Will on the day Grant brought the two letters to Will.

"You know, you are about the prettiest girl I've ever seen. And I really like that outfit." His eyes examined her from head to toe, lingering momentarily on her hips, breasts, then dancing up to her lips, and then her eyes. Grant was older than Jason by seven years. He had dark hair, deep blue eyes, and a chiseled chin with a reserved way about him. He disguised his confidence under his Southern gentlemanly behavior. For that reason, she found Jason to be playful and harmless, where Grant made her feel examined and uncomfortable. "Is there a special occasion today?" Grant asked.

"Thank you for your compliments, Mr. Grant. No, I'm just going into town this afternoon with Harriet and Fred and didn't want to wear my uniform. That's all. Is there anything I can get for you?"

"No, it's just—I was thinking I should take you to town for dinner at the Gardens; that's our town's nicest restaurant. And maybe I can buy you a piece of jewelry, some bobble you would like."

Niabi was surprised at what Grant was saying, but distracted by Sheila out in the hallway. She had stacked her two hands over her heart and was pushing in and out, simulating her heart bulging and retracting with each heartbeat.

"That's not necessary," Niabi replied.

But Grant interrupted. "Niabi, someday I will be the owner of Applegate Ranch."

Sheila cupped her hand around her left ear and leaned forward.

Grant added, "When that happens, I will be able to make you head household supervisor, provide you with your own cottage, buggy, and wardrobe. You will be financially fixed for the rest of your life."

Sheila's eyes bulged. She put her hands on her hips, started flapping her arms, strutting and working her neck like a head rooster, and glaring at Niabi as if to say take that deal!

Niabi replied, "You are most considerate of me, Mr. Grant. I don't know what to say."

"My immediate request though is that you . . ." Grant rose from his chair, coming closer to her. Within two feet, he continued, "Accompany me on my cruise to England."

Sheila fell backward on bundles of linen piled on the hallway floor. Witnessing her fall from downstairs, Harriet rushed upstairs to give aid. Almost out of breath with excitement, Harriet asked, "Are you alright, Sheila?"

Hearing all the commotion outside the office door, Grant quickly went over and closed the door. "Let me be clear," he said. "You can accompany me as my secretary. It will be all proper and above board."

"What is a secretary?" Niabi asked.

"Oh, that is a person that gets my papers for me, gets my coffee, and lets me know when I have visitors," Grant said.

"Oh, a kind of servant, a paid servant?" Niabi said.

"Yes, yes, a paid servant, of course. You will be paid for your time, and well, the big reward is that you get a free trip to England." He began to look puzzled that she wasn't showing more excitement. He stepped back and partially sat on the big desk. "Jason mentioned that he kissed you."

Wringing her hands in agitation, Niabi said, "That was a mistake."

Raising one hand, Grant said, "I understand perfectly. A young, inexperienced man like him is not for you. He will eventually run out of things to say or do and you will become bitterly bored. Where I, if given the chance, will keep you looking forward to the next day. I have an extended list of ideas to keep you happy, Niabi," he said, glancing across her bosom and licking his lips. "Even Will, a fine young man in his own right, is too young and can't offer you what I can. You need to think about your future, what kind of life you want to have. Where do you want to be in ten years? Life has a way of moving in the direction you aim it. But you need to determine where to aim it. You can decide to continue being just a servant, and there's nothing wrong with that, or become headmistress."

"Do you mean become your wife, Mr. Grant?"

Grant jerked and moved back to sit behind the desk. "There's no need to create hurdles for ourselves until we get better acquainted. For now, we can consider an amicable relationship that satisfies both of our immediate needs, and it can begin on our cruise to England."

She responds, "I must refuse." Niabi rose from her seat and moved toward the door, looking at him, thinking, *He too is a man in season for my body; disguising it as a fun-for-me cruise to England.* "I thank you for your in-vi-tation to England. Your suggestion that I think about my future is well founded. But I plan to go back to my village when Will returns." Having said that, she turned, walked out of the office, and went down the hall to the back staircase leading to the kitchen area.

In Baltimore, Maryland, Sam Egglesby, Jr. arrives at his job as a Pullman porter on the Baltimore and Ohio railroad. Dudley, a man he met in Baltimore, where Sam lives with his mother, recruited Sam to work as a porter. Admired for his well-groomed appearance, Dudley first saw Sam Egglesby Jr. helping a store owner unload food staples off a truck for the general store. He stands five feet, seven inches tall, chocolate brown, with short hair. The anguish and worry from his enslavement on an Alabama plantation are carried in his deep-set brown eyes. On his way to work one day, Dudley purchased items from the general store and struck up a conversation with Sam. His good manners and tone prompted Dudley to help him apply for a porter opening. Dudley gave Sam a uniform, a navy-blue tailored suit, starched white shirt, shiny black shoes, black socks, and navy-blue cap matching the suit with a label on the cap that read "Pullman Porter." Sam Jr. is grateful for the job. He overcomes his inability to read or write by being very sociable, well-mannered, and energetic. All that is expected of him as a porter is to greet passengers, carry their baggage, make up the sleeping berths, serve food and drinks brought from the dining car, shine shoes, and keep the cars tidy. He has to be available night and day to wait on the passengers. He is also expected to always wear a smile on his face.

Sam Jr. and his family have taken as their surname Egglesby, the name of the plantation they lived on in Alabama during slavery. They thought about changing their names, but didn't in case anyone needed to locate them. Sam Jr.'s porter job requires him to be away from home for almost a whole month at a time. He works fourteen-hour days and only gets three days off most months. He gets paid seventy dollars a month, but has to buy his own uniforms, shoes, meals, and pay for any dishes, towels, or other train fixtures the passengers confiscate. His duty is not only to help passengers, but to slyly keep watch over the linen, dishes, and utensils that are walking off the train. But being so watchful of passengers conflicts with how he earns tips from the same passengers. Passengers tip according to how accommodating and lenient the porter is with them.

After three years of working as a porter, Sam is getting worn out by the job. Only twenty-eight years old, he feels like a man of fifty. He gets minimal sleep, more like cat-naps, and eats on the run. He longs for those three days he has at home with his mother and brother to eat decent meals, take a long, hot bath, and sleep in his bed to his heart's content. The pay is good; it helps his family a great deal. They rent a small two-bedroom house in Baltimore with an outhouse and backyard. His mother takes in wash and does seamstress work. His brother works as a laborer for the city cleaning streets, picking up trash, cleaning buildings, whatever is needed. They are surprisingly making a good life for themselves considering none of them can read or write. Each night they are together, they pray that someday their entire family will be reunited, but how that will ever happen escapes them for now.

Before one three-day off period, while they are serving light snacks to onboard train passengers after dinner, Sam talks with Dudley about locating his father. It's evening, and the train rides smoothly coasting along an uninterrupted stretch.

"Make sure the tray for compartment five has cheese and wine," Dudley says after dressing the tray with a starched brilliant white cloth, white cloth napkins, and shined utensils.

"Checked and checked," Sam Jr. says scrutinizing the tray ordered by the customer in compartment five. Looking up, he asks Dudley, "I was just curious. Do you have any ideas about how I could go about finding my father?"

"Well, let's just put the word out," Dudley says. "We've got porters working the lines from New York to San Francisco. We'll have everyone looking for a Sam Egglesby, Sr., a former U.S. Army soldier."

They work as a tag team. Dudley leaves to deliver the evening snack to compartment five, while Sam sets up the next tray for compartment four. Dudley returns to the porter's station to share an idea with Sam. "Hey, have you thought about going to Washington, District of Columbia, and making inquiries at the Veterans Pension Office? If he's collecting a pension from the Army, they could give you his address."

"No, I would not know how to get there, and where to go once I'm there. This tray is ready," Sam Jr. says.

"OK, you deliver this one. About getting around Washington, well, I can help you with that. I have loads of family there. I will put you in touch with my nephew," Dudley says.

On one of his days off, Sam Jr. makes his way to Washington, DC, and Dudley's nephew directs him to the U.S. Army Pension Office. Sam Jr. arrives and nervously approaches a female attendant at a counter in the pension office. The attendant's blonde hair is pinned up revealing pale skin and keen facial features including a narrow nose holding up a pair of steel wire spectacles.

Sam Jr. clears his throat. "I'm trying to locate my father who fought on the Union side in the war."

"Of course, he did," the attendant says sharply.

Sam Jr. does not let her sharp tone deter him. "His name is Sam Egglesby, Sr."

"Young man, we do not give out our veterans' information and addresses." The attendant stiffens her shoulders.

"I just want to know if he is alive or not. Someone said he is eligible for a pension from the Army and —"

"I know, but we have files for *our* use only, and not for giving out our veterans' information to anyone that walks in here."

"Please, ma'am. It's just that my mother and I are desperate for news on him. We escaped the South when the war ended, escaped with nothin'. We hope to reunite with my father if he's alive, and we don't even know that much."

The attendant looks at him and takes a breath. "OK. Wait right here."

She comes back with a big brown envelope with the name "Sam Egglesby" on the front of it. She looks inside and pulls out papers. "Well, he was alive last April. It appears he comes around April of every year and collects an amount covering in arrears payments. That's all I can share with you."

Tears well up in Sam's eyes. He exits the pension office building walking aimlessly and continues down the street until he sees a church. This news has drained him and he wants to sit, so he goes inside the church. It is a Negro church, and he finds a seat in the very back close to the entrance. In the front of the sanctuary, the pastor converses softly with a man, and the sound of Sam Jr. entering attracts the pastor's attention. When their conversation ends, the man quietly disappears down a hallway. The pastor, who is a tall, commanding figure, a light-skinned Negro man with straight, slightly curly black hair, groomed mustache, and a bellowing voice, looks to the rear of the church where Sam Jr. sits. The pastor walks down the aisle of the sanctuary and approaches Sam Jr. "Good day to you, young man. I'm Pastor Gregory. Can I be of service to you, or do you want to sit alone in prayer?"

Sam lets out a deep sigh. "No, sir, I'm in need of much prayer. I've been trying to find my father and I'm not able to get very far, because I'm what you call an illiterate. I can't write anybody a letter or message to seek out information on his whereabouts. I just left the Army pension office down the street, and they say he's collecting his pension once a year, but they cannot give me his address. I'm so glad I know he survived the war. But I'm still without a father."

"When did you last see your father?" asks the pastor.

"He left the plantation in Alabama to join up to fight back when I was seven. He left behind me and my mother. When the war ended, we escaped the plantation and just ran, ran north, scared, and half-starving most of the time. Good Samaritans gave us biscuits and beans. We drank from creeks and wells. We were able to work, so we worked our way north, all the way to Baltimore because we were told there was plenty of work there for people that can't read or write. But before Baltimore, we befriended a young girl who had gotten herself in trouble. Her name was Clara Belle. We took her in, and she worked right alongside us up to when her baby was due. Unfortunately, she died giving birth to Youngster—that's what we call him. I guess he needs a proper name; we were moving too fast to give him one. Momma and I adopted him. We're the only family he knows, you see.

When we find Pops, he will have another son." Sam Jr. chokes up and drops his face into his hands.

"Now, now there. Listen, your story is not unlike those of many of our people coming out of the South, coming out of slavery. I tell you what. There is a network of us pastors that I can tap into, and I can send inquiries about a war veteran named . . ."

"Sam Sr., Sam Egglesby, Sr.," Sam Jr. says.

"I can send some inquiries to our sister churches. If he comes to Washington, DC, once a year, he may be in a neighboring state," the pastor says.

Reaching for two dollars, Sam Jr. says, "Please allow me to give you something for postage and your trouble. And I will tell you how to reach me and my family."

———•———

Miss Catherine exits a carriage for hire and bounces upstairs at the Applegate Ranch calling back to have someone bring her bags upstairs. She darts into Mrs. Applegate's room. Mrs. Applegate rises from her chair and hugs Catherine. "Ask Grant if he can bring up the heavy bags. They may be too heavy for Harriet and the girls," Mrs. Applegate says.

"OK, Auntie." Catherine exits the room, calls to Harriet from the top of the stairs, and asks her to get Grant to bring up her large bag. Catherine returns to Mrs. Applegate's room. She half-dances and twitches around the bedroom looking through the decorative perfume bottles on Mrs. Applegate's dressing table. "Have any new fragrances?" Catherine asks.

As Catherine twirls around to see if Mrs. Applegate points out a new perfume bottle, her eyes catch a glimpse of Niabi passing by the bedroom door, helping Harriet take her bags to one of the guest rooms.

"Who's that Indian girl?" Catherine asks as she continues investigating items on Mrs. Applegate's dressing table.

Browsing through papers, Mrs. Applegate answers, "Oh, she's Harriet's new assistant." Catherine removes the top on a perfume bottle and smells it. Mrs. Applegate continues, "She is a friend of Will's. Her name is Niabi."

Catherine abruptly stops what she is doing and arches one of her eyebrows. "A friend of Will's?"

"Yes," says Mrs. Applegate who finally looks up at Catherine, perplexed by her curiosity about the servants. "You never said what brought you to our door?"

Catherine goes to the doorway of the bedroom, looks down the hall, and sees Harriet and Niabi coming out of the guest room. Niabi waits while Harriet goes to Grant's room and asks him if he'll get Catherine's one heavy bag.

Still looking Niabi over, Catherine answers Mrs. Applegate. "Oh, I'm joining Grant and Jason on their trip to England."

"That should be fun and exciting," Mrs. Applegate says returning to her papers.

"Hmmm, hmmm," Catherine says and then steps out into the hallway to engage Harriet. "Harriet, I wonder if this little lady," she's pointing at Niabi, "can help me put my things away?"

"I can help you, Miss Catherine," Harriet says.

"No—um, I would prefer getting acquainted with Nee-yah-bee. I am sure she has stories; I'd like to hear, like how she met Will."

"I'll be faster Miss Catherine. You won't be entertained by her stories," Harriet insists.

"Nonsense. I'm on my way to England with Mr. Grant and some of Niabi's stories may be just what I need to make interesting conversations during the crossing."

"If you insist, Miss Catherine," Harriet says, grinding her teeth. Harriet turns and speaks to Niabi, "Niabi, help her unpack. Then I need you back in the kitchen to get dinner served, *right-a-way.*" Harriet has her back to Catherine. Facing Niabi, she rolls her eyes to the left toward the kitchen, warning her to hurry up and come downstairs.

Miss Catherine moves toward Niabi and gently places her hand on Niabi's back, directing her back into the guest room. As they proceed into the guest room, Catherine watches Harriet leave, and then she leans toward Niabi and says, "She's a real taskmaster. Won't even let you have some friendly conversation with me."

"Which bag do you want me to unpack first?" Niabi asks.

"Oh, forget those bags. I want to hear all about how you met Will, and what's going on between the two of you?"

"He's just a friend. Nothing is going on between us." Niabi feels her face begin to flush.

"How did you meet?" Catherine asks.

"We met near my village in the Indian Territory. Then he brought me here to see where he lives," Niabi says.

"Hmmmmm, hmmmmm." Catherine scans Niabi from head to toe. "How long were you two on the trail?"

"Weeks," Niabi says.

"Did you—how do I say this delicately? Did you and he make love?" Catherine asks.

"No! Why do you ask me such questions? What gives you the right to ask me that? Are you close to Will?" Niabi erupts.

"Well, yes. We're as close as two young red-blooded people can be. I let him kiss me, I mean a long, deep, juicy kiss, with his arms wrapped around me. I could barely breathe as he squeezed me so tight up against his healthy body," says Catherine. Niabi turns beet red.

Catherine continues, "You look a little disturbed about hearing this. He didn't tell you about us?"

"No, Miss Catherine. He didn't." Niabi's throat tightens.

"Well, that should make you think before going any further with him. You are pretty and all, but I think he prefers a woman who knows how to really make him happy."

"Is that all Miss Catherine?" Niabi says, her voice cracking.

"Yes, you may go." Catherine motions for her to leave, feeling quite satisfied that she has ruined any possible relationship between Niabi and Will. Although she knows her family would never let her couple up with Will, in the back of her mind, she secretly likes him a great deal and can't bear to know that he may have eyes for someone else instead of her.

With her skin flushed, eyes red, and on the brink of crying, Niabi barrels downstairs and almost bumps into Harriet. "Child, what did she say to you?" Harriet asks.

"I'm going to the cottage," Niabi says holding back her tears.

"Yes, go ahead. I'll be there directly."

Once inside the cottage, Niabi gets a fire going and pours herself a glass of water. She is infuriated with Will for lying and saying she is the only one he ever kissed. Since he lied to her about that, she feels no need to keep her promise to him.

Harriet rushes through the door. "Now tell me, tell me what got you so upset?"

"That girl, that Miss Catherine, she said she and Will kissed!"

"What? I know she is very . . . Well, there are no other words for it. Spoiled and undisciplined," Harriet says.

"Now, what I tell you next is only to get your help to make him take me home," Niabi says.

"Tell me, child," Harriet insists.

Niabi takes a deep breath, and then says, "Will took me from my village. I didn't want to leave my home. He took me."

"What? Am I hearing you right? Are you saying my son kidnapped you?" Harriet's eyes widen in disbelief.

"Kidnap? Yes, he forced me to come with him," Niabi says.

"Oh, my God, Oh, my God, you poor child. Yes, I will get him to take you home right away." Harriet wraps her arms around Niabi. Then she pulls away and looks into her eyes. "He . . . he didn't abuse you or harm you in any way, did he?"

"Oh, no, no. Nothing like that happened. He just tied me up with ropes so I couldn't run away," Niabi says.

"Oh, my goodness." Harriet takes deep breaths. "I can hardly believe you are talking about my son," she says.

"He promised to take me home by next spring. But now that I know he lies, I am not sure he will take me," Niabi says.

"Rest assured. He will be taking you home, or he will have to find a new home for himself. And from what I have heard, I may still put him out!"

After Harriet learns this startling news, she gets on her knees and prays every night. She leaves church right after services with Niabi because she is afraid she may let her worries leak out to the pastor while seeking his help to get this burden off her heart. For the first time in her life, she is ashamed of her boy. Niabi begins to see that divulging that information is taking its toll on Harriet, and tries to comfort Harriet. "Other than that, Will has been a perfect gentleman to me," she tells her. But Harriet refuses to accept her excuses.

"You don't need to make any excuses for him. It's his terrible deed; he knows better and he needs to answer for it."

Niabi sees that her confession has really hurt Harriet, and understands now why Will never wanted this story to see the light of day. Niabi starts to feel bad that she let her rage get the better of her, because her stay here hasn't been that bad. She is actually glad she came to visit. She's learned a lot and met interesting people.

One afternoon, Mrs. Walker drops by the cottage to see Harriet because they hadn't talked in a while. She is wondering why Harriet wasn't waiting around after church services to say hello and catch up on what their children are doing.

"Why don't you come to dinner tonight and bring Niabi? I'm sure Rita and Martha would love her company," Mrs. Walker says.

"I would love to come and bring Niabi. It would be nice for her to visit another Negro home while she's here. Sure, we would be happy to join you and your family. What time do you want us there?"

"Five this evening is good," Mrs. Walker replies and then goes on her way.

Later that afternoon, Harriet and Niabi leave the cottage and walk down to the Walkers' home. They are greeted at the door by Rita Mae Walker. "Welcome, welcome. I am so glad you accepted our dinner invitation," Rita says ushering them inside.

Niabi enters the Walkers' home and immediately notices many books on the bookshelves in the sitting room. They have schools in her village with a few donated books, but nothing like this in a home. As she walks around, Niabi also becomes impressed with the china closet filled with beautiful dishes and tea sets that Rita and Martha are removing and placing on the table.

"May I help you prepare?" Niabi asks.

"No, Niabi, you are our guest tonight," Rita says.

After dinner, Rita brings Niabi out on the front porch to sip hot tea.

"Have you heard from Will?" Rita asks.

"Mother Harriet has. He should be back here soon," Niabi says.

"I'm thinking about going to nursing school. Mother Harriet said you were training to be a healer," Rita says.

"Yes, I help with birthing, wounds, fevers, and other treatments."

"You are perfect for Will. He wants to make a life out on the frontier. I am happy he found someone he can make a life with. He is very dear to me." Rita starts to tear up. Niabi grabs her hand and looks at her helpless, not knowing what to say to stop her tears. Rita uses the back of her hands to wipe the tears. "I know I am acting just foolishly. I prayed about it and received comfort and understanding that my life is headed in a different direction. You see, I thought since I was a little girl that I would marry Will. But as I got older, I became interested in more than being a wife and mother. I thought I was betraying someone or somebody when my interests changed, but the one I was betraying with my doubt was myself. I'm glad you came to dinner. I wanted an opportunity to wish you and Mr. Will all the happiness."

"Miss Rita, Will and I have made no promises to each other," Niabi says.

"Oh, I just assumed you coming home with him, staying in his home, and the way you two look at each other, even in church. The sparks from you two fly off the ceiling."

"I had no idea . . ." Niabi stares at her. "Has he ever mentioned a Miss Catherine to you?" Niabi asks.

"No, but I have heard others talking about her saying she's a terrible flirt."

"A flirt?" Niabi asks.

"Ummmm, that's when, say, a female and sometimes males do it, too, but a female person tries too hard to get a man's attention. Just being, too, too friendly, even if the man is not interested."

Niabi develops a bad feeling in her gut. Has she misjudged Will too harshly, based on what Miss Catherine said?

The two bring their visit to a close, leave the porch, and enter the parlor in preparation for Niabi and Harriet to depart the Walker home. Pastor Walker trails behind Mrs. Walker and Rita as they follow Harriet and Niabi to the front door, and then suddenly raises his hand. "Oh Harriet, I almost forgot. During Will's travels has he ever mentioned coming across an ex-Union Army soldier, named Sam Egglesby, Sr.?"

"Soldier . . . Union Army. Maybe that's Dakota Sam," Niabi says looking at Harriet.

"The man traveling with Will?" Harriet asks.

"Yes, he fought in the War and lost track of his wife and son. When he returned after the War they were not at the plantation, and he searched and searched and couldn't find them," Niabi says.

"I wonder if it's the same man?" Harriet says. "I should check with Grant. I think Will asked him to help find the family of this man."

As Niabi walks back to the cottage with Harriet, she thinks about what Rita said about how she thought her life led down one path and found herself on a different path. And although Rita is sad about leaving the old path, there is a glimmer of joy in her face when talking about her new path. When she and Harriet reach the cottage, they see a lit lantern in the front room and Will lying on his pallet on the floor in the far corner of the sitting room. Harriet had kept the pallet freshened up in anticipation of Will's return. They both stand there examining him, surmising he came home while they were out, washed the dust off, put on his nightshirt, crawled onto his pallet, and fell into a deep sleep.

With her hands on her hips, Harriet firmly says, "Rest assured, I will speak to him in the morning." Her lips tighten on a face frozen with pain, and she looks over at Niabi before entering her bedroom and shutting the door.

Now standing alone watching Will sleep, Niabi says to herself: *What have I done? He lies there so peaceful, unaware of what is about to happen. How did I let Miss Catherine send me out like a bullet to injure the two people that have cared for me like family since I've been here? Yes, he shouldn't have taken me, but as it stands now, I'm a better person for it. Maybe the Great Spirit moved Will to take me so my feet would be on a new path, a different path.*

The next morning, Niabi rises and dresses before anyone else in the cottage. She sits in a chair near Will, watching his chest expand and contract with each breath. She feels anxious for him because he has no idea of what she has unleashed on him—the wrath of his mother.

Will stirs, opens his eyes, and says, "Hi, there." He yawns, stretching his long arms and legs. "You're awful quiet and still." He senses her somber mood and asks, "Is there something wrong?"

"Yes, I need to explain something," Niabi says wringing her hands. But before she can start her explanation, she is interrupted by Harriet, exiting her bedroom fully dressed with a pronounced scowl on her face.

"Niabi, why don't you get something to eat at the main house, and give me and Will some space here."

"But, Mother Harriet, I want—" Niabi says.

Harriet interrupts her, "Go on, now. I will see you in a few minutes."

After Niabi leaves, Will gets up wearing only his long night-shirt, walks to his room, and pulls on some clean but old pants. His thoughts are on getting a good hot bath to soak off the road dust and sweat. So, he returns to the kitchen to prepare to boil water for his bath. Harriet remains still, seething with anger, glaring at him.

Will detects something's amiss and finally looks at her. "What's wrong, Momma?"

"Don't call me Momma. Because a child of mine would not kidnap a young girl! And drag her around by a rope! Across the country!" Inflammatory accusations spill from Harriet's lips.

Will collapses into a chair and drops his head staring at the floor.

"Do you know how shocked I was to hear about that?" Harriet continues. "I said to myself, 'Not the child I bore. Not the child I took to church every Sunday. Not the child I taught right from wrong.' And a Negro child, who knows our history of being taken from Africa, and put into bondage. Not to mention the lynchings by rope! What were you thinking? Who are you? Your father would ..." Harriet stops; her hand flies up to cover her mouth.

Will looks up at her with red, watery eyes, starts to open his mouth, but the words do not come out.

"No, there is nothing you can say to me. All I want you to do is— the first chance you get—take that girl home. And maybe, before I close my eyes for the last time, I will forgive you for what you did. You broke my heart." Having said all that, Harriet rushes out of the cottage, closing the large wooden front door hard behind her.

Dazed, Will sits there a moment, wanting desperately to be somewhere else, to be someone else at this time. Tightening his jaws after these futile thoughts, he then decides to finish preparing his hot bath. With large pots on the stove, he makes repeated trips to the well nearest his cottage, carrying in pails of cold water to fill the pots on the stove and to fill half-way the bathtub located in the bathroom adjoined to Harriet's bedroom. On his trip bringing in the last pails of water, Niabi, who had been watching him and simmering in her own regrets, walks up and accompanies him into the cottage.

"Thanks for telling on me, and making my momma hate me," Will groans.

"Thanks for lying to me about only kissing me. You seem to have forgotten about Miss Catherine," she says stomping one foot with fists balled up.

Will retrieves the pots of hot water on the stove, carefully carries them through Harriet's bedroom to the bathroom, and gingerly pours the hot water into the tub. He sets his drying and wash cloths next to the tub and is ready to disrobe.

"Turn around so I can get in the tub, or leave. Suit yourself," Will demands.

Niabi turns around displaying an attempt to give him some portion of privacy, similar to the amount of privacy he gave her during their trip to his home when she was bound and needed to relieve herself on the side of the road or away from camp. This routine for them is well rehearsed.

He removes his pants, then his nightshirt, and totally naked steps into the tub. As he slowly squats down into the hot steaming water, he inhales deeply through his teeth making a hissing sound that increases louder as his loins submerge deeper into the heated water. Once he settles in, he drapes a cloth over the tub covering his body's private area, grasps a bar of soap, and lathers his hair.

Turning back toward him and seeing him lathering his hair, she pulls up a chair. "Let me do that," she says taking the soap out of his hand. She continues lathering his hair and massages his scalp.

"God, that feels soothing," he says. "But I'll need some strong whiskey to soothe the rest of this pain I bear."

———•———

When Harriet arrives at the main house, she begins making her rounds, determining the day's menus, supervising breakfast, changing the linen upstairs, and whatever else is to be done that day. The scolding she gave Will this morning makes it hard for her to focus on the work at hand. During her rounds, she does not see Niabi. She asks Ethel and Sheila if they have seen her. "No, not yet," says Ethel.

"Didn't you say Will is home?" Sheila asks.

Harriet looks at Sheila and hesitantly nods.

"Well, if I was her, I'd be after a little hello sugar after being away from him that long." All three laugh.

"You are just impossible," Harriet says entering the pantry to inventory food supplies.

Niabi squishes soap through his thick hair, rubbing the top of his head and temples. In those few moments, she observes the tension withdraw from his body. Once she is convinced Will has calmed down, she swallows and readies for another attempt to broach the subject. "How do you feel about Miss Catherine?" Niabi asks.

His eyes closed, body relaxed, Will emerges from the tranquility produced by her hands kneading his scalp. He takes a deep breath. "I didn't tell you about what happened with her because she forced herself on me. I have no interest in her." He turns around breaking her hold on his head, and looks her in the eyes. "No interest at all!"

Niabi only responds with a deep gaze into his eyes, savoring what she heard, feeling a wave of deep satisfaction come over her. "You should turn around. I'll rinse the soap out now." After rinsing his hair, she dries it with a cloth, continuing to apply a gentle rubbing. With eyes closed, he floats to the edge of serenity. She stops and lays the used cloth aside.

"Thank you," he says continuing to slumber in the tub with a cloth over his face. "You can start making plans for the trip back to your village. You may want to go into town and do some shopping. I can give you money for any things you want to buy and take back with you."

"That is very kind of you," she says her eyebrows raised, surprised at his continued kindness even though she has tampered with the most precious of bonds—his bond with his mother. Evaluating this new development and her clashing mixed feelings, she leaves the bathroom.

In his bedroom, she paces the floor. She's in turmoil. *Haven't I gotten exactly what I wanted?* she thinks. *He is committed to taking me home as soon as possible, and it is practically guaranteed by his mother's wrath.* In contrast, she ponders how she'll miss her adopted way of life with the Lawtons on the ranch. Before coming there, she detested washing clothes. However, working with Sheila doing the laundry became part of a game to see how fast they could get it all done. And afterward, there was time left to sit, talk, and laugh, or choose other things to do. She continues pondering how she'll miss cooking on Harriet's cast-iron Dutch ovens in the cottage and the main house's wood-burning stoves, working with Sheila using scrub boards in the large wash tubs, and the spacious clothesline; working with Clarence in the vegetable and flower gardens, and creating an herb garden. She'll also miss going with Harriet on excursions into town, buying fabrics, groceries, goods, and supplies for the main house, catering the Applegates' fancy dinner parties, attending church, helping out at church socials. In the review of highlights of her stay there, she finally gets around to the most compelling reason for her turmoil—her feelings for Will. She has been burying them so often and for so long, she didn't realize the depth of her passion for him until Miss Catherine spoke to her and something inside her snapped. She further thinks, *He's in there thinking he should take me home because I don't want him, that I don't choose him. Not that I ever told him I choose Nashoba or any other male suitor —he thinks I do not choose him!*

Niabi's pulse races. Her body becomes flushed. She unfastens the top buttons of her gray uniform attempting to cool down. She knows what's happening to her, but she's unsure about how he will respond. She returns to the bathroom. With his face still covered, he hears her footsteps approaching.

"Have you forgot something?" Will says exhaling deeply.

"Yes, I forgot to tell you something."

"Can it wait? I'd like to relax a few minutes more before I have to prepare to face my mother again."

"No, Will. I need to tell you now—there has been a change." Looking up at the ceiling she continues, "I am now traveling on a different path. I wasn't sure what I wanted before, but now I am. You see, I too want to live on *my* own farm, with *my* own vegetable, flower and herb gardens; I want to have babies and the love of a good man."

Will snatches the cloth off his face, rolls his eyes back, and gasps. "Well, I wish you and Nashoba well with your farm, gardens, babies— all of it! Good riddance to the two of you!" Will tempers his rage and anguish at hearing her revelations and drawing him out of his moments of peace. He tries to regain control over how he's reacting to this news. "And this you couldn't wait to tell me."

"Will, you don't understand me."

"That's a mouthful. I've never understood you. For example, why did you kiss me back, if . . . if you . . . never mind. I do understand one thing; I understand that I've had nothing but trouble ever since I laid eyes . . . on you."

Niabi gasps. "I hope you don't mean that," she pleads.

"What difference does it make now?" Will says in despair replacing the cloth back over his eyes and throwing his arms down by the sides of the tub.

Niabi blurts out, "Because I don't want Nashoba to give me babies. I want . . . Choctaw-Negro babies . . . from Will Lawton."

Dazed, Will snatches the cloth off his face again. He turns his head around. She moves from the rear to the side of the tub. "I thought you wanted to go back to your home, to your village, back to Nashoba, to your life, where you will someday become the wife of the chief."

Looking into his eyes, she squats down next to the tub. "I could never be with anyone else after getting to know you. Since I met you, I've observed the caring nature you show to humans and beasts alike, and it tugs on my heart. Yes, you were an idiot for kidnapping me, but from the start, the tenderness of your kisses caused my body to want you. That is why I was so mean to you from the beginning. I didn't understand these feelings I had toward a complete stranger. And I thought your desire for me was like smoke, would start hot and soon disappear. I waited for that to happen. And after at time, especially after I was so mean to you, you never stopped being loving and kind to me. But I need to know, Will. Right now—do you still have a fire burning inside of you for me?"

Will takes his hands and grabs her face and kisses her passionately. "Yes, the fire still burns for you and you only," he whispers.

She stands and hands him his large drying cloth. He stands up. Not meaning to display himself to her, he quickly wraps the cloth around his waist and lower body, and steps out of the tub dripping water onto the floor. He's oblivious to the water dripping because she moves close to him, and he wraps his arms around her. The kissing resumes and moves into a more intense level of passion. His lips softly bite her along the neck down to her collarbone, and then across the tops of her breasts. Then she is frantic to reconnect to his mouth. Breathless and pulsating, he stops and backs away. "We better stop, Niabi before we go too far. I have promised so many and myself that no harm will come to you."

She takes hold of his hands. "Will, things are different now with us." She steps back and puts her two hands out in front of her, palms facing. She moves them all the way to the left and clasps her to hands together with fingers curling around the opposite hand, and then says, "Remember, husband and wife. I need to know right now, that you agree." Her eyes locked on his.

His body now throbbing, sending messages that cloud his thinking. He wants to do right by her, and yet he desperately wants her. This is what he has wanted all along: her to choose him. He is cornered by his carnal desires and her willingness. No obstacles remain preventing them from being together. There is no other answer for him to say, but, "Yes, Niabi. Yes."

Niabi eases closer to him and looks deeper into his eyes. "Then, we choose each other. Come to the bedroom; I allow you to lie with me."

His brain and certain parts of his body are in complete celebration, none communicating with his legs, or his knees that are buckling. He leans against the tub and gathers himself. Yes, he heard right: *She said come to the bedroom and lie with her.* He watches her walk away looking back for him to follow.

———•———

Harriet starts to go back to the cottage to look for Niabi, but remembers that she needs to check with Grant about Sam Egglesby. The events of the morning have zapped half of her day's energy. She finds herself slowly climbing the stairs that she normally scoots up rather adeptly, as she goes to the office on the second floor where Grant works on the Applegate business. Harriet stops at the entrance of the office where the door is open and knocks. "Mr. Grant, may I have a moment?"

"Sure. Come on in, Harriet. What do you need?"

"My pastor received a communication from a man named Sam Egglesby, who is looking for his father, an ex-Union Army soldier. Is he . . .?"

"Yes, yes, ma'am. Ah . . . oh . . . Will's friend . . . ah," he stutters while scattering papers on his desk, looking for a paper that he soon finds and holds up to read. "Yes, Dakota Sam is Sam Egglesby, Sr., and he asked me to try to find his wife and son. I sent out inquiries, but have not heard anything on my end. But that is great news. Is Will at home, or still traveling?"

"He is home. I will send one of Fred's boys to town to locate Dakota Sam," Harriet says.

Grant is looking down at his desk when he says, "I guess Niabi is glad Will is home."

"She will be glad when she returns to her village. Thank you for your help, Mr. Grant," Harriet says.

"Ah, I did minimal here. But let me know if I can be of further assistance, Harriet."

"I'll let you get back to your work," Harriet says and leaves.

———•———

Will and Niabi, gripped in blissful satisfaction, lie naked and moist on the bed in Will's bedroom. With his body now tucked under hers, his right arm is weaved between her right arm and right breast, and across her waist, his right hand grasps her stomach holding her in place. Relaxed, breathlessly and with a touch of humor he says, "I am so glad you choose me, Niabi. I was worried there for a while." With her eyes closed and smiling, she twists her head toward him allowing her cheek to intercept his wanting lips.

Up to this point, Will had meager experience in lovemaking, only what he heard about on the cattle drives and once when he was drunk with a lady during the crew's layover in Dodge City. It was over lightning fast, both kept most of their clothes on. The only other appropriate information he received surfaced during his trip returning his father's body to Canada. At a family dinner there, an elderly male relative, a distant cousin of his father's named Wendell Ralston, beckoned a fifteen-year-old Will to come sit with him in the corner of Auntie Maise's parlor.

"Will, you find yourself on the brink of manhood without a father. A challenging position but not insurmountable. Search your mind, son. Is there anything, any information that your father hadn't gotten around to sharing with you before his passing that I might be able to attempt to provide some kind of explanation?"

Feeling rather melancholy after days of prayers, obituary, eulogy, and receiving messages of sympathy for the loss of his father, Will said, "I think he taught me the most important things about handling myself, horses, and farming. What is your expertise, sir?"

"Women. You are looking at a man who is married to his fourth wife. You ask how or why I am with wife number four? I didn't get it right until number four. You may not know the questions to ask, so let me offer this advice. There are two kinds of women in this world: those who know how to make a nest, and those who have never made a nest. For the former group, watch the fixed habits to ensure they complement your own. Fixed habits are like freight trains moving fast on a track. If they are going your way, fine; if they're not going your way and you get in front of them, they will run you down. For the latter group, you can get one totally untried, and the only thing that will make that go right is being patient and gentle because you are the only man that has come behind the curtains, so to speak. Where your natural instinct is to pounce like a wolf on a cornered injured rabbit, you should refrain, and instead pet and fondle to build trust and put her at ease. After so much petting and fondling, I'll be surprised if she doesn't pounce on you. Ha-ha-ha. Few men know that to be a husband is more than her obeying you, it is her wanting to please you. Is there any other advice I can give?" Mr. Ralston said, lighting up his Italian tobacco pipe.

In those tender moments lying in bed with Niabi, snuggled together, Will took heed of Mr. Ralston's advice. He proceeded in the gentlest of ways, asking her if he can do this or that, asking how she feels and if he can continue or go farther.

"Was I gentle enough for you, my sweet?" Will asks while kissing Niabi on her neck.

"Yes, my love. You are a wonderful mate. Worry not. I was forewarned by the women elders of the pain and pleasure of married life. Although their talk was only in preparation for marriage, and not for what we've done. Of course, we will correct things when we receive our marriage blessings from the chief on our return to my village. Am I wrong?"

Will, looking for more places to kiss, says, "Hmmm. Hmmm."

"Will, am I wrong?" she repeats looking at him.

"No, no, honey. Not wrong."

"As for now, no more talk about what has happened between us today. I fear I will be shunned by the others, and especially your mother. In fact, I had better be on my way to the main house," Niabi says. "Harriet may think I have been kidnapped again." They both smile as she dislodges her body from being encased by his. She exits the bed feeling his grasp about her waist loosening.

"Why don't you stay longer and we can just take our time learning more about each other?" Will pleads. "It feels so good to lie with you, hold you in my arms, and rub your soft skin." He catches a glimpse of her staring back at him.

"That doesn't sound like learning more about me, the person," Niabi says.

"And ... and hearing more stories about your village, the women elders, your herb garden," Will adds fighting back a grin.

"I find myself having difficulty believing you," she says smiling. "But, not to worry, there will be time for more talk." Now standing, she leans over and kisses him. Seeking to freshen up at the wash table, she pours water from the pitcher into the bowl and takes a cloth to clean herself. He watches with delight, wondering how can this be happening to him. Putting her undergarments and next her dress back on, she says, "I will be back here before you know it, but we can't do this again until we have our own home."

"Honey, oh, no. Who knows when that will be?" Then he leans back and says, "But we have a more pressing problem."

"What?" She slips into her shoes.

"I promised Nashoba I would bring you back to the village. To assure him of that, I left Rodeo at the village with him."

"What? You left Rodeo?"

She sits down on the bed staring at him. "We need to get a message to him that I have chosen my mate. He will understand. He knows I never made a promise to him. He knows that. But we have to get Rodeo." She moves closer to comfort him. "Oh, my love, I know how much Rodeo means to you." He grabs her pulling her back into the bed. The heavy kissing resumes, and he whispers, "Please, come back to bed. I need you."

She pulls back and stands up again. "I would love nothing more, my love. But right now, there are plans we must make, and decide how we are going to handle everything, including Nashoba, Rodeo, you and me. Think on these things. It won't be long before I'm back here, my love, later today."

"You are really going to leave me now?" Will sits up straight.

"Yes, I've been here too long already," Niabi says affectionately.

"Well, you have left me weak and I'm gonna lie here a while." Will lies back down. "In case my mother returns and questions why I am sleeping in here, tell her I am not feeling well; that my energy is completely down and I am too weak to walk, think, or breathe."

"You really want me to tell *your mother* all that?" says Niabi with both her eyebrows raised.

"No—What was I thinking? Only tell her I'm not feeling well and want to rest in the bed instead of on the pallet just for today."

"Yes—I can tell her that. Now, rest until later today, my love." She puckers a kiss at him.

"You have a lot of nerve doing that, and then leaving me," Will says and then leaps forward, his arms reaching for her, causing her to quickly scoot out of the room giggling. She feels happy and fulfilled leaving out the front door of the cottage.

Fred, the Applegate Ranch's foreman, was trained under Will's father, and he and his boys are more than willing to help with errands into town. Based on Harriet's request, Fred instructs his boy, Jasper, to go to town and ask Dakota Sam to come to Will's cottage, a cottage bourgeoning with a vibrant new love under its roof.

Dakota Sam arrives to the cottage that evening.

After opening the door, Will says smiling, "Welcome to my home, Dakota. This is my mother, and you know Niabi."

Dakota nods at Harriet. "Yes, how could I forget Niabi, the woman that caused an uprising?"

"Please have a seat." Harriet waves her hand directing him to one of the chairs at the kitchen table. They all sit down near him around the table. "It seems, that your son, Sam Egglesby is looking for you, too. He sent inquiries through the Colored churches," Harriet says.

Water starts to swell in Dakota's eyes. "My son?" he asks.

"Yes. Do you want us to send for him, or give you his address?" Harriet asks.

"I —ah, I should go to him. Most likely my son is hopefully with my dear wife, and I don't know if she can travel. I think I should go to them. Yes, I should go to them." Dakota nods and wipes a tear from his face.

"Well, we will have to get your son's address from Pastor Walker. I will go there tomorrow and ask him if he has it, or can get it," Harriet says.

Will looks at Niabi and their eyes lock. Both blush, smile, and then look away.

"Well, that is the best news I've had in a long time. Thank you, God!" Dakota says looking up, his face beaming as he raises both fists in the air.

"Good. We can now eat dinner and give thanks for this wonderful news," Harriet says.

Harriet goes back to the pot-bellied stove where pots of food are making bubbling sounds. Niabi gets up from the table to go and help her. As she gets up, she extends her hand toward Will. He reaches out and grazes her hand with his, as their eyes lock again momentarily.

Dakota says to Will in a whisper, "You know, I've been around animals mating, and I am pretty sure..."

Will interrupts him, "I'm taking Niabi back first thing come spring. Wish you could make the trip with us, but you will probably be with your family then, right?"

Speaking again low to be unheard by Harriet, Dakota says, "Why are you returning the cow, when you obviously like the milk so much?" and then chuckles.

Will doesn't appreciate his humor on the matter and says low, but firmly, "Quiet! She's decided she wants to be with me."

Dakota continues in a low tone, "And when did this happen? Before or after I was dodging arrows and bullets from her Indian suitor?"

Will says low, "Quiet. She and I are going to get married."

"Mary, Martha, and Joseph. Have you forgotten that a love-sick son of a chief is holding your prized horse until you return his woman?" Dakota says.

"What is that about Mary and Joseph?" Harriet asks. "And Will, where is Rodeo?"

Niabi and Dakota look at Will with expressions that say he needs to tell her everything. Will takes a deep breath. "Momma, when we rescued Oscar from Niabi's village, I had to leave Rodeo so the son of the chief would let us all go."

"What?" Harriet says as she starts setting dishes of hot food on the table.

Dakota doesn't wait for them. He digs in making his plate.

Will continues, "The chief's son wants to marry Niabi."

"Oh, that's nice for Niabi," Harriet says looking at Niabi.

"No, wait, Momma. Niabi decided she wants to marry me," Will says.

Harriet falls into her chair.

"He's right, Mother Harriet," Niabi adds walking over to them. "Remember the conversation we had about how one man makes me feel as compared to another man? Well, it is Will who gives me the tingly, bell-ringing, and skin-crawling feeling." Niabi comes toward Will and touches his face.

"Sweetie, did I hear you say something about another man?" Will asks, eyebrows raised.

Niabi kisses him on the cheek. "Let me make your plate," she says to Will.

Harriet is so shocked; she can't even prepare her own plate. She looks at Niabi and Will dumbfounded and thinks, *That's why I wanted to stay out of his personal business.*

Dakota chimes in, "Let's eat, and then figure out how to get Rodeo back on a full stomach."

CHAPTER 10

INVITATIONS

————

OSCAR'S grandfather, Phillipe LeGrande, grows anxious to complete his visit to the United States and head home to Canada. During his stay at the Hastings Ranch, when Oscar was missing, Phillipe tormented himself with worry for his grandson's safety. To distract Phillipe from worrying, Mrs. Hastings entertained him with guided tours of the ranch and impromptu jaunts into Waco. In return for her hospitality, Phillipe made an effort to cajole her during their rides and excursions. But when Will and Dakota Sam brought Oscar home wounded, Phillipe discontinued all his recreational activities and devoted his full attention to providing Oscar the medical care the doctor recommended.

Phillipe thought that Oscar had left Montreal abruptly because he had not permitted him to become a chef in the family restaurant. Oscar's absence created an unbearable void for Phillipe. He doesn't know how many more days he will have on this earth and wants to spend his last days surrounded by his loved ones. He desperately wants Oscar to return home, but decides to wait until he fully recovers to bring the subject up.

One morning after breakfast, weeks after Will and Dakota departed for Tennessee, both Phillipe and Mrs. Hastings make their way to Oscar's room. "Oh, I'm feeling a lot better," Oscar declares, waving his left arm around in the air in wide circles. "I have hardly any pain whatsoever. I guess it's time for me to whip up a fantastic dinner for you, Mrs. Hastings."

"Only if you're sure you are up to it—but, oh my, that is wonderful news," Mrs. Hastings says softly clapping her hands.

"Perhaps I can interest Grandpa in joining me, and together we can create something really special for you and Mr. Hastings. Maybe start with tomato bisque soup, followed by the main course of almond-crusted pork chops, green peas, beets with Spanish onions, artichokes, scalloped potatoes, baked bread, muffins. And for dessert, some kind of mousse."

"Oh, my goodness! Can I invite others to dinner?" Mrs. Hastings asks, eyes glazed.

"Well, of course, you can," says Oscar, cautiously. How many are you thinking of inviting?"

"For such a special dinner, I would have to include, say the mayor, sheriff, president of our bank, the doctor, and our neighbors, the Haywoods, and the Grants," Mrs. Hastings says counting the guests on her fingers.

"OK. Well, I will need time to prepare. Hmmmm." Oscar raises his eyebrows looking up at the ceiling. "At least seven days to check the meat in the smokehouse, the pantry, garden, and I may have to go into town and buy anything we are low on. I'll say, seven days at least before I can bring together a banquet for, sounds like, nearly ten people. What do you say, Grandpa? Are you up for it?" Oscar asks looking at Phillipe.

"I thought no one would ever ask." Phillipe smiles and thinks, *This may be the last supper of suppers for these folks. I take no pleasure in seeing my grandson's talents wasted in these backwoods.* "Yes, of course, we can cook up something fabulous."

"Very well. We can look at next Saturday, which is over seven days from now," Mrs. Hastings says shaking her hands in the air quickly. She is beside herself with excitement over planning such a special dinner party, and is frantic to get to her desk and start dispatching invitations to her guest list, which includes people she considers to be the town's movers and shakers. She turns to the maid, Marcie, and asks her to go fetch Ben who is somewhere working on the ranch. As soon as Ben is able, he comes to the main house and finds Mrs. Hastings in the office, busy drafting invitations.

Strolling up to and stopping in the doorway of the office, Ben takes off his hat and says, "Ma'am."

"Ben, yes, come in. Thank you for coming. I need you to deliver some invitations, no later than tomorrow afternoon."

"I can go as soon as you like," Ben says.

"OK. Let Mr. Hastings know, so I don't have hell to pay with him for using one of his ranch hands without permission."

Ben goes to the barn and saddles his horse to ride around the property looking for Mr. Hastings. Upon finding him, Ben lets him know that tomorrow he was asked to deliver invitations in town for Mrs. Hastings. When Mr. Hastings returns to the main house from working with Tom out in one of the pastures, he looks for Mrs. Hastings whom he finds still sitting at her desk. "What is this errand you are sending Ben on?"

Mrs. Hastings looks up from her papers. "Since we have two master chefs in our home, who have consented to prepare a delicious and special meal for us, I think this might be a splendid time to create some goodwill for ourselves, and invite the doctor, mayor, sheriff, banker, and some of the neighbors here for dinner. Don't you agree?"

Frown lines deepen in Mr. Hastings' face. "I don't mind the neighbors so much, but those other stuff-shirts. They are of no use all year. That Doc Stevenson is forever away to settlements or back east to conventions. The mayor has his perpetual hand out all the time. The sheriff embarrasses me saying I hire no-counts when I post bail to retrieve my ranch hands from jail. And the banker—oh, the banker, he's just robbing us right in our faces with high interest on payments and extra fees on transactions. Now you tell me, what kind of cheerful conversations am I gonna have with this bunch of vipers seated around our dinner table?"

"Well, I'm sending Ben to town to post their invitations tomorrow, and he should be back in a couple of hours," Mrs. Hastings says and refocuses on preparing her invitations.

"Oh yeah, invite those time wasters, and use one of my scarce ranch hands to do it! I'm only short-handed to take care of branding, fencing, birthing, worming, but go right ahead! Your dinner party means more than running this ranch," he grumbles words under his breath and lumbers out the office door.

Escaping to the veranda wearing their winter coats and covering themselves with furs, Oscar and his grandfather sit together on two white wrought-iron chairs separated by a matching white wrought-iron table drinking hot cider and brandy and sucking warm from a small fire pit masoned on the veranda. During a mild winter, like the one they are experiencing, these outdoor seats serve as a retreat from the household for reading a book or enjoying the fresh air, depending on which way the wind is blowing. The veranda is not completely isolated from the business of the ranch—branding irons burning beef hides, birthing cows, and sparring bulls—because such activities can either be heard or smelled. However today it provides Phillipe the privacy he is seeking.

"I meant to write you all more often, but my days are so full, especially when I'm on the cattle drives," Oscar says.

"I do not understand your attraction for cooking on the side of a dusty road for cowhands, people who have no appreciation for fine food. I've been told the dishes you cook for them are beans, rice, biscuits, grits—such a waste of your talent, my boy." Phillipe shakes his head.

"It is mostly for the pay, Grandpa, but I do enjoy seeing the country up close."

"Your parents were extremely worried when I left," Phillipe continues. "I had to plead with your father not to come. I panicked when I wired the Hastings to let them know I was coming and learned you were missing. After I arrived here, I held off sending any notice to your parents until I learned of your whereabouts. While you were recuperating, I sent them a wire to let them know you are well and safe. By the way, you never told me how you got injured?"

"My friend Will and I just crossed paths with the wrong Indians. We'll be more careful from now on."

"That brings me to what I wanted to talk to you about. Everything changed after you left. I felt I had let you down by not letting you work as a chef in the restaurant. I'm getting older, and am gradually turning more and more of the business over to your parents. I'm sure they would love to have you back there working alongside them."

"Go back home?" Oscar straightens his back. "That would mean giving up on my plans of having my own restaurant."

"You already have a restaurant, The LeGrande! Come home and we can explore any ideas you have, like expanding the services we offer. But that will be yours and your parents' decision. Not mine. I want you to seriously think about coming home with me. You are needed at home."

———•———

At the Applegate ranch, everyone is excited about the up and coming wedding between Will and Niabi. Harriet insists they have a wedding in Covington before they leave for Niabi's village, and has taken it upon herself to organize a group to plan the wedding. Mrs. Applegate has permitted Harriet to hold wedding planning meetings in her dining room; the meetings will be with Mrs. Walker, Martha, and Mrs. Fenton, Clarence's wife, and another fellow church member. Niabi's presence is essential, but she is avoiding them by lurking around the garden, supposedly helping Clarence deal with the frost. The ladies proceed with the meeting anyway.

"Is the bride-to-be coming to this meeting?" Mrs. Walker asks.

"We can go on and plan for the basic wedding things, which need to be done, and I can review everything with Niabi later," Harriet says.

"But she needs to participate in the planning of her own wedding, doesn't she?" Martha asks.

"Yes, she will come, but for now we can make a list of what's needed like flowers, invitations, the meal, whether we serve lunch or dinner," Harriet says counting the list on her fingers.

"What about her dress and his outfit?" Mrs. Walker asks.

"I will take care of that," Harriet says in a firm voice. Taking a deep breath, Harriet asks, "How shall we organize the actual marriage ceremony?" Her eyes circle the women seated at the dining room table.

"I will take care of that," Mrs. Walker says raising her hand.

A rather shy Mrs. Fenton looks around the large table, and then nervously says, "I'm a seamstress. So, if she wants me to make her a dress, I can do that, but she will have to show up to have it fitted on her."

"I will speak to her," Harriet says.

"I can handwrite the invitations. We need a guest list and a way to determine how many invitations we need?" Martha asks.

Harriet responds, "I will talk to her about that. In the meantime, I know we need to invite the Applegates, the Walkers, Fentons, Fred's family, and just let an announcement be made at the church for any others here in Covington. Also, Will's friends Oscar, Dakota Sam. I will check with Niabi and Will for any other names."

As the meeting winds down, everyone agrees a second planning meeting is a must. After thanking the other ladies for pitching in and seeing them out the door, Harriet makes haste to finish her few remaining tasks scheduled for that work day. She strolls through the kitchen, sees dinner is finished and ready to be served, and says, "Well done, Ethel." Ethel had collapsed on a stool pushed against the kitchen wall.

"Whew. I thought there was no end to the peeling, cutting, and boiling. We need to look over these menu selections," Ethel says further slumping down on the stool. Sheila scurries into the kitchen from upstairs, announces she is done for the day, and heads to the basement to her storage cupboard to fetch her coat and hat.

After having avoided the ladies' wedding planning meeting, Niabi finally enters the kitchen, walking in with her head tilted down, asking apologetically, "Can I assist with serving dinner?" She avoids eye contact with Harriet and Ethel. Harriet beams a look at Ethel suggesting she respond to Niabi. Harriet says, "I'll go and check on the state of the dining room."

"Yes, Niabi," Ethel says. "You take it all in, so I can stay off my sore feet. Mrs. Applegate and her guests should be entering the dining room shortly and waiting to be served." Niabi begins the process of placing dishes of food in the dining room on the buffet table along the wall.

Harriet sees Niabi has decided to work late serving dinner and uses that as an opportunity for her to find Will and speak to him alone. After checking the dining room and notifying Mrs. Applegate dinner has been set up and made ready, she gets her belongings and leaves for the day in search of Will.

At the end of the work day, Will has a habit of checking in on Rodeo. Only now he spends that quality time with FireTip. Harriet finds him in the barn brushing FireTip. She takes a deep breath, and then approaches him. "You need to help me with Niabi. She is not coming to the wedding planning meetings and we need to get invitations done, decide about flowers. Heck, I don't even know her full name. Can you speak to her? I'm nervous about the whole thing falling apart!"

"Calm down, Momma. Sure, I'll speak to her and find out why she's not going to the meetings," Will says.

After dinner at the cottage, Harriet and Niabi wash the dishes, dry them, and put them away. Harriet eyes Will, reminding him of their talk, before she turns and heads for her bedroom; his eyes communicate back to her that he will talk to Niabi. He has moved to one of the cushioned chairs near the fireplace in the front room. Harriet exits the kitchen, enters her room, and shuts the door. Niabi is all smiles as she pulls up a chair next to Will, glad they have these moments alone. Will takes one of Niabi's hands and asks if they can talk about something. She takes her other hand, rubs his hand, and says, "What do you want to talk about?"

"My dearest, you know I support you and want you to be happy. So, I ask, do you want to plan a wedding, or just not have a big ceremony and the two of us go to Pastor Walker on our own for a quiet private ceremony?" Will asks.

"This is about me missing the planning meeting, isn't it?" Niabi stops smiling and pulls away, but Will hangs on to her hand. "I don't know your ways, so I didn't feel I needed to be there; I would have nothing to say. How can I plan something I know nothing about? I only know the Choctaw way and . . . and . . . the more I think about it, I won't feel married until I have a Choctaw wedding."

"I don't know how we can do that . . . other than I take you home, and we have the wedding at your village." He caresses her hand and says, "But dearest, I like the idea of marrying here in Covington. Please don't make me travel all the way to your village before I can," he leans in for a kiss, "lay with you again."

What Will says gives Niabi an idea.

———•———

Blackie's horseshoes make crunching sounds against the powdery snow on the dirt road, as he plods down Poplar Grove street in Baltimore, Maryland, carrying the weight of Dakota Sam on his back. As Dakota nears the house that is said to contain the family he has been searching for, for the past twenty years, he wonders how would they look upon him now. Will they see an old man with no prospects, only a Civil War pension?

In front of an old wood-frame house with a wide front porch, Dakota pulls back on the reins, signaling to Blackie to halt. He ties Blackie to a railing, and climbs three steps to a front porch that wraps around the front of the house to midway on both sides. The heavy wooden front door stands open, pulled back, with only a screen door separating the front porch from the front room. Dakota knocks on the wood framing of the screen door, and an elderly lady, tall and slender, comes to the door. Her eyes gape, and her mouth drops open. She gasps and grips her face with one of her hands. Dakota removes his hat, and then quickly uses his hand to wipe the road dust off his face.

"Are you my Sam?" she asks, trembling with anticipation.

"Are you my Loma?" Dakota Sam asks, eyes watery, smiling with deep satisfaction at reaching the end of an arduous twenty-year search.

Caught up in the moment of seeing a character that only frequented her dreams, she slowly opens the screen door. He moves toward her beaming, confirming this is not an apparition. She extends her arms wide to receive the weary traveler. They embrace and kiss each other on lips and cheeks, letting out sounds of cheerful moaning. They remain locked in an embrace for a minute or two.

"Come on in and sit down. Oh, it gives my heart such pleasure to just see you, touch you, and know that after all these years, you have come back to us."

Loma takes his arm and guides Dakota to a chair in her modest front room. They seat themselves in two large adjacent wooden chairs fitted with cushions and stationed in front of a brick fireplace. Glancing around the wall, Dakota recognizes Loma's added touches: candles, curtains, and small porcelain vases filled with wild flowers.

"Can I get anything for you?" Loma asks.

"No, I don't need a thing. Right now, all I need is to gaze my eyes on my wife, whom I haven't seen in nearly twenty years. How is the boy?"

"You would be so proud of him. He's a man now. Working hard to keep a roof over our heads, and very much like you in his steady and calming spirit. He's at work—but Dakota, I must tell you something. We adopted a child who lost his mother. While Sam Jr. and I were moving from city to city, we encountered a young girl on the road. She joined us traveling and eventually we stopped at a contraband camp in Nashville, Tennessee. The young girl was named Clara Bell. Clara Bell had gotten herself in some trouble. She worked alongside me and Sam Jr., we three pooling our money to cover lodging and food. Clara Bell worked up until her baby was due. It was a difficult birth. We were in a contraband camp and made arrangements with a midwife. But at the appointed time, the midwife was nowhere to be found, and our need was a desperate one. To our deepest regrets, Clara Bell died. Before she passed, she squeezed my hand and begged me to get the baby out. The midwife came shortly after Clara Bell died. She examined her and said, 'We hadn't a moment to lose.' She asked for the clean linen we had ready, cut Clara Bell open, and pulled that baby right out of her belly. When he hit the open air, he began kicking and screaming. But all was not settled. We were not in the clear yet. The baby, losing its mother like that, now needed a wet nurse. The midwife told me of a young woman who worked at the Restless saloon and had given birth to a stillborn baby. She said that the woman may still have plenty of mother's milk in her breasts. Sam Jr. and I took the baby over to Restless. I recount in detail what happened, so you know what we know. A woman named Marge oversaw the girls working at the establishment. We were escorted into a room used as an office and for liquor storage. As Marge unlocked the door to let us in the room, she commented that Keri, the girl that lost her baby, was sadder than an old farm dog. She drooped around all day and cried all night.

"Marge saw our baby and asked, 'Are you gonna give her your baby?'

"I said, 'No! We just want her to wet nurse him.'

"Marge told us to wait there. I had never been to one of those places before. Ladies were walking around scantily dressed. Howls and shrills were heard upstairs and music spewed throughout from the parlor. When Keri entered the room where we waited, her eyes went straight to the baby squirming in my arms. Marge grabbed Keri's arm and stepped between us. Facing Keri, she said low so we could barely hear, 'Let me do the talkin'.' Putting one foot out and leaning back on the other, Marge next said, 'OK, she'll do it, for fifteen cents a session. You got that much?'

"We agreed to leave him at the saloon during the day and pick him up in the evening.

"Two days in, and the process was working. I would drop off Youngster in the morning on the way to my various cleaning jobs, and pick him up in the evening after I got off from work. She nursed him all day because he was growing fast. He was so full of milk when I picked him up, he slept through the night.

"One night, Keri said the baby was fussy and he hadn't finished taking in his milk, so I told her to come home with us. Later that night, Marge came looking for Keri. She stormed into our camp area and loudly asked Keri what she was doing there.

"Keri told her she was nursing the baby 'til he got to sleep. But that Marge got upset and told her to get back to Restless or else.

For that short while she was visiting us, I forgot, Keri was that kind of girl, and Marge was her overseer. Marge reminded me of the plantation overseer who whipped us slaves that got out of line or worked too slow. She threatened Keri, and I didn't like being around

Marge and didn't like the baby being near her, too. We doubled our efforts to have money ready to leave Nashville. I decided we were leaving as soon as Youngster reached nine months, an age I could wean him off the breast milk.

Youngster's nine-month birthdate eventually came, and I dropped by Restless to pick him up as usual. Keri had a gentleman customer, so the baby was with the other girls. I didn't give it away that we were leaving that night. I wanted to let Keri know, but I didn't know how Marge would take her income stream being shut off. Sam Jr. and I had already packed our things the night before. We hitched a ride on a delivery wagon to the Northern Tennessee border. From there we walked, hitched, camped, and made our way to Baltimore. I weaned Youngster by buying a cup of milk, warming it, and spoon-feeding him. I hard-boiled carrots and yams, mashed them, and fed them to him on my finger.

"I raised this baby. He's truly mine now. We call him Youngster, and he's fourteen years old. Oh, Dakota, my one wish now, and I prayed nights on this, is that when we were reunited, you will accept him as your boy, too."

Dakota lays his hat on a nearby table and takes Loma's hands. "If you have adopted him, my sweets, I see no reason why I can't adopt him, too," Dakota says and smiles.

"Thank you, my husband, thank you." Loma squeezes Dakota's hands, and asks, "Tell me, my dear husband, how did you find us?"

"When the war was over, I went to the Egglesby plantation and saw nothing left of my family. I asked around, searched some south, then some north. I wandered the countryside asking anyone and everyone if they knew people from the Egglesby plantation. My wandering, in fact, earned reasons for people to call me loco. Finally, a friend asked his boss, a White man, to put out some inquiries. I hear a pastor in Tennessee was in contact with Sam Jr. I guess all those inquiries paid off." Dakota pauses, and then asks, "How did you get out of Alabama?"

"When the soldiers stopped fighting in Decatur, there was like an empty void, no one around, no one patrolling to force us to stay. So, we stole away in the night. Running down roads, dipping into creeks to keep from getting caught, hiding in bushes—just runnin' 'til we made it to Tennessee. Many ex-slaves could go no farther than contraband camps, where food and shelter were scarce, and disease and sickness would break out from time to time. We found work in Nashville doing laundry, cleaning, cooking—you name it. Several migrators said conditions were better in Maryland, so we set our sights that way. Sam Jr. lucked out and got on with the railroad doing Pullman portering, and Youngster got on with a general labor group. He does whatever they ask, it seems, collecting garbage, trash, street cleaning, building cleaning, an assortment of work. I do laundry and maid service on call, like for fancy banquets and dinners. It's a living, and a darn sight better than slavery. At least I don't have nightmares about my babies being sold away from me, or any of us getting whipped to an inch of our lives because a piglet got loose."

"What did the overseers do when they saw I was gone?" Dakota asks.

Her eyes water. She swallows, and says, "They wanted to hurt me. I was sure 'nuff willing to submit my body to any kinda punishment, knowing you got free. But those clever rascals knew exactly where to aim. They brutally whipped our child, Sam Jr."

Dakota balls up his fists, and his lips squinch together. He breathes forcing air in and out hard, in anger, and with a cracked voice says, "I should have been there for you, been there to protect both of you."

Loma lurches over and grabs his arm, saying, "No, you did like we agreed. Get North and make a place for us to come to."

"That's why—why I enlisted, Dakota says stammering still reeling from what she just told him. "I figured I had nothin'. If I didn't survive the war, I'd be just where I started, of no use to you anyway. But if I survived, I'd get a monthly pension for the rest of my life. Now, I have something to offer you. However, now that I am with you, I don't want to be a burden. What can I . . .?" Dakota asks.

"No, no, honey, you can never be a burden," Loma says squeezing his hands again. "You are my joy sittin' here right next to me. If I go to my grave in the next five minutes, I will have known true joy that the Lord has brought you back to me. As the head of our family, I ask you, what do you want our family to do?"

"Well, my pension will give the family some relief. Maybe it can help Youngster come off his job, and go to school to get an education."

"Yes, that sounds good. I know Sam Jr. is not happy working his long hours. Maybe we can save some money, and that will give him time to switch to another job where he can have more time to rest and do some real thinking about his future—time so he can sort things out in his mind."

———•———

After Rita had her talk with Will on her front porch many months ago, she had allowed herself to imagine her life in other ways. One aspiration she toyed with was to become a nurse. She even went so far as to write to the Saint Mary's Nursing School in Washington, DC. Harriet solicited a letter of recommendation from Grant Applegate, and Pastor Walker wrote a letter heralding her work in the community, organizing church activities and helping the children and elderly. The letters, plus passing an aptitude test, have earned her a slot in the class starting January 1, 1887.

Exhausted after a long train ride from Covington, Tennessee, to Washington, DC, Rita checks her trunk at the train station before being picked up by the wagon from Saint Mary's Nursing School. Several other young ladies arrive around the same time as Rita, and all are told to wait in a particular area for the school's wagon. After checking into the nursing school near downtown, she hires a carriage to retrieve her trunk and take her to the home of Pastor Gregory and his wife, where she will room and board during school.

"Hello, young lady," Pastor Gregory greets her at his door. "Your parents wrote to me and told me to look out for you." The carriage driver sets Rita's trunk inside the house near the front door, and Rita tips him handsomely. Friends and neighbors of Covington had given her a loving send-off with cake, lemonade, and small gift sacks and handkerchiefs holding coins and dollars.

"Have you gotten registered at the school yet?"

"Yes, my classes start next week, and I'm looking forward to learning and living in a new place and all," Rita says setting down her bags. She looks around the pastor's home and is in awe of the high ceilings, staircase, and massive brick fireplace. Portraits of the pastor, Mrs. Gregory, and others are neatly arranged on the fireplace mantle and walls of the front room. The rooms are stylishly decorated with rugs, drapes, and chair cushions in purple prints with gold tassels and trims.

"Are these all of your bags?" Pastor Gregory asks.

Rita stops her gazing. "Yes this is everything."

"I hope you will be joining us for church services on Sundays."

"Yes, I will be there." Rita smiles and nods.

Pastor Gregory picks up her bags and ushers her into the front room. "Your mother says you are an excellent cook. I wonder if I could impose upon you, and ask you to grace my home's kitchen with some of your culinary delights."

"It is not an imposition at all. When do you want me to prepare something?"

"I want to invite a family to our home to celebrate their reunion, after being separated by the war for twenty years. And I want to also celebrate your new beginning as well," Pastor Gregory says.

"I would be happy to, but only if you have gotten your wife's approval for me to be in her kitchen," Rita says and laughs.

"Oh yes! I know who wears the pants around here. She has given her approval."

The Egglesbys take the train to Washington, DC, to spend a few days. They come in on a Friday, and on Sunday plan to attend church services at Pastor Gregory's church. After church services, the Egglesby family, absent Sam Egglesby Sr., pays their respects to the pastor in the front of the sanctuary near the altar. The pastor reminds the Egglesbys, Loma, Sam Jr., and Youngster, of an invitation to dinner at his home that evening. Pastor asks if Sam Egglesby Sr. will attend dinner as well.

"I will ask him," Loma says. "He stayed in the hotel room this morning because the only clothes he has are his Army uniforms."

"His Army uniforms would be a welcome sight in our church," Pastor Gregory says. "Tell your husband he is a hero in our eyes, and he will be very welcome here in whatever outfit he chooses."

The Egglesbys' opportunity to be in Washington, DC, at all was due to Sam Jr. finding a new job as a butler at the Reese-Hays Luxury Hotel in downtown Washington. Sam Jr. makes good pay, plus tips, and works a shift where he has three days off every week instead of once a month. He is in a much better mood, and the Egglesbys can stay at a nearby hotel in the Negro section of town to look the city over and consider whether to move the entire family to Washington, DC.

Sam Jr. has mixed feelings about them all moving there. He is starting to want some independence and privacy. There have been developments in his life that he wants to keep hidden from his family. Effects of the ravages of slavery are yet to be understood. For Sam Jr., unfortunately, the effects have manifested into nightmares, paranoia toward Whites, and waves of fury, then depression. He is aware of the effects and has done a good job of hiding them from day to day.

But after he acquired more personal time, easing up from being a round-the-clock caretaker for his mother and Youngster, the demons once held at bay by those responsibilities have made their appearance. One night retrieving a hotel guest's food tray of half-eaten plates and half-drank glasses of wine, Sam Jr. sipped from a leftover bottle of wine retrieved from the guest. At first, the alcohol in the drink tasted sharp and bitter. However, after a second and a third sip, what was sharp began to numb his entire mouth and began to permeate a numbness throughout his brain and body. He had never felt such freedom from aches and stress. He began to sample other leftover drinks from trays he picked up. To know which guests ordered drinks, he avoided assignments as a bellhop transporting guests' luggage or as a server serving guests in the parlor and patio, and instead voiced a preference for delivering and retrieving room-service trays. On occasion, if he knew the guest was a big spender, he would encourage them to order more than needed amounts of liquor to ensure they had a good time, and consequently there would be plenty of leftover drinks for him.

Latimore was the head Negro in charge of butlers and food servers at the hotel. Negroes were relegated to food servers instead of waiters in the restaurants because waiters were paid more, received larger tips, and were visible on the floor. Negroes were confined to housekeeping and food serving tasks.

One night when Dakota Sam is out, Youngster catches a horse-drawn street car into Washington, DC and comes to the hotel because of an emergency. Loma has slipped and fallen on the front steps and her wrist has swollen up and is hurting something awful. After making her comfortable in her bed, Youngster did not know what else to do, so he has come to the hotel hoping to get help from Sam Jr.

"He hasn't checked out, because his time card has not been stamped," says Latimore to a bright-eyed Youngster. "I will check the locker area. You wait here."

Sam Jr. had downed one-half of a bottle of wine a guest had discarded when he retrieved the room service table. He had changed out of his uniform and had drunk the wine in the hotel's basement. After he drags himself back to the locker area to get his hat and coat, he is confronted by Latimore.

"Your brother is here. There's an emergency with your mother at your home."

"Oh. Thank you." He wobbles while closing the locker and slides his hat on his head.

Latimore moves close to him. "Have you been drinkin'?"

"I'm off duty! And . . . I'm in control of myself and headed home. You have no reason to fire me."

"I'll let you go this time with only a warning. But never again bring liquor and drink it on these premises!" Latimore says raising his voice, and storms out of the locker room.

———•———

Dakota agrees to attend the dinner at Pastor Gregory's home. The pastor lives a thirty-minute walk from his church. He gives the Egglesbys detailed directions, and they walk from their hotel to the pastor's residence for a 5 p.m. dinner.

When the Egglesbys arrive at Pastor Gregory's home, the pastor greets them at the door. "Welcome, welcome."

"Thank you for having us," Loma says, and the Egglesbys remove their hats and file into the parlor.

Pastor Gregory asks Mrs. Egglesby to make the introductions. She begins by acknowledging Pastor and Mrs. Gregory to her family, and then introduces Sam Sr. first, followed by saying they have already met her oldest son, Sam Jr., and their youngest, whom they call Youngster.

"I understand I owe you, Pastor Gregory, for reuniting me with my family," Dakota Sam says extending his hand for a handshake.

"There was more than me at work, I assure you; and I attribute it all to God's good grace. It was messages to fellow pastors, messages through the Pullman porters, messages coming from Applegate Ranch, and somehow it all came together, and we gladly celebrate this wonderful reunion tonight." The pastor invites all to take a seat and adds, "I'm sure dinner will be ready shortly."

The Egglesbys begin to gawk at the purple and gold décor of the Gregorys' front sitting room. The Egglesbys' home is a small barren pinewood cavern compared to this chamber lush with rugs, cushions, and wallpaper.

Mrs. Gregory excuses herself to check on the dinner. In the kitchen, Rita says to Mrs. Gregory, "The food is ready to be served." She and Mrs. Gregory enter the dining room and place dishes of fried chicken, greens, cabbage, and yams on a buffet table against the wall; ham, corn, and biscuits are placed on the dining room table.

Mrs. Gregory returns to the parlor and announces, "We can go into the dining room." Everyone moves from the sitting room to the dining room where aromas from the food dance in the air. Mrs. Gregory continues, "Please sit wherever you like." Dakota Sam glances at the buffet table and the ham on the dining room table and is overcome with cheerfulness, making it difficult for him to pull his chair out from the table to sit.

"And, everyone," says Pastor Gregory, waiting for Rita to finish setting the food down, "this is a fellow church member from Covington, Tennessee: Miss Rita Walker. She'll be staying with us for a while. Tonight, we also celebrate her starting nursing school here in Washington, DC."

Pastor Gregory addresses all and says, "Before we partake of the delicious food prepared for us by Miss Walker, let us bow our heads and give thanks." All bow their heads and join hands. Pastor continues, "Heavenly Father, we do humbly thank you for what we are about to receive, and for all the days and nights you have fed and sheltered us, by way of good Samaritans, or others doing better or worse than ourselves; however, we are just so thankful that you held each of the Egglesby family members under your protection, safe from harm. And we thank you for making it possible for Miss Rita Walker to join us, as she embarks on her education to become a nurse. We give these thanks in the name of your Son and our Savior, Jesus Christ. Amen."

Mrs. Gregory announces, "Dinner is served."

As Dakota Sam starts lifting a plate, Loma grabs it and says, "Remain seated. Your wife is happy to make your plate tonight."

"Well, I want a little of everything," Dakota says, grinning from ear to ear.

"I know; you haven't changed," Loma says with a sparkle in her eyes.

Sam Jr. moves swiftly down the serving line at the buffet table to get behind Rita. She sees him walking up, moves to the side, anticipating he wants to begin making his plate, but he motions for her to proceed to make her plate first. As she begins to place spoonfuls of food on her plate, Sam Jr. says, "Pastor Gregory said you are from Covington, Tennessee."

"Yes, I am," Rita says.

"Did you know my father's friend Will of Applegate Ranch?" Sam Jr. asks.

"Yes, we grew up together as children. I know him very well."

Sam Jr. notices a slight tremor in her voice when she speaks about Will, as though the words are loaded with emotion. He adds food to his plate and follows her to the dining room table to make sure he sits next to her. "Why did you choose Washington, DC, for nursing school?" he asks.

"I like that there are a lot of ambitious Negroes here, and I wanted to get away from home."

He smiles and says, "Well, that is downright convenient, since I am working in Washington, and desiring to take a young lady sight-seeing of course when she has a break from classes."

"You are mighty sure of yourself Mister . . .?"

"It's Egglesby, Sam Egglesby, Jr."

"Then, Mr. Sam Egglesby Jr., what makes you think I will go with you sightseeing during my breaks?" Rita asks.

"Because fate has brought us together, Miss Rita, and it would be foolish for you to tempt fate." He completely stops eating and beams a smile of confidence directly at her face. As she slices a piece of ham on her plate, she inadvertently looks up and their eyes connect for a moment. They both blush, and she taps him on the arm. He returns to eating, and she steals another look at him. Before she knows it, she begins examining his face. Her eyes drift from his eyes to his nose and finally settle on his lips. He's talking to Youngster about how good the food is and is unaware she's examining him. She thinks, *Who is this dapper-dressed man, that's giving me a tingly feeling?* He returns his gaze toward her and pretends to try to take food off her plate. This ignites an exchange of affectionate taps and giggles. Realizing that they are having too much fun, they both look around the table wondering if the others see their mild flirtations.

———•———

Back in Covington, it's the end of February, and plans for Will and Niabi's wedding are coming together. The wedding date is set for June 18, 1887. Martha comes to the Applegate Ranch, and locates Niabi in the wash room in the basement of the main house. Martha shows her the draft invitation she has prepared. "How does this look? Martha asks.

W E D D I N G
Invitation
*You are invited to come and bear witness
to the marriage of Niabi to Mr. Will Lawton.*

At   On

*Colored Methodist Episcopal   Saturday, June 18, 1887
Church in Covington, Tennessee   7:00 pm*

"Just think—once these are sent out, your lovely wedding gifts will come rollin' in," Martha says.

Niabi looks at the paper. Then her eyes drift up and dance around, and she breathes deeply, formulating how to get one particular wedding gift. "This is good, Martha. Can you help me write notes to send with these invitations to my guests?"

"Yes, of course," Martha says.

"Also, can I take you into my confidence regarding the contents of the notes? I especially want my words kept from Will, for now."

Martha writes personal messages to accompany invitations sent to the trading post at Fort Townsend and Oscar. Invitations are also sent to Dakota Sam, Mr. & Mrs. Hastings, Rodrigo, Matt, and Tom. These are names of persons she remembers Will speaking of when telling her about different cattle drives.

———•———

The sound of metal hitting metal rattles through the window of the front bedroom. "Is that the mail?" Loma yells. There is no reply, because Dakota Sam, the only other person at home, is in the backyard of their recently acquired home in Washington shoveling Blackie's dung. Loma walks from the front bedroom to the front door, and steps out on the porch where the mailbox is stationed on a wooden post up against the porch railing. She opens the mailbox and finds inside a tan envelope which is addressed to Sam Egglesby Sr. and his family. She goes to the back door, and yells to Dakota Sam, "There is a letter here. I can make out Sam Egglesby."

Dakota walks over and looks at the envelope. "I can make out Apple; maybe it's from Applegate Ranch."

Still holding the envelope, Loma asks, "Open the envelope?"

"Yes, sweetness."

She opens it. Because his hands are dirty, he motions for her to hold on to the document inside and just show it to him. "I see something is happening on June 18. I could ride over to Pastor Gregory's, or do you know a neighbor who could read it to us?"

"I see the neighbors and speak to them. But I would feel uncomfortable asking them to read something to me. Wait, I know a lady, a White lady, one of my customers. She's very nice. I can ask her to read it to me."

Loma finishes her order for laundry, and takes it to her customer who is the wife of a naval officer.

When she returns home that evening, Loma holds the invitation and speaks from memory. "OK, let me sit down and remember what she said. It seems this is a wedding invitation. The wedding is between your friend Will Lawton, and a girl named Niabi. The wedding is June 18, this year like you said, and at the Colored Methodist Episcopal church in Covington, Tennessee."

"Well, I'll be! That Will is really gonna do it. He and that Indian gal are still stirring things up. I told you about the Indian gal, and how we got outta her Indian village by the skin of our teeth. And it was all because the chief's son was worked up over this same Indian gal."

"Will the chief's son simmer down after he learns she is marrying Will?" Loma asks.

"I doubt it. We may have another uprising on our hands, requiring calling out the troops and organizing peace conferences. I hope he knows what he's doing. And, from the mouth on her, knows what he's getting into." He looks at Loma and takes her hand, and says, "She's not a sweetie like my sweet Loma."

Loma smiles.

————•————

At the Hastings ranch, the maid distributes the mail to Mr. Hastings, Tom, Matt, Rodrigo, and Oscar. Oscar receives the letter from the maid in the kitchen as he is on his way upstairs to visit with Phillipe, who is staying in one of the guest rooms at the ranch.

Oscar stares at the envelope as he enters the guest room.

"Who is the letter from?" asks Phillipe.

"It's sent from Applegate Ranch. It must be from Will." Oscar opens the envelope and pulls out the papers it contains. He stares at the first document in surprised fright.

"Well, are you going to share, or is it private?" asks Phillipe.

"No, I can share it. It appears to be a wedding invitation. Will is marrying Niabi, an Indian girl, on June 18."

"Ah, Will. He's your good friend, no?"

"Yes, he is my good friend. I'm—wait, there is also a note from Niabi.

Dear Oscar,

Hope this letter finds you well. Will told me you were hurt during the rescue.

I was saddened to hear that, and in my prayers, I ask the Great Spirit to quicken your healing.

Now, I would like to help Will bring Rodeo home. I have sent a message to Nashoba with a wedding invitation, asking him to return

*Rodeo as his wedding gift to us. I ask you to do whatever you can on
that end to help get Rodeo returned from Nashoba to Will.*

  If this is too much for you to do, do not worry. I understand.

                                                                  Niabi

"What does she mean by 'rescue'?" Phillipe asks.

"Will met Niabi on a cattle drive. He decided to take her to his
home in Tennessee. The chief's son took me hostage to force Will to
bring Niabi back to their Indian village. I was tied up and held in a
dwelling in the village. When Will and Dakota Sam rescued me, I was
shot with an arrow by one of the villagers. Our release from the village was based on the chief's son keeping Will's horse Rodeo, a horse
Will loves like a person, until Will returns with Niabi. And that's the
whole story, Grandpa," says Oscar.

"This is almost like a Penny Dreadful story," Phillipe says, his
mouth gaped amazed at this tale.

"The chief's son is a proud man, and I can't believe she wants me
to convince him to release the horse when he said he would only do
it—when Will returns with her to the village," Oscar says.

"My goodness. This Niabi is asking the son of the chief to swallow his pride. Put yourself in his position, the position any man would
be in under these circumstances. You are swallowing your pride, and
giving a wedding gift to your adversaire to support the wedding
between the woman you love and your adversaire," Phillipe says.
"Imagine that."

"Yes, Grandpa," Oscar says snippily since he's not concerned over
Nashoba's plight one bit.

"That's a lot to ask," Phillipe says in a high-pitched tone. Then he
lowers his tone. "But, if this chief's son really and truly loves this
Niabi, I would think he would do this last one thing for her. But if
she was to be a mere badge of conquest or an ornament in his life, he

will not. I have learned, and someday I hope you will learn, too, that true love cannot be bought, bargained for, begged for, or forced. It just arises between two people; it is the caring feeling that one has for another, that grows effortlessly." Phillipe pours two glasses of water for him and Oscar. "I would be curious to see how this chief's son responds." Phillipe pauses, and then asks, "Are you going to this wedding?"

The day arrives for the special dinner at the Hastings Ranch. Mrs. Hastings hurries about making last-minute preparations for the arrival of her invited guests. The best china has been taken out of the china closet, washed, dried, and properly arranged on the dining room table at each of the place settings. Each place setting has the fork on the left side of the plate. On the right side of the plate is the knife, with the spoon to the right of the knife. At each setting, the bottoms of all eating utensils are lined up with the bottom of the plate. Glasses are to the right above the plate, and above the left side of the plate is a small bread plate with a butter spreader or small knife laid upon it. Mrs. Hastings had demonstrated to the maid how she wanted the place settings arranged. The nicest lace tablecloth covers the dining room table, and a matching one drapes the buffet table against the wall. Days before the glamourous crystal candelabra in the center of the dining room table and others on the buffet table were cleaned to a sparkle for the special dinner.

In his study, Mr. Hastings finds among his mail a tan envelope sent from the Applegate Ranch. He opens it and heads for the dining room where Mrs. Hastings is still putting the finishing touches on the room.

"Dear, there is an invitation here from Will Lawton, the Negro boy I hired to wrangle the horses on the drives," Mr. Hastings says.

"Oh, an invitation! What kind of invitation?" Mrs. Hastings asks while continuing to remove items from her china closet.

"A wedding invitation. It seems he is marrying the missing Choctaw Indian girl; I recognize the name from Captain Horton's notice."

"The missing Indian girl?" Mrs. Hastings arches her eyebrows.

"Now we know what happened to her," Mr. Hastings says glibly shaking his head.

While Mrs. Hastings continues taking glasses out of her huge china closet, Mr. Hastings walks toward the kitchen, swings open the door, and sees Oscar, Phillipe, and Marcie busy preparing dinner. "Oscar, have you heard about Will Lawton's wedding?" He says holding the tan envelope in front of him.

"Yes, sir. I've received an invitation." Oscar looks up from the food he is preparing. Phillipe and Marcie are busy looking for a pan in the shelves. After Marcie hears what is said and sees the envelope, she offers, "Mr. Hastings, similar tan envelopes were received in the mail for Tom, Matt, and Rodrigo."

"Oh, how interesting," Mr. Hastings replies, and then asks, "Oscar, are you going?"

Oscar sets down the large stirring spoon he was using. "Yes, I was going to ask you about time off to go," Oscar says.

Hearing the conversation through the open kitchen door, Mrs. Hastings says, "Psst, psst," to get Mr. Hastings's attention. He stops and looks at her. She motions for him to return to the dining room and close the kitchen door.

Frown lines appear on his forehead as he turns back to Oscar. "Let's talk about your plans later." Mr. Hasting closes the kitchen door and, still puzzled, asks Mrs. Hastings in a whisper, "What is it?"

She moves near him and responds in a low tone, "I don't like the sound of that. Time off to go to the wedding! He's young and talented, and liable to go off and keep going," she says as she throws up her hands. "What's gonna make him want to come back here?"

Mr. Hastings bristles and replies, trying to keep low tone as well. "So, what do you want me to do about it? Put him in leg irons to keep him locked down in your kitchen, woman!" The maid comes into the dining room bringing clean and pressed dinner napkins.

"Let's take this conversation upstairs," Mrs. Hastings says. She shows the maid where and how to place the napkins, which glasses are to be arranged on the dining room table, and which glasses are to be used for drinks before dinner in the parlor. Then, the Hastings go upstairs.

While the maid double-checks the table, Oscar tastes the prepared dishes and Phillipe monitors the baking bread and cakes. In their bedroom, Mr. and Mrs. Hastings begin to dress in their finery. Portions of their outfits for the evening lie on the bed and hang on the clothes closet door. While dressing, Mr. Hastings says to Mrs. Hastings, "Your time having Oscar work for you may be coming to an end. You can't expect him to be satisfied with being here forever. Just find someone else. Or even better, have him train someone for you. Speaking of cooking, I'm still wondering what is the purpose of this gathering in our dining room tonight? Did you have something particular in mind you want to campaign for?"

"The difference between you and me is that I plan ahead. Nothing is pressing now, but when you have people in, feed them, compliment them, and appear to be one of their supporters, it makes it much easier to get a yes answer out of them down the road, when you do need them for something. It costs us nothing to have these people out to our home for dinner."

"Well, it's costing me something—a restful night I would have otherwise spent reading a paper or a good book, smoking a cigar, and drinking warm brandy. I can think of a lot of ways to spend an evening after being out in the pastures monitoring for sick and pregnant cows."

"Oh, you just follow my lead and be your old charming self, and if you can't do that, just get yourself a glass of something, swig on it, and stay quiet," Mrs. Hastings says.

Doc Stevenson, Mayor Parker, Sheriff Dandry, and Bank President Collins all ride out from Waco together. The mayor and banker share a carriage ride, while the sheriff and doctor ride their horses. They arrive after the Grants and Haywoods, who are the Hastings' neighbors at adjoining ranches.

There had been contention between the Hastings and their neighbors when the Hastings first moved there. The land boundaries had to be confirmed, and the cattle had to be branded until all the fencing was up. Once the boundaries, fencing, and branding were done, the families began attending the same socials and interacting and exchanging pleasantries. Mr. Hastings is the only rancher with enough cattle to drive to market. The Grants have a few cattle and horses, but earn their money primarily from corn and cotton. The Haywoods earn their living in the same way.

The maid shows all of the guests into the parlor, which is located on the right side of the entryway. After she closes the front door, the maid stations herself behind a trolley decorated with a lace cloth, mounted with different drinks including whiskey, wine, beer, and iced tea. There in the parlor, she offers them the variety of drinks available from the trolley. Sheriff Dandry asks for whiskey. After being served, he walks over to Doc Stevenson and says, "You know my ankle is still bothering me, Doc."

"Did you wrap it as I told you, and stay off it for at least a day?" Doc asks.

"I can't stay off my feet and do my job," complains the sheriff.

Coming down their grand staircase to the entryway, Mrs. Hastings first, and then Mr. Hastings, enter the parlor, greeting their guests, "Welcome, welcome everyone. I hope you had a pleasant ride out?" Mrs. Hastings says.

"Yes, the roads were clear and it wasn't windy," remarks the sheriff.

"Has our maid, Marcie, offered you a drink of water, iced tea, or something a little stronger?" Mrs. Hastings asks her guests.

"Yes, she did," says the mayor.

Mrs. Grant and Mrs. Haywood draw near to Mrs. Hastings. "I love your dress," says Mrs. Grant. "Hmm, hmm, me, too," agrees Mrs. Haywood. The ladies salivate over her dress, which has a burgundy velvet top with a matching velvet belt. The top has a low neckline and its bottom drapes low over a beige chiffon lace floor-length skirt. For jewelry, she accented the outfit with magenta earrings, necklace, and bracelet.

"Thank you, ladies. Your compliments are much appreciated. But please excuse me for a moment," Mrs. Hastings says. Now directing her attention to all of her guests in the parlor, she says loud enough for all to hear, "Continue enjoying your drinks, and I'll check on our dinner."

Different ones make their drink selections, and the maid pours their beverages into small goblets. Mr. Hastings forms his lips into a smile, as he makes his rounds in the room, forcing out pleasantries to each male guest—pleasantries he deplores extending to particular ones of his guests.

Mrs. Hastings returns to the parlor with a reluctant Phillipe LeGrande and announces, "Ladies and gentlemen, may I introduce you to a special guest tonight, Mr. Phillipe LeGrande, who is a renowned chef from Montreal, Canada. He is a guest in my home, and I am so grateful that he is treating us tonight to a first-class meal with all the trimmings and dessert."

The gentlemen respond with, "Hear, hear," and the ladies look to each other and emit mild shrieks accompanied by gloved hands clapping.

Phillipe responds to Mrs. Hastings, "Oh, mademoiselle, you are too kind to Phillipe."

"Now, his grandson, Oscar, is our regular chef here at the ranch. He is also preparing our dinner and will be bringing out our food soon. I will have an opportunity then to introduce him. Though unusual for a master chef, I've asked Mr. LeGrande to join us at the table, which is something he rarely does. Ha ha ha," she laughs nervously. "But again, I want to thank him *and* his grandson for making this splendid evening possible," Mrs. Hastings concludes and everyone claps. Phillipe bows.

The maid steps away for five minutes, returns, and nods to Mrs. Hastings.

"Ladies and gentlemen, dinner is served," Mrs. Hastings announces.

The guests follow Mrs. Hastings into the dining room, located on the other side of the entryway, as she glides with her shoulders back, head high, and back straight. Mr. Hastings follows behind the last guest to leave the parlor. In the dining room, Mrs. Hastings directs each one of the guests to sit at a seat at the large dining room table, which comfortably seats twelve persons. She and Mr. Hastings take seats perched at each end of the long table. Platters and bowls emitting aromatic smells are already on the dining room table. Oscar enters the dining room bringing in a porcelain dish of scalloped potatoes and sets it on the buffet table. Mrs. Hastings uses this time to introduce Oscar as the other chef and Phillipe's grandson. That announcement immediately draws startled looks from all the guests. They struggle to hide their surprise as they look from Phillipe, the White man with a French accent, to Oscar, a Negro. Their startled looks cause Phillipe to lean back in his chair, his eyes circling the table, defying a show of any signs of being uncomfortable. Oscar, undaunted, steps forward, stands stiff and straight, then bows his head and returns to the kitchen.

Exasperated, Mrs. Hastings tries to squash the insensitive attention this news is getting. "Oscar is an equally marvelous chef. He's my regular chef at the ranch, and we are very pleased to have them both cooking for us tonight."

Phillipe LeGrande finds himself seated between Mrs. Hastings and the sheriff. Everyone has taken up the napkin that lay pressed flat on their plates and put them in their respective laps. Those nearest to the platters and bowls of beets, artichokes, and pees on the table dip out generous spoonfuls onto their plates, and pass the bowls around the table to the guest seated next to them. Some leave their seats to continue filling their plates with almond-crusted pork chops and scalloped potatoes from porcelain dishes on the buffet table. "There are more delights over here," says Mrs. Haywood anxiously inspecting the dishes on the buffet table.

Standing at the buffet table, the sheriff says, "We've been getting reports of Indians outside of the reservation. Have any of you seen any Indians on or near your property? They've been described as a hunting party."

"Quoi, I mean what is a hunting party?" Phillipe asks.

Returning to his seat next to Phillipe, the sheriff responds, "A hunting party is a group of young Indian males out hunting buffalo, deer, rabbit, whatever meat they can find to eat. Now that's what we hope they are hunting for."

Doc seated across the table in front of Phillipe joins in the conversation. "Sheriff, you don't know for sure there was a hunting party; you have no proof there were any Indians at all off the reservation."

"You're just an Indian-sympathizer, visiting settlements and contraband camps," the sheriff replies. "As far as you're concerned, they all can run free throughout the territory, thieving and frightening folks."

The maid comes in and goes from guest to guest, refilling their water glasses and wine glasses, and then looks to Mrs. Hastings for anything further. Mrs. Hastings shakes her head, not uttering a word. The maid then exits to the kitchen.

"You can't blame them for leaving that uninhabitable land they've been sequestered to," Doc responds. "If they leave the village or reservation, and I'm not saying they did, it's probably because the land lacks enough wild game to hunt and feed on, or the land isn't fertile enough to grow a decent crop. You have to understand, for some, their culture is to be a nomadic people, used to moving with the buffalo herds, relocating when the seasons change. They don't kill for sport or profit as we do. They only kill what they need for food, and leave no rotting carcass. They use the hides for their shelter, their clothing, the bones for tools, and other objects. On the other hand, their tribe may be a stationary one, living as farmers and quite skillful at it. Our grave mistake is that we disregard whatever culture they have and try to make them live like us."

Seated next to Mr. Hastings, the banker asks, "How safe is it if they're marauding around?"

"You surely don't fear the Indians?" Phillipe says. "I thought they were given land and resettled, and there is peace between them and the States."

"As Doc says, they may not be satisfied with the land given to them to live on, and choose to scavenge around on our land," Mayor Parker says.

Doc responds, "Listen to yourself—*our land?*"

Mayor Parker replies, "OK, the land we live on now! It's all settled now, by the Indian Wars, the Alamo, the Civil War. Blood was spilled to get us where we are now. Mexicans back to Mexico, Indians on the reservations, Negroes in contraband camps. Everybody has a place now. We need the Indians and the Negroes to be corralled because they come to our towns, go into our hotels, our saloons—our women aren't safe."

Jarred when the mayor references Negroes and possibly offending Phillipe, Mrs. Hastings speaks up, "Perhaps this isn't the best conversation for dinner."

"Mr. LeGrande, all of us don't share the opinion of the mayor," Mr. Grant contributes. "I have several Negroes working on my property. We have never had any trouble with them. I think this Indian hunting party business is just a rumor. It's a rumor until we have real evidence something is going on."

"Well, no disrespect to Mr. LeGrande or his grandson," Banker Collins says, "but we're talking about those *others*, that invade our property, squatting. They can bring down property values."

"Collins, is that all you're concerned about, property values?" Doc asks. "People around us are trying to survive—through bitter cold winters, food shortages, illnesses. Come down from your summit on the hill and take a look around you!"

"Hastings, have your drovers had any run-ins with Indians on the drives?" Mr. Haywood asks.

"No, nothing's been reported since I've been driving herds to Dodge City," Mr. Hastings says.

Seeing Mrs. Hastings in distress about the topic, Mr. Hastings attempts to change the subject. "We've just received notice that an Indian girl from the village near Red River is marrying one of my drovers, and we have been invited to the wedding."

"Yes, my grandson and I are going," Phillipe adds. "I hope I am not betraying him if I talk on this matter, but the bride of this wedding was pursued by the son of the chief, and she chose the drover. I met this drover briefly, and he seems to be a fine, upstanding person."

"Now that right there gives me a reason to be concerned," Sheriff Dandry says. "We could be sitting right on a powder keg. This chief's son might be angry about losing out to the drover. A drover from your ranch, Hastings."

"I would feel better, sheriff, if you would contact the fort, and let them know what's going on," Mayor Parker says. "You have to get out ahead of these things. If you don't, a wagon train is attacked, a ranch is torched, women raped."

"Oh dear, are you saying we are not safe?" Mrs. Haywood looks at the sheriff. "We don't have a lot of ranch hands that are good with guns as compared to the Hastings Ranch."

Doc Stevenson raises his voice. "Mayor, stop scaring the women!"

"Surely, mayor, you jest," Phillipe says, smiling. "Love triangles like this happen frequently where I come from. Is it not common in the States as well?"

"Not with the son of a chief. These are the Plains Indians," Sheriff Dandry responds. "They are fierce warriors. It has taken the government years fighting them before things settled down. And memories run long in this part of the country among settlers and the tribes."

Doc Stevenson throws his napkin down on the table. "You know nothing, sheriff! Just throw them all into one bucket, calling all of them plains Indians set on violence, and spewing fear and distrust."

Seeking to diffuse the current tension, Mr. Grant turns to Phillipe. "Mr. LeGrande, where will the wedding take place?"

"I believe it's in Tennessee. The groom is a close friend of my grandson. I don't share your fears. I see them all as people. I will go there, and make a toast to the bride and groom, a toast to their health and happiness," Phillipe says.

The dinner plates are taken up by the maids, and desserts are presented to the guests. The guests eagerly partake of the delicious desserts prepared by Phillipe: Bavarian cream pudding, and chocolate soufflé cake. Mr. Hastings chooses to forego the usual after-dinner practice of the men breaking off to his study to smoke, have more drinks, play cards, or talk politics. The women have become anxious to get home after the unnerving talk about roaming Indians, so Mr.

and Mrs. Hastings encourage the husbands to get them home to settle their nerves. Similar comments from the Hastings are made to the
mayor and banker, that they should head back and limit the time they
are out on the road in the dark.

Banker Collins responds through his wine-laced mouth, "We are
traveling, after all, with the sheriff. What shall we fear?"

Doc Stevenson replies, "We can't be certain that at the first sign
of danger, the sheriff won't take off, leaving us." They all let out a
laugh, and proceed to mount their horses or carriage, respectively.

When the last guest is seen moving away from the main house,
Mr. Hastings closes the front doors and bellows, "What a night!"

Mrs. Hastings speaks with Phillipe at the bottom of the staircase.
"I want to apologize if my guests made you feel in any way uncomfortable. They are people shaped by this land, and by the time we find
ourselves living in. They mean no disrespect to you personally."

"Since Oscar's father married my daughter Yvette, I have learned
that some of my acquaintances speak words of dissent, but would
never act harshly, while other acquaintances speak words of dissent
and then act accordingly. This state of affairs leaves me with no other
choice but to always be vigilant for the sake of my loved ones," Phillipe says.

Phillipe bids Mr. and Mrs. Hastings goodnight and goes to the
kitchen to assist Oscar and the maids with the cleanup.

As the Hastings head upstairs to bed, Mrs. Hastings says to Mr.
Hastings, "I am completely disgusted with tonight's dinner. These
people, who are the leading figures of our town, are nothing more
than outright petty bigots and racists."

"Where do you think you are, Mrs. Hastings? We are in Texas, the
last hold-out for ending slavery. Th people here fought the government to keep slavery, drove out the Indians and the Mexicans. The
towns are segregated. You know this! And, your little dinner party is
gonna mean a hill of beans to how they think about things."

"I know. I just thought they would show some class about it. They gawked at Phillipe being related to Oscar, said Negroes and Indians are torching ranches, insinuated raping white women. This was an outright insult to our great chefs, who are my special guests. I wouldn't be surprised if Phillipe didn't pull his boy outta here altogether, tonight. I'm so boiling hot, I could go to that wedding, and hope all the Negroes and Indians come. And if I live through it, come back, and host another dinner party, and recount the whole affair to them. See how they like that!"

———•———

The trading post inside the Fort Townsend complex receives its mail regularly delivered through the railroad service. When the mail arrives that evening, Captain Horton reviews it for dispatches from Army headquarters. Among the correspondence he finds one tan envelope addressed to Nashoba, Trading Post, Fort Townsend, Indian Territory. Captain Horton sends a soldier to ask Chief Samuels for an audience with him tomorrow before noon. The soldier is directed to share that a letter has come for Nashoba. The chief agrees to the meeting.

The next day, Captain Horton arrives at Chief Samuels' dwelling accompanied by two soldiers: his clerk, Nelson, to record the meeting, and one additional soldier for security, who waits outside. The agreement established between the fort and the tribe includes that all communications between the fort and the village are handled through the captain and the chief only. Nashoba is allowed to be present, and the captain asks if they are ready to begin. Chief Samuels nods, indicating yes. The captain speaks to the clerk, "Let the record show:

The day and date are Monday, March 7, 1887.

The time is 1100.

Captain Horton delivers to Chief Samuels a small tan envelope addressed to Nashoba, care of the Trading Post at Fort Townsend,

Indian Territory and sent from Applegate Ranch in Covington, Tennessee. Pause record."

The chief shows no reaction. Nashoba stares at the envelope with curiosity.

Captain Horton clears his throat. "Chief Samuels, I can leave the envelope with you, or if you need me to, I can read the letter to you. Your choice."

Chief Samuels asks, "Nashoba, were you expecting this letter?"

"No."

"Since I have no contacts or reasons to receive communications from this Applegate Ranch, you might as well read the letter, captain, in case I need your assistance to respond," the chief says.

"Let the record show that Chief Samuels consents to my reading the letter to those present. Let the record show that I am opening the tan envelope and I find two documents inside. The first document appears to be a wedding invitation, which reads as follows: 'You are invited to come and bear witness to the marriage of Niabi to Mr. Will Lawton at the Colored Methodist Episcopal Church near Covington, Tennessee, on June 18, 1887, at 1 p.m.' Pause record."

"Lies! Lies!" Nashoba blurts out, leaping to his feet.

"Wait, Nashoba," says the chief. "What is the second document?"

"Let the record show the second document is a letter addressed to Nashoba from Niabi. Pause record," the captain says.

"More lies," Nashoba says as he turns his back to them and steps away, clenching his fists and holding back a rage to scream. Then he turns, moves back toward the chief, and says, "I tell you, Father, they have sent lies here. Lies!"

"You say these are lies, my son" the chief says. "Before you are final in that thinking, hear the letter and then tell me that you know these are not the words of Niabi. Continue, captain."

"Let the record show I will read the contents of the letter to Chief Samuels. It appears to be private so I will pause record.

Dear Nashoba,

You are the Great Wolf of the forest. I am a mere fawn on my way home. If you have fed, I can make it home. If you are hungry, I must be clever and swift. I must run fast through the forest; make the tree trunks and bushes places to hide me, aid my escape, so I can live another day. I ask you now, to be the fed Great Wolf and let me keep my tears, and live in your forest as the fawn spared by the hunter.

Nashoba, it would lift my heart to the sky, if you would send the horse named Rodeo home. Show all that the Great Wolf has fed, and for now, the weaker creatures in the forest have nothing to fear. We bow in silence, as you walk past our hiding places.

Niabi

"That is all that is written here," Captain Horton says, his eyes wide open searching the faces of the tribesmen for understanding of what he just read.

Nashoba stands dismayed. He unclenches his fists.

"Are these the words of Niabi, my son?" the chief asks Nashoba.

A weak utterance tumbles from Nashoba's lips. "Yes, they are her words." Then, he storms out of the chief's dwelling.

"Thank you, Captain Horton, for bringing these documents to us. We can handle it from here."

Captain Horton places the two documents in the hands of Chief Samuels, walks over to the recorder, and asks him to go and join the other soldier and wait for him outside. He turns around and asks the chief, "Forgive me, Chief Samuels, I am curious. How was Nashoba so certain that these are the words of Niabi?"

"We believe in spirit guides, captain. They can come to us in the form of an animal. Nashoba in Choctaw means wolf. I imagine anyone of our tribe could have divulged that fact to someone passing through our village, and that someone could have used that information to create such a letter. But Niabi had a secret ceremony regarding her spirit guide. Niabi means 'fawn spared by the hunter.' The only ones that would know the full name is her, myself, and someone she often played with as a child in the forest. She saw that someone one day shoot an arrow into a fawn, causing her to cry. The someone promised her, he would never kill another fawn. That someone is Nashoba."

CHAPTER 11

GOOD NEWS

———

PART of Tom Morgan's job as the ranch foreman at the Hastings Ranch is to monitor the cattle feeding across the ranch's pastures, see to it the cattle are rotated around the pastures, and make sure areas are reseeded when needed. Tom has at his disposal the cattle drive drovers who are now working as ranch hands for moving the cattle between grazing pastures, and to watering holes and troughs on the property. The ranch hands begin their days early, usually before or near sunrise, and spend most of the day moving cattle, isolating those appearing ill, mending fences, and watching out for would-be cattle thieves.

This morning, Mr. Hastings gets an early breakfast consisting of coffee, a biscuit, and bacon, before saddling his horse and riding out to the west pasture to join Tom. After cordial greetings and an exchange regarding work for the day, Tom asks Mr. Hastings, "What do you make of this invitation to Will's wedding?"

"It's something, months ago, I would have responded to by sending them a nice tablecloth or a cute tea set," Mr. Hastings replies. "But now that Mrs. Hastings has a burr in her boot about the whole thing, I've gotten hog-tied into going."

"Noooo, you're foolin' me?"

"Yeah, in fact, I'm riding into town tomorrow to look into train tickets, and not just for me and the missus. Oscar and his grandpa are traveling with us."

"Matt, Rodrigo, and I received invites, too, but I think only Rodrigo wants to go," Tom says.

"Well, if I get train tickets, I'll include one for him. If he's goin', he might as well join our party," Mr. Hastings says.

———•———

Saint Mary's Nursing School of Washington, DC, has a small campus with greens covered by elm trees that screen the sunlight, usher through occasional warm spring breezes, and sway as those breezes whisk across the grounds stirring chirping robins and sparrows. The campus greens provide the perfect atmosphere for enjoying a basket lunch outdoors.

Sitting on a blanket sprawled out on the grass under an elm tree near the school, Rita one by one empties a large basket filled with lunch for her and Sam Jr. Sitting next to her, drawing glances from her in between arranging the food, she notices he is always immaculately clean, groomed, and tailored in his dress. He is about five-feet-seven, a little shorter than Will, and weighs about the same as Will. His eyebrows are thinner than Will's, and so are his lips. She makes these comparisons, but Sam Jr. scores higher than Will because he constantly sends her notes requesting her company, and she doesn't mind that at all. His notes are whimsical and amusing. One of his notes reads, "Roses are red, violets are blue, I'd swim the Mississippi, scale the Rockies, and walk through the badlands to again see you." Rita has no idea that he is getting one of his co-workers to write these sweet notes for him. Because she is a college student, he is ashamed to tell her he can't read or write.

"What did you bring in your lunch basket?" Sam Jr. asks.

"We have fried chicken, and," she points from bowl to bowl identifying different dishes. "There is potato salad, green beans, oh yes, and sweet potatoes. I hope you like everything."

"If you prepared it, I'm sure I will like it," Sam Jr. says and inhales the delicious aromas.

He makes a small plate of fried chicken, scoops out food from the bowls, and begins eating. "You know, my father received an invitation to your friend's, um . . . um . . . Will's wedding. He's thinking about going and wants my mother to go with him." He pauses and looks at her as she pretends to show no interest in this topic. "I don't mean to make you uncomfortable, but I'm curious about something and hope you don't mind me asking."

"Oh, you've got my curiosity piqued. What do you need to know?" Rita lets out a sigh.

"Was there something between you and Will?" he asks.

Rita rubs her arm. "I might as well tell you. Will and I *were* close. You see, we grew up together. Our parents are close, and we spent lots of time at each other's home, him at my house the most because my mother tutored him. After we got older, I think everyone in our little community expected us to marry, settle down, and have children. But there were never any commitments made between him and me. As it turns out, the last time I saw him, we parted as very good friends."

"If I may impose further upon you, may I ask if you are going to his wedding?" Sam Jr. asks.

"About that. It still stings a little to see him with his bride. I suppose I should go, though. You know, the wedding is at my father's church, my home church. My father is the pastor and will most likely be the one conducting the ceremony."

"You mean I'm courting a pastor's daughter?" says Sam Jr. smiling.

"Who said you were courting me? This is only the second time I've set eyes on you, Mr. Sam Egglesby Jr. One time out alone does not equal courting." She pauses, and then continues, "We're just two mature nineteenth-century people out for lunch."

Then Sam Jr. breaks in, interrupting her. "Out for lunch, then a walk, then sitting in Pastor Gregory's parlor for a little sparking."

"Sparking?" she laughs.

He laughs covering his mouth with his napkin. "Ha ha ha, I dare not do that out *here*." He takes the napkin and wipes his mouth. "I want our time together to always be special, and I want to always show you respect, Miss Rita."

Rita watches him talk with such sincerity and delights in his confidence and positivity. "What would you do, Mr. Egglesby, if you weren't so respectful right now?" She gazes into his eyes as she did at the dinner the last time they were together.

Sam Jr. hurries chewing his food and swallows. He wipes his mouth again with his napkin, licks his lips, and leans toward her. She remains absolutely still. The only slightest movement she makes is to tilt her face to intercept his. He kisses her gently and then leans back. "That's what I would do, Miss Rita." Taking her hand, he continues, "And I'll let you know right now that I'm not gonna rest until I clear your mind of all memories of your former suitors, and have you telling your girlfriends about me."

As he says that, her body quivers. She smiles maintaining eye contact with him. He continues holding her hand and smiling at her as if to confirm there is indeed some courting going on here.

"Finish your lunch," she says, slipping her hand from his to place cloths over the bowls of food.

"Yes, ma'am," he says.

———·———

Breakfast is brought to Chief Samuel's dwelling and placed on a table next to chairs fitted with blankets or quilts as cushions. The breakfast consists of cornmeal mush, nut bread, a bowl of berries, and hot tea with honey. Some of the items are received as part of rations provided from the U.S. Government to the region care of the trading post to supplement shortfalls from the land, crops not harvested, and hunted game not found. After sitting with the dwelling flap for the entrance pulled open, enabling him to look out and watch the sunrise, the chief ends his morning meditation. Seated on one of the cushioned chairs next to the table, he then begins to eat his breakfast. He expects Captain Horton by 10 or 11 a.m. that morning. Near meeting time, he changes into his more formal meeting clothing, and waits for Captain Horton.

After the captain arrives and is seated on one of the four chairs available in the chief's chukka, the captain motions for his clerk, Nelson, to sit next to him and record the meeting. Both captain and chief, seated across from one another, exchange a look as if to say we can begin. Chief Samuels states, "We need to go to the wedding we spoke of the last time you were here. We need to deliver the horse named Rodeo to Niabi. That is our request for you today."

"Let the record show," Captain Horton dictates, "Chief Samuels is requesting an authorization for travel for . . .?" He looks at Chief Samuels and waits for him to finish the statement, identifying the travelers.

The chief names the travelers. "Nashoba, Talako, and Koi."

The captain continues, "Travel for Nashoba, Talako, and Koi. They request an authorization for travel from the village at Red River to Tennessee for a wedding of a fellow tribe member in June 1887. Pause record."

Nelson whispers to the captain, and the captain turns to Chief Samuels. "I will need to consult the written invitation for the exact date and city to finalize this request."

Chief Samuels reaches for a document on his desk. "Yes, I have it here." The chief hands the document to the captain.

"Of course, I will be contacting my commanding officer at U.S. Army headquarters seeking approval for this travel authorization," the captain says.

The chief examines the captain squinting his eyes. "Captain, we live here," the chief says. "Not like you live in this world. You are free to come and go as you please. We live here with our bodies in these chukkas, our bodies meeting around the fires, our bodies walking back and forth to the garden, but our spirits, our hearts do not live here. They are floating down the river, riding through the valleys, and scaling the mountains. Have confidence; we live here, captain." The chief rises and goes away from the captain to the other side of the dwelling. Another tribesman, who tends to the chief's needs, sees him walk away, enters the dwelling, and ushers the captain and his soldier to take their leave of the chief and return to their horses.

After leaving the village and returning to the fort, the captain drafts a wire message based on the recorded meeting with the chief, and sends it to his commanding officer at Army headquarters in Washington, DC. Three days later, he receives the following reply:

> **To: Captain Horton, FT. Townsend**
> Authorization denied for travel by land. The destination is too far, and there is no funding for travel by train.
> **From: LT. Gen. Stewart, Washington, DC**

Upon receiving this wire, Captain Horton decides to send a wire to the Hastings Ranch.

> **To: Mr. W. John Hastings, Hastings Ranch**
> Chief's son wants to return the horse called Rodeo to Will Lawton at the Applegate Ranch and attend the wedding. The U.S. Army denied authorization for travel by land, but may approve travel by train for their three passengers and one horse, if the fare can be raised.
> **From: Captain Horton, FT. Townsend**

Captain Horton's message is received at the Waco Telegraph office and is given to a rider to take to the Hastings Ranch. Upon making his delivery, he is generously tipped for his trip. After Mr. Hastings reviews the captain's message, he pours himself three-quarters of a glass of his most potent whiskey. He feels the blood warming in his veins as he ponders whether to share this news with Mrs. Hastings. With time, he had hoped she would forget about going to the wedding and be on to another one of her projects. He has nothing against Will or Negro people in general; he just doesn't feel comfortable participating in their event when he doesn't have to. It's not like Will is marrying his daughter. But the dye has been cast. His wife views their attendance as some kind of pilgrimage, and he might as well work to make it as pleasant an adventure as possible.

Later that day, Mr. Hastings, Mrs. Hastings, and Phillipe sit down at one end of the large dining room table for dinner, as they usually do every evening during Phillipe's stay. After they begin their desserts, Mrs. Hastings implores Phillipe to present the name of the dessert he prepared and explain how it was made. Phillipe is delighted to share how the peppermint puffs are made. When the culinary lecture winds down, Mr. Hastings rings the bell for the maid. She enters and he says, "Please have Oscar join us here in the dining room."

"What's going on?" Mrs. Hastings asks wide-eyed, looking at Mr. Hastings.

"Give me a moment, dear, and everything will become clear."

Oscar enters. "Sir, you need me for something?"

"Yes, take a seat, please. You are involved in this, too," Mr. Hastings says.

Mrs. Hastings opens her mouth to speak, and Mr. Hastings' hand flies up to stop her. "I have received a wire from Captain Horton at Fort Townsend. It seems three Indians and a horse require train fare from Red River to Covington, Tennessee, for the wedding in June. The first-class fare one way is twenty dollars per passenger. Mrs. Hastings and I have talked about going to the wedding; I also received word that Rodrigo wants to go. And, well, I am considering responding to Captain Horton's wire by saying I will pay the Indians' fares."

"Oh, dear. How open-minded and completely magnificent of you," Mrs. Hastings says, her eyes and mouth jolted open. Sitting next to him at the table, she reaches over to rub his arm smiling in awe of his decision. He pats her hand, and swallows, looking at her and displaying a wry smile like a cow just released after branding. Phillipe looks on, appreciating the significance of Mr. Hastings' gesture, beaming with excitement for the two.

"Do you know who the three Indians are?" Oscar asks.

Pulling his gaze from Mrs. Hastings, Mr. Hastings replies, "I know one of them is the chief's son."

"Nashoba," Oscar mutters, then thinks *Most likely he'll be accompanied by the other two road bandits, Talako and Koi.*

"I didn't price out the shipment of the horse, but that will be easy to get," Mr. Hastings says.

"Let Oscar and I foot the bill for the horse being shipped," Phillipe interjects. "That's the least I can do for your more-than-generous hospitality. I am so indebted to you—to both of you."

"No, Phillipe you have been a breath of fresh air in my home these last few weeks," Mrs. Hastings says. "And Oscar, you know I feel you are a treasure, just a treasure."

Mr. Hastings places his napkin on the table. "If that is what you would like to do, I'll get that price for you and help you make the arrangements," he says to Phillipe.

"After I have gone and committed myself, I ask you, do you think it will be very expensive shipping a horse?" Phillipe asks.

"I don't think so," Mr. Hastings says. "They ship carloads of cattle all the time. The only problem, like with the cattle during a trip like that, is having it fed, watered, and disposal of its droppings."

Then Mr. Hastings turns to Mrs. Hastings. "Now dear, are you *sure* you want to go to this wedding?"

"Hell yes!" she shouts. "And now that the Indians are coming, I wouldn't miss it for the world!"

Accompanied by Phillipe, Mr. Hastings makes another trip into Waco to talk with the train ticket agent at the depot. He completes purchases for the fares and the horse shipment. With a confirmed departure date, they go over to the telegraph office and send a wire to Captain Horton at the fort.

> **To: Captain Horton, FT. Townsend**
>
> Have made arrangements with Grand Pacific Railroad. The train will have an empty cattle car for the horse when it stops at the Red River depot on June 13, 1887, at 1 p.m. Have the three passengers and the horse at RR depot for pickup. Their fares are paid in full.
>
> **From: Mr. W. J. Hastings, Hastings Ranch**

Standing at his desk, Captain Horton pours hot coffee as he reads a wire message that was placed on his desk. The message distracts him causing him to miss the cup and send steaming hot coffee pouring down on his desk, his boots, and the floor. "Damn it! Nelson!" he yells. "Get in here! Clean this up. Salvage any pages on the desk that you can. And we need to send a message to HQ, ASAP!"

> **To: LT. Gen. Stewart, Washington DC**
>
> Have obtained train fare for three Indians and horse to travel from Red River village to Covington, Tennessee.
>
> Will depart June 13, 1887. Wedding is June 18th. Expect travelers to return by June 23rd.
>
> **From: Captain Horton, Fort Townsend**

In three days, Captain Horton receives a dispatch from Army headquarters.

> **To: Captain Horton, FT. Townsend**
>
> Travel approved. Authorization contingent on you escorting them to Tennessee and back.
>
> Take two or three privates with you. Do not want an incident.
>
> **From: LT. Gen. Stewart, Washington, DC**

When Captain Horton receives the message from Lt. General Stewart in the morning, he pours his coffee before he begins to read it. After reading the dispatch, he calls Nelson. "Set up a meeting this afternoon with the chief," he orders.

On this afternoon, the chief normally has a council meeting with the village elders and heads of various operations in his large dwelling, his council comprising men and women. The first topic on the agenda concerns the school that has been set up with the help of missionaries. The council is questioning using the Bible and other unapproved documents as the only reading material and excluding curricula based on ancestral teachings. However, an incident has leapfrogged to the top of the agenda. There has been a shooting of one of their young village males out near the border of their land. This incident has dominated the meeting and roused much friction among the council members. It seems the young male was chasing a rabbit with his bow and arrow. When the rabbit stopped, the young male cocked his arrow, readying to shoot, but gunshots rang out from behind trees targeting the young male. The shooters, presumed to be White men, had lain in wait behind fallen trees, intending to ambush anyone coming to the edge of the village boundary.

The chief has scheduled the meeting with the captain at a time long after the regular council meeting is expected to end. Captain Horton arrives on time; however, the council meeting runs over. Horton is allowed to wait at the entrance of the chief's dwelling until he is permitted to enter. He begins standing there not long after the council receives the news about the shooting, which leads to a precipitous flaring of tempers and blustering outbursts. Chief Samuels asks his council to suspend the meeting for two hours and reconvene after the captain leaves. Chief Samuels regrets having to stall the meeting for hours because the favored choice of reaction to this news is more of revenge rather than diplomacy, and he needs to put a clamp on that. Members are walking out of the meeting not giving the captain any greeting whatsoever, where in the past he had at least received a few nods. After Horton enters, Chief Samuels suggests Horton utilize his contacts to put a stop to the harassment of his people by White people. Right now, no one has been killed, but he is not going to sit by and let Whites come onto their land and shoot them down. The captain responds with an assurance that he will look into the matter, put up more signs stating imprisonment and fines for trespassers, and circulate a notice of a reward for information about anyone breaching the border onto their land, or harassing villagers.

Chief Samuels walks over to a table to prepare himself some tea. "Now to your meeting, captain. Have a seat," he says.

Captain and Nelson sit down on one of the many seating places left from the suspended council meeting. They have their choice from chairs and pads that rest on the cane platforms fixed along the walls of the chukka. Smoke from burning incense drifts through the dwelling. The captain strolls through the slight fog finding seats nearest the chief.

Remaining at the table with his back turned, Chief Samuels asks, "Would you like some tea, captain?"

"No, no. I had coffee earlier. Too much drinking of stimulants has adverse effects on my stomach," Captain Horton says placing his hand over his stomach.

"What news do you bring to me today?" the chief asks.

"Good news!" The captain continues, "Nelson, begin recording. Yes, let the record show I am informing Chief Samuels that travel authorization has been approved and received for Nashoba, Talako, and Koi to travel by train, leaving the Red River depot going to Covington, Tennessee, on June 13, pick up at 1 p.m. The train will include a cattle car for the horse they are taking with them. Pause record."

"Travel by train—that is a big change given our journey here to this territory from Mississippi was on foot." The chief pours hot water into a mug of tea and stirs in some honey. "Where will Nashoba and the other young men be allowed to sleep, or to make camp in Tennessee?"

Captain Horton's face reddens, and he looks at Nelson desperate for help. He soon realizes this pause, his delayed response, is creating a problem within itself. "I am not sure, but I can find out and get back to you right away," he finally says.

Taking a seat, Chief Samuels says, "If necessary, captain, Nashoba and his friends can raise a tipi anywhere." The chief turns to look directly at Captain Horton, giving him a piercing stare. "I just want to make sure they are in a safe place where they won't have to fear falling asleep, being poisoned, infected with disease, or whatever your people have contrived over the years to punish us for being alive on this land you kill to possess. Do you understand me, captain?"

"Yes, of course," the captain says. "To ensure safe passage, I and two other soldiers will escort them, there and back." Captain Horton thinks, *If Nashoba raises a tipi out in a field, I will be required to pitch a tent right next to him based on my orders from headquarters.*

———•———

Rodrigo finishes his day's work, puts his gear up in the barn, and walks over to the main house. He enters through the kitchen, finds Oscar eating his dinner, and takes a seat on a stool in the corner. "Do you think it is a good idea for me to go to the wedding?" he asks.

"Yes. I'm sure Will would be glad to see you," Oscar says.

"Matt said I should go," Rodrigo adds. "He's willing to even pitch in on my train ticket. I haven't been anywhere since I stumbled upon this ranch after leaving Juarez."

"We'll have fun seeing Will again. And seeing him marry his pretty Indian girl," Oscar says and smiles before scooping more food into his mouth.

"Yeah, Matt goes on for some time about how if he had known she wanted off the reservation he would have taken her." They both smile. Rodrigo removes his hat and runs his fingers through his black curly hair, whipping up dust.

"Hey, watch it. I'm gonna have to sweep up after you leave," Oscar complains.

"I don't see any dirt on the floor," Rodrigo says looking around on the floor where he is sitting. "But, amigo, do you have any ideas about where I can stay while I'm there?"

"We can get with Will after we arrive, and ask him what we should do. However, as a backup, take one of the drover's tents in case we both are stuck outside. My grandpa can always get a hotel room in the town."

During the next few days, several wires go back and forth between Horton and Mr. Hastings. Here they are in chronological order:

> **To: Mr. W. J. Hastings, Hastings Ranch**
>
> Authorization received for me to accompany the special three passengers from the village in Red River to ensure safe passage. Let me know if you learn anything further on lodging for me, two additional soldiers, and our Red River passengers.
>
> **From: Captain Horton, FT. Townsend**

To: Captain Horton, FT. Townsend

Will make inquiries regarding possible lodging. My party will include my wife, cook, guest, and a drover.

From: Mr. W. J. Hastings, Hastings Ranch

To: Mr. W. J. Hastings, Hastings Ranch

Is your drover available to help monitor the safety of Red River passengers?

Can pay him a daily rate. Would appreciate an extra set of eyes and can save on bringing another soldier on the government payroll.

From: Captain Horton, FT. Townsend

In the middle of spring on a clear morning, Mr. Hastings rides out to the pastures and seeks out Rodrigo. When he finds him, he informs him that train tickets have been purchased, including one for him. Next, he asks Rodrigo if he is willing to assist the soldiers in guarding the Indians. "I don't expect there will be any trouble," he says, "but the captain at Fort Townsend is also coming to make sure there are no incidents, and you will be compensated for your time if you choose to help out."

Rodrigo answers, "Sure, Mr. Hastings. I don't mind helping out. Now, Oscar said I should take a drover's tent in case there is no lodging, and we have to make camp somewhere."

"That's a good idea," Mr. Hastings says. "Take whatever you need in case you have to make camp. We don't know anyone at the other end, except Will, so we are unsure what we're faced with. But that's not to say we are not up for the challenge and adventure." And with that, Mr. Hastings turns his horse back toward the house and leaves.

Rodrigo walks away feeling a lot better about going on the trip. This guard duty gives him another good reason for going.

As Mr. Hastings enters the house, Mrs. Hastings approaches him. "Do we need to reserve rooms in Tennessee at the nearest hotel?" she asks.

"Maybe. I told Captain Horton I would look into that. Have you heard where Oscar and Phillipe are staying?" Mr. Hastings asks.

"I will ask him about it, but if you get hotel rooms, get them one also," Mrs. Hastings says.

A wrinkle creases Mr. Hastings' forehead. "Well, there may be objections to Oscar staying in the same hotel, you know."

Mrs. Hastings bristles. "We will just inform them and that he is in our employment, a manservant, valet, whatever it takes to convince them that he has to be at our beck and call."

Before dinner later that day, Mrs. Hastings corners Oscar in the kitchen. "Has your friend, Will, said where the guests coming to the wedding should obtain lodgings? Mr. Hastings and I would like to be nearby, but in a comfortable establishment. And then there is the captain and soldiers who are coming along on the trip from Fort Townsend, you know, to keep everyone safe." She maintains a motionless stance looking at Oscar waiting for an answer.

"Yes, ma'am. I will ask and find out. I will post a letter to them right away," Oscar says.

"Fine," she says nodding her head, and then turns to leave the kitchen and go about her afternoon until dinner is ready.

After the kitchen falls silent from cleanup after dinner, Oscar retreats to his room to write a letter to Niabi.

Dear Niabi,

Wonderful news. Nashoba has agreed to bring Rodeo to Tennessee. He is coming himself. Everyone coming from Hastings Ranch will meet up with those coming from your village, and together

will board a train at the Red River depot on June 13th at 1 p.m. The
train destination is Memphis.

I will be traveling with my grandfather and Mr. and Mrs.
Hastings of Hastings Ranch. This is the ranch that pays Will for
cattle driving. Also traveling with us is a ranch hand named Rodrigo
and three soldiers from Fort Townsend; I was told they are to escort
and provide safe travel for your tribesmen.

We are wondering where we should get lodging. I can camp
anywhere, or sleep on the floor in Will's house. The same can be said
for Rodrigo. My grandfather and the Hastings, being White, can get
rooms at a nearby hotel if necessary. The soldiers will want to stay
near the villagers. Do you know the name of the nearest hotel? Please
provide that name, so I can give it to Mrs. Hastings. Do you have
ideas for lodging for the three Indians from your village and the three
soldiers from Fort Townsend, also?

Hope to hear from you soon.

Oscar Kintoole

Sitting in the main house going through the mail, Mrs. Applegate
laments about not receiving correspondence from her two sons who
are galivanting around Europe with her niece Catherine. With all that
is going on, she is somewhat glad Catherine isn't there to stir up
mischief, but she misses her boys.

In the mail she finds a letter from Oscar Kintoole at the Hastings
Ranch, Waco, Texas, addressed to Niabi. She hears someone in the
hallway and calls out. Sheila steps to the door. "May I help you,
ma'am?" she asks.

"Yes, Sheila, can you find Niabi and send her to me?" Mrs. Applegate asks.

"Right away," Sheila says, and hurries down the hall.

After Harriet had such a fit about which flowers would be in her
bouquet, in her hair, and on the altar in the church, Niabi is out in

the garden looking over the flowers. She sees no reason for Harriet to get worked up over it, but has promised to look at what is in the garden and yard. Sheila calls out to Niabi. "Mrs. Applegate wants to see you in the office."

"What now?" Niabi says, then thinks, *Is she gonna get on me about the planning meetings too?*

Niabi enters the office. "You asked for me?"

"Yes, Niabi. I have a letter here for you. From an Oscar Kin-toole, I think?"

"Oh, that's Will's friend from the ranch that does the cattle drives," replies Niabi.

"Well, here you go," Mrs. Applegate says and hands the letter to her.

Niabi takes the letter, goes outside of the office near the stairs, and reads it. After reading the letter, she returns to the office, stands in the doorway, and sighs.

Mrs. Applegate inquires, "Is there something wrong, Niabi?"

"Yes, ma'am. They are asking about hotels and lodging for about ten people."

"Well, let me take a look at the letter," Mrs. Applegate says holding out her hand.

After Niabi hands her the letter, Mrs. Applegate motions to Niabi to take a seat. Niabi sits there wondering if it is even safe for Nashoba to stay at the hotel in town. After finishing reading the letter from Oscar, Mrs. Applegate gets up from her desk and walks around taking long strides and holding her hand on her face. "Well, we got the Hastings couple," she says. "They can go in the guest room. Then we have Oscar and his grandfather. Hmmm, I can add a cot in Jason's room, and he and his grandfather can take that room. Now for the ranch hand, soldiers, and Indians, we can clean out the foaling barn where we do the birthing, and put the Indians in one compartment and the soldiers in the other. It's not the main house, but it's well built, holds its heat, and is near a water well and an outhouse."

Niabi's face brightens. "Oh, oh, I'm sure that will be quite alright," she says.

Mrs. Applegate continues, "If one or two don't like that, there is maybe one or two beds in the bunkhouse near Fred's cottage. I'll ask Fred if the empty beds need to be cleaned out. I can get some additional cots and chairs out of storage. But don't worry; we've got plenty of room."

"Thank you, Mrs. Applegate. Oh, thank you." Niabi presses her hands together against her chest. "This is good news! I can't wait to share it with Will."

"I've been intending to ask Will about what happened to Rodeo," Mrs. Applegate interrupts. "I usually see him taking Rodeo for an evening ride, or sometimes he puts him in that nearby pasture right out there." Standing near the office's window on the second floor, she points down at the nearest pasture. "Under that tree, I have watched him basking in the sun or stretched out napping."

"Rodeo got hurt and Will left him at my village. My people are bringing him on the train. I wonder if I may ask you to keep this to yourself, since Will doesn't know he's coming, and it's my surprise for him," Niabi says.

"Good. But, no, no. I will keep this under my hat," Mrs. Applegate promises.

"Thank you, and thank you for all you are doing for Will and me." Niabi quickly turns and walks briskly out of the office, down the stairs, and tells Sheila she is going to find Will to give him some good news.

Niabi goes to the barn, and walks around inside looking for Will. She exits it and stands in front of the barn, searching from near to far, and then walks to the back of the barn, again combing the fields and pastures as far as she can see. She then looks for Fred, and finds him replacing a horse's shoe. "Fred, do you know where Will is?"

"I think he's at the foaling barn in the far pasture, setting it up for two possible foals that are gonna drop within the week," Fred says.

"Which way to the foaling barn?"

"Come here, child," Fred says. He walks her out to the back of the barn, and points to the far west end of the pasture. She sees a building she had noticed in the past but never asked about.

Fred looks around the area. "I don't see FireTip. Do you want me to saddle another so you can ride over there?"

"No, I will walk," Niabi says. She has never told Will, but walking helps her control her emotions whenever she thinks about him and the way he touches her and kisses her. He never knew that, after that first kiss, she wanted him just as much as he wanted her. Now that they are getting married, there is some relief in knowing that she will not have to hold back her passion for him.

After a long walk, she nears the foaling barn and sees FireTip grazing nearby. He whinnies and gallops over to her. As she greets him with pats and rubs, she hears thrashing inside the building, walks in, and finds Will inside busy working. She stops and puts her hands on her hips from being winded. "So, this is the foaling barn," she says looking around the room. "What is this used for?"

"Hi, sweetie," Will says. Will has a rhythm going using a pitchfork spreading hay over the floor of one of two large stalls in the foaling barn. "The foaling barn—well, this building has two of these large stalls. The stalls themselves are for the mares that are ready to give birth. We bring them here where it's quiet; they like being away from anything that might appear to be harmful to their new foal. Many animals like to go off and be to themselves when they give birth. Our mares are more comfortable giving birth out here isolated and all." Will pauses to catch his breath, and then he continues, "And on the end, next door, there is a small office with a cot, chair, and desk. As soon as the foal is born, we take its weight, dimensions, record when it stands, whether it is nursing properly; we gather a lot of data. But you've got a grin on your face. I know you didn't come all the way out here just to ask me what a foaling barn is."

She twirls around in the large stall laden with freshly padded hay. "I've got good news. In fact, I've got great news."

"Well, don't leave me wondering here. What is it?" Will asks continuing to work giving her short glances.

"Your friend Oscar is coming to the wedding." Will swings the pitchfork.

"Oh, I coulda told you that," he says. "He's like my closest friend. Of course, he's coming."

"That's not all," Niabi says.

"What else?"

"His grandfather is coming, too."

"The old Canadian man?"

"Yes, Oscar is concerned, though, because the grandfather is White and Oscar wants ideas about where they can stay, their lodging."

Will pauses, and then says, "He can stay—"

She interrupts him. "I have that all worked out. The grandfather will stay in the main house with Oscar in Jason's room. And in addition to that, Mr. and Mrs. Hastings will stay in the guest room in the main house."

Will stops working. "Mr. and Mrs. Hastings? Are you sure they are coming? I can count on my hand the number of times I've talked to him and her. Hmmm, maybe once or twice."

"Well, they are coming!" Niabi says.

"Now, is Mrs. Applegate OK with these plans?" Will asks.

"It was *her* idea," Niabi says. "Also, Oscar said a ranch hand named Rodrigo is coming."

"Ahhh . . . Rodrigo. I thought he didn't like me," says Will as he returns to pitching hay.

"Well, evidently you are wrong." Niabi twirls again in front of him. He watches her while he works spreading hay.

"You are acting as though you've been in Mrs. Applegate's liquor closet," he laughs and continues breaking a small bale of hay, and spreading it around on the floor with the pitchfork.

"No, I'm just so very happy today," Niabi says. "This news has me in such a good mood; it makes me want to dance with joy, and I want to celebrate with my future husband."

The way she said those words "future husband" make him stop swinging the pitchfork, and give her his full attention. She twirls over to him, takes the pitchfork out of his hands, and puts it in the corner. "We won't run into it over here."

"Ha ha ha. What are you talking about 'won't run into it'?" She continues twirling and swaying as if performing a ritual dance. He looks over at the pitchfork, and then back at her. "Honey, I really need to finish this tonight. We've got mares ready to drop any day now, and that dancing you're doing is . . . well." His skin prickles. She locks eyes with him and slowly walks over to him and begins rubbing her hands up and down his chest, and then unbuttons his shirt, throws it open, and continues rubbing the skin of his chest, up and down. Waves of passion sweep over him from head to toes. She then rubs his arms and then his neck, smiling at him. He wraps his arms around her waist, and matches her swaying movement, now both are swaying their hips from side to side. "Oh, I know what you want. You want me to kiss you, and hug you the way I did that day when I stole your basket of herbs. I can do that, Miss Niabi," he says.

She pulls his neck down, bites it with her lips, and whispers, "I want more than just a kiss and hug from you right now." She pushes away from him, sits down on the soft floor padded with hay, and pulls on his hand. She whispers, "Lie with me, my love."

No further words of invitation are required. He lies down, and they kiss and caress. His body moves like a puppet on strings, responding to her hands that position his lips to hers, his body over hers; he is transfixed by her imploring him to respond to a most impetuous desire. Mindful they are still new to their lovemaking, he acts with restraint, performing with gentleness and loving care. After all, this is the angel that captured his heart, his young bride. Soon, there will be adequate time and the right place to fully satisfy themselves. But for now, she summons the love he has for her. "Oh, my Niabi," he whispers in her ear. "We better hurry before someone comes looking for us."

After almost three-quarters of an hour of lovemaking, their erotic stupor winds down, because they both agree to stop before someone finds them. Still in each other's arms, they take turns, each giving the other one the "last kiss," him saying "this is the last one," and they laugh, and then her saying "now this is the last one," both again laughing at their unwillingness to be the one to receive the last kiss. He gives in to be the last recipient, jumps up, buttons his pants and shirt, and dusts the hay lent off his pants. He helps her get the hay out of her hair, and she straightens her dress.

Will grabs the pitchfork from the corner and locks it in the office. She turns to him and says firmly, "We need our own place."

"Yes, I agree," Will says as he follows her out of the foaling barn. Sensing her frustration about ending their lovemaking before she was ready, he gazes at her and says, "It won't always be like this."

He signals to FireTip. FireTip has been waiting next to the foaling barn, untied. He gallops over, and Will mounts him, and extends his hand down toward her to lift her onto FireTip. "You want a ride back?"

"No, I need to walk."

"You sure? It's a long walk."

"I enjoy a long walk," she says squeezing his hand. "I'll see you at the cottage, my love."

"OK, see you at the cottage." He eases FireTip away giving him an extra tug to get him to stop looking her way.

After putting FireTip up for the night, Will knows he has a few minutes before Niabi reaches the cottage on foot. He leaves the barn, walks briskly into the cottage, and finds his mother preparing dinner. "Almost done, and we can sit down and eat," Harriet says.

He looks at her and asks, "Momma, may I talk with you about something?"

"Sure, son."

"Is there any way you can stay with the Walkers or the Johnsons the night right after Niabi and I are married?"

Harriet turns to him with a surprised look on her face.

"So, my new wife and I can have a little honeymoon here in the cottage?" Will adds.

"You don't want to go off somewhere?" Harriet asks.

"Immediately after the wedding, I've got to take her home to her village and get Rodeo, so there is no need to go somewhere and then take that long trip to the Indian Territory. I think we can just have our honeymoon right here."

"Will Niabi be satisfied with just staying here?" Harriet asks, looking around the room.

He thinks, *Niabi would be satisfied if we stayed all night in the foaling barn; she just wants us to have uninterrupted privacy.* But he answers her, "Yes, I will explain to her that we can have our honeymoon here, and then as I promised I'll take her home. Her enthusiasm may be low because she wants to have a Choctaw wedding ceremony. I can go and pick up Rodeo; we'll do a Choctaw wedding, and after that, we will both be very happy."

"Son, you sure the honeymoon hasn't already started?"

He goes over to a pitcher, pours a bowl of warm water, wets a cloth, and wipes his face and arms, but can't look her way. "What do you mean?" he asks.

"I'm not trying to pry into your business, but I saw her enter the foaling barn earlier today and you two were forever coming out of there. You are your own man now, but son, you have to be careful. I know you are betrothed, the wedding day is approaching, and the two of you have every right to be together and express your feelings. But if her belly is going to be sticking out come June, we need to change the style of her wedding dress. Right now, it has a tightly fitted waist."

"She hasn't said she's with child," Will answers, a flush heating his face.

"This is April. Can you wait two more months?"

How impossible is this request? Will thinks, *Now that I've been to heaven a couple of times now.* "Yes, Momma," he says continuing to think about this matter and concluding this is really Momma's fault. She hadn't sufficiently warned him about how hard it would be to refrain from lovemaking when it's with the right woman. Yes, she warned him about the effects of liquor and fast women, but what about when you fall in love with that special woman, one who is sleeping in your house right on the other side of a wall next to you? *I'm only human,* he thinks. *And Niabi doesn't help the situation. She acts like a mountain lion that's claimed her territory, and her territory is where ever I'm standing.*

Niabi walks through the front door, huffing, her face glistening with sweat. "Where were you, missy?" Harriet asks while checking her pots and appearing ignorant of their recent tryst. "I missed you at the main house, and you weren't here."

Looking dead at Will, Niabi answers, "Oh, I took a long relaxing walk." She then slowly steps over to the pitcher and bowl and washes her hands and face using another clean cloth. Then she asks Harriet if she needs her help.

"No, I have everything under control," Harriet says. "You can take a seat next to your husband-to-be."

Niabi and Will exchange looks, puckering lips, winking, and smiling, all done without making a sound to alert Harriet of their mischievous flirtations. Niabi sits down near Will at their small table for four in their kitchen, reaches over, and takes his hand. Speaking with the slightest amount of arousing tone, she asks, "Are you ready to eat your dinner, Mr. Will?"

Will jumps up and walks away saying, "I'm not doing anything 'til June."

Niabi looks baffled at his abrupt walking away.

The next day, Niabi drafts a letter back to Oscar.

Dear Oscar:

Mrs. Applegate informs me that Mr. and Mrs. Hastings will stay in her guest room in the main house at Applegate Ranch. Phillipe and you will stay in one of her son's rooms with you on a cot. The soldiers, Rodrigo, and members of my tribe will stay in what we call the foaling barn, but it will be completely cleaned out and furnished with cots, chairs, tables, and lanterns. There is an outhouse nearby and water well. Rodrigo can lodge with the soldiers or in the ranch's bunkhouse.

Niabi

The wedding planning committee meets again in Mrs. Applegate's dining room. Niabi walks in and takes a seat at the table. "Well, it's nice to see the bride here for a change," Mrs. Fenton says sarcastically. "I cut the dress out of the muslin material Mrs. Applegate gave me and it will be stitched up this evening. If you want to come by tomorrow, you can try it on," she says to Niabi.

"How many days are left?" Martha asks.

Looking at a calendar, Harriet answers, "We have ten days until my baby belongs to Niabi." Everyone laughs.

"He will always be yours, Mother Harriet," Niabi says with a smile.

———•———

It's ten days before the wedding. One evening, Dakota Sam and Sam Jr. meet a man who worked as a porter with Sam Jr. The man takes them to the train depot to purchase train tickets for travel from Washington, DC to Memphis, Tennessee. After speaking to the train agent at the caged ticket window, he explains to Dakota Sam that they can buy two one-way tickets now, and get the return trip tickets when they are ready to leave Tennessee. However, Dakota figures he'd be in the same predicament then, unable to read the schedule and select a route and price. But the man explains he may not be able to predict the exact time they would want to leave. "Just wait," the man says. "I'm sure there will be some friend or acquaintance that will help you buy the return tickets."

Finally, Dakota gives in and decides to leave three days before the wedding date and to buy the return tickets in Tennessee after their visit. The man purchases two tickets for Dakota Sam and Loma. He writes down instructions for a friend to help them buy additional tickets in case Sam Jr. and Youngster decide to travel with them. With two tickets in hand, Dakota Sam goes home to Loma to make plans for their trip.

When Dakota Sam leaves, Sam Jr. thanks his porter friend, says goodbye, and makes a beeline over to Pastor Gregory's home. The hour is 8:30 p.m. and generally considered too late in the evening to receive polite company, especially gentlemen callers. Sam Jr. knocks on the door. The pastor, his wife, and Rita have finished dinner and are talking in the parlor. Hearing the knock, the pastor excuses himself to go see who is at the front door. "Well, hello, young man," he says. "To what do I owe this pleasure?"

"I'm sorry, Pastor Gregory. Ah, my family is headed to Tennessee in a few days for a wedding, and I wanted to know for sure if Rita is going or not?"

"Well, come in. That sounds urgent. She's right here in the parlor. But please keep your visit short, lest I will break one of my promises to her parents."

"Yes, sir," Sam Jr. says.

"Hi, Sam, good to see you," Rita says, as she greets him with a kiss on the cheek.

The Gregorys excuse themselves and take their leave of the young couple.

"I apologize for the hour," Sam Jr. says. "It's just that my father has purchased train tickets to go to the wedding and he asked me if I am attending. I would not need to go unless you are going."

"I may go up the day before because I can't get the time off from classes. I am doing all I can do to keep up with my lessons," Rita says.

"OK. Well, that works for me because I can't take off for a long period either. So, I will gather up Youngster and we can all go together, get our tickets at the same time, and then leave," Sam Jr. says.

"Sounds good," Rita says.

————•————

Ten days before the wedding at the village near the Red River, Nashoba requests entry to Niabi's dwelling that she shares with Liola.

"You may enter," Liola says.

"Good day, Liola. Ahhhh, I am here bearing news . . . Niabi is getting married."

"To you Nashoba?" Liola asks.

Nashoba takes the question like a spear to his side, and then answers, "No, she has chosen the Negro man that kept coming to our village, the one who left the horse."

"Oh, yes. I remember him," Liola says, "but she never expressed love for him. You know this to be true?"

"Yes, Liola," he answers impatiently, wanting to complete his visit and leave. "I go to see her soon and return the Negro's horse. I want you to pack up whatever she needs for her wedding and her new life. I will carry it to her."

"Nashoba, you are taking on the spirit of a great man. The strength to put aside your own feelings for a woman you chose for your own, and do this for her is of a man standing above men. The Great Spirit has found our tribe worthy to have our great Chief Samuels; now it seems we continue to be worthy of having our next great chief."

Nashoba feels rewarded for coming to see her. He nods and says, "Thank you for your words. I will collect her things from you after four sunsets."

———•———

The bunkhouse at the Hastings Ranch has a common room where the ranch hands congregate to eat and talk. A smaller crew is resident year-round, and others join the crew when a herd is forming to head north. Rodrigo is in the common room with Ben, Zeb, Matt, Tom, and Clancy.

"I hear you are headed to Will's wedding," Ben says to Rodrigo. "Have you met the bride?"

"No," Rodrigo says.

Then Matt joins in the conversation. "I saw her when Will was sniffing around her dwelling." The group laughs. Matt continues, "I think he was hooked before the line went into the water." The group laughs again.

"You saw her?" Zeb asks.

"Yeah, if he's marrying the one I saw. I never got her name."

"How'd the squaw look?" Zeb asks.

"There's no need to speak disrespectfully," Tom interrupts.

"About a Negro and a squaw?" Zeb frowns. "OK, I won't call them any names, but you got to admit, Will didn't do himself any favors marrying an Indian. He's gonna have a small herd of little mulatto papooses running all around his place, and have to feed and clothe 'em, and—"

"Well, Zeb, that's what any father has to do. What's your point?" Tom says, squinting his eyes with irritation at Zeb.

"He should have married another Negro. At least the papooses have to deal with one reason for being despised and not two," Zeb says, and then laughs. The others fall silent. Rodrigo gets up causing his chair to tumble and walks outside.

"You're someone to despise, Zeb," Matt says. "Will is a very lucky man. That Indian girl is a real looker if you know what I mean; I mean she fills out her little dress," Matt says waving his hands in the shape of a female figure. "And not only that," continues Matt, "the chief's son has eyes for her, and I suspect that's why Will didn't come back to this territory."

Ben joins Rodrigo outside, leaning against the bunkhouse's hitching post. "That Zeb is a real pain in the rear," Ben says.

"Sometimes I wonder, Ben, if my people, Negro people, and Indian people will ever be able to live with your people. We are always the brunt of the jokes, the last to get served, and easily rejected."

"I think in time, things will get better." Ben continues, changing the subject, "Hey, have you started packing for your trip?"

"I'm not taking much. Just something clean to wear to the wedding, and a drover's tent and camping gear, in case I have to make camp somewhere," Rodrigo says.

"Well, I sure wish I could go and see him with his bride. Matt says she is a real looker; even the chief's son wanted her to be his bride," Ben says.

"Did you say the chief's son?"

"Yeah," Ben nods, and then cocks his head to one side looking at Rodrigo for more.

Rodrigo doesn't tell Ben, but he knows some Indians will be traveling with them on the train, and he is expected to assist the soldiers with escorting and protecting the Indians. After hearing this news, he wonders if he needs to protect Will from the Indians.

CHAPTER 12

ALL ABOARD

———

THE train whistle begins blowing more than one hundred feet out from the Waco station. The clanging of the train bell continues as it slows and comes to a complete stop in front of the depot. Individuals run to the caged ticket window demanding a ticket. The train conductor steps out of one of the train carriage cars and places a portable step near the steps built into the train's entrance, steps which lead up onto the train. Mr. and Mrs. Hastings, Phillipe, and Oscar had ridden to the Waco depot in the Hastings' four-person carriage loaded with luggage, camping gear, and gifts. The carriage is driven by Ben and drawn by four quarter horses. Rodrigo hitched a ride sitting next to Ben on the driver's bench. Tom accompanies them, riding alongside on his horse to take note of any last-minute concerns of Mr. Hastings. Ben and Rodrigo unload everyone's luggage and packages and place them on the platform for the train personnel to sort out.

Mrs. Hastings keeps her purse and one bag with her at all times. While Mr. Hastings looks for the train conductor, she waits on the platform with Phillipe, Oscar, and Rodrigo. When Mr. Hastings finds the conductor, he says, "I'm the party that reserved the cattle car for a horse and our party has five passengers, four first-class and one second-class. We have additional passengers to pick up at the Red River Depot."

"Don't worry, sir. The agent at the Waco station explained to me what you're trying to do." Under his breath the conductor says, "I hope he knows what he's doing, messing with Indians."

When Mrs. Hastings steps to the entrance of the train where the conductor waits to let passengers board, the conductor looks at her ticket and tells her to go up the steps, then go to her right, and find her seat in first class. The conductor says the same to Mr. Hastings and Phillipe. When Oscar starts to follow Phillipe onto the train, the conductor yells, "No, no, not you, professor. Go to the left for second class. There's plenty of seats in the back there for you."

Phillipe turns around. "Why do you tell him a different thing? He is traveling with me," he says with indignation.

Hearing his accent, the conductor answers, "I don't know how things are done where you come from, but around here, you see, we don't have Negroes in first class."

Phillipe's face reddens, a vein swells in his neck. Rodrigo steps forward, displays his ticket, and squeezes by them to board saying, "I go to the left." The conductor nods at Rodrigo, but his eyes stay fixed on Oscar and Phillipe. By this time, Mr. Hastings walks back to the entrance now crowded with him, Phillipe, and Oscar. A line of people waiting to board forms behind them along the side of the train.

"This man is my personal valet," Mr. Hastings says. "He's in my employment. Of course, he travels with me. He's at my beck and call."

By now, the people in the line waiting to board start verbally complaining and shouting, "What's the holdup?"

"All right, all right. He can be up there with you. But he better not look like a passenger. He needs to be on duty, working," the conductor says.

Mr. Hastings, Phillipe, and now Oscar proceed into first class and find seats. Mr. and Mrs. Hastings sit in two seats on the front row, and Phillipe and Oscar sit in two seats of the second row directly behind the Hastings, but facing the Hastings with a table between the two pairs. Because there is no dining car on this train, this first-class car comes with eight sets of four plush, padded seats around a table where there is ample room to distance yourself from the other passengers at the table, if you are not traveling as a party of four.

Rodrigo has made his way to the second car of the second-class section, which is the class in which the majority of the people travel. The first car of the second class is filled with Whites, who look to be laborers, farmers, and who don't look hospitable toward Rodrigo sitting among them. He sees more empty seats in the next passenger car of the second-class section where there are more Whites, but they congregate in the front of the car, and the Negroes are in the back of the car. Three rows of seats are available between the two groups, the Whites and Negroes, and in one of those rows sits a young lady he could tell is of Mexican descent. He sits down in the row of seats across the aisle from her, leaving two empty rows between them and the Whites in front, but no empty row between them and the Negroes. Behind the Negroes are two rows of empty seats. After he sits down, he tips his hat at her, and the young lady nods back.

The conductor steps out and yells, "All aboard! All aboard!" He grabs his portable step, hops on the train, and then signals to the engineer. Soon, he goes down the aisles checking tickets in first class. He stops to chat with Mr. Hastings, and informs him they would be stopping at the Red River depot to pick up the remainder of his party and a horse. As the conductor continues checking tickets, a porter follows behind him asking if refreshments or snacks are desired.

Mrs. Hastings whispers to Mr. Hastings, "If he is perturbed by Oscar traveling with us in first class, wait until he sees our traveling companions waiting at Red River."

"Well, considering our Red River travelers, the ticket agent and I determined it would be best all around if they are seated in second class," Mr. Hastings says.

Still whispering, Mrs. Hastings is alarmed and says with emphasizes, "Second class for the son of the chief. You agreed to put the son of the chief in second class?"

Mr. Hastings responds, "It's either second class, honey, or a replay of the Indian Wars. You see how the sheriff is all riled up about a *rumor* of Indians being off the reservation. Now, we're putting them on this train. These people on this train are not much different from the sheriff."

The whistle blows, the bell clangs, and the train pushes off from the station. The start is a little jerky, but once the train gets moving, passengers experience a soothing rocking motion while gazing out the window at the myriad of people, buildings, and animals on the landscape that all swish by.

Rodrigo asks the young lady across the aisle, "Are you from Waco?"

"No, I am from Arkansas," she says.

"What brings you to Waco?"

"I am a teacher. I wanted to go to the reservation to teach the children to read and write but was denied entry. So, I will go home and teach where I can."

"Sorry you couldn't get in. There has been a lot of uneasiness between the townspeople and the Indians, and it's probably best that you not get caught up in that anyway."

After a while, the conductor walks through the aisle yelling the name of the next stop. Only a few passengers exit and even fewer board. With a jerking motion, the iron wheels begin to roll and regain their smooth glide along the rail, coasting through green and brown fields, rolling hills, and clusters of trees. Deer, red foxes, and other wildlife seen through the window dart in and out of view as the train passes. Just as steady and deliberate as the minute hand sweeps around the clock face, so does the train, riding its passengers and cargo to a schedule, from stop to stop. A rider naps during a long stretch of gentle rocking, only to be awaken again when the conductor walks through the cars yelling, "Next stop, Red River. Red River!"

Mr. Hastings, Phillipe, and Oscar all get up and go to the exit to wait until the train stops. As they step down, they see the conductor standing on the platform looking around. Rodrigo steps out, too. Mrs. Hastings stays onboard but positions herself on the entryway steps of the train where she can see what is going on.

The Red River depot is situated in the middle of nothing but dirt, grass, and a few trees. The platform itself is only a weather-beaten wooden canopy, and next to it stands a wooden post for hanging a lamp. The conductor impatiently yells, "Mr. Hastings, there's not a soul out here. Normally, I would tell the engineer to just keep going when I don't see anyone out here, but for you, we've stopped."

Everyone looks around. Even some of the other passengers begin getting off to stretch their legs. Seeing others getting off the train, the conductor speaks up. "Now, only five minutes for this stop. Please don't wander off."

"Like there's somewhere to go," a man remarks and other passengers on the platform laugh.

"We will be boarding in five minutes," the conductor repeats. Just then a dust cloud clears and a band of Indians is seen heading their way.

"Here they come!" Mr. Hastings yells.

The passengers standing outside point and say, "Look!" Some hurry back on board the train.

"Shouldn't you open the cattle car so we can load our horse?" Mr. Hastings says to the conductor.

"Yes, right away," the conductor says. He calls a Negro worker named Rayburn out from the front of the train. Rayburn runs to the rear of the train and opens the cattle car, and with the conductor's aid places a sturdy ramp slanted up from the ground to the floor of the cattle car.

It is a sight to behold. Chief Samuels, Nashoba, and Captain Horton riding in front, followed by Talako, Koi, two U.S. soldiers, and behind them are two elder Indian males, and two additional young Indian males. Another soldier drives an army cargo wagon with the travelers' belongings. The additional riders accompany the chief for protection. Nashoba bolts ahead riding up to the train, and dismounts Rodeo.

"Is this one of the horses?" asks the conductor.

Captain Horton rides up close behind Nashoba. "Yes, and we have three more from the U.S. Army," Captain Horton says as he dismounts. "I have confirmation from Grand Pacific Railroad, if you care to see it."

"No need," says the conductor.

The conductor directs Rayburn to escort the horses up the ramp to board the cattle car and secure them, so they will not get injured during the train ride. When Rayburn seizes Rodeo's reins, he rears up on his hind legs refusing to go up the ramp. Nashoba walks over and waves Rayburn off. He takes out some carrots, feeds them to Rodeo, and then walks him up the ramp and into the cattle car. Rayburn follows them into the car and installs some padded partitions creating a makeshift narrow stall. Two padded partitions fitted to both sides of the horse lock into the sidewall of the cattle car and the floor. After the saddle is removed, Rayburn ties Rodeo's reins loosely to the sidewall, so the reins have enough slack to give him room to back up a little. But the padded partitions help the horse keep its balance when the train rocks hard from side to side. Rayburn escorts the other three horses onboard, once their saddles are removed. He secures them in the same manner as he did for Rodeo. When Rayburn finishes, the four horses are in stalls near the rear of the cattle car. Other train workers pitch in storing the saddles in the baggage car. A shovel hangs from the cattle car's side wall for scooping horse dung; two troughs protrude from the side wall in front of each horse in each stall, one filled with feed and another with water. When the train is stationary, access to these troughs is provided from the top of the cattle car.

Talako and Koi dismount and hand their horses over to their tribesmen to return to their village. They unload their gear from the

U.S. cargo wagon and hand it all to Nashoba, who is still inside the cattle car. Nashoba begins storing their gear and items in the front of the cattle car away from the horses. The conductor asks, "What are they doing? They should put that in the second-class car or the baggage car." After he sees all of their things have been loaded into the cattle car, he continues, "Well, alright. Let's load up and move out of here."

A man standing on the depot platform yells, "Conductor, you not putting them filthy Injuns on this train, are you?" Chief Samuels gives Captain Horton a deadly stare.

Captain Horton stutters as he asks Nashoba to come down so they can all board the train. "We, uh . . . are all going to ride together in this last passenger car," Horton says loudly and firmly.

"No, captain, I find the company more to my liking right here," Nashoba says calmly and firmly. Nashoba motions for Talako and Koi to board, joining him in the cattle car. Observing what is happening, Mrs. Hastings becomes flabbergasted that no one is stopping Nashoba.

"You're going to be uncomfortable riding back there," Captain Horton says. "There is no place to—damn it! Can't you just come to the next car on the train?" Horton says lifting his arm shoulder height, pointing at the last passenger car. Rayburn, hearing the exchange, runs to the front of the train, picks up a large brass chamber pot, brings it to the cattle car, and places it in the corner in the back of the cattle car across from the horses.

Glancing at the chamber pot, Nashoba says, "You see, captain, we will be OK, but back here."

Captain Horton rubs his chin and glances from Nashoba to the chief. He turns and instructs his soldiers to prepare to board the last car near the cattle car. Rodrigo returns to his seat, and the Hastings, Phillipe, and Oscar go back to first class. Rayburn and the conductor replace the ramp on the side inside of the cattle car, and Rayburn runs ahead and boards the train in the baggage car in the front of first class.

Chief Samuels gives one last goodbye look to his son, who stares back standing in the doorway of the cattle car as the conductor closes it. Each soldier, carrying a pistol and Springfield rifle, board followed by the captain.

The conductor walks to the middle car and yells, "All aboard! All aboard!" He steps up onto the train, leans out to wave his hand to the engineer, and they push off. The engineer blows the whistle, and the bell clangs as the large iron wheels chug from slow up to about twenty miles per hour. Gradually, the train returns to the soothing rocking it had before stopping at the Red River depot.

The young lady sees Captain Horton directing his soldiers about where to sit and what to watch for out the window. Horton says, "I want you to call out if you see anyone approaching that cattle car, or anyone exiting that car. You watch this side, and you, soldier, watch the other side. If it gets boring you can switch sides, but under no circumstances are both of you to not be watching that car. Do you understand?"

"What if we have to go to the privy, captain?" asks one of the soldiers.

"Just let me know, and Rodrigo or I will relieve your watch 'til you return," Horton says.

The young lady moves closer to the aisle, beckons Rodrigo to come to the end of the aisle on his side, and asks, "Are there Indians on board?"

"Yes."

"Are they in the cattle car behind us?"

"Yes, we are escorting them to Tennessee."

"Why?"

"Ahhh . . . to a wedding, and returning a horse," Rodrigo says.

Her eyes widen. "This sounds like there is a good story with this. But I will spare you from sharing it for now, at least until it's convenient for you to share it with me," the young lady says, smiling.

The next stop is McKeevers Junction, and again the train slows, the whistle blows, and the bell clangs. When the train comes to a complete stop, Talako pushes open the cattle car door and jumps out. One of the soldiers yells, "Captain, one of 'em is out of the cattle car. Look!"

Talako walks about fifteen feet from the tracks and vomits. Koi jumps out as well to dump the chamber pot. The captain followed by the soldiers stream out carrying their rifles. The conductor and people on the platform exiting the train and waiting to board come to a standstill, watching the goings-on at the back of the train. Finally, the conductor turns and yells, "Those with tickets line up here, facing me." Everyone lines up, their bodies facing the conductor, but their heads swivel looking back to watch the soldiers get the Indians back in the cattle car.

Once Talako and Koi are back on board, Talako says he wants to sit in the doorway, keeping the door cracked to get some fresh air. "I think that's a bad idea," Captain Horton says.

Nashoba speaks up. "He's not used to the rocking of the train. It's making him sick. The fresh air may help him."

Captain Horton frowns. "Keeping the door open lets the people know you are back here. I just don't want you getting any unwanted attention."

"I understand your concern, Captain," Nashoba says. "But we can take care of ourselves."

Word quickly spreads that Indians are on the train. The conductor helps the last of the passengers on board and yells, "All aboard! All aboard!" and signals the engineer. The train pulls off slowly before it picks up speed. Two riders, young White males, start racing their horses so that when the train exits the town passing the last buildings, they will be able to match the speed of the train riding parallel to the tracks. Their horses reach the maximum speed of the train and are parallel to the second-class section. When they are even to the cattle car, they yell expletives at the Indians. Captain Horton and the soldiers watch for signs that it will go beyond name-calling. They can withstand name-calling.

After a while, Nashoba has his fill of the name-calling. He asks Koi, "Is it time to throw some of our four-legged friend's packages off the train?"

Koi laughs. "Yeaaaah, good idea," he says. He unhooks the shovel from the side of the train car. He scoops up a pile of horse dung, and walks toward the sliding car door, which is already opened one-third way allowing Talako to sit next to it inhaling fresh air. Talako sees Koi carrying the dung, and pushes the sliding door further open. Koi slings the dung straight out, and it flies as if he knows the physics of how it would react. On the train, the dung is moving at the speed of the train. When he throws it out, it still moves at the speed of the train, and is carried out by the additional force exerted on it from Koi, a force in the direction perpendicular to the train's direction. The dung appears to go out and suspend in the air until the force of gravity takes over, and then it enters a parabolic curve headed down toward the ground. The riders now lag in speed compared to the train. The rider closest to the sliding cattle car door sees something thrown out of the train and rides right into it. Zap! The rider is hit and slows to wipe the smelly dung off his chin and chest, causing the other rider to stop. Koi swings his fist. He shouts, "We got him," and lets out a war cry. Nashoba smiles and returns to his meditating in the corner. Talako continues inhaling fresh air, and Koi closes the door back to where it was.

The train has a long stop at Hot Springs, Arkansas. The soldiers get off the train and walk back to an area near the cattle car. Rodrigo goes forward to exit near first class, sees Oscar, and begins talking with him. Nashoba comes to the front wall of the cattle car, nearest to the last second-class passenger car, and knocks on it asking for more feed and water, but no one responds. Hearing Nashoba, the young lady sitting across from Rodrigo in second class goes to the back of her train car, walks past where the Negroes sit, and then past where the soldiers sit until she is out of the car. Standing on a metal platform between the last second-class passenger car and the cattle car, she can see through the slats of the cattle car's front wall that someone is standing there. "I heard you. What do you need?" she asks.

Surprised to hear a woman answer him, Nashoba says, "The horses are low on feed, and we are completely out of water."

"I will get someone," she replies. She tells a porter, and before long, Rayburn goes to the cattle car and places a bag of feed and keg of water inside. She watches him load them into the cattle car, and then she returns to the metal platform and says, "Hi, did you get what you needed?"

"Yes, thank you," Nashoba says.

"Are you from the tribe at Red River?" she asks.

"Yes. Why do you ask?"

"I traveled to New Paris, Texas, at the Texas border hoping to come to your village, but there was some trouble, and no one would bring me out. I was going to contact the fort, but the sheriff at New Paris told me it wasn't safe for me to travel in that direction."

"Those good town people hate us for no reason. Why did you want to come to our village?" Nashoba asks.

"Oh, heavens, I should have told you that I am a teacher. I wanted to teach Indian children. My mother is Indian, and my father is Mexican," she says.

"What is your name?" Nashoba asks.

"My name is Louisa, but my dad calls me Lou because he wanted a son."

"Lou," Nashoba says lifting his tone.

"What is your name?"

"I am Nashoba. If you come back to Red River, come to Fort Townsend. Our village is very near there. Tell them at the fort, Nashoba invited you to teach the children, and you will be admitted."

"Oh, how can I thank you? I can barely see your face, just barely make out your beautiful hair and eyes."

A grin slides across his face, and Koi pushes him.

The others begin to return to their seats. She quickly turns and walks back to her seat. The conductor yells, "All aboard! All aboard!"

Rodrigo rushes back to his seat. "Did you get a chance to get out, walk around, and get some air?" he asks Lou.

"No, and I'm glad I didn't. I met one of the Indians in the back," Lou says.

"Which one?" Rodrigo asks.

"His name is Nashoba."

Rodrigo winces.

"You don't approve," she says.

"I just hear he's dangerous and would recommend you stay clear of him," Rodrigo says.

Louisa wonders how someone who speaks so kindly to her can be dangerous.

The train settles into another long session of rocking. She wants to give her address to Nashoba so they can correspond. She gets up and walks to the rear of her passenger car. One of the soldiers asks her, "Are you looking for the water closet, ma'am?"

"I want to give this information to Nashoba, so his tribe can receive a new teacher," she says.

Half asleep, Captain Horton looks up when he hears someone talking to one of his soldiers, but goes back to sleep. The soldier tells

her, "I'll get him." He walks out on the metal platform next to the
cattle car and calls out, "Nashoba, there is a lady here for you."

Nashoba comes to the front wall of the car and looks through one
of the slats, so he can get a good look at her. Her hair is black and
rolled up under a black printed bonnet. Her dress matches her bonnet and is also black taffeta with red, white, and green print. Filling
out the dress, her body looks solid and healthy, not skinny. Her eyes
are deep set behind long lashes, under thick arched brows, and above
plump lips. He looks at her and smiles. "Lou?"

"Yes, it's me." What she sees through the slats is attractive. He is
bare-chested and muscular. His chest and arms are burnt copper. He
has a strong chin, long black hair, piercing eyes, and smells of burning incense that can barely be made out over the smell of horse and
dung. Rodrigo implies she should be afraid of him, and yet she feels
she would be safer on the other side of that wall standing next to him.
Her imaginings start with wondering how tall he would be next to
her, but she composes herself quickly. "I'm getting off at the next stop
and I wanted you to have my address, so we can correspond about the
teaching work at your village." She hands a piece of paper to him. He
accepts it.

"Have a safe travel to your home, Lou," he says.

"I wish you the same Mr.—I mean, Nashoba."

The train starts to slow. The whistle toots and the bell clangs. They
arrive at Little Rock. Lou begins gathering her things. "Is this your
stop?" Rodrigo asks.

She says, "Yes." Rodrigo hops up, grabs her largest bag, and follows her off the train car. When they get outside to the platform,
Rodrigo asks if he can get her address, too.

"I have need of an English teacher, also," he says and smiles.

"Of course, Rodrigo. Let me find another piece of paper and write
it down for you."

As she writes, Nashoba slides the cattle car door open and jumps out. One soldier says, "Captain, Nashoba's out."

The captain says "I see him." Captain Horton and one soldier rush out, and stand between the cattle car and the depot's passenger platform. Louisa finishes writing her note and hands it to Rodrigo. Then her eyes become fixed on Nashoba. He's walking around, swinging his arms in circles, squatting up and down, flexing his leg muscles. She knows then and there that, if she ever sees him again, she will need a chaperone for sure because in her eyes he is spectacular. He glances around the area then looks over at the platform and stops. He recognizes the coloring of her dress and how it is filled out. He nods at her. She nods back at him, and smiles. They hold a gaze at one another for a few seconds, then she turns toward the depot to go through to exit the station.

"All aboard! All aboard!" yells the conductor. Mr. Hastings informs Mrs. Hastings that the next stop is theirs. He informs Phillipe as well.

The conductor walks through the first-class car and sees Oscar fast asleep. He abruptly stops and starts to say something, but Phillipe interjects, "We have worn this poor Negro out, working, but hey, we took pity on him and let him get a little nap until we get off, and then he has to start earning his keep all over again!" The conductor seems happy to hear that kind of talk and walks on.

"Bravo, Phillipe," Mrs. Hastings says.

Mrs. Applegate is expecting her guests. All accommodations have been cleaned, fresh linen set out, and made ready to receive the wedding guests. The only shoe left to drop is Will finding out there are three Indians and a horse arriving on the 2 p.m. train from Little Rock, Arkansas.

———•———

At the Applegate Ranch, Will helps Fred and his son, Fred Jr., harness horses to a covered wagon and a four-passenger carriage. Each rig gets four horses each.

"This is a lot of hauling power for picking up five people," Will says to Fred as he hitches a harness to a horse.

"I just do what Mrs. Applegate and your sweet Niabi tell me to do," Fred says bringing over another horse to harness.

While they are working, Niabi walks up. "Will, I received word that Dakota Sam and his wife are coming to the wedding. I told them we would find them a place to stay. I was wondering if there is room at Pastor Walker's home. Can you go there and ask if they can take them in?"

"Go now?" Will looks at her in disbelief. "Fred's gonna need someone to drive one of these rigs," Will says fastening the last harness on a horse for the covered wagon.

"There's plenty of time for you to go and come back," Niabi says as she nears Will getting close enough to grab one of his ears, rubs it three times, and smiling, releases it. He quickly becomes enamored, smiling back at her. However, he is reluctant to grab her in the presence of Fred and his son. He starts working on the carriage and repeatedly glances at her. She saunters around him knowing she's put him into a playful mood.

Not taking his eyes off her, Will asks, "Fred, what time did Mrs. Applegate tell you to leave to go to the station?" Will is trying to decide why she rubbed his ear, and if he has time to investigate. He turns to Fred awaiting his answer.

Standing behind Will, Niabi shakes her head and mouths the word, "No." Fred sees her, but Will can't. Realizing she does not want Will to go with him to pick up the guests, Fred says, "Oh, later on. Much later. I'm gonna go up to the main house now to get the correct time. Will, you go ahead and help out Miss Niabi for the time being." Fred and Fred Jr. continue getting the carriage ready.

Will walks to Niabi, takes her hands, and looks into her eyes. "OK, Niabi. Is that what you want me to do right now?"

"Yes, I want you to go and ask the Walkers because the Egglesbys are the last of our guests who are in need of lodgings."

Disappointed that the ear rubbing wasn't a prelude to some type of affectionate contact between the two, Will says, "Alright. I'll take FireTip, and will be back as soon as I can."

"Don't ahh rush such a request. After all, you are asking them to host people in their home that they don't even know. Umm, make them aware of your friendship with Dakota Sam and what he means to you. That should help smooth the way," Niabi says.

As Will rides down the path leading away from the Applegate property and is too far to see what is going to happen, she walks out of the barn and waves, summoning Clarence to come and drive the other rig.

"Fred, here's your other driver for the covered wagon. Go now, before Will comes back," she says.

"I hope you know what you're doing, Miss Niabi. Will is on that FireTip, and can easily catch up to us when he returns," Fred says. He pauses, and then adds, "Will also might not like you tricking him."

"Dakota Sam and his wife *do* need a place to stay," Niabi says. "And anyway, I'll tend to Will. You go on to the station. Oh, here is a note containing Mrs. Applegate's instructions for you to give to Mr. Hastings. At the station, ask around among station workers for a passenger named Mr. John Hastings, and give this note to him."

The train slows when it starts to cross the bridge over the Mississippi. Nashoba, Talako, and Koi brace themselves standing near the cattle car's partially opened sliding door holding on tight, to look out and marvel at the expanse of the river. As boys, they were told about this river, its width, and length. Elders of the tribe lived in the region before being forced to the Indian Territory. They look in amazement at how the heavy metal train moves on tracks built over the great river

below them. Scanning farther down the waterway, they see an exqui-
site white steamboat with paddles pushing its glide through the water.
This is an everyday sight to the people who inhabit this area, but for
these travelers from the Red River village, it is an awakening—a new
awareness about how the land is developing around them. They were
aware such building feats are possible, but to witness it first-hand has
a remarkable effect on them. Nashoba was taught to believe such skills
and know-how would have had to come from the Great Spirit; therefore, just as the land comes from the Great Spirit, the White man is
not entitled to keep all the land, nor all of the knowledge.

As they stand in the doorway, Nashoba tells Talako and Koi he
will wear his formal headdress when they leave the cattle car to show
his pride in his ancestry. "We are the original people of this land. Our
ancestors welcomed the White man when he came to our shores, and
our generosity was rewarded with death and suffering," he says. "We
are a proud people, proud of our heritage. While we keep the treaty
to live in peace, that doesn't mean we must forget who we are."

The conductor calls out Memphis as the next stop about twenty
minutes before the train rolls into the station. Captain Horton walks
out of the passenger car onto the metal platform next to the front wall
of the cattle car. He calls out Nashoba's name. When Nashoba reaches
the front wall, he asks, "What do you want?"

"Memphis, Tennessee, is the next stop and where we get off. Prepare to unload all of your things. I'll work out how we're getting to
the ranch where we will be staying," Horton says.

The train whistle blows and its bell begins clanging as it deceler-
ates into the Memphis station. Memphis' Calhoun Street Railway Station bustles with customers, passengers, concession stand operators,
and porters checking tickets and sorting luggage. On the far west end
of the station, a covered wagon and a four-passenger carriage await a
2 p.m. pick up for passengers arriving on the Little Rock train. The
noise from the density of people milling about the station drifts
through the train car windows before the passengers on the train can

see them. When the train pulls into the station, the on-board passengers see the throng of people swarming over every portion of the station platform, and moving in and out of the station building. A station worker sorts the throng, telling boarding passengers to line up on the side facing the train to give those arriving room to get off and collect their luggage. The train pulls to a stop. Mr. Hastings is the first of their party to exit the train. He is followed by Mrs. Hastings whom he helps down the steps leading off the train. She is followed by Phillipe and Oscar. Fred approaches a station worker. The worker has travelers on both sides of him waiting with questions, luggage to be checked, and tickets to be reviewed. Fred gets his opportunity when the worker bends over to tag a trunk for the baggage car. He darts forward. "Sir, I have a note from the Applegate Ranch for a passenger named Mr. Hastings on this here two o'clock train."

The worker points to the conductor and says, "Ask him."

Fred walks over to the equally busy conductor. Dressed in his good suit and mimicking the ways of Orin Applegate and Sir Jeffery Clements, he gets near the front of the line and bellows, "Pardon me, sir. I have a note from the Applegate Ranch for a passenger named Mr. John Hastings. Might you help me locate the passenger? I have his transportation." The conductor immediately points to a tall mid-forty-ish White man wearing a tan felt hat with a matching tan coat. Fred surmises the name Applegate Ranch is what got the stone over the fence. Fred goes to the man in the tan hat and asks, "Sir, are you Mr. Hastings?"

"Yes, I'm Mr. Hastings."

"I have a note for you from Mrs. Applegate of Applegate Ranch," Fred says, and hands Mr. Hastings the note.

Mr. Hastings reads it, and says, "Good! Very good! Where are your rigs?"

"Right this way, sir."

"Come, my dear. It seems our transportation may be all taken care of," Mr. Hastings says to Mrs. Hastings.

Phillipe and Oscar stand near the train and look in amazement at how busy and large the station is compared to the one at Waco and the dismal Red River station. With Mrs. Hastings at his side, Mr. Hastings waits for the conductor to get the cattle car open, but he continues being swamped with passengers. Railroad workers bring the soldiers' saddles. Rayburn soon comes running to open the cattle car, and Mr. Hastings takes Mrs. Hastings by the arm and follows him. He asks Fred if he can assist Rayburn in setting up the ramp to get Rodeo and the other horses off the train.

"So that's where Mr. Rodeo got himself to," Fred says.

Fred helps Rayburn, and Rayburn and the U.S. soldiers lead the horses out of the cattle car. Nashoba leads Rodeo out. When Nashoba emerges from the cattle car, his body is fully covered by a red shirt with white diamond-shaped trim, tan buckskin pants, breechcloth, and his feathered headdress. Fred gawks at him. This is the first time Fred has been close to an Indian. His knowledge of them is from hearing bits and pieces about Indians raiding settlers' camps, and claims they were in response to the White settlers brutally attacking their camps. This was the basis of the Indian Wars that went on for years, each side attacking the other in retaliation, resulting in the merciless killing of men, women, and children.

Captain Horton walks over to Nashoba. "With all due respect, Nashoba," he says, "we are trying not to draw attention to ourselves. Your headdress is doing just the opposite."

Nashoba says, "Captain, you wear your blue uniform because you are a soldier. I wear my headdress because I am the son of Chief Samuels, and we are of the Choctaw tribe. I can no more remove my current status than you can remove yours. We both are in our uniforms."

Talako and Koi completed unloading all of their things, and Mr. Hastings directs them to load them onto the covered wagon driven by Clarence. Talako and Koi look to Nashoba, who nods in agreement. Captain Horton, his soldiers, and Nashoba are busy fitting their saddles and gear on their horses, before Horton commands the soldiers to help Rodrigo, Oscar and Mr. Hastings finish loading all their satchels and bags onto the carriage and wagon. After all the baggage is loaded, Mr. Hastings tells Mrs. Hastings, Phillipe, and Oscar to take seats in the four-person carriage. Mr. Hastings then tells Captain Horton, "Seats are available for the Indian guests in the covered wagon." Talako and Koi again glance over at Nashoba. He nods a confirmation, and they climb into the wagon and seat themselves. Rodrigo moves to the front of the covered wagon, greets Clarence and hops onto the bench next to Clarence. Horton and the other U.S. soldiers mount their horses, and Nashoba mounts Rodeo.

Captain Horton gives Fred the signal to move out. The four-person carriage moves out first, followed by Captain Horton and the soldiers who surround Nashoba riding Rodeo, and last is the covered wagon. Horton is conscientious about being able to block any attack that might be made on Nashoba. However, it is impossible to avoid the jaw-dropping attention their procession draws as they proceed down the main street to pick up the road to Covington and on to the Applegate Ranch.

When Will returns and goes into the barn, he is mystified to see that both rigs are gone, and no one is around. Niabi runs into the barn. "Why did they leave me? Who's driving the other rig?" he asks her.

"Calm down. Everything is fine. In fact, everything is perfect, my love," she says and starts tearing up.

Will dismounts. "What is it, honey?" he asks. You have been acting strange all morning." He hugs her and continues, "Don't get all upset about the wedding. You will get your Choctaw wedding when I take you back to your village, OK?"

She chokes up, smiles, and nods.

After removing the saddle from FireTip, Niabi joins him, escorting FireTip to a far east pasture where he can romp alone, away from the other Applegate stock. When they return to the barn, he notices she can't hold back a devilish grin, so he grabs her. "What are you grinning about?" She kisses him to get his mind off that question. As they are kissing, hugging, and enjoying moments of privacy, they hear sounds outside the barn—the clatter of moving wagon parts, harnesses being jiggled by the movement of teams of horses, wheels rolling, unleveling carriages and wagon beds, and then hearing two people call out whoa! Whoa!

Once the rigs are stopped, Mr. and Mrs. Hastings are the first to exit.

Will steps out of the barn with one hand towing a smiling Niabi. At first, he can't make heads or tails of the scene. Familiar is the White couple, and then a somewhat familiar older White male. "Oh, there's Oscar," he says and begins walking toward them. When he sees the Indian headdress, he slows his approach. By then Rodeo sees him and rears up whinnying.

"Let him go. Let him go to Will," Oscar yells to Nashoba.

Nashoba dismounts Rodeo and hits him on the butt. Rodeo gallops, kicking and leaping, until he gets to Will. "Oh, buddy, I'm so glad to see you, I missed you," Will cries out, mounts him, and they take off for the far east pasture where FireTip is located.

Harriet directs those with rooms in the main house to come inside and says, "The ranch hands will help you unload your things onto the back porch."

Niabi walks over to Nashoba.

"You came. Nashoba, you came," Niabi says with tears glistening in her eyes.

"After your letter, did I have a choice?" Nashoba says.

"Thank you for coming," Niabi gushes.

Captain Horton overhears their conversation and approaches Niabi. Tipping his hat, he says, "Captain Horton, ma'am. Glad to make your acquaintance. Where did Mrs. Applegate say we—that is your fellow tribesmen, my soldiers, and the ranch hand—are to have lodgings?"

"Welcome Captain. Out in the far west pasture at a building we call the foaling barn," Niabi says, "but it's been made accommodating for guests to stay in. The floors were cleaned and inside are cots, chairs, and lanterns. I will ask Clarence to take you out there to get settled, and then you may be expected to gather in the main house." Nashoba notices a change in her. She turns to Clarence. "Clarence, can you take them and their things out to the foaling barn?"

Clarence nods in agreement.

Horton and the soldiers decide to ride over on their horses; Rodrigo, Talako, and Koi decide to ride over in the wagon. Nashoba says he will walk over with Niabi.

As Nashoba strolls to the foaling barn alongside Niabi, he turns around 360° glancing at the vast property, admiring the lush greens, the clean well-kept buildings, the peacefulness and beauty of the entire ranch.

"Are you happy, Niabi?" Nashoba asks.

"If we are not beyond the young people we were only months ago, I dare not tell you my true feelings about another. Because I value your friendship and know how proud you are, I don't want to hurt your pride. But if we are older and wiser and see the world with clear eyes, I can feel free to share my feelings; to tell you that my heart floats on bird's wings, and my soul rests peacefully in a river's deep when he is near me."

"That's enough." Nashoba says and tightens his jaws. "I just wanted to make sure you had not been tricked in any way to be here," he says. "I believed you were taken by force because—I couldn't imagine you went from wanting to become a healer to wanting to be that man's woman."

"You were always capable of discerning things happening to me. Someday I may share with you how I really came to be here. But now is not the time," Niabi says.

Nashoba becomes curious about her statement.

"What news do you bring from Liola?" Niabi asks changing the subject.

"She packed some things for me to bring to you, and I have a surprise for you, too."

"A surprise?"

"Yes. Father reviewed the wedding ceremony with me and gave me his authority to wed you to Will, in the Choctaw way, if that is what you want." He pauses. "You two will be man and wife in the eyes of both nations," Nashoba says gazing at her through softer eyes.

She leaps up, hugs Nashoba, and kisses him on his cheek. Overcome by her affection, her scent, and softness of her body when it pressed against his, he fights his desire to fully embrace her, and show her how much he cares. So, he restricts the movement of his arms, but harbors a scant hope that until the wedding ceremony, he may be able to win back her heart.

It is a great distance between where Will has ridden and the foaling barn. Will can barely identify persons on the other side of the ranch. However, he can make out certain figures, such as an Indian in a headdress who hugs and kisses his Niabi. His guts wrench. What he fears has come true—Nashoba has come for her, and she is being wooed back into his clutches.

CHAPTER 13

ACCOMMODATIONS

————

As Niabi and Nashoba continue strolling to the foaling barn, she points out different structures, corrals, and clusters of stock. She laughs telling him she came all this way and ended up learning to become a contributing worker on the ranch and receiving monthly pay to work. "I did almost this same work at the village for free, ha ha ha." She explodes with excitement when she points to the herb garden she started. As she happily shares her stories she jumps, twists and points causing parts of her body, her breasts and hips to bounce. Nashoba watches her with pleasure and can't take his eyes off her. Being near her again reminds him of the void her absence from the village created for him. It is akin to a time without water. Suddenly he has an overwhelming desire to quench his thirst. He abruptly stops and asks, "Niabi, tell me, is there nothing I can do to win your heart? I know I have acted proud, but I need you. I need you in my life. What can I give you, be to you, for you to give up this man and come back home with me?"

Her animated sharing stops. She is stunned to hear this. "Oh, Nashoba, I thought we were past this. I love him. You did nothing wrong." She takes his hand. "We will always be close, like family. You are dear to me. Can you accept me and him together, so that in the future, you will always be welcomed into my home, and me in yours?" Niabi holds her head to one side, shoulders slumped.

"Forgive me," he says, bowing his head. "You know me. I don't give up easily." He looks at her with desire in his eyes. "And you are a prize worth fighting for." He then looks toward the structure ahead of them, takes a breath, and says, "Now, show me the lodging you have for us."

Talako and Koi have already arrived at the foaling barn and begin to unload their gear, baskets, and satchels, and decide to dig a pit for a campfire in front of the foaling barn, which causes Harriet to come running their way. The soldiers settle in with Rodrigo in the stall next to the Indians. Each stall is thirty-by-thirty feet square, with sliding doors, which, when open, allow a six-foot wide doorway. Feeling he deserves separate quarters owing to his rank, Captain Horton is not pleased with the arrangements, but he knows he should stay near the Indians. After Niabi shows Nashoba and Captain Horton around the foaling barn and points out structures of interest on that side of the ranch, Harriet finally reaches them, out of breath and winded.

"You don't need to cook," Harriet says panting for air. "I will have meals ready for everyone each day."

Niabi speaks up on their behalf. "They like the fire, Momma Harriet. It's just our way. It's not only for cooking but for warmth against the night air, to scare away bad spirits, and smooth the way to speak to the Great Spirit."

"Well, we all can do with a bit of prayer, and keeping bad spirits away. Oh, yes. Captain Horton, Mrs. Applegate said there's been some kind of mix-up, and you are to take her son Grant's room in the main house. Somehow that got lost in the communications. As I said, all will be dining at the main house, breakfast at 9 a.m., lunch is served at 12 noon, and dinner at 4 p.m. So, there will be no need to do any cooking out here." A bell will sound thirty minutes before each serving time. Harriet starts to walk away, and then stops and adds, "Oh yes, and there is a tub for bathing in the office there at the end of this building."

Captain Horton ties his horse to the back of the wagon and loads his gear. He and Harriet ride with Clarence back to the main house.

"Who is this Negro woman to order us not to cook for ourselves?" Nashoba asks, a frown creasing his brow.

"She's Will's mother. Please, you have come this far. Just for these days eat our cooking. I have planned dishes to eat that I think you will like. If you don't like our food, I will tell her you want to cook for yourselves—like you are anxious to cook, ha!" Niabi says throwing her head back.

"Do we come to the main house to eat, too?" Talako asks.

"Yes, of course." Looking between Talako and Koi, Niabi adds, "You are all my special guests. But, Talako, are you alright? You look a little pale."

"The train made him sick. I want to make him some tea, but ..." Nashoba says, shrugging his shoulders.

"Yes, go ahead. Make him some tea," Niabi says.

Nashoba looks at their baskets and satchels. "Where do you want me to take these things sent to you from Liola?" Nashoba asks.

"When you are ready, you can follow me back to the cottage, and I will show you where I live on the ranch," Niabi says.

Oscar steps out on the back porch and watches Will ride Rodeo, trailed by FireTip, into the corral closest to the main house. Will removes his saddle from Rodeo, lets them both run loose, and then he crosses the yard going to the back porch. He approaches Oscar with his lips tight and a scowl on his face. Oscar knows when Will's upset and looks at him bewildered.

"I'm glad you came, Oscar," Will says still scowling.

"Well then, why do you look so displeased?" Oscar asks. "You've got your Rodeo back, soon to have *the* woman in your bed. What more can you want, my friend?"

Speaking low, Will says, "First, I've had the woman in my bed a couple of times already now."

"Nooooo, before the wedding? What . . . what is it really like, being with a woman you have such passion for? You know, I've had that saloon girl, who jumped around, and I never felt anything in particular. Then there was the seamstress. She rocked me to sleep."

"All I can say, O," Will says holding onto the porch railing, leaning back, "it's like . . . every nerve in your body is focused on every spot where your skin is touching hers. The two of you are rushing to the top of a mountain, and then you jump off together, sliding down the other side of the mountain, sliding on something warm and soft. When you get to the bottom, you're left feeling limp and spent, yet miraculously you recover enough energy and strength to go again," Will says followed by a sigh.

"Fabulous! Just fabulous!" Oscar says.

"But, Nashoba is here, and I think he's here to convince her to go back," Will says wrinkling his brow.

"No, Will. He came to bring Rodeo back. Did she not tell you he was coming?"

"No. She knew?"

"Ahhhhh, it must have been your surprise. All of this is happening to reunite you with Rodeo. She wants to please you. I don't think she has any intention of leaving you now, especially if those mountain slides are happening for her as they are for you. Ha ha," Oscar laughs and slaps Will's shoulder. Will laughs a little, too.

Phillipe steps out on the porch. "Is this the groom, Will?"

"Yes, Mr. LeGrande, it's good to see you again," Will says, shaking his hand.

"Oh, it is my pleasure to be here. Please call me Phillipe. My grandson holds you out as his best friend and wanted to be here to celebrate your wedding. And I am glad to be here, also. Although, I must say you have assembled a rare collection of wedding guests."

"Yes, I'm afraid I owe that to my bride. She sent out invitations to more people than I knew were on the list."

"Oh yes, we received, or rather Oscar received several letters from her, or were those wires from Captain Horton? Not sure now."

Oscar interrupts, "Grandpa, give us a moment. I'm trying to settle Will's concerns about Nashoba showing up."

Returning to the main house, Niabi sees Will, Phillipe and Oscar on the porch.

After she strolls up, Will says, "Phillipe, this is my bride, Niabi." He turns to Niabi and asks, "You remember Oscar, don't you?"

"Yes, you were with him at the trading post. I remember you," Niabi says. "Glad to finally meet you, and see you standing before me."

"Well, this is his grandfather," Will says. Niabi nods at Phillipe.

"Won't you come in and greet your guests from Texas?" Phillipe asks Niabi.

"Of course," Niabi says. She follows Phillipe into the parlor where the Hastings are seated. Will and Oscar enter behind them, Oscar expressing how beautiful the ranch grounds are and that he can't wait to have Will introduce him to his mother.

Phillipe introduces Mr. and Mrs. Hastings to Niabi. "How was your journey?" Niabi asks. Mr. and Mrs. Hastings reply that it was comfortable for a train without a proper dining car. After they exchange various pleasantries, Mrs. Hastings pulls Niabi aside, tells her about Nashoba riding in the cattle car, and asks her to convince him to ride in the passenger car on the ride back. Niabi reassures Mrs. Hastings that she will speak to Nashoba. The ladies rejoin the others who are admiring a collection of guns and rifles in a display case. Will introduces Oscar to Harriet.

In the parlor, Mrs. Applegate excuses herself from her guests and gestures to Harriet to follow her to the pantry in the kitchen. "I noticed you've moved Captain Horton into Grant's room."

"Yes, Mr. Hastings recommended the move, saying he and the soldiers would be more comfortable with separate quarters. And frankly, I think it's a great idea. He's about the right age to appreciate a woman of your status," Harriet says.

"Oh, Harriet, I don't know about that. It has been ten years since I lost Orin. For a marriage my parents arranged, it was loving and good security for me. I never regretted becoming his wife. But he was the only man I was ever close to, and ... I admit, I do occasionally wonder what it's like to be wooed by an exciting lover." Both ladies use their hands to muffle a spontaneous soft giggle.

"Well, I think this Captain Horton fits the bill. He's a gentleman, courageous for sure to be escorting Indians, and I've already noticed he puts a smile on your face," Harriet says.

"Are you trying to play matchmaker? You are overstepping your bounds, Mrs. Lawton."

"Don't get formal with me in private. You need to have some fun. Just put on some of your perfume, sashay by him, and let nature take its course," Harriet says. They both laugh.

At 3:30 p.m., Harriet rings the dinner bell, and Clarence takes the wagon out to the foaling barn. The soldiers and Rodrigo ride back in the wagon, but Nashoba and his tribesmen decide to walk. Everyone subsequently assembles in the parlor. As Nashoba, Talako, and Koi look around the massive entryway and parlor as if it's a museum, Mrs. Applegate asks Niabi for introductions.

"Mrs. Applegate, I am proud to present two of my tribesmen, Talako and Koi," Niabi says. Mrs. Applegate nods at both of the young men.

Niabi asks Koi if he would bring Nashoba to her. Mrs. Applegate asks Talako if his name has a meaning in his language. He says, "Yes, Talako means eagle."

Nashoba walks over with Koi. Niabi says, "Mrs. Applegate, this is Nashoba, the son of our great Chief Samuels."

"How does one greet an Indian prince?" Mrs. Applegate asks.

"In my case, like any other man," Nashoba says, standing in a wide stance with his arms folded. My father is a chief and not a king. But I thank you for the royal compliment."

Mrs. Applegate continues, "I am honored to meet you, Nashoba."

He responds, "The feeling is mutual, Mrs. Applegate." Looking around he continues, "You have a rather large home. We can fit my whole village and the garden in here." Everyone laughs.

"I will take that as a compliment. I must apologize for your accommodations. All of my cottages are occupied, but I hope the foaling barn is comfortable for you and your tribesmen, and gives you some privacy."

"We are quite comfortable," Nashoba says. "We like being together and near the outdoors. You must know, we were prepared to pitch a tipi, so your foaling barn is an improvement, and yet gives us exactly what we need to enjoy our stay."

Mrs. Applegate nods again at Nashoba, and then moves away to formally greet Captain Horton. "And you're Captain Horton?"

He removes his hat, brings his body to attention, clicks his heels together and nods. "Yes, ma'am, at your service."

"Impressive," she says quickly raising her voice from a low to high tone. "And how about your soldiers and the Hastings' ranch hand? Are the accommodations agreeable to them?" Mrs. Applegate asks pulling her shoulders back and throwing her head up.

"No complaints," says the captain, looking at the soldiers and Rodrigo. They each respond, "Everything is fine." "Yes fine."

Although Mrs. Applegate is in her late forties, she is a fine-looking woman, and Captain Horton is picking up signals from her, causing him to find further items to talk about with her. The captain stands leaning back into his legs, shoulders back, chin erect, and speaking in a low charming tone. Mrs. Applegate thinks maybe Harriet is right.

Captain Horton asks, "Mrs. Applegate, perhaps during my stay will you honor me with a tour of your beautiful ranch?"

"Please call me Lorraine. I would be delighted to give you a tour. But will riding around looking at horses being trained and bred be fascinating to you, captain?"

Captain Horton looks into Lorraine's eyes, intending to coyly convey an ardent interest far beyond that of guest to hostess. "Lorraine, being an officer in the Army, I have a natural affinity for observing any type of training," he replies, "but I must admit I haven't witnessed much breeding of late. As a mammal myself, you never know when such knowledge will come in handy." A mischievous grin crosses his lips.

"Captain Horton, I think you are going to blush before I do," she replies, and they both smile.

Sheila returns from the corridor between the kitchen and the parlor where she spies on the menagerie of guests assembled in the parlor, and reports back to Harriet and Ethel. "The Indians are very healthy looking, so are the soldiers," she says. "And that ranch hand is no pass-up either. I would be glad if any of them come courting me."

"Stay in here and help us get this food ready to serve," Harriet says.

Mrs. Applegate decides to go with a complete buffet dinner, and asks for all the food to be set on two buffet tables three feet from the wall. The guests have to line up and proceed down the line to be served by Sheila and Ethel from the choices of dishes displayed. Niabi goes ahead of her tribesmen and identifies the dishes, which ones she cooked; and she encourages them to try ones they aren't familiar with like the beef stew, chicken and dumplings, and roasted lamb. The guests are treated to sweet potato pie and chocolate cake for dessert.

After dinner, Mr. Hastings, Captain Horton, and Phillipe settle in the office upstairs to smoke and drink. The two soldiers walk to the foaling barn with the Choctaw tribesmen, Rodrigo, and Oscar. On the way, Talako says to Oscar, "It's good to see you in good health."

Oscar replies, "Let's keep me that way."

Rodrigo walking, leans in close to Oscar and asks, "What's that about?"

"I'll explain when we have privacy."

Niabi and Will depart for their cottage. After they enter the cottage and begin preparing for bed, Will frowns and says, "Well, I'm just gonna say it. I saw you and Nashoba hugging and kissing. As painful as it is, I'm man enough to allow you to go back with him if he is the one you truly want."

Undressing in his bedroom, she heard him through the partially opened bedroom door. "Come in here!" she demands. Will walks into his bedroom. The only light in the room is from a lantern on the wash table in the corner. Walking through the doorway he first sees her dress laid on the chair near the door. Then he sees her standing in front of him in a thin undergarment with the lantern's light flickering behind her. The lantern's light filters through her thin undergarment accentuating each curve of her breasts, hips and thighs. He immediately wants to take back what he said. He would be crushed if she leaves him now. Unbeknownst to him, a mixture of anger and passion floods her body, but she controls her impulse to draw him to her. "Do you still want me as your woman?" she asks.

"Yes, of course, I do," Will answers.

"I have given you my body two times now. Along with my body, if you care to know, came my heart and my soul. When I stand here in front of you nearly naked, I feel no shame because I already feel you are my husband. That's why it hurts me so to hear you say such words that make little of what has passed between us."

Will's eyes roam from her face to torso. He licks his lips and thinks how this scene reminds him of the first time he saw her rise up out of the Red River, drenched in a thin undergarment. He sighs deeply, connecting his eyes with hers. "I am very sorry, Niabi. No, you have my body, heart, and soul, too, and I want to keep yours."

"OK, then. I asked Nashoba to bring Rodeo as a surprise for you," Niabi says through clenched jaws.

"I ... I didn't know," Will squeezes out.

"Then know this, Will Lawton. Not a day has gone by since I agreed to marry you, where I have had any doubts in my mind at all!"

He stands there fixed on her, hoping that this moment will end with a kiss, hug, or some kind of touching.

"Now, please leave and close the door behind you," she says firmly not moving an inch.

He walks backwards heading for the door, dragging his feet with a roguish grin, giving her one final look over, from her thick mane of black hair to curvy hips. He closes the door behind him.

———•———

After days of staying at the Applegate Ranch in the foaling barn, milling around the ranch grounds, observing the horse training then gardening, Nashoba is getting bored, especially from being sequestered to the view of the soldiers. Talako and Koi know Nashoba wants to go into town to look around. The three contrive a way for him to slip into town. When he carried those things he brought from Liola to Niabi's cottage, he noticed a brown, wide-brimmed hat she wears to keep the sun off her. One day, he asks her if he can use it. Earlier when he toured the ranch, he saw spare field-worker clothes on a shelf in the bunkhouse. They are clean, folded, and available when ranch hands soil their clothes and need to change. The plan they contrive consists of telling one of the soldiers that Nashoba is taking a bath in the foaling barn office. The other soldier accompanies Rodrigo, Talako, and Koi on a ride out to the lake ten miles from the ranch. While the one soldier is watching the doors of the foaling barn office where Nashoba is supposed to be bathing, Nashoba saddles a horse he stashed in a far end of the pasture the night before. Unaware that Hastings, Phillipe, and Oscar have also gone into town, Nashoba uses this opportunity to go alone into Covington.

———•———

On the second floor of the main house, Mrs. Applegate works in her office. Captain Horton leaves Grant's room wandering the hallway. He sees her, and enters the office. "You surely don't spend every day working, do you?"

She lowers the document she is reading and looks his way. "Not every day, but I get done what needs to be done." Watching him mill around the room looking at pictures and plaques of times gone by, she leans back in her chair. "Have the others gone into town?"

"Yes. But, back to you. Is there even time for a male suitor?" Horton asks with his back to her, examining a picture of Orin and Jeffery Clements posted on the office wall across the room.

"Oh, heavens no. After my husband Orin passed, I was more concerned about keeping the ship afloat."

Careful not to let him see she is admiring his physique, she remains seated at the desk scanning him up and down from his blue uniform to his shiny black boots. She sees a thirty-to-forty-year-old gent of medium height with a fit frame, dark brown hair, and a matching thin mustache. As she watches him meandering around the office, she wonders what is he up to.

"And a fine job you are doing, too. But you are a very attractive woman," he says, easing his way in her direction. As he abandons his review of the wall mementos, his words draw her eyes to his face. Coming closer, he locks eyes with her.

Her pulse quickens. "Won't you have a seat, captain?" Breaking her gaze at him, she extends her open palm, motioning for him to have a seat in one of the chairs near her desk. "I suppose you see me as a lonely and vulnerable woman who would easily succumb to your gentlemanly charms," she smiles and says in her polite Southern drawl.

"On the contrary," he says, finding his way to a chair facing her desk. "I see you as a capable, intelligent woman who intrigues me to no end. And I would be lucky if such a woman favors me with at any level of attention."

"Before such a woman can engage in one of these levels of attention as you say, might she know your full name and a little of your background, sir?"

"Ha ha, of course. How rude of me. My full name is rather ostentatious, not one I would have chosen. I'm Montgomery Bradford Horton. How is that for a monogram to carry through life?"

"There's nothing wrong with your name." She looks upwards and, with a twinkle in her eyes, says, "I can call you Monty." They both laugh. "And what about your family? Where do you come from?"

"I grew up in Massachusetts. We were people of modest means. My father and his father were military men, so choosing this life came quite easy to me and my oldest brother. My youngest brother appears to be the smart one, though. He chose to get a good education and is now a successful tradesman. Because I was so well-suited for command, the department sought to give me a real challenge and posted me out in the frontier. I was assigned an odd assortment of young men they want to be whipped into shape."

"How long do you have to serve out there?"

"I've got one more year before I can apply for another assignment. Wouldn't it be splendid if I was placed near Covington, Tennessee?" As he speaks his eyes never waver from hers. She finds herself hanging on to each word exiting his mouth, being lulled by his soothing tone, calmed by his confident demeanor.

Watching the movement of his mouth as he speaks, she seeks to break the romantic spell she is falling under and blurts out, "Let us go down and see if lunch is ready." She stands and then proceeds to the door.

Feeling he hasn't made the most of that time alone with her, he restrains his desires for another time. "After you, ma'am."

The soldier guarding the empty foaling barn office finally goes in and doesn't find Nashoba. He panics. His thoughts race. He thinks there aren't too many places Nashoba can be. The soldier rides out to the lake, looks around, and sees the others, but not Nashoba. Realizing he has lost him and needs to inform Captain Horton, which could mean the end of his career, he races back to the main house.

After the captain and Mrs. Applegate finish their lunch, the bashful pair leave the dining room and stroll into the parlor deep in conversation about exciting events of the day, including the dedication of the gift from France, the statue of liberty. He scans the parlor room, moves near a settee, and motions for her to join him there. She cautiously draws near, sits down, and then he sits next to her.

"Sitting here, I am reminded of teachings that a debutante is not to sit this close to a young man unless she is chaperoned," she says.

"Well, thank God that is of no concern to us. I'm a full-fledged gentleman, and you are a beautiful widow. Besides, a man would be foolish to take liberties with you in your home."

"Especially when I have my gun rack right there in the corner," she says shifting her eyes and nodding her head toward the gun rack.

"Ha ha ha. Yes, and then there's that. Lorraine, if I may speak directly, I *would* like to get to know you better, if that is acceptable to you."

"I . . . I don't have a problem with that."

He moves closer to her. "You don't know how happy I am to have met you."

As he leans close to her, his lips are but a breath away. Her mind tells her to back away, but her body invites him to taste her lips. His muscular arms enclose her into an embrace. They lean against the back of the settee locked in a kiss. Drawn to her soft and fragrant skin, he tirelessly kisses her about the neck. Softly he says, "I'm so glad I came on this trip."

"I'm glad you did, too." She puts her hands against his chest and pushes him back. She sits up, pats her hair, and straightens her blouse. Taking a deep breath, she says, "I'm surprised at how fast we've gotten close to each other."

He calms his breathing, maintaining a gaze on her. "There is no surprise here. We each have been alone too long, and we have found each other. The real concern, though, is," he says, causing her anxiety to build awaiting his next words. *Is he betrothed or, worse, married?* she thinks.

He continues, "I never thought a day about deserting until I held you in my arms." She smiles relieved. He leans in again putting his hand on her waist. "Lorraine, I want you," he says as he nibbles on her neck.

She feels her body responding to his request. "One last kiss," she says, holding up just her index finger.

Inside the kitchen, the soldier appears and asks Harriet if she knows where Captain Horton is. Harriet knows he and Mrs. Applegate are in the parlor. She doesn't want to disturb them, but the soldier insists, telling her Nashoba is missing. Harriet tells him to wait there in the kitchen. Before entering the parlor, she clears her throat loudly, "Uh, ummm," and then calls out, "Mrs. Applegate."

Horton and Mrs. Applegate untangle themselves and return to a more presentable state. "Yes, Harriet. I'm in here," Mrs. Applegate says.

Harriet enters and tells them that a soldier is in the kitchen with an urgent message for Captain Horton, that Nashoba is missing.

"Tell the soldier I'll meet him in the barn," Horton says. Harriet returns to the kitchen.

Horton takes Mrs. Applegate's hand and kisses it. Maintaining direct eye contact he says, "I must take my leave of you, my sweet."

Captain Horton meets his soldier in the barn. "Where was the last place you saw him?" After the soldier explains about the excursion to the lake and that Nashoba wasn't seen around the ranch, Horton exclaims, "Let's go to town!"

Nashoba walks along the wide boardwalk which flanks the dirt road, running down the middle of town in front of all of the town's storefronts. The boardwalk extends from one end of the town to the other. Folding his hair up into Niabi's brown wide-brimmed hat and wearing a brown shirt and brown cotton pants he found in the bunkhouse, he is unrecognizable as an Indian, without a closer look. People walk along the boardwalk, in conversation or looking at store window displays. They stroll past him; some even nod a hello. He peers through different storefront windows: a bakery, fabric store, hat millinery store and gun shop. He is amazed at the variety of stores. A White gentleman, tall and stocky, walking by dressed in the finest business attire, bumps into him. Nashoba nods and continues on his way. The White gentleman stops and asks, curling his lips, "Have you forgot your manners, sir? I believe I am owed an apology." Nashoba has no intention of giving him an apology; after all, the White man bumped into him, not the other way around. The gentleman removes his hat and coat and asks his companion, "Hold these, while I teach this no-count a lesson." While Nashoba is not good at gardening, cooking, or building a shelter, from years of wrestling with friends and other men—whoever would challenge him in the village—he is excellent at stickball and hand-to-hand fighting. "Put up your dukes," the gentleman says and prances in a circle around Nashoba, who holds his ground. The gentleman swings, and Nashoba ducks. He jabs, and Nashoba bounces from side to side, avoiding any hits from the jabs. Finally, Nashoba pulls his strength into his core, centers it to get the maximum burst of power, and kicks out sideways, hitting the gentleman in the gut with his foot, sending him flying off the boardwalk onto the dirt road that makes up the main street. Lying in the road, the gentleman curls up into the fetal position in gut-wrenching pain. The crowd is not dense, but the few who stand by and watch the two sparring are wowed and delighted to have this to discuss.

Just as the gentleman hits the dirt, the Applegate Ranch four-person carriage pulls up carrying Phillipe and Oscar. They are curious to see what is happening. Seeing a man that resembles Nashoba, Phillipe beckons him over to the carriage. "What is happening here? You are in disguise and fighting?"

"That White man wanted to fight me because I didn't apologize for him running into me!" Nashoba explains out of breath.

Phillipe opens the carriage door. "Get in. Get in. We're on our way to the Gardens for lunch. Come with us. Leave here before you are found out," Phillipe says.

Nashoba climbs into the carriage, and they move off.

A short while later, Captain Horton and the soldier gallop into town. The captain dismounts from his horse, and questions random store owners and persons walking along the boardwalk about whether they have seen a tall, tan man with black hair. He is reluctant to provide more details than that for fear of starting a panic. No one recollects seeing a person looking like that. The captain soon hears about a man brawling with a finely dressed tradesman and then riding off in a large carriage. Captain Horton remembers that the Hastings and Phillipe were to travel into town in the ranch's carriage, and had left word with the kitchen workers that they were going to the Gardens for a late lunch after shopping. So, Captain Horton and the soldier head to the restaurant. Since Captain Horton was caught metaphorically with his pants down when the crisis with Nashoba arose, he decides not to report the incident to his superiors, and tells the soldier with him he would fare better if he never mentions it as well. At the Gardens, squinting his eyes, Captain Horton approaches Nashoba, preparing himself for what he needs to say.

The next day, Mrs. Applegate gives Captain Horton some of her husband's old work clothes and takes him on a tour of the ranch on horseback. The tour ends with a jaunt, racing their horses out to the lake. When they arrive at the lake, she hops off. He hops off coming toward her, and she runs from him. Catching her, he grabs her and pulls her down on top of him onto the low soft grass. As they land on the ground, laughter bursts from her. She looks at him blushing, and then he flips her over and kisses her. "You take a lot of liberties for a guest in my home, Captain Horton," she says, pulling their lips apart.

"I thought you were going to call me Monty," he says, looking into her eyes. He releases her and stretches out next to her on the low blade grass. Head raised, resting on his elbows, he looks around at the scenery. "No, I just believe in not missing an opportunity like this to enjoy myself. I'm in tranquil, beautiful surroundings with a beautiful and admirable woman."

She sits up. "This lake was the only place Orin would bring the family when he took breaks from work. While I imagined he and I could make it a romantic retreat somehow, he would spend all the time here teaching the boys to swim, fish, or make fires." After gazing out at the lake, she connects her eyes with Horton again. "Am I sport to you, Captain?"

His forehead wrinkles for a moment. "Lorraine, I know you've just met me. But surely two mature adults can determine if they've found something special. And from what has been going on between us, I think we give each other a joy that is amazing and precious. Aren't our feelings mutual?" He takes her hand, kisses it, and jokingly continues kissing up her arm, over her shoulder to her neck, face, and lips. They both laugh.

She pushes him away saying, "No, I don't think so." Then she runs, laughing, and hops onto her horse.

He yells, "I know you don't mean that." She glares at him, and then races back to the ranch, and to the main house. He chases behind her.

Entering the kitchen, so out of breath she can hardly speak, she asks the staff, "How is dinner coming? Will it be on time tonight?"

Harriet answers in the affirmative, but squints her eyes at her. Harriet suspects the preparation of dinner is not the real concern here. The conversation with the staff about dinner is merely to give Captain Horton time to catch up with her. He and Lorraine exchange glances, pretending to be surprised to run into each other in the kitchen and trying to hide their playfulness.

"Mrs. Applegate, may I speak with you in the office?" the captain asks.

"Alright," she says and turns slowly to exit the kitchen, and ascends the staircase with him trailing behind her. Norms and conventions of the time, dictating a man isn't to see a woman's naked body until they are wed, overtake her mind. Getting married is not currently in her cross-hairs, but the captain is right. She is lonely and longs to be touched. It will be to her detriment if he's actually a scoundrel hiding under the uniform of a respectable U.S. Army captain. They enter the hallway, pass by the office, continue to the end of the hallway, and stop in front of her bedroom door.

He fidgets and immediately moves away. "Well, I'll bid you a good day, my lady, until dinner, if ... that is what you truly want," he says, looking her way with a bleak expression.

Pausing at the door with her back to him, she can feel his eyes on her watching and hear him breathing through his mouth. She opens the bedroom door and pauses again. Slowly, he backs up, anticipating he will enter Grant's room located next to hers, if she is indeed done with him for now. She turns, her face flushed, locking eyes with him. These circumstances entice him to hold his position and hope. Holding the door with her left hand, she throws the door open wider, allowing enough room for him to walk in. She stands to the side maintaining a lock on his eyes. He squints one eye, uncertain about what all this means, but moves forward. His eyes are still locked to hers. She leans against the wall, parting her lips; her face softens into only the beginning of a smile. He slowly moves toward her, and then walks past her, entering her bedroom, maintaining locked eyes, concluding this must indeed be an invitation. Once he's through the doorway and inside of the bedroom, she closes and locks the door. "You've got my complete attention, Monty," she says.

A half an hour before the dinner bell is rung, he rises to search around the room for his clothes. She watches him dress and then helps him button his shirt in between short playful kisses. Once fully dressed, he pulls her into him and kisses her again but hard and passionately. "This went unexpectedly well. Don't you agree?" he asks. Still floating from their lovemaking, she nods, her eyes twinkling and lips swollen. He releases her to leave, but before he opens the bedroom door, he says, "I can't wait until round two." He cracks the door. Seeing the hallway is empty, he slips out and into Grant's bedroom to wash up and dress for dinner.

That evening after dinner, before going upstairs to retire, Mrs. Applegate strolls into the kitchen to tell the staff dinner was wonderful. After she exits the kitchen, Harriet corners her near the staircase. "You are just glowing," she says. "I see you are spending a lot of time with Captain Horton. Is it working out with him?"

"The man is decent company."

"Oh, well, then he is a good match for you," Harriet says and smiles.

"Orin was the only man I ever experienced. He was conservative in his professional and personal life. The captain, on the other hand, is very conservative in his professional life, but in private, behind closed doors, he's as creative and inventive as he is energetic. Not what you'd expect."

"He's not offending or being inappropriate with you, is he?" Harriet whispers, frowning.

"Any woman I should think would enjoy this kind of inappropriateness," she adds and quickly covers her mouth with her hand. "Apologies for speaking so unrefined," Mrs. Applegate says. "Let's just say, I am thoroughly enjoying his attention. More so than I would care for him to know. But it's you, Harriet, that I will blame for all of this." Pointing her finger at Harriet, she continues, "It will be your fault when I'm sad after he leaves. Dear Harriet, what am I going to do when this charming gentleman returns to his fort?" Lorraine clutches Harriet's hands, and they both smile at each other.

———•———

Several days pass, and the day comes for Dakota and Loma to board their train for Memphis. Mrs. Applegate sends Clarence to pick them up in her small carriage, and take them to Pastor Walker's home. She gives Clarence, who can't read and write, another note written on her stationary to give to the conductor at the Memphis station.

The Egglesbys get off the train and wait by the station building. Clarence walks up to the conductor. "Sir, I'm here to pick up some more folks coming in on this train. Here are their names on this note." He hands the note to the conductor.

The conductor is a different one. He reads the note and recognizes the names, Mr. and Mrs. Egglesby. While he knows exactly who the Egglesbys are by sight, he is inclined to be ornery toward Clarence. He tells him, "Go stand over there by the station door until I'm not busy." His directions force Clarence into the densest part of people moving around the busy station platform; he has to half-step, stop, and then side-step, offering several "pardon mes" until he finally reaches a spot against the building. The conductor looks his way and feels a crooked pride about getting Clarence to go and stand about three feet from the Egglesbys.

Dakota keeps looking around for a face he recognizes.

"Maybe they forgot we were coming today," Loma says.

"No, the pastor wouldn't forget, and that gal Niabi wrote a sincere letter. Let me ask this conductor," Dakota Sam says and walks over to the conductor. "Sir, has anyone inquired about the Egglesbys, or is there an office or somewhere I can go to ... ahhhh ... to gets some information?" he asks.

The conductor is busy directing persons exiting the train, and organizing a line of folks waiting to board. Wondering if Mrs. Applegate's guests have missed the train, Clarence starts walking away slowly back to the wagon.

The conductor looks at Dakota Sam. "I think that nig—Negro with the dirt farmer's hat came for you," he says with a smirk on his face while pointing at Clarence. Dakota looks in the direction he pointed and spots a big Negro man in a hat slowly walking away. The conductor continues, "You better git your things and follow him."

Dakota Sam has wiped the smile off a man's face for lesser offenses, but he is traveling with Loma now, and though he is carrying his gun, he reasons he can't give that man the good pistol-whipping he deserves and get away clean, leaving her to suffer for his rash actions.

He has to chase Clarence down before he can go back for Loma and their satchels. He yells to be heard over the throngs of people at the station. "I say—pardon me, are you from Niabi and Pastor Walker?"

"Yes! Yes! I saw you, but wasn't sure you were the ones. Come on here," Clarence says.

"Let me get my wife and bags."

When they reach Clarence next to the carriage, Clarence says, "Get right onboard Mrs. Applegate's fine carriage she sent out here just for you." Tears well up in Clarence's eyes, because he is glad he doesn't have to go back and tell them he couldn't find the passengers and is overcome with joy that he has them. Tears also collect in Loma's eyes because they are in a strange city, and she sees how difficult it is to get help. She's just tired of being scared.

"The good Lord is with us today," Loma says settling in next to Dakota in the carriage. Dakota wraps his arm around her and hugs her.

"Yes, indeedie," Clarence says. "We found each other, and now I'm taking you to Pastor Walker's home."

"What's the pastor like?" Loma asks.

"Oh, he's a good pastor. Gives us food for thought every Sunday. You will enjoy being in his lovely home."

Dakota hides his feeling insecure and awkward by being overly attentive to Loma as they ride in their handsome carriage. He thinks part of this insecurity is because he is without Blackie and has to depend on this sniffling darkie driving them to get them where they want to go. While he is grateful he and Loma will have clean, safe lodging, he hates having to be pleasant and beholden to another man, especially one he does not know. He has his pistol on him if any real danger arises, but from what he observed during his last stay in Covington, he may very well be the most untamed being for miles, with maybe the exception of the Indians. He resolves to get through this visit by squeezing in his butt cheeks and thinking before he speaks so no swear words or farts spill out during conversations with the Walkers.

CHAPTER 14

THE CEREMONY

_____

It is the Thursday before the wedding. Oscar and Rodrigo walk around the ranch looking for Will and after not finding him, they approach Fred in the office within the barn.

Fred extends a hand to Oscar and says, "I know you are Oscar, Will's friend. He has talked about you. And who is this here, vaquero?"

"Ahhh, you know the language?" Rodrigo asks.

"No, just studied horses and ranching from different experts and visitors to the ranch. You can't get around the history of the old ranchers in the West coming from Mexico, and then the Spaniards who introduce horses to the States. Unfortunately, I recall the care and training of horses, but I know no other Spanish word, except vaquero. Fred again extends his right hand, but to Rodrigo, and says, "I'm the ranch foreman, Fred Johnson. Glad to meet Will's friends."

"Well, I am Rodrigo Figueroa. I work with Will on the cattle drives."

"Have you seen Will? We thought he may be finished with his work," Oscar remarks.

"He's out on the grounds somewhere, probably giving Rodeo and FireTip a romp," Fred replies. They all walk out to the back of the barn.

Rodrigo sees Will in the distance, riding toward the foaling barn. He knows the Indians and soldiers are there, but only sees Nashoba sitting outside.

"He's headed toward the foaling barn. Let's go over there," Rodrigo says, slapping Oscar on his arm in a panic.

Will rides up to the foaling barn on Rodeo, with FireTip tagging along, and sees only Nashoba sitting outside on a chair. There is no fire burning in the pit that Nashoba and his tribesmen had dug. Will dismounts, reluctantly. Nashoba remains seated, but gives Will his full attention.

"I never got a chance to thank you for returning Rodeo, and taking such good care of him," Will says.

Nashoba stands, walks toward him, and stops five feet in front of Will.

"How did you do it, Negro man? How did you convince Niabi to be *your* woman?"

Will looks away from him, looks out at the pastures, not allowing Nashoba to draw him into a dispute. "I just came over to thank you. That's all," Will says, and abruptly turns to leave.

Nashoba swiftly responds, "And I accept your thanks. I am just— what's the word? Puzzled, as to how she went from wanting so much to be a healer to now wanting to bear your seed."

Will quickly twists back around to face Nashoba and blurts out, "And not your seed?" Again, Will tries to calm himself. "Niabi told me how proud you are. I'm not going to turn our wedding celebration into a brawl with you." He pauses, before continuing, "Is any answer I give you going to make it right for you?"

"I have known her since we were children. I watched her blossom into the woman she is now," Nashoba says.

Will interrupts him. "She said there were no promises between you two."

"Yes, that is true," Nashoba says stepping closer, now within one foot of Will, locking eyes, each staring the other one down. In a low threatening tone Nashoba says, "How did you do it, Negro man? How did you take her from our village without a trace?" Nashoba again stands within arm's reach, face to face, with Will as he did when they were in the village when Oscar was rescued.

"You are *not* in your village now, Nashoba," Will says.

"Do you want to hit me?" Nashoba asks in a low menacing tone with a stone face. "That is one way to settle things between us."

Nashoba hears others approaching and glances over to see Oscar and Rodrigo. He backs off Will, walks over near FireTip, and asks, "Is this the tan horse she rode before she disappeared?" Will is still steaming and doesn't answer. Nashoba walks closer to FireTip, and he rears up at him. "You control these horses like a shaman. Did you train this one against my kind?" Nashoba asks.

Will takes a deep breath, and lets it out slowly. "He doesn't like anyone except me and Niabi."

"Good evening," says Oscar.

"Everything OK, Will?" Rodrigo asks, nervously looking from Will to Nashoba and back.

Nashoba answers, "He is fine. We were just recalling our past encounters. After he and Niabi are married, he and I are going to be like family."

"Where's Talako and Koi? I feel better with you and them in front of me and not darting out from behind me," Oscar says smiling and squinting at Nashoba.

As Nashoba walks back to his chair, he says, "Your food is too heavy for them. They fill themselves like pigs and can barely walk back here after lunch, and always get sleepy early. After the wedding, I will run them and get their bodies strong again; get them ready like we have to be for the stickball games. Come, sit with me. Let's make the nice talk."

———•———

Youngster, Sam Jr., and Rita dart through the rain to the train depot in Washington, DC. They board the train for Memphis, traveling in second class. After arriving in Memphis, Rita has them follow her over to the livery stable to ask the Negro worker who tends to the horses if she can pay to use a wagon to get home and return it the next day. "Do you know how to handle a wagon?" Rita asks Sam Jr.

"I've done every job but one requiring that. What about you, Youngster?" Sam Jr. asks.

"Nope," Youngster says shaking his head.

"OK, you gents are going to be driven by a lady to your destination," Rita says smiling.

They ride out to the Walkers' home. Pastor and Mrs. Walker do not know she is bringing more guests needing lodgings. Their house is full of guests: Dakota Sam and his wife, Loma.

"This is Sam Jr.'s father and mother," Rita says to her parents. "I have been seeing a lot of Sam Jr. in Washington, DC."

"This is your son, Dakota?" Pastor Walker asks looking surprised because the son looks so poised and tailored compared to the father.

"Yes," Dakota Sam says proudly.

"Small world," Pastor Walker says.

"And real small in this house," says Mrs. Walker. "Rita can share a room with Martha, and we can ask Harriet if the bunkhouse at Applegate Ranch has some beds available. They have a lot of room there. You two young men just need a clean spot to lie down. You can spend most of the day down here with us, and have your meals here. Rita, you want to take them down there and talk to Harriet?"

"OK, mom" Rita says.

Driving the wagon with Sam Jr. and Youngster sitting beside her, Rita comes down the path from her home to the Applegate Ranch. Working with horses in a pasture near the path to the Walker home, Will can see the wagon coming. He calls Rodeo, and he comes over, allowing Will to mount him bareback. FireTip, who has been playing with Rodeo in the corral since morning, and is enjoying Rodeo being back with him, follows Rodeo over to Will. Will loves the two horses so much he doesn't object and lets FireTip tag along to meet Rita.

"Well, Miss Rita, I was told that you are in Washington DC, making yourself into a nurse. Was I misinformed?" Will asks.

"No, you weren't. Will, I want to introduce you to Sam Egglesby Jr. and Youngster Egglesby," Rita says.

"Egglesby?" Will says.

"Yes, you know our father, Dakota Sam," Sam Jr. says.

"Well, I'll say. Yeah, Dakota's boys. Welcome! Welcome! When does your father arrive?" Will asks.

"He's already here at the Walkers' home. Since he doesn't have Blackie, he's probably waiting to walk down when he thinks you are free from work to talk," Sam Jr. says.

"Oh, I can ride over and visit him," Will says. "But tell him to come anytime. Anytime. We have a couple of orders to finish, but I'm free to stop and talk to him anytime. I owe him a lot."

"Do you know if there are spare beds in the bunkhouse? Our house is full," Rita says.

"Well, we can go take a look," Will says.

Will, Rita, Sam Jr., and Youngster walk over to Fred's office in the barn, and Fred shows them the bunkhouse and determines, with the crew he has working on the grounds, there are five beds available.

"I'll let Mrs. Applegate know they are staying here. What are you folks doing for meals?" Fred asks.

"Oh, they will be eating at my house. They can sleep here, and spend the day at my house," Rita says. She looks at Will and feels emotionally naked. She feels that he sees how she has moved on from him, and now has interests in Sam Jr., who now walks around the barn like a competing rooster. When he and Youngster walk out of the back of the barn and look around, they see on the other side of the far pasture Indians sitting outside and talking.

Sam Jr. says, "Now, that's a sight I didn't expect to see. What are Indians doing here?"

"I'll leave the whole story for your father to tell you. But for now, they are like my new relatives," Will says.

Rita walks over to Sam Jr. "OK, it's settled. You can come back here tonight and sleep." She pauses, takes his hand, and then continues, "I'll meet you at the wagon. I want to say something to Will." They exchange glances, the she waits, watching him slowly walk begrudgingly to the wagon.

Rita walks back to Will. "I want to express how happy I am for you," she says.

"We are such good friends. I know that without you having to say it," Will says.

Tears sparkle in Rita's eyes. "I'm sorry," she says. "I feel a lot of emotions right now."

"Come here," he says as he reaches for her. She moves closer to Will, and they embrace in a loving bear hug. "You will always be very special to me, and I want you to be happy, too," Will says.

"I know. I know that," Rita says. They separate, but Will holds on to her hand. He kind of did that to mess with Sam Jr., who watches them, trying to look like he isn't.

"Is this man, a possible ...?" Will asks.

"He may be a possible, but for now he's a lot of fun," Rita says, dabbing her eyes with her fingers.

"Well, good. You deserve some good fun, as long as he's respectful."

"Oh yes, he's a good man. I just don't know his heart like I know Will's heart," Rita says, placing her hand over her heart.

"Let me put you on this wagon before you have us both teared up," Will says.

At that moment, Oscar walks up with Rodrigo. "More wedding guests?" Oscar asks Will.

"Yes, Oscar, this is Rita." Looking at Rita, Will says, "Hmm, how do I describe you?"

"Try, we grew up together, we played together as children, and our parents are close. There's a lot you can say, Will," Rita says, shaking her head and pretending to be annoyed.

Will strides over to the wagon. "And these are Dakota Sam's boys!" he says.

"Dakota Sam's! How do you do? Your dad helped save my life," Oscar shouts as he shakes each of their hands.

"What?" Sam Jr. says.

"Another story Dakota Sam needs to tell you," Will adds.

Will helps Rita climb onto the wagon. She takes the reins and heads back to her house. Sam Jr. shouts back at Will, "Now if my father doesn't tell me these stories, I'll be back here to find you two."

When they arrive at the Walker home, Dakota is waiting out front with two saddled horses. All file into the Walker house, but Dakota asks Sam Jr. to wait. "The Walkers need that rig-for-hire returned to Memphis. Why don't we do that for them, son?" Dakota Sam asks Sam Jr.

"Sure, but I'm not the best rider," says Sam Jr., ashamed he cannot ride.

"Nonsense. All you need to do is hang on. The horse does all the work. I'll tie the reins to the back of the wagon, and take the wagon back to Memphis. On the way back, you get your first lesson from me for free. And anyway, a son of mine should know how to ride well."

Both sit on the wagon bench harboring bourgeoning frustrations. "I needed to get out of that house for a while," Dakota says. Sam Jr.

looks at him surprised. Dakota continues, "The pastor's family are good people and all. But that's it—they're too damn good. I have to watch what I say, how I say it. I've been holdin' in a healthy fart for goin' on a day."

"Just fart, Poppa!" Sam Jr. says grinning. "I'm sure they know about farts."

"You know what I mean. I don't want to be an embarrassment to my Loma. And now that you have taken up with their daughter, she's to be impressed, too."

Dakota Sam returns and checks in the rig Rita rented. Sam Jr. does not relish the trip back. Dakota and Sam Jr. mount the horses they brought and start their arduous journey back to the Walkers' home. To the observer, Dakota Sam rides very slowly while Sam Jr. appears to be meandering from one side of the road to the other and into the thickets off the road while being bombarded by Dakota Sam's instructions. Sam Jr. has a time keeping the horse going in a straight line.

"Keep your heels from tapping him. Press with your calves. Now just let him settle into a trot, and don't pull on either side of the reins," Dakota says. "Yeah, that's good. He's moving a lot better."

"I need to talk to you about something," Sam Jr. says, after feeling he can keep the horse moving in a straight line.

"I hear you," Dakota says.

"I really like this girl, Rita. I don't know how she feels about me," Sam Jr. says, wrestling to get the horse heading straight again. "Doggone it! Come back to the road. So, Pops, I'm worried that she won't want me when she finds out I can't read or write."

"What makes you think that?"

"She's an accomplished young lady. Why would she want to get with me?"

"You can't think like that, son. Women get with men for different reasons. Some want a protector, a provider, a lover, or a patient. If other men fear you, you're a protector. If you provide a roof and food, you're a provider. Excitement in the bedroom, you're a lover, and frailties of the mind or spirit, and you're a patient. Now, what category do you fit in, and is that the category she's looking for?"

"I don't know if it's that simple, Pops. And anyway," Sam Jr. says, letting out a deep sigh, "I don't know what she wants."

"Well, lying to her won't increase her devotion to you. I would suggest coming clean to her and then seeing how she responds. You might as well find out now before you get in any deeper. Of course, I never had to be anyone but myself with your mother. I was kind and thoughtful to her. It also probably helped that I found ways to curl her toes, but that's way down the road for you. She's a proper girl, your girl, and will want to be courted for a while before you get a chance to curl any toes. But I say, break this tension you have growin' over the matter, and tell her the truth now. How she reacts will give you all the reason you need to stay or leave her."

On the Thursday before the wedding, Mrs. Applegate processes an order for forty horses to a vendor in Philadelphia. She wants to get the paperwork done in case one of her current very special guests wants another tour of the ranch or a brisk ride out to the lake. She has refrained from letting her mind explore what has already transpired or of future possible entanglements with Captain Montgomery Bradford Horton. This work, her work, is the bloodline of the ranch, and she must see to it that the work gets completed to specifications and on time.

Mr. Hastings, Phillipe, Oscar, Rodrigo, Captain Horton, the soldiers, and tribesmen ride out to the lake. Harriet and her staff had packed them lunch, and they plan to spend the day there. Will is busy fulfilling the last of the orders after extending his apologies for not being able to accompany them. Workdays after the wedding date have been removed from his work schedule, allowing for a honeymoon, so he must get as much as possible done now to stay in good with Mrs. Applegate, especially after all she has done for him and Niabi.

The only visiting guest left in the main house is Mrs. Hastings who, after breakfast, had returned to her quarters, the guest room, and now exits that room strolling down the hallway on the second floor. With the other Texas contingent out to the lake, she seeks out the company of Mrs. Applegate whom she is told is working in her office. Perusing the hallway passing alcoves with closed doors, she finds the office door open, knocks, gains permission to enter from Mrs. Applegate who is sitting at her desk. "Mrs. Applegate," Mrs. Hastings says.

"Please call me Lorraine," Mrs. Applegate replies.

"And you may call me Abigail."

"Lorraine, I was told you have children; may I ask where they are?"

"Yes, I have two grown sons, Grant and Jason. They are off running around Europe. We were looking at sales opportunities over there, but I haven't heard from them, so I'm not sure if they are spending money on business or pleasure," Mrs. Applegate says, and pauses. "I informed them about the wedding, but my sons only offer their best wishes to the happy couple with no commitments to return. In contrast, my niece, Catherine, who's traveling with them, surprisingly questions my judgment for supporting the event. While I expect some of my family and acquaintances will question my actions, I was quite surprised to hear such remarks coming from her— someone I thought was fond of everyone that lives and works here. Do you have children?"

"No. Mr. Hastings and I were so busy building up the ranch, and I had trouble carrying one to term, so I said well, we gave it a good try, and now let's get on with living we're blessed with. I enjoy that it is just him and me. We entertain his business associates regularly, and occasionally we enjoy a trip here and there. I wonder about what it would have been like to have children, but we're happy for the most part."

"Where will your property and your assets go when you leave this earth?" Mrs. Applegate asks.

"Mr. Hastings has some relatives that will get it, I'm sure. My people are in New York and have no stomach for life in Texas. They don't like the heat, the distance, or the conversation."

Gesturing toward a chair directly in front of Mrs. Applegate's desk, Mrs. Hastings asks, "May I?"

"I've completely forgotten myself. Of course, have a seat," Mrs. Applegate says. "You know, a lot can be excused, but poor manners is not one of them." Both ladies smile and nod in agreement.

"You and I have a lot in common. We are—and in your case were—married to powerful men, and as bubbling brides were probably underestimated as far as what we are capable of. We were desired to be their homemakers and bearers of heirs. We sat on the sidelines of our husbands' rich and exciting lives and after a while, if we had an ounce of intellect, we became bored with organizing our face powders and perfumes," Mrs. Hastings says.

"I know what you mean. I was never allowed in the room when ranch business was transacted. As Grant got older, I convinced Orin to let me at least listen in, so I could reinforce the points he was teaching Grant. Thank God, I did that. Because when Orin died suddenly, Grant was still too young and immature. So, I had to take control. Initially, that didn't mean much since customers and supporters didn't see me as a serious business person. But, through my contacts overseas, I invited a few aristocrats from Europe who weren't put off by a woman running what heretofore is a successful ranch. Before you know it, the rich American social climbers were arriving here by the droves to fraternize. It also helped that my brother-in-law lent his name as a sponsor, but we have had good business ever since. Are you involved in your husband's business?"

"You have to understand, he met me at a gala in New York, where gaggles of debutantes from wealthy families surrounded him as prospects for his bride. He knew he had his pick of the pack. He was rich, handsome, and wasn't boring. I don't know if he was looking to marry right then, but I was. I hung back across the room, glancing at him occasionally, then wetting my lips during an alluring stare at him before retreating out to the balcony. His curiosity was piqued. Once out on the balcony, he tangled with a wild cat. My quick wit, and confidence to challenge and engage him, satisfied an appetite he had no idea he had. We were married within the month. At first, the ranch, the land, and the prestige of being Mrs. W. John Hastings were all I ever longed for. I went about making our home comfortable and efficient. He made the money, and together we determined how it was spent. But as time rolled on and our family never grew, I find myself at a crossroads. I think I am going to do more traveling. If he's smart, he'll join me. Otherwise, I don't know what's next behind the curtain for us." She pauses, looks at Lorraine, and then asks, "Do you mind me asking you, how do you cope with the loss of companionship provided by your husband?"

"In the beginning it was grim. Right after Orin died, I would lie in our bed and find myself reaching out for him. I am reluctant to accept the attention of suitors, because it would be so easy for a new husband to take over, take charge, and relegate me back to just the role of a wife. And the mechanisms in our society would support his claim to all that I have. No, I have tasted being in control of my own life and the zeal of keeping our operations out of the red. I want my boys to feel that way about running the ranch, too. I believe I can nurture that kind of drive in them too."

"I want us to stay in touch. Strong women need to support each other," Mrs. Hastings says.

"I ardently agree," Mrs. Applegate says.

Later that evening carrying his suit coat over his arm, Phillipe wanders down the hall to the backstairs, and down to the kitchen where he finds Sheila. "Beautiful lady, do you have an iron to press the clothes?" he asks.

"Yes, I can iron it for you," Sheila says.

"Ah, it is a delicate weave. You can't have the iron too hot," Phillipe says.

Sheila nods. "I promise to be really careful. Is this all you need to be pressed?"

"Yes, my pants are perfect," Phillipe says.

Sheila goes to the basement to press Phillipe's suit coat. Ethel hurries there to speak to Sheila and asks, "How many bottles of wine did we set out?"

"Five red, five white, and five champagne. Why?" Sheila replies.

"I just looked in the cabinet in the dining room and one of the reds is missing," Ethel says.

"You think one of the guests took it?" Sheila asks.

"I hope not. But if anyone took it, let's hope that's all they wanted, because we have more guests coming and we can't watch each one to find out who's takin' stuff. Do you think I should tell Mrs. Applegate?" Ethel says.

"No, her nerves have got to be fragile by her stretching her hospitality to hosting Negroes and Indians, opening her house to strangers, and none of her kin bein' around. Now if she learns things are going missing, she may break out in hives. Let's hope someone was just desperate to quench a thirst," Sheila says.

Youngster has finished playing with Fred Jr. and wants to get to the Walkers' home in time for dinner. He had seen Sam Jr. earlier entering the bunkhouse and decides to see if he is still there so they can walk to the Walkers' together. Youngster enters the bunkhouse and hears faint talking coming from the area where he and Sam Jr. are bedding down.

"Why would she want me after chasin' after that Will Lawton? He rides horses and handles rigs. Ho, hoooo, that's a protector and a provider for sure," Sam Jr. says.

Youngster looks around and sees no one other than Sam Jr. "Who are you talking to?" Youngster asks. He does see an almost empty bottle of wine. Sam Jr. clumsily tries to hide it under blankets. A look of disappointment flickers across Youngster's face.

"What do ya . . . you want, Youngster?" Sam Jr. says, slurring his words.

"I need to know you are OK. Why are you drinking that, putting that in your body? I'm sure you know what too much of that does to a person. I've seen other men get out of control after drinking too much. It's not good for you!" Youngster pleads.

Sam Jr. takes a deep breath and exhales. "You wouldn't understand."

"Try me!" Youngster demands.

Sam Jr. closes his eyes. Then he looks down and says, "Your mother, Loma, and I went through a lot before you came to us. The stench of slavery still burns my nostrils. As far back as I can remember, I lived in fear of being separated from Mom and Pops. They were all I had. If I had to pack my valuables and run, all I would pack are them. I've tried to adjust, especially after we escaped. But I fear I'm a damaged man. I can't read or write. Don't know numbers. What use am I? That's why the wine; it helps me forget, and temporarily dulls my pain."

Youngster's face snarls. "What use are you? How can you say that? You are my big brother, the one I look up to. I don't care about whether you read and write. I know you are a good, hard-working person that Momma Loma and I depended on, and still do. How are you going to explain to Momma, Poppa, and now Rita that you are drowning yourself in wine?"

"I'm not gonna, and you not gonna tell, either," Sam Jr. says and leans back on his bunkbed, glaring at Youngster.

"Sam, come on with me. I won't say a word. We'll just go and have dinner," says Youngster.

"I'm fine. I have some bread, ham, and an apple from the kitchen. Sheila got it for me. I think she's a little sweet on me. You head on back now, and tell them I ... I turned in early."

On the eve of the wedding, everyone on the planning committee meets at the church to put all the flowers in place. Decorating the altar is Martha and Mrs. Fenton's job; putting flowers near the entrance is Mrs. Walker and Harriet's job. Rita, Sam Jr., and Youngster decorate the center aisle end of each pew with a small bouquet of white and varying shades of orange daylilies and lilac irises, tied with orange, white, and yellow ribbons. While the committee is at work, Will walks in with Oscar and Rodrigo and looks around the room for Niabi. Not seeing her, he goes to the front of the church and asks Harriet if she has seen her. Harriet says she is in with the pastor. The two Indians, Talako and Koi, and the soldiers are seated in the rear of the church. Will thinks it is odd for them to be there without Nashoba, but suddenly Niabi walks out of the pastor's office located in the back of the church, followed by Nashoba and Pastor Walker. Instantly, Will's face changes from pleasant to one of defiance as he stares at Nashoba. Niabi rushes to Will, greets him with a hug and kiss on the cheek, while he continues staring at Nashoba. "What was he doing in there?" Will asks through clenched teeth.

Nashoba hears him and strolls to them grinning. "I am the one who will marry her to you tomorrow," he says with an even wider grin showing his teeth and folding his arms across his chest.

Will looks at Niabi. "What does he mean, he's marrying you to me?"

A smile creeps across Niabi's lips. "Yes, my love, Nashoba has permission to perform the Choctaw wedding ceremony for us tomorrow. Isn't that wonderful?"

Will lets out a deep sigh. Hugging her, he answers her, "Yes, that is wonderful."

The morning of the special day finally arrives. Niabi awakes and watches the sun's beams overtake the small window in Will's bedroom. She had a good night's sleep. If she were at her village, she would have slept in a dwelling with other maidens who would feed her, wash her, and dress her for the ceremony. She will miss the camaraderie of her village sisters. A day or so before this wedding day, in preparation for her honeymoon, the women elders would have pulled her into a meeting about the details of mating. That part is unnecessary now. Before she met Will, she benefitted from limited counseling from the women elders, counseling reserved for brides, and from what she gleaned from talking to young wives in her village whom she aided during childbirth. She had noticed how attentive husbands could not be held outside the birthing room, while others waited patiently until the woman and child were cleaned and made presentable before they approached. She lies there, watching the sunrise confident that Will will be an attentive husband.

She hears Harriet in the kitchen preparing breakfast. After putting on a plain cotton dress, she enters the kitchen and notices Will is up and out. "Good morning," she says to Harriet.

"Good morning," Harriet displays a smile from ear to ear.

"Has my groom gone to ground?" Niabi asks.

"He'll be back," Harriet says continuing to smile. "I couldn't stop him from going so early to the Johnsons to get boot polish from Fred. I think he's a bit nervous and doesn't know how to settle himself. You'll have to help him when he gets like that."

A mood of festive gaiety fills the cottage. Harriet floats around the kitchen, humming a tune and coating the bride and groom with adoring smiles. She has the bride and groom's day completely planned. They would have breakfast in the cottage, and then separate for Will to dress in his bedroom while Niabi dresses in her bedroom. After that, they are not to see each other until they reach the altar. Once Niabi is dressed, she will be ridden to the church with Harriet in a carriage. After a wait of twenty minutes, the carriage will return to the cottage to bring Will to the church.

Will had been given one of Grant's old dress suits. The suit was cleaned, tailored by Mrs. Fenton to fit him, and pressed. He will wear a black jacket, black waistcoat, black trousers, a white dress shirt, and a black string tie, all complemented with his shined black boots. His hair is cut shorter and oiled; his face is shaved and eyebrows trimmed.

After breakfast, Niabi watches him shine his boots. Harriet is in her room, setting up to do Niabi's hair, and waiting for her to bring her dress and undergarments in.

"Are you excited?" Niabi asks Will.

"Yes, but I can manage it. I just want you to be happy." She gets up from a chair at the kitchen table, walks around the table, and sits on his lap. They gaze into each other's eyes and kiss. "Just think, by this time tomorrow you will be all mine," Will says.

"Aren't I yours now?"

"Yes. We do belong to each other and have been since you invited me to the bedroom," he says pinching her on the side of her stomach, causing her to squirm, giggle and say, "No, stop." He continues, "The ceremony today, my love, only informs everyone what we have in our hearts." She kisses him, and he sets the polish down to embrace her. They immerse themselves into passionate kissing.

Harriet exits her bedroom and catches them wrapped around each other. "OK, there will be plenty of time for that tonight. I need you in here, young lady, so I can get you ready."

Almost filled to capacity, the church bulges with wedding guests. Talako and Koi sit in the first row of the right section of pews. Behind them is the Texas contingent, comprising the Hastings, Phillipe, and Rodrigo. Mrs. Applegate, Captain Horton, and the two soldiers sit in the third row. Dressed in a gray satin dress trimmed in beige lace, Harriet sits in the first row of the left section of pews. Behind her, Dakota Sam, Loma, Youngster sit and, along with everyone in attendance, anxiously wait for the ceremony to begin. Extra chairs are brought in for several town merchants who do not want to snub Mrs. Applegate by their absence at the event.

People continue to stream in as the hour grows near. Sam Jr. and Rita serve as ushers at the front doors. As they direct in the last few guests to empty seats, Pastor Walker enters and asks everyone to take their seats. Rita and Sam Jr. walk down a side aisle to the front, and sit in the third row on the left side with Mrs. Walker. After Pastor Walker calls for the church to bless this day, he asks Talako and Koi to come forward. They light incense, arrange themselves on chairs with two drums and flute in the front near the right side of the altar, and begin playing a slow and methodical beat, accompanied by flute music matched in soft tones and tempo. A few guests gasp at the sight of the Indians, and then settle into an appreciation of their musical serenade. The pastor nods to Will. With Oscar by his side, Will takes eight steps down the aisle, and stops in front of the altar on the left side.

Moments later, Niabi appears, floating from the church office in a dress made by Liola. Liola does not make the traditional Choctaw cotton dress with long sleeves, an ankle-length flowing skirt with ruffles, and a white apron cloth in the front. This wedding outfit is a mid-calf length dress made of tan deerskin, trimmed with white half-diamond-shaped applique, and she wears matching tan deerskin moccasin boots. The trim is above the bustline and three inches above the hem. Three feathers brought by Nashoba, one from a white dove, one from a falcon, and one from an eagle, adorn her hair. Her outfit is accented by a bouquet of white and shades of orange daylilies and lilac irises that she carries, picked from the Applegates' garden. Martha, who serves as her bridesmaid, follows Niabi in a pale violet dress and violet ribbons in her hair. The last to enter, Nashoba, wears a pale, near white, buckskin suit with white cotton breechcloth and his feathered headdress. He carries a smoking smudge bundle, which he carries to the altar and stops in front and between Will and Niabi. There, he waves the bundle through the air above them before bringing it to rest in front of him. The smudge emits a burning sage scent and dark gray smoke.

Nashoba addresses those assembled in the sanctuary. "It is our tradition that on the wedding day, members of both families gather at a designated site. The day before, relatives of the bride begin preparing food for the wedding feast. At a given point during the day of the wedding feast, the girl is moved away from the group to start her run, and her intended husband must pursue her. If he catches her too soon, she is considered indifferent to the match, and the wedding might be called off. On the other hand, if he is unable to catch her in a reasonable length of time, he might be considered indifferent, and the wedding is called off."

Looking at Niabi, Nashoba whispers, "Niabi, you may start your run."

Niabi looks at Will, and then turns, handing Martha her bouquet, before running out the side door of the church near the entrance to the pastor's office. Will looks on confused. He doesn't know what this is all about. Smiling with great delight, Nashoba looks at him and says, "Catch her, if you truly want her." Will looks at Oscar, and then blasts out of the church. At first, he doesn't see which way she ran. He runs to the road next to the church, looks both ways, and sees her heading in the direction toward town, walking fast. When she turns and sees him coming, she picks up the pace, running leisurely. Inside, wedding attendees are wondering what to do. Fred Jr. and one or two others exit the church through the main doors looking for the bride and groom. Most stay seated, bound by the ceremonial atmosphere of the drums beating accompanied by the flute's melody, amidst the circulating incense smells. The turn of events does ignite a whispering chatter among them.

Niabi runs into a thicket of trees just off the road, and slips inside. Will runs up, and looks in the thicket to see her standing there with arms open wide inviting him to her. He walks forward and upon reaching her, kisses her. "Did I pass this test?" he asks.

"You have already won my heart many times over. Now, you need to take my hand and pull me back to the church to show all that I am yours."

"Here they come!" yells Fred Jr.

The couple returns to the sanctuary, walks down the center aisle together, and repositions themselves in front of Nashoba. Nashoba continues the ceremony by taking a feather and using it to guide the smoke over his head to his back, and then to the front of his body.

Next, as part of the ceremony, he speaks words in his language as he waves the feather, directing the smoke over Will's head to his back, and then guides the smoke to Will's front. Speaking in his tongue, he continues waving the feather, guiding the flow of smoke over Niabi's head, first to flow over her head to her back, and then to flow down the front of her body. This is done to cleanse the area of bad spirits and clear the area for the entrance of good spirits.

Nashoba asks Oscar and Martha to pick up the blanket that has been placed on the first pew, bring it forward, and wrap it around Will and Niabi. After this is done, Nashoba says, "Will and Niabi, you are wrapped in the blanket to first symbolize that your separate individual lives have been brought together. I ask Martha and Oscar to help you turn when I direct you." He now recites the words given to him by Chief Samuels.

"Now we ask for the blessings of the four winds.

"Will the couple turn, and face east?

Blessings to this couple with gifts from the east and of air.

From the east comes the rising of the sun, the gift of a new day.

With each breath of air, you seize an opportunity to erase the pain and sorrow of yesterday, and continue, each day fresh and anew enriching each other's lives,

With each new day building a better tomorrow.

"Will the couple turn and face south?

Blessings to this couple with gifts from the south and of Earth.

Toward the south flows most rivers, flowing around Terra, Mother Earth, from which food is harvested, foliage sustained, and shelter abounds.

Since spewing lava, through the rains, snows, and winds, give respect to Terra,

She returns giving fertility, health, and stability.

"Will the couple turn and face west?

Blessings to this couple with gifts from the west and of water.

In the west are storm clouds and the ocean's high waves.

The water shows the capacity to rise in emotion and fall into silence with trust between one another, knowing that help to stem a raging tide is always there because the Great Spirit will reach your hearts and minds in spiritual time.

"Will the couple turn and face north?

Blessings to this couple with gifts from the north and of fire.

From the north comes guidance and a fiery passion that will guide your hearts to seek each other out.

And when one mate carries the torch through the darkness, the other mate follows, and when the other mate carries the torch, the one mate follows, and when both find themselves in the darkness, seek the other with open hearts and purity in spirit, for this is the making of a loving home.

"May you walk gently on our Mother the Earth, sheltered under Father Sky and from Brother Wind, disciplining Sister Human Nature, remembering the Sun renews and the Moon restores in your prayers to the Great Spirit all the days of your life.

"May the Great Spirit give blessings to this couple!

"Let us all repeat, Blessings to this couple!"

All the congregants say, "Blessings to this couple."

To close the ceremony, Nashoba walks around the couple three times with the burning smudge. To conclude the blessing, he says, "Will and Niabi, the blanket now symbolizes that your two lives are no longer. There is only one life under the blanket."

Nashoba instructs Martha and Oscar to remove the blanket.

Then he looks into the eyes of groom and bride and says, "I am authorized to announce to all before us that you are blessed by the four winds to be man and wife." Nashoba then steps aside and sits next to Talako and Koi, who suspend their drumbeat and the playing of the flute.

Pastor Walker comes forward and says, "Dearly beloved, we are gathered together here in the sight of God, and in the face of this congregation, to join together this man and this woman in holy matrimony; which is an honorable estate, signifying unto us the mystical union that is betwixt Christ and his Church; which holy estate Christ adorned and beautified with his presence, and therefore is not by any to be enterprised, nor taken in hand, unadvisedly, lightly, or wantonly, to satisfy men's carnal lusts and appetites; but reverently, discreetly, advisedly, soberly, and in the fear of God; duly considering the causes for which matrimony was ordained.

First, it was ordained for the procreation of children, to be brought up in the fear and nurture of the Lord, and to the praise of his holy Name.

Secondly, it was ordained for a remedy against sin, and to avoid fornication.

Thirdly, it was ordained for the mutual society, help, and comfort, that the one ought to have of the other, both in prosperity and adversity. Into which holy estate these two persons present come now to be joined. Therefore, if any man can show any just cause, why they may not lawfully be joined together, let him now speak, or else hereafter forever hold his peace."

Will has had his eyes fixed on Pastor Walker up to this point. But when there is a call for objectors to the union, he can't help nonchalantly glancing Nashoba's way and observes him grimace, mouth closed, jaws clenching. Will quickly returns his gaze to Niabi then to Pastor Walker.

Pastor Walker after receiving no objections proceeds with the ceremony. "Will Lawton, wilt thou have this woman to thy wedded wife, to live together after God's ordinance in the holy estate of matrimony? Wilt thou love her, comfort her, honor, and keep her in sickness and in health; and, forsaking all other, so long as ye both shall live?"

Will answers, "I will."

Pastor Walker continues, "Niabi, wilt thou have this man to thy wedded husband, to live together after God's ordinance in the holy estate of matrimony? Wilt thou obey him, and serve him, love, honor, and keep him in sickness and in health; and, forsaking all other, so long as ye both shall live?"

Niabi answers, "I will."

Pastor Walker then asks, "Who giveth this woman to be married to this man?"

Nashoba rises, steps forward, and says, "I, Nashoba, son of Chief Samuels of the Choctaw giveth this woman on behalf of Chief Samuels and all her many loved ones in the Indian Territory."

Upon hearing this, Will gawks at Nashoba; then realizes how he may look and stops himself. He thinks, *Didn't see that one coming.* Nashoba squints his eyes at him. Will returns to his original stance and Nashoba returns to his seat.

Pastor Walker says, "Let us pray. O eternal God, creator, and preserver of all mankind, giver of all spiritual grace, the author of everlasting life; send thy blessing upon these thy servants, this man, and this woman, whom we bless in thy name; that, as Isaac and Rebecca lived faithfully together, so these persons may surely perform and keep the vow and covenant betwixt them made, and may ever remain in perfect love and peace together, and live according to thy laws; through Jesus Christ our Lord. Amen."

Pastor Walker joins their right hands together, and says, "Those whom God hath joined together let no man put asunder."

Pastor Walker then addresses the congregation: "Forasmuch as Will Lawton and Niabi of Choctaw Nation have consented together in holy wedlock, and have witnessed the same before God and this company, and thereto have pledged to the other; I pronounce that they be man and wife together, in the name of the Father, and of the Son, and of the Holy Ghost. Amen."

The congregation says, "Amen. Amen."

Pastor Walker says to Will, "You may kiss the bride."

Will and Niabi embrace and both gently kiss each other on the lips.

Pastor Walker asks the couple to turn and face the audience, and says, "Ladies and gentlemen, I present to you the new Mr. and Mrs. Will Lawton."

Beaming, Pastor Walker thanks the members of the Choctaw tribe for the beautiful music and inspiring ceremonial services. He then announces the wedding couple invites the attendees to a late lunch, or early dinner at the Applegate Ranch in the backyard.

"You'll have plenty of food, music, dancing, and lemonade. Ah, just lemonade. Remember we have children in the crowd. This concludes the ceremony. Go, and enjoy the festivities, and God be with you."

As the guests begin to stand and greet one another, Harriet, Martha, Oscar and Mrs. Walker come forward and surround the happy couple bestowing on them smiles, kisses and hugs of congratulations. When his aisle is clear to exist, Phillipe maneuvers to get himself in front of Nashoba and says, "English is my second language, but I even find no French words that can adequately express how gracious and gallant your actions have been to this couple. You, sir, have my complete respect." He brings his hand up to his forehead symbolizing a salute to Nashoba then turns and walks away.

Dressed in his Sunday best suit, Fred Jr. approaches Youngster. "They are going to be forever getting over there and putting all the food out. Feel like taking a ride on one of our horses till then?"

"I don't know how to ride," Youngster says.

"It's easy. I can show you how."

They leave and get two horses out of one of the pastures. Fred Jr. picks out a mild and gentle horse for Youngster and puts saddles and harnesses on both horses.

"Now, just pull to the right to go right, pull to the left to go left, and pull back to stop. To get him going, press with your lower legs or use your heels, but very softly. See, you gettin' it," Fred Jr. says.

Youngster is wobbly as he rides around aimlessly. "Let's go," Fred Jr. says. "There's a creek close by on Mr. Bannister's property, and there's usually no one around." As Fred Jr. starts moving off, he puts his hand out at Youngster's horse like he has a treat, and the horse begins to follow Fred Jr.

When they reach the creek, Fred Jr. strips all his clothes off. With a surprised look on his face, Youngster asks, "Swim naked?"

"Yeah, I do it all the time," Fred Jr. says. "I would never get to swim if I had to wait 'til I got swimming clothes."

Youngster takes all his clothes off. Since Loma had cleaned and pressed them, he takes time to neatly fold them and place them on the ground where he is sure they won't get wet and minimally dusty.

A more enjoyable time could not be had. The boys frolic in the prior tranquil, clear creek water, causing large surges to slap its banks as each one takes turns running from the side, leaping in, sometimes head first, then feet first, and always accompanied by screeches and laughter. While diving in and splashing water, suddenly Fred Jr. says, "Listen, someone's riding this way. Grab your clothes and let's go! Just come on naked!"

"Naked? Wait I've got to at least put on my pants," Youngster says.

"I'm telling you; we don't have time for that," Fred Jr. yells holding his clothes in a bundle and sitting on his horse ready to go. While Youngster struggles to get his pants on, Mr. Bannister rides up, pointing a rifle at Fred Jr.

"Please don't shoot, Mr. Bannister. We were just swimming," Fred Jr. pleads, lowering his eyes avoiding eye contact with Mr. Bannister. Trembling, Youngster stares directly at the rifle.

Bannister turns the rifle on Youngster. "Who is this young Negra?" Bannister growls.

With teeth chattering, Youngster says, "I'm Youngster, sir. Visiting from Washington, DC. I came to the wedding celebration at the Applegate Ranch." Words tumble out of his mouth. "My mother, brother, and father are here, too. My father is a veteran of the U.S. Union Army. Sir, we mean no disrespect using your creek. We just wanted to swim and then go back home."

Mr. Bannister rides over to Youngster and strikes him across the face with the butt of his rifle, knocking him to the ground. Bannister glares at him. "That's for offering more information than I asked for, Negra, ... and for your pappy fightin' for the wrong side. Now git before I plug holes in the two a-you." Dazed, Youngster manages to get to his feet. While holding his clothes, now bunched up, he tries to get back up on his horse. Blood streaming from his mouth, he finally mounts and rides out behind Fred Jr.

Bannister ends his rant by saying, "And don't ever swim in my creek again!"

As they ride, Fred Jr. looks back. "Are you hurting badly?" He slows and, when he is even to Youngster, leans over to see if the blood is coming from his lip or out of his mouth. "Let me see where the blood is coming from."

"No, you've done enough," Youngster says, knocking his hand away.

"I told you to get on the horse and go," Fred Jr. argues.

"And what, get shot in the back?"

"He wouldn't have shot."

"You don't know what that crazy bastard would do," Youngster says sharply.

"Well, we gotta think of something," Fred Jr. says. "I can't take you back to the celebration lookin' like that. Let me find my mother, and meet you in front of our cottage. She's stern but is willing to work with me, giving me a long rope to mess up. And I never do anything to really rile her up."

"Will she tell my mother? My mother might understand, but I don't know what my new father will make of this. He may punish me or decide to take revenge on Bannister and end up in jail, or lynched."

The two stop and dress at the property line in a cluster of trees. After dressing, they proceed to the Johnsons' cottage. Fred Jr. leaves and returns with his mother, Mrs. Johnson. They go inside the cottage, and she begins cleaning the blood off Youngster and seeing what damage has been done. "I can't believe you boys had nothing better to do than run out and mix it up with that racist cracker. You know how he is, Fred Jr., and how he feels about us," Mrs. Johnson complains.

"We didn't approach him; we went to the creek to swim," Fred Jr. says.

"Get it through your thick head: the creek is on *his* land. It's trespassing. Did he invite you over? No! Stay off his land! Ride out to the lake to swim!" Examining Youngster's mouth, she says, "I think your lip is just busted. Your teeth seem stiff enough." Addressing Fred Jr. again, she says, "Yes, you have to remember you are nothing to him. You are like a cat or a dog he found on his land. Please, please stay away from that man."

"When he pointed the rifle at me, I felt helpless," Youngster says. "I remembered how helpless my mother said they were when they wanted to take a break and the overseer told them to keep working, working over their hunger, working over their pain." Youngster speaks softly, "Loma is not my real mother. She raised me, though. My real mother worked while I was in her belly. She saw a need to work up until the moment I was due. The night I was born, she had problems and died right before they got me out. As my new father says, we live from one stark peril to the next." Mrs. Johnson rolls her eyes wondering why his daddy is telling him that. Youngster continues, "When does the hate stop, Mrs. Johnson? When does it stop?" The tears begin streaming from his eyes.

"Oh, child. It will get better. Fred Jr., let's sit a while here with Youngster, 'til he feels up to rejoining the wedding celebration."

The wedding guests are awed as they file into the backyard of the Applegate Ranch. On wooden posts covering chairs and tables, two large white canopies run from the top of the back porch of the main house into the yard. In a corner of the porch, a table is set aside for gifts. Below, at the far end under the canopies, a quartet of church members plays a lively ditty on fiddle, harmonica, guitar, and a banjo; their feet pounding a fabricated wooden stage platform add deep percussion to the melody. Holding hands, Will and Niabi enter the area under the canopies. The musicians immediately stop playing and announce, "The bride and groom will now dance." Guests call them to the front where there is an area to dance. The only preparation Niabi had for this nuptials dance was Harriet advising her to step from side to side in unison with Will. Their bodies move in time with the music. It was moments after the vows were recited, when Will realizes he's now the head of a household and the level of responsibility that accompanies it. He also may have already done the groundwork to grow that household. As they dance he develops a desperate wish for a drink to steady his nerves. Then he looks into Niabi's face; she is glowing, her eyes dancing from the musicians to the porch, then around the guest tables while stepping on his feet, and then back to his face, laughing, saying "ha ha, Sorry." And at that moment, he is calmed and strengthened by the love they share, the intimate partnership, and just in awe of how something so right emerged from his initial misdeed.

After a while, they are joined in the dancing by Dakota Sam and Loma, as well as Rita and Sam Jr., then Mr. and Mrs. Hastings, Mr. and Mrs. Clarence Fenton and Oscar and Martha. Captain Horton, who enters fixed at the side of Mrs. Applegate, looks at her and motions an invitation to dance. She mouths, "No." He smiles and follows her to a table. After they are seated she leans her head toward his to hear what he's saying. "Did I tell you that I like you with your hair down?" says Captain Horton.

"Get a real good look, it's just for today," says Lorraine smiling. "And, if I have too much to drink ... maybe it's still down for the whole night."

In the nearby pasture, Rodeo and FireTip put on a show, chasing each other and rearing up on their hind legs as though they are celebrating, too. At the end of the song, guests are invited to form a line up on the back porch where the food is spread out on long linen-covered tables. Sheila tells Talako she is fixing his plate, Ethel tells Koi she is preparing his plate, and Harriet makes a similar announcement to Nashoba. They are not used to dealing with strong Negro women and find it more expedient not to argue with them. With his plate in hand, Nashoba is followed by Talako and Koi, looking for a table to sit at. Dakota Sam speaks up, "Village brothers, please join me at my table," he says. The three Indians find seats with Dakota Sam and sit down.

"Haven't seen you since you had a rifle on me," Dakota Sam says and chuckles.

"And I didn't shoot, as you remember too," Nashoba replies.

"Thank you for that. Lest my pretty Loma would be a widow today," Dakota Sam says, watching Loma standing on the porch preparing his plate.

"How many of your seed is here?" Nashoba asks.

"I have two sons," Dakota Sam says, looking around, but only seeing the one and not the younger one.

"I see you wear the White man's blue uniform. Why do you do that after what he has done to your people? Why...do you wear it still?" Nashoba asks.

"Well, Nashoba, first, there's not too many haberdasheries out in the backwoods and out on the frontier where I've been travelin'. Second, yes, there is a lot to be angry about, a lot my generation will never forget. But because I have been told what their constitution says, I want to help bring those beliefs to the top, out of and above the ruckus," Dakota says. "I want to make it so. It may not happen during my lifetime, but maybe it will during my children's lifetime."

Loma approaches the table carrying two plates. "Beautiful ceremony, sir," she says to Nashoba.

Nashoba casts his eyes on her, nods, and smiles, noticing that she is a Negro woman who is a little more to his liking—soft-spoken and more agreeable in comparison to those others.

As Loma places Dakota's plate in front of him and sits down beside him, Dakota Sam looks at her and says, "Thank you, sweetie." He continues addressing Nashoba, "That constitution they have speaks of all men as equal, and justice for all."

Nashoba says, "Huh. You came by train, right?"

"Yes," Dakota Sam says.

"When you rode in, in the second class, in the back of the train car, was that equality and justice for all?" Nashoba asks. "I rode here in a cattle car. I know that's what they think of me. I don't desire to sit with them and make the nice talk with them. I was in the cattle car where I could choose to be in the front, or in the back, could burn my incense, talk and laugh freely, and commune with my spirits. You see, I have learned something on this trip. They don't want to ride in the cattle car, so they say nothing. You are equal and get justice for all, as long as it doesn't interfere with them getting something they want."

"You are right. But I still believe as long as good men, good men like you and me, fight evil men, there will be changes," Dakota Sam says.

Niabi walks over to the table and rests her hand on Nashoba's shoulder. "I can't thank you and Chief Samuels enough. Are you okay? How's the food?" she asks.

"The food is good," Nashoba says.

"I told you," Niabi says.

"What about you, Talako and Koi? Are you pleased with the food?" Niabi asks. Nashoba gushes a chuckle. Talako and Koi both nod their heads, and can only do that and smile because their mouths are full.

Nashoba adds, "Yes, they have been nothing but pleased with the food, like perpetual grazing cows." Niabi smiles, but Talako and Koi scowl at Nashoba.

She bends down close to Nashoba and whispers, "I look forward to your wedding day."

Nashoba looks up, surprised at her comment. Then he motions for Niabi to come in closer, again to talk. "I did meet a young woman on the train."

"Yeah?" Niabi sits down next to him. "Tell me about her."

Nashoba slowly inhales, his cheeks fill with air and he visibly pushes the air out. "Her name is Louisa. She is a teacher from Little Rock, Arkansas. She wanted to come out to our village, but the local town sheriff stopped her."

"Will she come back?"

"Not sure."

"Nashoba, I know it's hard for you to accept help. But one thing my relationship with Will has shown me is that some people who are not in your tribe deserve your trust. I can ask Mrs. Applegate, or her sons, to make inquiries about the young woman. If they find something, I will get word to you."

Nashoba nods but says nothing. He wonders if he has told her too much.

The sound of a spoon clinking a glass rings out. Seated at a table with Mr. and Mrs. Hastings, Phillipe stands up. Having had way too much wine, he leans against the table to balance himself. "All aboard! All aboard!" he says. Guests at his table burst into laughter, and others at nearby tables chuckle with a puzzled look.

"Oh, wrong toast," Phillipe jabbers.

"Grandfather, what are you doing?" Oscar asks.

"Please, ladies and gentlemen," Phillipe continues. "Please raise your glasses for a toast to Will and Niabi. My heart is full tonight. If the world could see the brotherhood and family of friends joined here under this canopy tonight, it would be an inspiration to make the world a better place. We, are better individuals because you, Will and Niabi, have brought us together to celebrate this most happy occasion. Unending health and happiness to the bride and groom." Phillipe continues holding his glass raised high in front of him.

With raised glasses, the crowd repeats, "To the bride and groom."

After several dances with Harriet, Rita and Martha, and now flanked by Oscar and Rodrigo sitting at a table, Will finds himself wanting to loosen his tie. The hour is about 8 p.m., and the length of the day weighs heavy on him. He doesn't want to sleep through his honeymoon. Several guests have already stopped by to say their goodbyes and express how beautiful the ceremony was especially the Four Winds ceremony. Niabi stands in a corner, talking to Ethel, Martha, and Rita. They ask questions of Niabi, ranging from the meaning of the smudge smoke, who made her dress, to how many children she wants to have. Before Niabi can get a word out, Rita offers an opinion. "Due to economics and keeping daily schedules from being a burden, I can see one or two being an ideal number. That's as many as I would have."

Passing by, Sheila overhears her answer and sticks her head in the group. "That will be *way* in the future if you don't snag this Mr. Sam Jr., or I will!" Sheila says.

"Go away from us," Ethel says and the ladies laugh.

After having a couple of drinks of wine from all the toasting, Will's head is foggy. He tries to walk it off. Heading to the back of the barn, he stops when he hears Harriet calling him.

"Son, this will be the last time we talk as just mother and son before you take on the responsibility of a husband. Are there ... experiences, advice that ... that I should share with you?"

Will's wit and tongue are quite loosened by the wine he's imbibed. He looks at her with a half-grin. "I can see the sweat beading up on your brow. This is not a conversation you are wanting to have with me. So don't pretend, Momma," he says, shaking his finger at her. His head rolls, he looks down, then to the side, and continues, "I've observed things, from on the ranch, and talking to other men."

Harriet takes a deep breath before interrupting him. "And I have forgotten. You and Niabi are already affectionate to one another, and thus my concerns are in vain," she says snippily and turns to walk away. But he grabs her arm.

He nears her and kisses her on the forehead. "Ignore me. Your concerns are always welcome and will never be ignored by me, so long as I have a breath in me. You are my momma." Harriet, teary-eyed, hugs him and drifts away toward the remnants of the party.

Will watches her walk away and ponders whether the wine made him too flippant with his mother and turns to walk back to the party to apologize, but then he hears, "Will Lawton." He turns and is surprised to see an approaching Nashoba.

"I was on my way to my bed and saw you and thought, I didn't congratulate the groom."

"I wasn't expecting it; hadn't given it any thought."

"No. I must wish you well and a good life as the husband of my dear friend. She says she wants to feel welcome in my home and me in hers. So, I will come to your home one day, and should I find that all is not well—let's just say losing a horse will be the least pain you suffer."

Will blinks trying to clear the fog from his brain.

"But for now, we are brothers and I wish you...a...a good evening." Nashoba struggled to get that last part out, then abruptly turns and walks toward the foaling barn.

Will drags back toward the party, smiling and waving back at lively guests still drinking, laughing, dancing, and chasing after drinks and a last serving of food as Harriet doles out the remainder to the guests. After the food tables are cleared about half of the guests depart and the musicians pack up. Mrs. Applegate and her houseguests continue in lively conversation under the canopies.

When Niabi seeks Will out, he is leaning against a post. She says, "Harriet went home with Mrs. Johnson. Did you know about that?"

"Yes, I asked her to," he replies throwing his head up, inhaling air to fight off fatigue and dizziness.

"Well, I am getting really tired," she says, stretches her arms out, and yawns.

"Me too. Now, I won't have to look over my shoulder, once we are in the cottage tonight for, say some disgruntled Indians, do I?" Will asks.

"Are you bringing that up again?" Niabi asks.

"Sorry, just had to make one last comment about that," Will says. "Are you ready to go to the cottage?"

"Yes, I am ready. I thanked Mrs. Applegate, your mother, and Mrs. Walker. I'll see the others tomorrow and thank them."

"If I let you out of the cottage tomorrow," Will responds, and they both giggle.

"Why don't we walk out slow," Niabi says, and Will adds, "You mean don't run?" They both laugh, and she slaps him playfully on his arm.

Will puts his right arm around Niabi and raises his left hand at the remainder of the wedding guests still sitting or milling around the tables. He yells, "Everyone, thank you for coming. Good night."

"Whoooooo," comes from a few left in the crowd who tease them about leaving to go start their honeymoon. Everyone left in the yard starts laughing.

Grandpa Phillipe even gets in on the joke when he yells, "Try to pace yourselves."

From everyone comes another uproar of laughter.

Will and Niabi reach the cottage door, and he scoops her up in his arms before she can walk in.

"I was told by Oscar that this is a tradition that some people follow—that the husband carries the wife over the threshold," he says.

"Oh, I didn't know that."

Will sets her down and lights a lantern that he easily finds near the door. "So, are we in your room or Harriet's room?" Niabi asks looking around.

Spotting flowers have been laid on her bed, Will points and says, "I think she wants us in here. I'll wash up in my bedroom."

"I'll wash up in here," Niabi says, smiling walking backwards as she enters Harriet's bedroom. Will watches her, then turns to go enter his bedroom.

After he finishes washing up, Will douses all the lanterns in his room and the kitchen. There is only one lantern left burning and it is in Harriet's bedroom, on a side table next to the large bed where Niabi lies under the covers, waiting for him. Will wears only a large drying cloth, covering his bottom and tied at the waist. As he enters the bedroom, there is a faint scent of lavender oil, the same scent emanating from her body all those times he encountered her near the village. He walks over and stands at the side of the bed facing her. She scoots over to the opposite side and throws the covers open inviting him to get in bed under the covers next to her. As the covers whip open, a heavier scent of lavender oil rushes out and flows directly into his nostrils. The light from the lantern on the side table rushes in across her naked caramel skin, lighting up her rounded curves, dipping and tucking into folds and creases under her breasts and thighs. As she lies in front of him, his eyes gaze upon her as an amorous feast. She raises her arms and asks softly, "Will you lie with me, my love?"

He unties the cloth around his waist and lets it drop to the floor as he slides onto the bed and under the covers next to her. Lying there facing her, he says, "I don't feel different. I mean, I don't feel any different about you now that we have had the ceremony. I still love you so much, as I did before."

She puts her arms around his chest and pulls herself into him. He rolls forward, and she scoots under him. She gives him a passionate kiss, and says, "Well, there is one difference I've noticed."

"What's that?" Will asks.

"This is the first time you ever told me you loved me."

"Can't be?" Will says with a short bob of his head and raising his eyebrows.

"Yes, you have kidnapped me, roped me, forced your kisses and hugs on me, and a couple of times even made love to me, but you never ever said the words, 'I love you'."

The Four Winds blow around their bodies as they begin their rhythm of passion. The newlyweds decide to take as long as they need to satisfy their cravings for one another, cravings that had been building since they met.